Nothing

The bodies spilled around them in a bloody tangle. Shkai'ra paused for an instant to grab a handful of rag as she stepped over them, wiping the slippery soles of her sandals.

"Let's go," she said. They flung themselves up the stairs; in long strides; Shkai'ra checked herself to let the shorter woman keep pace. Their hands left faint red smears on the scrubbed white pine of the balustrade.

The stairwell exited on the flat central roof of the building. At the opposite end was another exit; beside it stood ten soldiers in heavy infantry armor, armed with shortened close-combat spears, huge oblong shields, and double-edged stabbing swords. Their officer wore the same round steel bowl helmet, but his carried a plume.

The Fehinnan's dark face was split by a white-toothed smile. "Shkai'ra! . . . Such a pity we'll never be able to toss the bones together again. On the other hand, I won't have to pay those thirty silvers the dice lost me, either.

"Kill them."

Dedication

Creativity

Dance with Siva!
                    In Joy we dance.
                            We dance destruction
and creation.
            Fly with eagles,
                    delve in darkness.

In joy and sorrow
                    are we free,
                to cleave a stormcloud

Ride the thunder.
                    Laugh!

                            For we are free.

sm 83/04/08

To both our partners

Karen and Jan

S.M. Stirling

Shirley Meier

BAEN
FANTASY

SABER & SHADOW

Copyright © 1992 by S.M. Stirling & Shirley Meier

A Baen Books Original

Baen Publishing Enterprises
P.O. Box 1403
Riverdale, N.Y. 10471

ISBN: 0-671-72143-7

Cover art by Larry Elmore

First printing, November 1992

Distributed by
SIMON & SCHUSTER
1230 Avenue of the Americas
New York, N.Y. 10020

Printed in the United States of America

CHAPTER I

The Fehinnan ship floated on a sea that glowed in the sun like a heated copper plate, becalmed with all sails set and hanging limp. The water stretched out to a sulfur-colored horizon in swells like ripples in thick oil. They'd lost the wind a week ago in the journey west across the Lannic.

The *Fair-Wind Flycatcher*, a barque-rigged two-hundred tonner, had weighed anchor out of the colony city of Nübuah near the Pillars of Heaven guarding the strait to the Closed Sea. She carried a tight-packed cargo of nearly five hundred slaves, ivory, dyestuffs, pepper and metal for Illizbuah, the capital of Fehinna across the Lannic Ocean; that had been over thirty-three days ago, more than long enough for a crossing with favoring weather. Over the days, the press of bodies in the hold had lessened as the dead were thrown to the sharks following the ship. When the coffles got small enough, they were brought on deck to be fed and hosed down and exercised. The stink of shit and blood and fear was soaked into the ship's

1

wood, hovering, clotting as it sat, trodden into the boards of the deck as the slaves shuffled to the sound of the slave-dance drummer. Now, with the ship becalmed, the sharks circled rather than following, waiting.

Megan Whitlock watched her feet lift, then fall, lift then fall to the drumbeat, pale toes gripping, a stinging sensation rising from the oak manacles where they'd torn old scabs off. There wasn't much bleeding though, for which she was thankful. *So tired*, she thought.

Tight-packing slaves was a gamble on good winds. The captain of the *Flycatcher* had lost.

The Zak woman was shorter than the rest of her coffle, though not by much. Along with black slaves bought from the *Poquay*, the fortified trading posts strung along the coast of the southern continent, there were a few criminals from Nübuah and its settlements—Fehinnan stock and shorter than most naZak she was used to. Where they were olive-skinned, she was pale as milk, and though her hair was as black as theirs, it fell like straight silk, when unbraided, rather than clinging in wiry curls. The sun burned her skin. How many times had they been dragged up to dance? At least the slavers had stopped demanding that they sing.

Dance. Dance to exercise us. Pound the stupid drum, pipe on the silly wooden whistle. I'm not going to die on this stinking tub. I have to live to have my revenge. The idea of revenge burned quietly now, put away in the back of her mind. There were more important things to pay attention to; like holding to life, fighting not to become a dumb beast in chains. She ignored the watching crewfolk with crossbows and spears, and the ones with long switches ready to keep the slaves moving sprightly.

The old Fehinnan in front of her stumbled. She caught his elbow though she felt weak herself. "Don't fall, Jaipahl. Don't you dare die on me." In the foul dark air of the hold, he had been teaching her Fehinnan, as she had been teaching him Zak.

"No. Not yet." His breathing was hoarse but steady. "Megan, it would be more correct if you used a formal tone, speaking Fehinnan."

"As if I should care to speak correctly to a master? High, formal, Fehinnan in a slave's mouth?" Jaipahl looked over his shoulder, raised and dropped one shoulder in a half shrug, and smiled, thin white stubble on his cheek creasing. Fehinnan had a fiendishly complicated system of honorific inflections, altering the whole meaning depending on the status of the speakers. Most of the sailors and slaves around her spoke a simplified pidgin.

"So, you plan to be a slave forever, a *mofoar*?"

She was panting too hard to answer, just shook her head, feet rising and falling, shuffling to the drum. She looked down at the links between them, concentrating on keeping her feet. This bit of exercise wouldn't have bothered her a few weeks ago.

Then, she'd been able to feed herself things like fish oil so that the growth of her claws wouldn't leech her blood of iron. The witch/healer who had given them to her had explained that it would strain her body just to have steel claws, that she would have to guard against blood-weakness by eating liver and fish oil. Megan could hardly say to a slaver, "Excuse me, but I need a special diet." Thank Koru, Goddess, that the claws grew so slowly or she'd have been dead by now.

In the darkness of the hold, she felt chilled even in the baking heat that made the ship's surgeon come down naked and leave after a few moments. She was exhausted just by moving, short of breath, wanting anything with iron in it. She tried chewing on her nails themselves, but only ended up worrying at the skin around them. The lock on the end of the coffle was just within her reach, the one bit of metal that she could lick, but it wasn't enough. She snorted to herself. *Never thought I'd live long enough to develop cravings for liver.* She kept her hands closed loosely so that her nails wouldn't catch the sun. The slavers hadn't noticed and she'd worn a deep groove in one link of the wooden chain strung through her ankle manacles, despite the metallic hardness of the tropical wood. The coffle was strung together with one chain looped through foot shackles. One good twist would snap the link and she'd be free; she and the other nine in the coffle. *I need a shoreline to swim to before I try anything, though.*

The lookout shouted and the piper stopped with a squeal, standing up; the drummer thumped on for a stroke or two then followed suit.

"Cap! Bad weather making!"

The slaves had stopped the moment the sound had, standing like fleshy posts in the deck. Megan raised her head, squinting at the horizon. There were clouds, a thicker haze on the edge of the sea. Then a tiny doll-sized flash of blue-white, horizontal lightning.

I never was much good at judging weather on a sea, Megan thought. *But . . .*

The captain stared for a long moment through the spy-glass, then spun on her heel, shouting.

"Get 'em below! Strike all sail but the jib, wind's comin'! *Uraccano.*"

The bosun's pipe shrilled, sending sailors clambering frantically to pull in sail before the wind hit. The slaves were urged back into the hold with a shouted command, and when they didn't move fast enough, a lashing. Megan blinked at the darkness, eyes refusing to adjust, watching the square of light and air above as the sailors quickly snapped locks into place and swarmed back up to the deck. Slanting across the tiny rectangles of sky, she could see the ropes shaking as people scrambled in the rigging. The hatch cover rattled onto its fittings with a hollow boom that echoed through the sudden darkness, leaving only a patchwork gleam through the grillwork in the center of the wooden circle. A mallet sounded a hollow *tock* as they hammered the securing wedges home. With the hatch shut and battened, dark and smell closed in.

"They're trying to run on jibs from the feel," she murmured to Jaipahl, next to her.

Sailcloth boomed above them, moving in the gusts that brought a stray jet of cooler air. The *Flycatcher* heeled over, sending Megan sliding against her chains and the rough wood, tearing the scabs on her back loose, bilge gurgling below. Someone cried out in the dark and a fight was starting further down the coffle. The wood of the ship cracked and groaned as she righted and ran before the wind.

"I believe we have a wind," Jaipahl said calmly, loud over the noise.

Shkai'ra Mek Kermak's-kin grunted and slapped at the mosquitos again, crouching on the sandspit and leaning on her scabbarded saber, long fingers wrapped around the bone hilt. The salt marsh whispered on either side, and the shouts and crashes from the villagers salvaging the ship echoed loud across it. The longshore swamp smelled of rot, and the overcast rolled low and threatening over air that shimmered with heat and moisture, over oil-smooth sea the color of grey bread mold. More knocking sounds, as the natives broke up the shipwreck with stone-headed hammers. They had stripped out everything of use, and now they were taking the remainder apart for the stout oak timber.

Miserable tub, Shkai'ra thought, spitting in the direction of the wreck.

It had been a three-master, a freighter out of the Kahab Sea; from Kyuba, heading north with sugar,

rum, molasses and coffee for Illizbuah, capital of Fehinna. And one down-on-her-luck mercenary, shipping
on as a marine to get passage back to the city that
was the closest thing to a home she had. The tall
woman slapped at the insects again and ignored the
greasy sweat matting her red-blond hair and running
down her face; for a moment she thought longingly of
her native land far to the northwest. Cool winds blowing the tall prairie grass like green-bronze waves, sky
wide and blue . . . She shook her head, the narrow
hawk-features brooding and sullen.

Luck—she made a sign with her sword-hand—had
not been good of late. No pirate attack, just a few
galleys coming out to sniff their trail off the Sea
Islands, so she had not even earned any hard coin.
Then the storm that caught them out to sea, blowing
them north past Fehinna and onto a sandbar on the
Joisi coast. The natives were miserable savages in mud
huts, but they had some contact with outsiders and
had taken the survivors in, for a stiff price.

A fresh shout brought her head up, and she
unclipped the binoculars at her waist, standing and
scanning out to sea.

Ia! she thought: *yes!* Sails, a middling-size schooner.
Fehinnan by her lines and the sunburst flag.

A smoke-signal went up from the village, hidden off
half a kilometer west behind dunes and scrub cedar.
The salvagers splashed back from their work. More of
the Joisi swarmed down to the beach; they were
armed with long spears and hide shields, blowguns
and wooden swords set with shark's teeth or pieces of
glass. Traders put in here to barter for muskrat pelts,
cedar oil and whatever else the locals had on hand,
but a village that looked too easy a mark might be
plundered and its inhabitants hustled off to the slave
markets of the Cayspec lands to the south.

Shkai'ra grinned slowly, standing. A black tomcat
left off its investigation of the long sawgrass and

sprang for her shoulder, climbing up the horsehide tunic she had worn ever since the wreck two weeks ago. She put up a hand to rub absently at the cat's scarred chin. The jacket hid her money belt quite handily. There had been considerable confusion when the ship went ashore in the storm, and she had paid a last-minute visit to the captain's cabin. *So unfortunate, the captain being up on deck trying to save his ship,* she thought.

And so fortunate, that trader coming in, her mind went on as she sauntered toward the landing-stage. The ship had dropped anchor offshore, and a longboat was stroking for the beach. These last few days, the savages had started looking at the metal of her weapons and harness with speculative eyes. It was a considerable fortune, by local standards. . . .

"Back to Illizbuah," she said.

"Meeorw," the cat crooned, squinting its green eyes at the ship. He *liked* ships—they generally had an interesting population of rodents.

Like being in a nightmare, only with your eyes open, Megan thought as the ship lurched and flung her against the ring-bolt. She grabbed and clung to it, feeling Jaipahl and the person beyond him catch onto the chain linking them together. She blinked to test that her eyes were open. *The Arkan Hell is like this: airless.* On the fairest of days, when the hold was opened as much as it could be, a candle wouldn't stay lit on the bottom deck, fading to a red smolder. During the storm the ship was sealed, and now it was like being smothered: you could fill your lungs till they hurt, but it did no good.

She licked dry lips, trying to swallow, bracing herself as she was flung on top of Jaipahl, both of them sliding in the mush of shit and piss, blood and vomit coating the boards. "Sorry," she shouted to make herself heard over the shrieking of the ship. She could feel him nod. It was like thunder in the dark; the hull vibrating as it slid into the troughs of the waves, numbing the ears. The moans of the sick and dying couldn't be heard.

The *Flycatcher*'s bottom boards, just above the bilge, were packed with slaves lying head to toe, four across the beam. Around the sides of the ship there were half floors, wide enough for one rank of slaves to lie, and one more above that, the half trestles made of cheap pine. Megan was lucky enough to be on the top tier.

There was no way to get water, and the shitbuckets at the ends of the rows had become dangerous missiles as the ship rolled, lurching out of their stands. For a moment, she shuddered at the thought of what it must be like down at the bottommost layer.

How many days: one? Two at most? She'd hesitated about doing anything as the storm hit, even though the crew would be busy. If the slaves could get loose in the tumult, they'd have to crew the ship. *I hate being unsure of what to do.* They were nowhere near land that she last knew, but with the storm blowing for more than a day they'd have to do something soon or all die of thirst. *I'd heard that storms on this sea could run for days, but reading it and feeling it are two different things.* The groaning of the wooden hull was an even, harsh grind, punctuated now and then with tooth-grating *crack-pop* sounds as the *Flycatcher* climbed up and planed down waves peaking high as the mizzen masthead.

Jaipahl reached out in the dark and fumblingly patted her shoulder. She swallowed again, trying to work up spit, tasting dry bile. Jaipahl leaned over and yelled in her ear.

"There's more water in the bilge, someone passed the word up. It's running through the slats on the bottom tier."

Her skin crawled as she realized the ship's seams

were going. The *Flycatcher* was filthy but sound, and the decking hatches were still tight. The rhythm of the waves was bad, though—a pounding twist as the slaver ploughed into each swell, wrenching as her bow broke free. Treenails were yielding, stringers working loose on the frame, caulking tearing out.

She had to do something. Just then the hull-note changed and someone yelled wordlessly from forward, a different sound from people fighting with each other, more panicked than angry. Something went *crack* above their heads as canvas gave way. *That was the last sail.* Seconds later the ship lurched and groaned, the bow not meeting the waves quite head-on.

She pulled her legs up as much as she could, pulling Jaipahl's up, too. *I'll explain later. If the ship goes down we'll never get out in the mess. I don't want to die.* She snapped the link of the chain, caught Jaipahl's hand and made him feel the broken edge because in the noise she couldn't explain. Even as the ship lurched she could feel him tense, though he didn't move immediately. The severed chain slithered through ankle-rings, leaving the coffle free.

Megan was short enough to sit up without hitting her head on the deck over her head but couldn't brace herself. The forward hatch was ripped open then, letting in a blast of wind and water foaming up over the hatch-combing, with a little light. Fear came with it, but clean air as well. Three of the *Flycatcher*'s crew held onto the hatch, yelling down that they needed everyone to bail or work the pumps. An ominous rending groan came from forward, and they swung down and started unlocking chains as Megan stood up, crouched, feeling the deck against her back.

The *Flycatcher* lurched, falling, and Megan lost her balance and fell three tiers onto the people lying below. For a moment she lay, gasping, as hands reached, touching in the dark. *I'm going mad.* Her chest was tight, the ship was screaming as Megan wanted to. Out—she had to get out.

She bit down on the edge of her hand, spat out scum that crusted on her teeth, forcing calm. Her teeth hurt and felt a little loose; not enough greens, she thought irrelevantly. She scrambled up to her knees, realized why the person she'd landed most heavily on wasn't protesting, and bellowed as best she could, using the command-voice she had developed as a riverboat captain on the Brezhan.

"DON'T FIGHT, *they need us to bail!*"

She had to yell to be heard, in all the languages she knew, hoping that someone had the sense to pass on the word. It was hard to tell, but clutching hands let go.

She clambered up to the forward hatch. Another wave washed over the deck, pouring in the open hatch with a cold impact that wrenched at her wrists as she clung to the ladder, stinging in all the wounds and grazes.

"Hang on, Jaipahl!" Megan shouted in his ear, as they cleared the ladder, falling flat on the pitching deck and grabbing for rope ends. It was day—black cloud, black water washing over the stern. Sailors were handing down buckets, calling the first out of the hold to the fixed pumps to relieve exhausted crew. The ceramic gears whined as slaves and crewfolk heaved at the crank handles, and spouts of filthy bilgewater scudded across the deck, lost in the wind-blown wrack.

"There's still a lot of headway on the ship." Even the rags were dangerous in *this*; bare poles would have been. The small spritsail at the bow was still holding, keeping the ship steerable, but the forestay to the mizzenmast thrummed like a harpstring. "Ach, Koru help us! The hull won't stand much more of this from the sound!"

The hatch flipped out of the crew's hands, grabbed

by the wind and ripped back off its hinges like paper tearing as Megan dug her claws into the deck to keep from being dragged loose, trying to breathe between waves.

She blinked salt water out of her eyes. Stays parted with deep musical notes, the cables flying wildly. Five or six crew were fighting to hold the two-meter circle of the wheel whenever the rudder was in the water. She craned her head to look as the bow rose, and fought an internal cringe: waves, waves mast-high in black water as far as she could see, the tops ripping off into spume under the shrieking wind until sea and sky mixed into wolf-grey chaos. Megan coughed, waves pressed water into her nose, wind driving air out of her lungs. She put her head down, clinging to water casks lashed to the deck. Jaipahl crawled over to her like a brown bug under a waterfall, a waterfall that poured past him through the opened hatch into the hold. Bursts of seawater smashed the bucket brigade back into the dark, and the motion of the ship grew more sluggish, as if she had sand under her keel and no sea room. Between one wave and the next, Jaipahl was gone.

"Jaipahlllll!!!" Megan screamed into the wind. There was no answer but the empty rope flailing on the deck where he'd been.

Below, someone screamed, and from forward the wooden shriek of the ship ran up the scale, making Megan's teeth hurt before the mizzenmast broke just below deck. It swayed forward, leaned to port and pivoted in its collar, grinding the broken butt-end through the holds. The oak deck ripped. "Jaiiiiipahhlll!!!"

The *Flycatcher* lurched, leaned to starboard and turned her bow out of the wind. A wave reared over the rail and seemed to hover for a second. The slats all along the ship's bow sprang, pouring water below. She started to roll broadside, hesitated a long, long instant on her side at the top of wave. The massed screaming of the slaves and crew could be heard even over the storm's sound.

Megan looked straight down the width of the deck and down the black wall of water stretching below. She leaped over the gunwale, onto the side of the *Flycatcher* as the ship rolled, ran down to the keel coming up out of the water, and threw herself into the sea, trying to get away from the suction of the sinking ship. A dark shape struck her, and she clung, driving her nails into wood and sisal cordage.

The coaster *Liquid Radiance* heeled in the wind. Shkai'ra looked up from relacing the shoulder-plate of her armor in annoyance.

It was two hours past noon, and the wind was at their backs from the east; with the tide working for them they should reach Illizbuah before sunset, tomorrow if the Captain decided to salvage more storm flotsam. The flat Fehinnan coast was already a low blue line against the horizon in the west. The dozen crew and four—what the captain euphemistically called "rescued"—castaways all turned longing glances toward shore.

At least I'm alive, Shkai'ra thought resignedly. That had been a question of some uncertainty, back half a week ago when the *Radiance* had picked her and the Fehinnans up off the beach, on receipt of signed scrip acknowledging the debt of passage money, as an act of well-paid benevolence to fellow Fehinnans.

Fellow Fehinnans or residents, Shkai'ra thought, wiping sweat from her face. She envied the sailors, clad in light tunics or stripped to their breechclouts. Half an hour of this sun would turn her into a baked lobster if she so much as took off her shirt.

The lookout at the mast called something in sailor's argot, lowering his binoculars and pointing. Shkai'ra rose to her feet and walked to the rail; behind her, Ten-Knife-Foot curled on top of her duffle. When the merchantman had beaten herself to pieces on the sand, the tom had clung to her shoulders, yowling at the water all the way as Shkai'ra had floundered and waded ashore; a small miracle, like others in the years since they met. Perhaps there had been the will of a spirit in that; she made the warding gesture to the gods with her sword-hand.

She knew no loose fingers would touch her things if they wanted to stay attached. Ten-Knife-Foot guarded everything he considered his very well. She shaded her eyes with a hand and peered ahead past the smooth ripple of the *Radiance*'s cutwater. The cat probably considered her among *his* possessions. All she could see was the glittering flat surface of the water, riffled by the steady onshore wind, and a few high clouds, land just visible on the horizon.

"What is it?" she asked the sailor next to her as he squinted at the waves. He was a typical low-country Fehinnan, short and mahogany-brown with close-cropped wiry black hair; he glanced doubtfully up at her long-limbed height, as if surprised someone with red-blond braids could speak the language of civilization. Tall fair folk were rare in Fehinna, although not unknown north of the Cayspec or west in the mountains, and most such tribes were savages.

"Wreck," he said shortly. "No wonder a't, wh'it storm blew itself out." The hurricane had torn itself into mere storms against the coast, and the *Radiance* had ridden out the worst of it fairly handily in the lee of the offshore islands.

Shkai'ra nodded, then drew up her binoculars. The sea leaped close, wavering with the motion. "It's . . ." she began. "Hmm. It's a big round piece of wood, with bits of ropes and canvas hanging off it, and a body . . ." The distant tiny figure moved, and a gull leaped away flapping ". . . no, with somebody alive hanging on to it."

. . . damn seagulls, . . . ow . . . get off. Megan waved a hand just enough to scare the birds. The sun shimmered in her eyes as she blinked, trying to clear the stinging of salt. Her left hand was still tied into the snarl of rope where she'd lashed it when she started to fear her grip slipping; the wrist-galls were newly chaffed open by the rope, stinging with salt. They wouldn't fester, though she worried that the blood would draw sharks or barracuda. At least she was clean, having been in the water for a couple of days—wrinkled and badly sunburned, but clean. She'd had nothing but a rag loincloth and a few scraps of sail against the sun's heat. She'd let her hair down at first to help cover her skin against the sun, but found it catching in every crack and tangling around her arms and legs whenever she was in the water, so had braided it up again.

She tried swallowing, but her mouth was too dry, tongue like boot leather. She worked her hand free and pulled herself higher up on the board though it exposed her to the sun. From that position she could make better headway, lying belly down with the wooden edge at her armpits, paddling with her hands.

The shore line was a tantalizing darker blue ribbon on the horizon, maybe ten *chiliois* away. Too far away to abandon the hatch-cover and just swim. Either way, the current she was in pushed her further away.

The water had warmed and changed color, tasting less of salt—an estuary of some kind. There were more birds in the sky and floating branches washed from inland. She paddled, started up as her face touched the water and paddled again, trying not to fade into unconsciousness.

I just have to make it that far. After everything,

I'm not giving up now. She edged back and laid
her cheek on the warm, almost hot wood, glad for
the water lapping over it, then pulled a flap of canvas up to cover her head, rinsed and spat salt water,
dribbling warm down her chin. *Gotta stop doin' that
. . . be too tempted to swallow . . . crazy with salt.*
She spat, waved a hand at the gulls that had settled
again. *Sun. Flapping air-rats . . . damn you, won't
get my eyeballs yet. Waves thundering in my head
. . . no, sails, dream ships chasing gulls away, dream-
ing tackle squeal, thunder's the sails.* What roused
her from her daze was the shadow of the ship,
blocking the sun that had burned down on her with
bone-biting intensity. *A real ship?* A reaching boathook snagged at the ropes at one end of her hatch
cover. *Koru, let it be real. . . .*

Shkai'ra had sauntered back to her duffle and scratched
under Ten-Knife-Foot's chin. She sat down, leaning
against the barrel, throwing her dice idly against the
deck rather than going back to the shoulder lacing.
*Have to figure out what to do once I get back to the
City. Not completely broke, for once. Jaibo'll probably still be visiting his kinfast up river. . . .* She
glanced over at the castaway they were just bringing
onboard.

A small, pale woman lying on the boards, black
braids knotted and crusted with salt, silver nail-paint
shining on her hands. *Captain might get a good passage fee from that one. Looks like she might clean up
nicely, though I don't recognize the race.* White-
skinned as a Payalach highlander, but tiny, like a dwarf
except that the proportions were normal. She craned
her neck, more interested, as the bosun looked up and
said something to the captain, smiling, pointing to the
woman's ankles and the wooden cuffs. The captain
smacked his palms together and clasped self-satisfied
hands in the small of his back as he turned back to

the wheel. The bosun sent someone below and held a cup of water to the woman on the deck. Ten-Knife put his paws out on Shkai'ra's knee and started to knead and purr. The castaway drank thirstily, coughed, drank more.

"*Ai!* Cat! Stop that!" Shkai'ra unhooked his claws from her horsehide breeches and her skin, dice clattering to the deck, and looked up again as the crewman brought up a length of rope.

They're counting her a found slave. If she lives, her sale will be more than enough to pay for her rescue. There's a good market for exotics in the City, and there aren't many races that small. She looked down at the dice and grinned at the three sixes showing. "*Ia*, Ten-Knife, always lucky when I don't know it or need it."

Her head snapped up at the sudden shouting forward, hand falling reflexively to the bone hilt of her saber. The half-dead castaway had exploded up off the deck when they'd tried to secure her ankle chains. One crewman stumbled back, bloody hands clamped over his face, the bosun lay on the deck with her throat slashed open.

No blade, how—

The castaway launched herself on the next, the one with the boathook, blocked the weapon with one forearm, snatched his belt-knife and slashed up with it in the same motion.

Shkai'ra's mouth pursed in a silent whistle. *Not bad.* Other crew answered the noise, grabbing up belaying pins and rope-ends as they ran. The captain jumped over the poop rail to the main deck, pulling his sword. The woman backed up against the rail, boathook in one hand, knife in the other, bloody to the elbows. She panted, swaying on her feet. Shkai'ra found herself watching, standing relaxed with her hand on her sword. She rather hoped the castaway would escape; that had been a good fight.

There was a black blur from the duffle beside her as Ten-Knife streaked across the deck, leaped up and landed, all claws out, on the captain's cotton-clad back. He shrieked with surprise and pain, spun around, trying to reach over his shoulder with the shortsword; the first mate reached to pull the cat loose and pulled back her thumb bitten to the bone. Ten-Knife jumped down.

"*Nia, nia,*" Shkai'ra said chidingly as the mate swung her wooden club back for a blow. Ten-Knife hissed defiance with arched back and bottled tail. "That's *my* cat."

The long curve of her saber flicked free; the captain turned at the sound, and she smashed the smaller Fehinnan sword loose from his grip with a harsh rasp of metal on metal. Snarling, the mate feinted Shkai'ra with her oak belaying pin, then leaped back from the bright sword edge as it hissed back and forth with negligent speed.

"It's not a fight unless you push it," Shkai'ra said helpfully.

The captain left his first mate to deal with the tall red head for a moment, staring at the small woman at bay at the rail. "You pay passage, mofoar?

"Passage, or you try and sell me?" The woman's voice was steady, her Fehinnan clear.

" 'f you got no coin, you a slave—or you 'kin go over 't side agin."

She looked around at the ring of sailors and nodded. Then she grinned, threw the boathook at one of the crew and somersaulted backward over the side of the ship and into the water, taking the knife with her.

Baiwun, she'd rather drown than be a slave. Not an ekafrek, that one, Shkai'ra thought, edging back as a few of the sailors turned her way. The oak railing touched the small of her back.

Ten-Knife tripped another sailor by running under his feet and skittered down into the hold.

"Rayab! Check t' water, get 't slave back," the captain snapped. "Lissayaz! Don't go aftr t' animal, see t' Tahm an' t'others!" He wrenched his small sword free from the wood of the deck. Then he turned back to Shkai'ra, weapon held point up. It was a Fehinnan infantry shortsword, a leaf-shaped blade with a central blood-gutter and a circular guard at the hilt.

Shkai'ra let her sword's tip make small circles in the air and set herself against the rail; her left hand drew the long double-edged knife she wore across the small of her back.

"You! Your animal cost us tat slave! You fishfukkin' for'n—"

He paused; the foreigner was taller than any of the Fehinnans onboard, and he had seen enough fighters to know the coiled look of a warrior.

Any sailor could fight, and there were weapons and corselets in the arms locker, but . . . that meter length of saber looked sharp enough to part a hair.

"I'll pay gild for the blow I struck you," she said reasonably; her Fehinnan had an unusual accent, staccato and guttural. "But the cat was sent to me by the luck-gods. I can't let any harm it, or my luck might go."

He growled and sheathed his sword with a snap. "Jest see I don see t' beast agin or ay'all do more'n add t' yer fee. I've alus had a hankerin' for catskin gloves!" She held his eyes and nodded once, slowly.

"No sign, Cap!" the crewman called. "No swimmers!"

He spat on the deck and stalked away. Shkai'ra looked over the rail into the green-brown water. *Rather drown than be a slave.* She sauntered back to her duffle and scooped up the dice in a thoughtful mood. *Spunky little bitch.*

Smyna Caaituh's-kin, General-Commander in the Iron House and Grand Captain of Fehinna, held a page of paper in the flame of the alcohol lamp on her desk. She poked at the ashes with the ivory stem of her pipe until they thoroughly mixed into the mess in her ashtray. Then she closed the folder in front of her with long wire-strong fingers, tying the ribbon, dropping on a glob of hot wax and rolling her sigil onto it with a small cylinder of inscribed stone. The smell of the wax mingled with the Iron House's old scents: ancient mass-concrete, well-tended woodwork, warrior's leather and metal, hints of tobacco and smoke.

A touch on the china gong, and an aide came to file the papers in the sanctum; another brought her a jug of pomegranate juice, sweating coolness through the unglazed pottery surface. The soldier leaned back against her padded wicker backrest, lighting her pipe and blowing a meditative smoke ring at the coffered vault of the ceiling, sipped at the astringent liquid and thought.

She was a tall Fehinnan and very thin in a muscular fashion, close-cropped black hair showing no sign of grey yet despite her forty years. The plain military tunic of dull scarlet cotton that reached to her knees bore few of the decorations she was entitled to, simply the golden sunbursts on the shoulders that marked her rank; for the rest she wore a family signet ring. A plain officer's longsword stood in its rack by the door, a single-edged weapon with a brass basket hilt. She glanced up at it, then stared down at her hands on the desk and traced the soldier's callus on the right as she considered the summary she'd just burned.

"Divine Solar Light, but things were easier when I only had a cavalry regiment to think about," she murmured softly; her accent had the liquid precision of a tidewater aristocrat.

As General-Commander she was one of the most powerful people in the City, as long as she didn't let either of the other two factions in the Iron House gain any ground. Which was difficult; the problem with being at the top of the heap was that it made you the only target for the ones a step or two below.

War is a great simplifier, she thought. *And I know just the war to start.*

The intelligence report had been fairly unequivocal. It had been fifty years since the Five Nations War, and Fehinna had recovered faster than any of the coalition that had fought her to a standstill two generations ago. They would be in no position to stop Fehinna expanding, as long as the armies of the God-King didn't try to move directly north. *And we're ready.*

Her eyes lifted to the map across the room. Fehinna held most of the lowlands around the Cayspec; five centuries ago they had finished pushing the last of the western savages out of the fertile Piedmont country, over the Blue Crests and the great valley beyond, into the rugged wastes of the Payalach Mountains. No profit in war there, against wild highlanders who had little worth taking; most of them were headhunters, many were cannibals, and all of them had damnable skill with their horn-and-elm bows.

Not north, no. Maailun and Eassho were both smaller than Fehinna but nearly as rich and much alike in customs and speech, properly worshiping the Sun, however heretical their fashion. Behind them the Penza city-states, Lankaz and Yawuc and the rest. The last great war had gone north, lasted a decade and killed every fourth adult in five great nations.

South is the prize, she knew. Kaailun. Huge, populous, but rather backward by her nation's standards; the people spoke dialects similar to Fehinnan, but they were pagans who slaughtered cattle and humans to the ancient spirits, Gawhud and Olsaytn, Jayskri and Ussay. She made the holy sun-circle over her chest. That would interest the priests, in their ever-eager hunt for heretics. More to the point, what had been a loosely united kingdom in her grandparents' time had fallen apart into feudal anarchy, an anarchy among which Fehinnan money and agents had laid the foundations of conquest.

Not an easy war, but well worth it. Rich land, needing only modern techniques to bring it to full bearing. A people advanced enough to make valuable and docile slaves and underlings, as well; the markets would be glutted. Glory and wealth for the leaders, estates for the younger-child gentlefolk who officered the Fehinnan armies, farms for settlers.

Not to mention converts for the temple to tithe, she added mentally; although sometimes she felt they were almost as eager for recalcitrants to send to the Holy Light.

One solution for several problems. *Maahk and Sanha, to start with.* Both corps-commanders, both able, and both from rival family coalitions. A serious war would leave many extremely honorable and extremely perilous positions to be filled . . . which they could not decline with honor.

Now to convince the priests.

Under the Sun-On-Earth, the God-King, She-who-lives-forever, the High Priest Cubilano was the power in the temple. Eager for expansion; not so eager to see the military grow in power and influence.

But. But. There was always a but. She got up and paced the office.

The merchants. Illizbuah had suffered less than the countryside during the Five Nations War, and the opening of the trans-Lannic trade was bringing in incredible wealth. All of which, and its attendant power, went to the urban patricians, not to the landowners who should have it, by ancient hereditary right.

Not to mention the Guild of the Wise. Scholars, officially—there were rumors of magic—were just

barely tolerated by the priesthood, who resented their
breaking the clerical monopoly on higher learning.
Very valuable as navigators and mechanicians, doctors
and numerators, and heavily patronized by the merchant community . . . and the state.

War was a long-term investment; taxes would go up,
they'd have to, and quite a few *shaaid*, the lowest
caste, would starve to death. She shrugged off the
thought. There were always more.

The merchants would see their profits squeezed and
the expansion of the trans-Lannic colonies slowed.
Military contracts could not begin to compensate, and
then again, with territorial expansion the aristocracy
would be fully back in the saddle again.

She looked out; the window was above the roof level
of much of the Iron House, and looked out over the
City, at the flame on the golden dome of the temple,
at hectares of jumbled red-tiled roofs, towers and gardens and tenement blocks.

*I'll get the High Priest on my side, however I do it,
and once this war starts I'll be secure. All I have to
do is get Cubilano to hear me and hope that the Sun-
On-Earth takes no notice what games her faithful are
playing.* She picked up the folder on her desk. *I'll let
him see these if he seems . . . reasonable.* She signed
herself again. The Sun-On-Earth might well listen to
rival voices . . . or not listen at all.

The God-King could be . . . alarming.

CHAPTER II

The *Radiance* slowed, coasting in toward the shore on her larboard tack. The water warmed a little, a sign that the bottom was shelving, and tackle rattled as the ship prepared to come about and head into the bay. Megan raised her head, trying to see in the spray, looking up from where she clung by one hand to the leading edge of the rudder of the ship; the other cramped, wrapping around the hilt of the knife driven into the hull.

When she'd gone over the side, the ship had been making two knots, just getting under way after having cast loose the hatch cover that had been her raft. She'd been scraped by the barnacles of the hull and knocked under once but stayed close enough to grab. The hull right here was fairly smooth, slippery because of a skirt of weed; the coaster needed to be hauled out and cleaned.

Koru, if I ever complain of having a boring life ever again I give you permission *to rain divine farts on me*.

She was hungry, trying to shake visions of barley

and mushroom soup out of her head, warm crusty amaranth bread sopping up the juices from a roast; honeynut pastries and maple sugar. Even remembering the mash on the slaver made her mouth water.

She'd driven the knife into the hull just in front of the rudder, hoping that whoever was on the wheel wasn't experienced enough to feel the drag.

I'm glad that I could speak to the cat, and that it felt like fighting, she thought, clamping her teeth together to keep them from chattering. Even warm water leeched the heat out a body, eventually—worse if it was moving. Back home a person could die in a few minutes if he fell into the river just before freezeup. Megan had always liked cats; dogs tended to be too sloppily disgusting for her taste. *Even if Shyll happens to like them.* For a moment, homesickness caught at her throat; Shyll and her cousin Rilla, the hard-won warmth of her own home, the House of the Sleeping Dragon she had built into a great trading firm from a single leaky riverboat. . . . *Enough of that.*

The moon was up, its reflection wrinkling in the water, as the long, slow ghosts of storm waves rumbled in among the mangroves and swamp cypress. She could swim that far, she thought, when it was just a bit darker, perhaps one more tack.

The sky was a deep blue silk, edged with orangey gold on one hem and jet on the other. The diamond embroidery of stars was just showing when she yanked the knife free and hesitated. She had never liked to hurt a ship if she could avoid it. On the other hand—

I know this type of merchant, even if they aren't of my race. They'd skin a tick for its hide and tallow and complain of their meager living while cleaning their teeth with ivory toothpicks. Trying to put shackles on a castaway was downright inhospitable and unsailorlike, too. She reached up and snaked her hand through the hole where the stempost of the rudder met the under-deck tiller, feeling for the wrist-thick ropes that ran through pulleys to transmit the torque of the wheel. They were just where they would be on a ship like this back on the *Mitvald Zee*. With exquisite care, she sawed at the rope until it was almost cut through. The mate's knife was excellent steel and half as long as her forearm, much better than the usual crewfolk tool; it was good and sharp, as well.

One more tack and you'll lose steerage; inconvenience you for a day. She grinned to herself as she let go and let the *Radiance* pull away from her. *A good-bye present to someone who tried to take me for a slave*.

Awkwardly, clutching the knife in her teeth, she swam with a slow, even stroke to the mangroves and hauled herself out of the water and the ooze, climbing up the main trunk. There, in a springy tangle of branches that were well above the wave action, she fell asleep.

Next morning she grinned at the distant speck that must be the coaster, driven further out by the estuary current while they tried to affect repairs.

"Good morning!" she said, as if the captain could hear her. Then she licked dry lips. First course was to find water. Then food. She slapped at the mosquitoes. And some kind of clothing against the bugs.

As the sun rose higher, she found a pool of cleanish water further in the swamp and drank through a handful of grass to strain it as best she could. Her claws were blunting but they wore through the oak around her ankles so she could pull her feet free and felt much better even though the thick, rot-stinking mud clung to her all over. Without the wood, her ankles were braceletted by black leeches where the skin was broken.

"Koru, I think the Dark Lord thought this place up as an antechamber to Halya," she muttered, looking at the fringe of leeches around one ankle slowly ballooning from tassels to lumps.

Later that afternoon, she avoided a pack of miniature alligators, watching them swarm a strayed cow, picking the beast down to bones in the time it took to count one hundred. The gators were barely the length of her hand, nothing like the man-sized creatures that hunted the warm rivers south of the Mitvald Sea, or the ten-meter oceangoing kind. . . . But a stray cow meant that humans lived somewhere near.

Climbing through the limber trunks of the tangled mangroves to avoid the gators' pond, she blinked to chase way the greenish-grey blotches swimming across her sight.

"Got to eat soon," she muttered, then clamped her lips shut against making any more noise than she had to. *I need something more orderly than all these stupid trees, something like pavement. Maybe a good building or two to block out this miserable wilderness.* The almost dry ground under her feet was enough of a shock to make her stumble, and the sounds she heard ringing through the trees cheered her no end; the rasp of saws, the squeal of a hand mill, dogs barking, geese, voices. The sound of a village carried for a couple of chiliois sometimes.

But they're probably the sort like that captain, she thought. *Besides, I've no money to buy with.* She found a relatively dry hollow to wait for the sun to go down, too hungry to feel hunger, only emptiness, trying to ignore her awful hair, matted with sweat, salt at the roots, grease, and crushed insects. She leaned her head back against the tree, looking up through the grey-green leaves festooned with strange grey moss that looked like hair. *First, after all the essentials, I have to find a city big enough to have a fair-sized port, and get back home before everything's in ruins.* The man who had drugged her and sold her off was *not* the sort to keep a shipping firm in good order.

The village was on the edge of a dredged canal, houses set up on long pole legs. The animal pens were clustered below, and from one house came the voices of the villagers, talking, singing. As the night deepened, they went their ways in ones and twos, the hum of their talk comfortable as hive-bees on a hot, drowsy day. She waited till the moon was up, looking to see Shamballah, the god's moon, then shook her head. She'd read enough sailor's rutter-books, and all reported if you went far enough west, or east, Shamballah wouldn't show in the sky at all. This country must be at least seven or eight thousand chiliois west of F'talezon, the full length of the Mitvald and the full width of the Lannic Ocean as well.

She avoided the pens full of geese, because they were better watchers than dogs. A tunic seized from a clothesline made her feel more human. *Someone's left a pie of some kind on the windowsill up there.* When the scratch of her claws on the wood roused no one inside, she paused just under the window. Suspicious of something so easy to take, she stilled herself, listening. She could only hear two sounds, and knew that the dog was below at the pigpen. Megan wrinkled her nose at the stray odor. Just as coffee smelled better than it tasted, live pigs smelled much worse than pork.

When she lifted the pie from the sill, careful not to scrape it across the wood, she bit her lip slightly because it was still hot enough to redden her hands. From inside came a fluttering snore and she froze. Another snore.

She clambered down carefully, changing her grip on the pie, saliva in her mouth as she smelled the warm fruit odor of blackberries. The first bite was Koru's Lap itself, and she closed her eyes blissfully, stopping herself from trying to cram the whole thing into her mouth at once, holding back the urge to gorge.

Now. We'll see how well the canoes are tied and what town that coaster was making for. A big freshwater estuary like this meant a river, and settlements usually clustered where river and sea met.

A long day later she looked across the water at the largest city she'd ever seen in her life. Even at a distance the low, wide golden dome bulked in the eastern quarter like a mountain, the long tongue of flame at its apex licking at blue-black undersides of clouds rolling in from the north. The setting sun picked out the tops of the towering clouds in orange and gold. The hectares of city below gleamed in the hazy sun, white seawalls tinted pink. Distantly, she could see the bulk of a fort at either end of the wall. Two more in the middle broke up the pattern of warehouses, docking basins and gardens, then more warehouses, more docks. She whistled to herself. This city sprawled, where every city she'd ever known coiled in on itself. There was nothing like this back in the Mitvald, except perhaps Arko the City Itself, the Imperial capital.

She paddled across the river, avoiding the wash of a four-masted warship, running under bare poles against the tide. It was propelled by no means she could see, though there was a beat being struck inside the hull, keeping time for someone. Her stolen canoe blended in with hundreds of others on the city side of the river, clustering away from the customs gates and forts, passing the sailing ships.

The seawall was impressive, presenting a blank, white stone face to the estuary. She assumed it would be difficult to get in without papers or clearance of some sort, especially considering what Jaipahl had told her. Her eyebrows furrowed in a frown. *Rather frown than cry.* After the storm had died, she'd searched in the wreckage, paddling from floating bundle to floating bundle, uselessly.

The memory of his dry old scholar's tone triggered

another thought. This city must be Illizbuah, Fehin-na's capital. She couldn't imagine a city larger than this. She floated a moment, noticing the measured patrol along the top of the city walls. They were far between, which made sense if this was the capital city in the heart of their home territory.

Her dugout scraped the low walkway disappearing under the rising tide. She tilted her head back. It was a smooth wall, but the cracks were enough to give her claws a grip. There was only a bit of shadow here, because of the angle of the wall. She sighed. She'd have to use more power. As tired as she was, as hungry as she was, she doubted she'd be able to hold any illusion longer than an instant or two.

She tied the canoe to one of the poured-stone rings in the walkway and stood up to her ankles in water. Breathing evenly, she blanked her mind, drawing on the pool of power she saw in her head, and was startled at how thinned down it felt. Almost startled enough to break her concentration, she steadied and imagined herself becoming part of the wall, fading from sight as she thought of flat, white stone and climbed. She lay on top of the wall for a long moment panting, nauseated, a headache beginning to pound behind her eyes.

Up, get up. The patrol is coming, and I don't *want anyone to see me getting in.* She tried not to shudder as she called on power a second time, to hide her climb down.

It took her a long time to recover from that, the ache fierce enough in her head that she didn't notice a sweeping thought arcing from the temple, seeking through the mind-world like a swaying cobra.

Her hands shook as she walked along the docks, a fact that she hid by jamming them in the back of her belt, swaggering as if she'd entered through the gate and had every right to be where she was. *Never look weak in a poor quarter, and conversely, never swagger enough to draw a challenge; especially if one is a foreigner.* That had been her mother's advice, years ago.

The streets nearest the dock were dark, a poured-stone pole standing at one corner with the lamp at the top broken, glass shards lying around the base. She emerged from the small streets into a roar of light and sound.

"I think I'm going to like this place, the short time I'm here," she said to herself, and leaned against the wall to look down the street.

Shkai'ra sank down and studied the view between her toes as they floated and dipped through the light wisps of steam on the surface of the bath water; there was more than enough room, since the tubs were the sawn halves of wine casks built to hold a tonne each. Dying evening light slanted down from the window opposite, picking out detail: the cool blue flagstones, the warm brown tile that covered the walls of the long rectangular room, the band of blue-flowered glazed tile around the edge of the ceiling.

Also the warning over the arched entrance, of course: *Patrons must soap and rinse before entering tubs. No food or fornication while bathing. Penalty for peeing in the bath water is clubbing to unconsciousness.* There was an attendant to enforce it, too; a black giant from the Sea Islands leaning on the weighted staff that was his people's national weapon. Fehinnans took cleanliness seriously, and the Weary Wayfarer's Hope of Comfort and Delight was a respectable inn, unlike many of its customers.

Shkai'ra ducked her head, scrubbing at the roots of her hair to get rid of the last of the salt; having been delayed while the ship affected repairs had been irritating enough to make her promise to sacrifice a sheep to Glitch, godlet of fuckups, if he would just *ignore* her for a while. Some people petitioned Glitch for *good* luck, but that was pointless. She surfaced, wallowing with luxurious content. In her homeland, folk bathed once a month, less in winter, and a hot soak was a special comfort for the elderly, to ease the pain of often-broken bones.

If you live on the Great River, learn to enjoy catfish, she quoted to herself, throwing back the damp mass of her hair.

A portly man bustled in with an armload of towels and a tray of stoneware jugs.

"Firehair!" he said, stopping. "Still alive! I thought the sharks would eat you sure, down south."

"Junno, you're *always* surprised when someone makes a journey outside the city and lives," she replied. He was one of the kinfast that owned the Weary Wayfarer, and an old friend of sorts. "Nothing down there but cheap rum and big bugs. They got you hauling wine again?"

He sighed and sat down, removing the stopper from a jug and refilled her cup. "Shorthanded," he said, and scowled. "Two of our people killed in a riot—times are hard, very hard. Plenty of scum we could hire, but we're waiting for trustworthy help. Glad to have you here again, by the Immortal Sun."

Shkai'ra nodded; she got a reduced rate, on the understanding she would help crack heads if necessary. This was not the quietest section of town.

"I noticed the harbor wasn't crowded," she said.

"War talk, and traders waiting till things settle down before they spend," Junno said. He refilled her cup again and took a drink himself. "Just when everyone was finally making a little coin, enough to pay their taxes and eat meat once a week —" Shkai'ra looked ironically at his well-padded stomach "—the Iron House has nothing better to do than think up a new war. Soldiers! Murdering scum—no offense."

"None taken," Shkai'ra said. In her native tongue murderer was a complimentary term, anyway. Junno chuckled and heaved himself erect; she snaked out an arm to ensure he left the jug.

The warm air smelled pleasantly of hot stone, soap and the screens of woven cedarwood strips between the tubs; the others were all full, to judge by the splashings and low sounds of conversation, but nobody had disputed her possession of a tub large enough for three—four, if they were Fehinnans. There were *some* advantages to being a foreigner here. Relaxing into the heat, she considered reaching for the wine cup on the floor beside her, then settled for reaching her hand down to Ten-Knife-Foot. A furred head butted against the fingertips; she rubbed and was rewarded with a deep rumbling purr.

Ahi-a, she thought. What to do? Feasting, fornication and fighting were the choices. . . .

Feet stepped into her field of vision. Woman's feet, small, well-formed but battered and callused, with half-healed circular scars around the ankles. Long legs . . . no, only in proportion. Good build; she noted the way the buttocks curved at the back but flattened even with the thighs at the sides—hard exercise. An old scar angling up along the muscles of her belly, breasts high and rounded, strong neck, shoulders sloping from the deltoids. Scars: knife fighter's scars. A good knife fighter, to have lived a score of years with a disadvantage in reach.

The face was alien here in Fehinna. It would have been more so in the bleak stone keeps and huddled villages of the watcher's northwestern home. Triangular, the eyes enormous and as black as the hair that tumbled almost to her calves. Strange, she thought. And beautiful.

"Mo'kta moi-trutka azhyt," Shkai'ra said suddenly, in her own language: "Well, dip me in dung." "I've seen *you* before."

The small woman tensed slightly. Shkai'ra smiled, lying back with her arms along the edge of the tub and reaching for the carved hickory wine cup.

"Don't worry; if I saw that shipload of bandits dying of thirst in a desert, I wouldn't spit on them. It might give them the strength to crawl to water. Very nice, the way you took out that kinless fishfucker's throat. Fast." She eyed the other woman. "I don't think you'd make a very good slave, anyway. Can't see you lying down peacefully for the master's horny teenaged off-spring, somehow." She sipped, continuing in a slightly different tone: "Room for two."

Pretty, she thought idly. *Interesting.* One of the compensations of exile was meeting odd types. Everything came to Illizbuah if you waited, went the saying. Although it was very odd that they should meet again; it smelled of luck. *Two sheep, Glitch*, she added mentally.

"I thank you," the other said, in Fehinnan still more heavily accented. She laid a fingertip to the white strand of hair at her temple and inclined her head slightly. "I hight . . . pardon, am Megan. Called . . . *Byeliy-skayishka*, ah, 'White-Hair-Bit?'" She indicated the silver strand in her hair.

"Whitlock," Shkai'ra said, pronouncing the word carefully. "I think. Godsdamned Fehinnan always sounds like they've got porridge in their mouths." She shrugged. "I'm being rude. Speed to your horse, strength to your lance, a straight shaft to your bow. Shkai'ra Mek-Kermak's-Kin, I am called: late Senior in Stonefort, in the Kommanz of Granfor. On the Sea of Grass, six months' travel north and west."

Megan examined her speculatively. The copper-blond hair was darker wet and she hadn't recognized the woman at first. Tall, eyes of a pale smoke-grey, startling against the dark-tanned face. A thin high-cheeked face . . . a saber must have caused that scar arcing from the corner of an eye down the cheek;

there were other white marks on right arm and left leg, below where the shield would cover. A cavalry fighter, then. That would accord with the greeting; and a plainsdweller, like those at home.

The appraisal flickered through her mind in the instant it took to slide into the water, submerge, and resurface, slicking hair back from her face. A few suds floated free, from the preliminary cleaning; the swamps took more than one rinsing to wash out of her memory, even if the mud was off her skin.

"A titled one . . . The only rank I claim is Riverguild Master, out of F'talezon in Zakos, and owner/captain of my own ship. Over the Great Sea—the Lannic, it is called here, and in the eastern end of the Mitvald." *No need to tell her any more than that. The company, ships, warehouses and all, may be down to rags before I get back.*

"Nice to hear someone who speaks Fehinnan with a worse accent than mine," Shkai'ra said, grinning. She was actually fluent, but the sounds were difficult for her after the staccato gutturals of Kommanzanu.

Resentful at being ignored, the cat stood on his hind legs, stretching up. She smiled, an odd closed curve of the lips, and scratched expertly behind his ears. The yellow eyes closed to slits.

"As for titles, 'penniless exile' would be better, here. Or 'sellsword,' as the Fehinnans say." She tipped more of the jug into her cup. "Just back from a long voyage south; little profit, damnably sober and chaste, and several shipwrecks. Seawater holds no luck for me."

"We have that in common, then. Hello, little shadowbrother." Megan said, regarding the cat. It returned her gaze and yawned, pink and white and cavernous.

"I picked him up two seasons ago, on the western border."

The arrows had come out of the scrub oak along the mountain trail at dusk.

"We didn't do too well."

*She had shot her quiver empty: the Kommanz wheel-
bow hit harder than anything east of the Great River,
but none of the others were horsearchers. . . .*

"I woke up with a broken arm; my horse lying
across one leg."

*Crusted blood on her eyelids. Yelling laughter from
the tribesfolk as they took their pick of heads and
melted back into the forest.*

"Ten-Knife was sitting on my chest, the next time
I woke up."

*The sound the wounded made, when the scavengers
found them.*

"Wine?" she said, raising her cup and admiring the
sheen on the swirling grain.

Megan reached over to stretch out a hand to Ten-
Knife, carefully. He sniffed, twice, then turned and
inclined his head, purring as she rubbed the indicated
cheek. "I've passed his first test, it seems," she said
lightly, lying back again and letting her hair drift free
in the soothing water.

Good, to feel clean again, she thought. *Very good.*
Though there had been plenty of water in the swamp,
all of it had left her feeling greasy.

She opened her eyes to the ceiling, glass skylights
and mosaics of colored stone showing seaweed and
fish, thinking that she never wanted to see grey moss
hanging over her again. It went with the smell.

They lounged in silence for minutes, comfortably.
"I'm starting to wrinkle," Shkai'ra said. "Odd habits
they have here in the southlands, soaking the whole
body in warm water. Nice, in limited amounts."

"In so warm a climate, I can ynerstun . . . understand it," Megan said. "Fehinnans seem offended by
smells. The wine smells good, but not on an empty
stomach."

She'd eaten several small meals over the day already,
not wanting to gorge and make herself sick, but was
hungry again.

"I could eat," Shkai'ra said. "After all that hardtack, I could eat half a roasted pig. Gods and demons, I got sick of coconut and pineapple down south."

Megan found herself wanting company. *I've always been comfortable alone*, she thought. *But that's always been in a familiar place or surrounded by my own people.*

Shkai'ra rose and wrapped herself in the cool fluffy towel held out by an inn servant. "The Weary Wayfarer sets a good table," she said, stretching with unselfconscious pleasure. "Among its other virtues. Neutrality is one; freelances stay here, from the City and the world." She looked down to the smaller woman; standing, the other's head just reached her breastbone. "We are not unfriends." There was a speculative look in her eyes, just for an instant. "Perhaps we may become friends." The narrow face lit for a moment in an oddly charming smile. "It would be dangerous for both of us if we were enemies, I think."

Megan looked up and imagined that face over a blade, all angles and planes, with not a soft line in it. "You'd have the weight and reach on me," she said casually as they proceeded through to the changing room. *Flattery. What does she want?* Attendants handed them long linen robes and cloth sandals. "But I'd be willing to wager on speed, if only for the first pass," she continued, tying the sash of the robe herself, forestalling the servant who tried to do it for her. *She knows this city, even if she's not native. We'll see.*

There was an outdoor dining area, tucked into the angle between two roofs at second-story level. Seaward, the masts of ships showed forest-thick over the warehouses. Harbor smells were overborne by roasting meat and garlic.

"Ach, that smells good," Megan said, looking around at the low tables and cushions. *Like home.* The table bore candles in glass bubbles, salt, spices, a platter of cornbread, a tall beaker, and cups of cool brown stoneware. The breeze blew crisp and strong, damp from the river but cool against skins still heated from the baths. The wind was rising before rain.

Shkai'ra shook herself and tucked her feet beneath her on the cushions. "Fish stew?" she said to Megan inquiringly.

"It sounds better than what I've been eating lately." *No need to mention slave gruel.* "But I have wished for good red meat."

"I was raised on steak myself," Shkai'ra said. "Well, then. Hmmm."

A rotund woman climbed puffing out onto the rooftop terrace, followed by several servers with trays. She presented them at a neighboring table, whisking off the ceramic covers to a round of applause as blue flames danced over the dish. Then she waddled over to Shkai'ra's table, mopping at her face with one end of the towel that lay around her neck.

"Ah! Shkai'ra!" she said. "So thin, so thin!" A sausage-like finger prodded at muscle that lay like smooth armor over the Kommanza's ribs. "You will starve without Annulu to cook for you." The fat woman's Fehinnan held a slight trace of a singsong accent, and she was paler than the run of lowlanders. She turned to Megan. "I tell her often, to be thin is a temptation to wickedness—only we fat people are to be trusted. We are too heavy to be wicked—not quick enough. She should eat!"

Shkai'ra sank a friendly elbow into the cook's side. "We'd decided we both want meat," she said. "What's good?"

"*Everything* out of Glaaghi's kitchen is good . . . especially when I do a special hire—then it is my kitchen!" Annulu said in mock anger. "But for you and your friend, it will be especially good. Wait. It will be a surprise." She nudged Shkai'ra with her foot. "Manners, outland barbarian."

"Ah." Shkai'ra started slightly, then made the introduction.

"I greet you and your family and look forward to your art," Megan said.

"More than art. Magic!" Annulu said, retreating to the stairwell.

At Megan's raised eyebrow, Shkai'ra spoke. "Old friends," she said. "I lent her part of the money to buy herself, back when." A reminiscent grin. "Long story. The price kept going up because she's the best cook in the New City . . . and she couldn't bear to do a bad meal."

A plate of pickled appetizers appeared; then red bean soup with prawns, hot in both meanings of the word, with a salad of greens; then roast of pork, honey-glazed and stuffed with truffles and onions; steamed seaweed; baked sweet potatoes on a bed of scented rice. The wine had a strange musky tang to Megan's palate, but it was pleasing.

They both ate with the slow enjoyment of those who have gone hungry often. At last Shkai'ra sighed, mopped up a corner of her plate with a heel of bread, and belched comfortably. Swift, efficient hands removed the soiled dishes and replaced them with platters of cheese and flatbread, more wine, and a pot suspended in a porcelain frame over an open flame. Megan discretely laid a clip of metal under the edge of the plate and never saw it disappear. In her estimation, it was enough to pay for good service; especially since she'd found she'd stolen quite a lot the evening before, not knowing the value of the metal. *Servers in inns are always underpaid anyway.*

Shkai'ra paused, considered, and poured herself a cup of the tea rather than more wine. "Ahi-a, at home I'd be eating jerked meat in the saddle, while we fought to keep the nomads off the crops. Exile can have its compensations." She smiled and glanced upward. Now the long twilight of summer was fading, and clouds rolled black along the western horizon. A small storm rolling in, one of the hurricane's children.

"Exile?" Megan began, raising an eyebrow.

"But for all the striving and slaying," Shkai'ra said, an hour later, "I've only what I arrived with: my sword and my wits." They had been exchanging bits of their life stories; suitably edited, Megan was sure—her own certainly had been, by omission. It was unusual that she felt as talkative as she did.

Shkai'ra linked her fingers and rested her chin on them; her smile was oddly charming on the long harsh face, and her eyelids drooped slightly.

"Since you're going to be in town for a while," she went on, "perhaps we could get to know one another better?"

Megan leaned back away from Shkai'ra and stretched. Lamplight glittered in her eyes, sheened off hair and the bright inlays of the low table. *She's interested in me for more than just company.* For an instant, she remembered Serkai. They had initiated each other into the first mysteries of sex when they were children. But that was before—the *River Lady*. Her face hardened a little. *But this one isn't being pushy. Women don't tend to be.* She couldn't bear the thought of being with a male and hadn't for the last eight years. Not since Sarngeld bought her from her aunt. *But with a woman?*

She swallowed and forced herself to lean forward casually. Somehow during the talk, she'd gotten closer to Shkai'ra than anyone else at home for years. It was a strange, cracking sort of feeling, like scraping ash off a log and finding it was still glowing underneath, however faintly.

"That might be—possible," she said. Pondering, she tapped one nail against the table with an oddly metallic sound.

Their fingers touched; Megan opened her mouth to

speak. A fat drop of water fell on their hands, and with a blaze of multiforked lightning the storm broke over their heads. They blinked away the dazzle and rushed for shelter, reaching the arcade just as the rain became a hissing downpour.

Megan's face smoothed into a mask, pale in the blue flaring light, carefully not showing emotion. "I hate storms," she said.

"*Eh'mex mekagro nai*," Shkai'ra replied, and shivered slightly. "Baiwun Avenger rides the Plains of Sky tonight." Over kilometers of darkened cityscape the flame of the Sun Temple twisted, lashing the sky.

She turned to Megan. "See you tomorrow?" she said.

Megan nodded. The weariness of days settled on her shoulders. "Goddess ward your sleep," she said.

It was after midnight, and Baiwun's hammer still rumbled in the distance. Shkai'ra sat cross-legged on the round bed that dominated her room. Hands rested on thighs, and the grey eyes were sightless as she meditated, unable to sleep. No Kommanza was easy in a thunderstorm; it was the most frightening of natural things to dwellers on the empty plains. In thunder the Avenger sought out lawbreakers.

A harsh scream broke the silence and the sound of dripping waters. It came from the next room—a long despairing wail of agony and terror.

CHAPTER III

Yeva Haacha's-kin, a master of the Guild of the Wise, sat before a silver bowl in a garden that whispered and rustled as rain pattered down, on vine and leaf and carved stone pergola. The rain somehow avoided the space where she sat. Long black hair fell in a curtain as she leaned forward over the bowl and passed a hand over the water; eyes the color of milk from corner to corner gazed into it.

With a chime the metal chilled suddenly as the water froze; frost-fog tumbling over the smooth edge, drifting down over embossed figures thick with hoar, to puddle and dissipate in the rain outside the circle of protection.

Thunder cracked overhead. The figures rising out of the ice wavered for a moment, then firmed as her concentration took hold. The symbol was the thing; she reached to hold firm the sympathetic linkage between the *here* and the *there*. *Ah, General-Commander Smyna, and the High Priest—unmistakable*. Their voices rang insect-thin from the images of

41

frost, speaking of war; dates, places, strategies. Yeva's lips thinned. Smooth conversation in a quiet room; the lives and homes of others wrecked by papers dropped across a table.

She touched the bowl with a finger, and the metal glowed white for an instant: time present. Then another image rose unbidden, flickering. She concentrated to firm it, for the unasked Sight was always valuable. A woman—no, two women—sat at a low table, a candle between them. Red hair inclining toward dark, a finger tracing on the table. A gust of . . . not-wind, and the scene vanished. She touched her finger again to the bowl, and this time the glow was red: time past. Earlier this evening.

The blind woman raised her eyes to the garden and thought for long minutes. *The unsought omen is always to be heeded.* No vision of the future was complete, for the future was not one path but many. Every living soul helped shape it, with every decision they made. Here were two more to play the game, two who had become crucial.

Faces called up in answer to her question. How were they to deal with Illizbuah? She smiled suddenly and gestured. The cold-formed fog billowed up, obscuring her from sight. Lightning flashed, reflecting a million shining droplets of frozen air as the rain fell freely everywhere. It puddled in the bowl, with the melting ice.

Cubilano, Reflection of the Everlasting Light, High Priest of the Sun in Illizbuah, Chancellor of Fehinna's God-King, sat in the silence he preferred. *Such undiscipline,* he thought, noting a slight movement of an acolyte's eyes. He made an almost imperceptible sign with one finger, and the acolyte moved forward, covered his eyes with his hands, and bowed deeply.

"Young one," Cubilano said quietly, "strength of will can overcome the need to move injudiciously. My child, go from here to the Great Altar; there you may assume the posture of submission and remain, contemplating what virtue lies in stillness, for as long as it would take the Sun to pass through the width of two hands."

The young priest began to stand. "You have not been given leave to depart," the hierarch said in mild reproof. "Meditate for the same length of time again, on the usages of proper respect. Go."

He watched the boy back out of the room, then gazed slowly around at the dozen others arrayed against the walls. These were the shaven-headed symbols of his power, identical in their robes of orange satin. One did not need *things* cluttering one's life in order to show strength.

The furnishings of the room were sparse, befitting a man of austerity; a low table, racks for books and scrolls and the pillows Fehinnans preferred for their cross-legged sitting posture. Tropical cedar from the islands of the Kahab Sea lay warm against tile, in light that the tinted skylight washed pale yellow. This deep in the temple the wild noise of the storm came muffled and the lamps never flickered on their serpent-carved stands.

The silence had been a physical presence to be felt; now it deepened to an unbearable motionless tension.

Cubilano might have been a figure carved of gold and mahogany, here in the centrum of his might. His face was the ordinary, wrinkled, thick-boned countenance of any land-bound peasant lucky enough to see sixty seasons; but his eyes were not ordinary at all. They were willing to see the world burn for the favor of his God.

One of the acolytes leaned close and whispered. The door opened, swinging on ironwood bearings.

That door . . . he thought. *How many Sun-turnings had it been? It had been his second week in the temple, still speechless with awe; even the little provincial*

*seminary had been impressive enough, after his kin-
fast's wattle-and-daub huts, but Illizbuah had been
stunning.*

All new acolytes were presented to the Reflection;
it was a tradition, but no great ritual. He had advanced
with eyes firmly fixed on the ground, a stocky boy of
ten in a saffron gown. The hand had fallen on his
head; he still remembered the dry cool feel of the old
woman's skin on his scalp.

"So this is the one who shows such promise," the
voice had said. That had startled him enough to make
him glance up. Their eyes had met, the young boy's
and the old woman's, for a long minute. Her face had
looked incredibly old to him, an aristocrat's face
seamed and worn to a blade of bone and skin, the
face of a dying eagle; beyond the indignities of hope.

"Who knows?" she had said at last, with a dry rasping chuckle. "He might sit on this cushion, one day."

As General-Commander Smyna Caaituh's-kin was
ushered in, the room flashed from warm yellow into
searing blue-white. Thunder followed, more felt in
bone and gut than heard. *A bad storm,* she thought.
Hopefully not an omen for what she planned. Then
again, when hail fell in high summer, someone was
struck; it might be her enemies, they were thick
enough on the ground. The uncanny figure before
her did nothing to ease her discomfort; priests
were . . .

She tuned her mind to a meaningless hum of unfo-
cused thought. One never knew how much they could
see in your head; the Sun-on-Earth could, that she
did know, having spent time in the palace. More than
one commander of her acquaintance had gone to the
flaying tables for disloyal fantasies. She closed her eyes
for a moment to allow them to adjust to the dim light
and heard Cubilano's voice, dry and whispery.

"General-Commander, enter and be welcome in

the House of the Sun." From where he sat, Cubilano could feel the room's effect on the soldier. It was normal enough to the eyes of the uninitiated, but subtle art had gone into the angles, the patterns of roof and floor. They dwarfed anyone who stood before him and gave the dais a dominating effect that mere size could not yield. Silently, he commended the spirit of the long-dead Reflection who had built it; had he been alone, he might have smiled. It was the duty of the Servants to increase the power of the Sun-on-Earth, generation after generation—which meant to diminish worldly powers, like mere general-commanders.

Smyna summoned the arrogance of thirty generations of aristocrats to stride across the floor that reason told her was of no great size. Reason lied, something in her said. It was vast, and she no more than an insect to be crushed beneath a sandal.

High Priest? she thought. A tenant's child, she reminded herself. Scarcely more than a slave, whatever the law might say; bound to the soil, barely fit to serve in her stables, but for the chance attention of some meddling priest.

"Great Light, I greet you," she said. There was deference in her voice, but her bow was merely that to an equal, and she failed to speak in the subordinate mode. The acolytes tensed, less a physical movement than a turning of attention. "Fellow Hand of the God Among Us," she added. That put her behavior within the canons, although barely. She had addressed him in private and in his capacity as chancellor, which was not, in theory, a priestly office. Usually the Reflection held it, but lay men and women had as well, within living memory.

Cubilano watched her as she stood with stiff-spined alertness, like a fighting quail ruffling before a rival. *Hard metal,* he thought. *But that is needful, for a sharp tool.* He gestured to one of the cushions before him and returned the hand to its place in the opposite sleeve. *When shoveling shit, one uses a dung fork.*

"Child of the Light, be honored among us"—*for the moment. This one,* he thought, *would bargain toe to toe with the Sun Herself for ambition's sake.* Anger threatened to cloud his mind, at the thought of the Servants of the Light seen as a stepping-stone to mere power and wealth. For a moment he concentrated on the smells of incense and warm wood and sunflower oil from the lanterns.

"Leave us," he said in his dry, quiet voice. The acolytes bowed and glided from the room, the muted rustle of cloth on cloth like dead leaves. The last paused to pull the door shut behind her. Another flicker from the storm outside gilded them both as they gazed at each other. *I have the advantage here,* he thought, looking down at Smyna. *She shows little reaction for one untrained; let us see what bait she takes.*

"You mentioned that you wished to discuss the darkness and heresy that surrounds us?"

Smyna took her courage in her hands: a Fehinnan would have said, caught her soul in her own net.

"Here are the staff studies, Radiance," she said, setting a thick leather folder of papers before him. "Essentially—not to be technical, we can take the Kaailun states to the south in two campaigning seasons. None of them are very large, and Intelligence swears that they'll be slitting each other's throats when our siege trains arrive beneath the walls." A brief smile showed white against the olive skin. "Encouraged by our, ah, subsidies."

She sat and watched him stare unwinkingly at the folder. Coming here openly had been a statement of intent, that the High Priest had demanded, and her rivals in the command would use it, but none of them would seriously suspect that she had given the chancellor the secret contingency plans; the penalties for divulging them would last three days at least, before death. The factions were delicately balanced in the Iron House; command of the Illizbuah garrison was prestigious, but of less real importance than one of the provincial army corps. With this in his hands, Cubilano could marshal unanswerable arguments with the Sun-on-Earth. Unlimited preferment would come to the commander who had been on the winning side, once the Sun-on-Earth spoke for war.

"The Kaailun are notorious unbelievers, who have rejected our missionaries most obdurately," Cubilano said.

Not altogether surprising, since they preach unlimited submission to the Sun-on-Earth, Smyna thought dryly, then caught herself. That was a dangerous thought, skirting blasphemy.

"The northern powers?" the High Priest continued.

Smyna shrugged. "No great problem, Radiance. We've recovered from the Five Nations War faster than they did."

As a girl she had played among the bones and broken catapults in the cleared fire zone beneath the walls of her kinfast's stronghold. "The Pensa are too occupied with each other; they've considered it beneath their dignity to fight outsiders since the Maleficent's day." The archpriest made a sign to avert evil at the name. "Maailun and D'waah will fight"—She spread her hands—"but that, however, is what the armed forces of the Tecktahate of Fehinna are for, after all." Smyna used the formal term: Burning Righteous Sword of the Divine Incandescence.

Flattery never hurts, she thought. *Nor unction. Smear it on—the arse of the mighty tastes of gold.* Fear stabbed at her again; the mind was open to the God of which it was a shadow. She shook herself inwardly. It was a common enough saying, and this one was only High Priest, not the Sun-On-Earth Herself.

The priest stared over her head, as the lightning cast the room in silver. "All those who do not believe . . . lost, lost in the darkness. The Fire that cleanses must be brought to earth, a healing cautery."

Like the great lens in the temple dome. He could almost see the fierce point of focus trembling in the incense laden air; almost hear the shocked, disbelieving first scream as another soul was freed to the only God.

Smyna tried to bring the conversation back to practicalities. "Radiance, there are still those who oppose the plan. Many of the landed families are afraid for their estates; loot is desirable, but burned crops and slaughtered workers . . . they remember the last war, and the navy is more interested in the Kahab Sea, and the new trade colonies across the Lannic."

Peasant hardheadedness showed on the other's face. For a moment Smyna was reminded of a formidable suspicious old farmwoman at market, shaking her fist over piled yams and raisins, refusing to be taken in by smooth city words.

"Aye," he said. "The shiplords of the city are so inclined; higher taxes and smaller markets disturb merchants. They seldom look beyond the swell of their fat stomachs, and they stir the shaaids, the city-scum, to complaint over the imposts we must have to hire troops and import metals." He stared at the soldier. "Only in burning is there holiness. They too will have their moment with the Flame."

Smyna Caaituh's-kin, who had hunted tigers and armed slaves for sport, inclined her head, controlling her shudder. Fanatics disturbed her; they were too unpredictable, and the chancellor was brilliantly so. To use him was to grasp the knife by the blade, but there was little choice, less glory, and no advancement in peacetime. Few of the officer corps in these days were the heirs to great wealth; the Righteous Sword was a convenient and honorable way of giving them a living without upsetting the delicate matrimonial alliances that were the warp of Fehinnan politics. Plunder would pay debts and augment niggardly pay and stipends; casualties and mobilization of cadre units would give the ambitious room to rise in the table of ranks.

Oh, yes, there would be many to follow and support; rotting in the border garrisons, in the endless boredom of drill fields, patrolling the western mountains against starving savages who could hide under an oak leaf and put arrows through a squirrel's eye.

"You are prepared for opposition, then, Radiance?" she asked. She was deeply committed; still, it would be well to be sure that he was not too far gone in mystical ecstasy to attend to the necessities.

He nodded. "They have overreached themselves. Trade is bad enough. Their rabble-rousers have provoked the shaaids beyond endurance and there will be troubles; I will use them to swing opinion against them in the council, and the House of Tecktahs, as you warriors use an opponent's strength against him."

"How does the Sun-on-Earth regard this matter?"

Both Fehinnans drew a circle over their breasts at the mention of the God-King. "The new Avatar of Her has authorized this." Cubilano produced a stamped document.

Smyna restrained herself from snatching and instead read it gravely. Cubilano allowed himself an inward smile as he saw her eagerness. "Radiance, this is everything we asked for!" She looked up, understanding in her eyes. "Ahhh, that is why there was an announcement that the proclamation would deal with an increase in taxes!"

Cubilano withdrew a hand from his sleeve and stroked his chin. It was the first gesture Smyna had seen him use.

"The Sun-on-Earth . . ." He paused. How best to explain? "The God is much occupied with other thoughts, of late. This matter is left in my hands. It would be well to have preparations made in the Iron House both to deal with possible civil unrest, and to use the revenues which will flow automatically once the new measures are in place. Since you are commander of the Illizbuah garrison, and have access to the necessary communications and staff personnel . . ."

"The shaaid will riot?"

"Of course. My information is definite, and it is in any case necessary." He managed to shrug without movement. "They are not so devout as the peasantry; still, however many you kill, there will be sufficient for the city's needs."

"In other words," Smyna said, greatly daring, "you feel a short, sharp riot will strengthen your hand against the merchants with the Sun-on-Earth, who will not love those who incite his subjects to revolt. You will be able to arrest the most vociferous of the merchants. By association, the navy and peace factions will be covered by the same shroud." The High Priest gazed at her, unblinking. "But the disturbances must not be allowed to get out of hand; that might convince the Radiant One that there was something to our opponents' predictions of ruin from a militant policy."

Cubilano gave her a smile as cold as duty. "Who are we to question the mind of the God? We serve the Avatar of Her with our human minds and wills." He paused. "Have you made your devotions to the God as the Law commands?" he said sharply.

Caught off balance, she struggled to regain the initiative. "I . . . the Caaituh's-kin are pious; nobody can dispute that."

"Yet a great kinfast is made up of many souls," Cubilano continued. "Dehanno, your kinelder, heir to the Tecktahship . . . he has been less than friendly to the Servants of the Light, disputing our ownership of lands." His expression became somber. "Such a one might have to be . . . set aside by the Sun-on-Earth for a more devout heir."

Smyna bowed her head. Here was the carrot, tailored to her alone. Hers if she succeeded; if she failed, the stick of disgrace for the one who had callously slaughtered the people of the Divine One, as they rightly protested measures adopted by misguided ministers. The God could do no wrong; Her servants were another matter entirely. There was a silken reminder that however high she climbed the temple would have its hand on the ladder. Still . . .

"I will order the regiments into the city," she said. "Obedient to your wishes, Mirror of the Eternal Light."

The priest made a gesture of dismissal. "Further communications had best be by the secure channels we established," he said. She had known his insistence on a public meeting was a demand for commitment. She replied with a deep obeisance and turned to go. At the threshold she hesitated.

"Radiance, I have heard that the Guild of the Wise favors the merchant guilds in this matter."

For the first time, Cubilano raised his voice. "The Conspiracy of the Foolish!" It cracked out across the chamber. "The Guild of the Damned!" Smyna blinked. "After the riots, the guilds will have no recourse. Except the 'wise.' And if they are so foolish"—his hands curled shut—"the Sun has fire to spare."

Yeva sat in the guest room rather than the garden now. Some stern ascetics would scorn to use the Art to keep themselves dry in a rainstorm, or to make ice to render scrying easier. She was not of their number, but there would be no energy to spare for luxuries this time. The glass stood before her, as milk-white as the magician's eyes, held in its frame like a pearl beneath the chin of a dragon.

War had been decided; that was certain. But it was necessary to know more, and temple alarms had certainly been tripped by her first scrying. She took one deep breath, then another, sank into light trance, and began very delicately to probe.

The circle of priests formed with swift ease once the Watcher had called. Heretical use of the Holy Sun's Power had been found again. Around the walls of a cone-shaped room, eyes focused unblinking on the pinpoint of flame that burned unwavering in the center; waiting, patient as a cancer breeding silently through the nerves.

There! The flame wavered in a certain nonphysical undirection. Hate surged within the circle, building into a swirling vortex, ready to be released when the Damned One of the Guild of Fools showed himself.

Soundless, the form of the magician drifted over the temple. She scanned the area carefully, averting her consciousness from the shape before her; on this plane one could confront nothing that was not elemental Truth; she had no desire to comprehend what two hundred generations of belief and agony had made of it. Here as ever, there was no unknowing.

Probing, she met a shell of glass. No, it was alive; pulsing rhythmically, tiny openings gaping as it moved. It tasted of sour yellow; she gritted nonexistent teeth and slid along the outer surface, extending a tendril . . . She stepped sideways, to the plane of Absolute Essence, and considered the Symbol of the Temple. *Ahhhh, perhaps* . . . Walking the time dimension was a physical thing here, studying the manifold branchings of probability. Yes: a high possibility of a gap *here*. Best not consider it too closely, lest the information gained fix the parameters when she returned to the time-inflow. It would be of no use to penetrate here, for there was no verbal language among absolute Symbol.

Sideways again, to the original plane. She picked the place/time, pushed, felt a sensation like icy slivers that rasped sadly grey on her skin, and was through. Yeva heard: ". . . not intend to *split* the Iron House; if division came to actual fighting, there would be disas—"

A wave of emotion broke around her, swirling the identity matrix that she was here, smashing her against the inner wall of the temple's protection. Rage, pain, fear, guilt, hate, lust flickered through the pathways of her consciousness, and far away she could sense the response of her immobile body as its glands opened slightly, beneath the iron control her training imposed on the hindbrain. The priestly circle fought to pin her mind there until emotion killed the body. Coppery taste of fear, savage adrenaline exhilaration of anger, grey meaninglessness of depression. With a single convulsive heave she snapped back through the opening of her entry and returned identity to the physical body. They followed her, using the window in time and possibility for the counterstrike. World and otherworld crackled as the bolt struck, and there was an ear-stunning roar of entopic noise as she shouted words of Containment. Darkness.

And rain. The servants arrived as fear overbalanced fear. They found her sitting unharmed amid the shattered glass and plants of the solarium; droplets misted her hair and seeped into the cushions as she regarded the crushed and smoldering remains of her surroundings. But for fortune and speed, they might have found nothing but charred bone and greasy ash, or a body probability-twisted into something that had no right to exist in time-present-here. As it was . . .

"The lightning rod needs replacing," she said, before signaling her bodyservant to carry her from the wreckage.

CHAPTER IV

The scream still echoed through the thunder-ridden night as the plainswoman came out of her crouch and flowed smoothly erect. That was the room directly next to hers, the one the outlander, Megan, had taken. The saber flickered into her hand as she twisted past the bedpost; three long strides brought her to the connecting door. Her dagger thudded into the wood beside the lock, and she threw her weight levering against the hilt until the ironwood lock mechanism broke from the softer oak with a rending crunch like the sound of tearing cartilage that went with a crushed knee. She kicked flat-footed, then dove forward into the outlander's room, the curved sword moving in a neat precise arc, up into guard position.

Megan had flung herself onto the strange bed, staring at the ceiling. Naked in the damp heat, she lay and listened to the storm, refusing to remember. Denying, as she had every time a storm had brought those memories crowding back. No, she refused to remember, she refused to feel that way ever again. She concentrated on her breath, forcing it to even out into deep slow rhythms; felt the sweat trickling down her flanks, the crisp texture of the close-woven linen beneath her. A pond of still water grew before the eyes of her mind. She slept. And dreamed, remembering.

The rough, prickly fiber of the rope dug painfully into her hands; that was nothing, a welcome distraction from the tearing pain between her legs. She leaned into the coil of rope, grateful for its support as she stared down into the dark track behind the ship, black against the slush-white surface of the freezing river. She was cold; the tears froze on her lashes. Blood trickled warmly down her thighs, cooling. Thunder crashed to the north. Muffled now, not close and overwhelming as it had when Sarngeld had raped her.

She looked down at the water with longing as it curled and chuckled to itself under the keel. Peace, and escape, and forgetting. A gloved hand speared down from above and caught the oak chain at her neck as she leaned toward the water. She twisted away, choking, trying to scream as he lifted her to the deck of the ship.

Shkai'ra scanned the room, instantly aware that there was no third presence. She relaxed as much as was possible for one who had spent her childhood under the Warmasters' instruction and laid the saber on a table before walking to the bed. The outlander, Megan, ground her teeth and wrestled with the sweat-soaked sheets. Shkai'ra stood, watching, contemplating her own emotions with detached curiosity.

She did not feel pity; her folk lacked even the concept. Concern, perhaps. On the Plains of Night, even the fiercest was driven prey, and she had night terrors enough of her own. What connection? The stranger was interesting, true. And attractive, but no more so than many men and women she met daily.

She sat on the bed and laid a cool strong hand on the other's shoulder. "Wake, Whitlock," she said in a calm conversational tone. "That fight is past."

Under her hand, Megan froze to utter stillness. With a shudder her body relaxed into wakefulness, and her hand went out to trace an ungloved hand, raised to touch the smooth line of Shkai'ra's cheek.

"Not him," she murmured, still in the dream's grip. She sat up. Unwelcome sobs forced themselves past clenched teeth. She had sworn that she would not weep again; shame added to her misery as she turned her face away.

"Sorry to break down your door," Shkai'ra said calmly. "Thought someone was chopping you up with an axe." A pause. "I always hated thunder-storms, too."

Megan stilled as she woke more fully. "Thank you, for, well, being concerned. But I'm all right." She tried to pull her barriers up, but they were still shat-tered by the dream. She felt the rasp of Shkai'ra's calluses. She sat up, slowly, feeling suddenly lonely as the Kommanza took her hand away.

The plainswoman was so close . . . "This binds . . ." Her voice also refused to work properly, and it came out so low that she doubted Shkai'ra heard it. Some-thing she'd walled away inside herself long ago finally broke free, and she cried; harsh and tearing, for she fought it still, but the tears still came.

"I felt him die . . . I felt his life go, leaking out of every wound, but I live that time again, when thunder walks. Why?" Then rage welled up in her through grief and she crooked a hand in a slash across the bedding. "I could kill him again. And *still feel pleasure in it.*"

Her tears were gradually slowing and her breathing becoming more regular. "So long. So long ago."

"They never leave us, those we've killed; we give them immortality," Shkai'ra said. "I'm not far," she went on, standing and taking up her sword. "Call if there's need." The broken door swung quietly shut behind her.

"Why?"

Shkai'ra paced like a trapped cat, her bare feet soundless on the brown tile of her own room. The shadows were deep, only a small flicker from the peanut-oil lantern in its niche casting a flickering ruddy light.

"Why did I do that?" *Why help the stranger?* Not a Kommanzanu thing to do, but there seemed to be something binding them. Unlikely that they would meet in the first place, cast together by the strange gods who ruled the sea. Then to turn up at the same place in this swarming anthill of a city. . . .

Unease crawled in her stomach, like the Fear Snake beneath the earth in the old stories. For a longing moment, she wished she was home; then she could go to the sweatbath and throw water on the rocks, maybe get a vision from the Red Hawk, her clan's totem. Or go to to the castle shaman for a spell against misfortune. Or at least take her horse and bow and ride out on the clean steppe, out past the villages and fields until there was nothing but the bowl of the sky and the cold northern winds. Sweat runneled down her bare skin and matted her hair; like a sauna you could never get out of.

She looked over at the door, wedged closed with a scrap of wood for privacy's sake. *She fights well*, Shkai'ra thought. Her mind played over the brief scrimmage on the ship's deck. *Strips well, too*, she added, feeling a familiar pleasurable itch between her legs. There had been a nice young sailor on the ship coming north from the Kahab Sea, but that was weeks ago, and he had died when the ship went aground up in Joisi. Nearly a month celibate. *I would very much like to take this Megan to bed. So strange, so tiny and so pretty. . . .* Which was one good reason to be pleasant, although she suspected more patience would be required than she was usually prepared to show. *Perhaps the spirits mean to throw us together.* A shaman had once said it was her fate to lie far from home, among witches and strangers.

At that she shrugged. *I can sleep now.* If the spirits wanted something, they generally got it; she only hoped that the Ztrateke ahKomman, the high gods of her people, were not involved. They had nasty dispositions. A small six-limbed joss stood in an empty lampniche, carved of bone and wood. Glitch, with his bulging bloodshot eyes and spikey red hair and snaggletoothed grin. One hand was extended with a single finger raised, another held a long pin, a third a feather; the others brandished mousetraps, buckets and gluepots. Shkai'ra lit a small stick of incense and stuck it into the blob of wax on the statuette's baseboard.

"*None of your fucking jokes,*" she said to the godlet in her own language. "*You just watch it, or my ghost will chase you down and tear off a pair or two of arms.*"

A slight grating sound woke Megan the next morning, and the entire weight of a tomcat placed on one paw at a time as he walked over her and shoved his nose in her ear.

"Ach! Cat, stop that!" But she scritched him carefully behind his ears. He meowed at her and jumped down from the bed.

From the next room came a subdued knock and Shkai'ra's husky voice as breakfast was delivered. Megan sighed, tried to go back to sleep, but the next time Ten-Knife-Foot pushed the door open, rubbing his cheek on it, she threw the cotton sheet off and called a servant to order her own breakfast. Ten-Knife insisted on sharing her bacon with her.

"This one—" She looked through the door to where Shkai'ra was finishing a sword exercise, empty-handed, and pointed down to where the cat lay on her foot. "This one wants to expand his territory and is insisting that we share too." She watched the plainswoman straighten. "Is he always this acquisitive of people?"

"Nia." Shkai'ra smiled, pausing for a moment and craning her head back to call through the gap between door and jamb. "He usually bites people he meets. Good morning."

"Goddess morning to you."

Megan found herself watching a droplet of sweat run down the underside of one of Shkai'ra's breasts. The Kommanza caught the glance and smiled back with a lazy grin. Then she took a deep breath, bent backward until her palms touched the floor behind her heels, did a handstand, and then dropped into a series of exercises, stretching first, then blocks, kicks, and handblows at an imaginary opponent.

Stop that, Megan told herself firmly, looking down at the tray in her lap as she ate and away from the rippling sweat-slick skin. The eating-pick was strange, with four tines rather than one. *You decided long ago that sex doesn't interest you anymore.*

Shkai'ra was wiping her torso with a towel as Megan came through the door. "No gods-damned point in this," she grumbled, throwing it over one shoulder and dropping an armload of clothes and weapons on a chair. "I'll be sweaty again in a breath, just standing still." She scooped up the cat and sat, fanning a piece of paper at him; he batted at it with claws out, and she read the Fehinnan cursive with her lips moving slowly.

A snuffle of laughter escaped her, growing to a throaty chuckle.

"An itemized bill," Shkai'ra said, ruffling the

animal's ears. "for Ten-Knife's depredations. A trail of
ruin he must have left. *In one night, cat?* Also a trail
of black kittens with yellow eyes and terrible tempers,
I'm sure." The cat endured her fingers for a moment,
then flowed through her arms and stalked away with
an air of purpose.

"How much damage can a cat do?" Megan said.
"And he must have caught his share of rats."

Shkai'ra picked up the list. "Also a pet dog, a roast
of beef, two pieces of imported sharksfin from the
table of a shipowner, upsetting a bottle of wine in the
process—" More laughter, to herself. "Well, I can
pay." She tossed the paper aside and moved to the
window, sighing and stretching in vast contentment. It
was early morning, and the rain had washed the air
of some of its tidewater sultriness; there was a fresh-
ness to the damp, a smell of coffee and food and silt-
laden water from the river.

Megan watched a moment, then poured herself a
mug of tea. She leaned back against the pillows,
heaped high and newly beaten into submission,
promptly scalding her mouth.

"Fishguts! I should know better." She put the mug
down and watched Shkai'ra for a long moment before
gathering her hair to rebraid it. "I knew there was . . .
ouch . . . a reason that I seldom unbound this mess. I
should hack it all off." She finished winding the braids
around her head and fetched her knife as Shkai'ra
drew her saber.

"On the lunge, wouldn't it be better to use the other
arm as a counterbalance?" Megan asked.

"Not . . . if . . . you're . . . using . . . a shield,"
Shkai'ra said, between deep even breaths. She shifted
her grip to the two-handed foot fighting stance and
snapped into the guard-against-spear, then whipped
down into the straight cut to the head, the pear-
splitter. The moves flowed one into the other, yet each
was sharp and definite, ending with a "huff" of

expelled breath at the moment of impact, the long flat muscles standing out under the skin in clean relief as they tensed and relaxed.

"Not that I really know much about those ox-stickers," Megan said. She began her own exercises, a series of fluid moves, one into the other, holding each pose a second or so, increasing the speed until she was blurring through a shadow fight that ended with the lunge; throat, heart, groin. She stood up, and nodded at her imaginary opponent, and walked back toward the bed, flipping the knife.

Shkai'ra had finished with a sideways flick of the sword and had stood watching, wiping the steel in her hands carefully, before starting to dress. "Ox-sticker it might be, but good for keeping small people with sharp objects in their hands at a safe distance."

Megan glanced out of the corner of one eye. "Oh?" She found herself wanting to show off her skill. *What is the matter with me?* She tossed the knife thoughtfully in her hand.

The Kommanza stuffed the last bit of bread into her mouth and finished buckling on her saber. The stiletto disappeared up one sleeve, and the dagger rode opposite the sword. Then she produced a shot-pistol from under the pillow, a heavy double-barreled weapon with a pistol grip. Breaking it open, she checked the brass cartridges.

Megan looked down at the cup left on her tray and picked it up with an expression of disgust. "Swill!" She threw the contents as far back into her throat as possible, so she wouldn't have to taste it, and shuddered. "Gahh, that's awful." She washed the taste of fish oil from her mouth with a swig of cold tea and sat on the pillow by the desk.

Shkai'ra clicked the firearm closed with a flexing of her wrist and walked over to run a finger around the inside of the china tumbler. She tasted and made a grimace.

"Zoweitz of foulness, what is this stuff?" She patted her pouch to make sure the other two rounds were in place; that was the price of a good horse, and the weapon would buy and stock a farm.

Megan held up her hands and looked at the light glancing off the silvery nails. *How much do I trust her?* "These are steel. The witch who gave me these warned me that the iron in them comes from my body. Fish oil has the most of what is needed, and rather than letting my claws leach me of my life . . ." She reached out and tapped them on the mug. The sound rang hard. "I've had them only about seven, eight iron-cycles; moonturnings, you would say."

Shkai'ra looked at her hands, halfway between nervousness and appreciation. That was a good magic, for a warrior; ten knives nobody would suspect and nobody could take away. Even the steel-sheen could have been paint.

"Sharp, too, from what I saw on board the *Radiance, kh'eeredo*," she said.

"Sharp? Oh, I don't have means of really honing them, yet." Megan lapsed into silence. The word "kh'eeredo" had a sense of kinship in it, but this one had been a stranger to her just yesterday. On the ship she had distracted the sailors, but that had been for the cat's sake. . . . Bonds could be used against you. They opened you up to feeling and emotion. The old habits died hard; even the donning of clothing had put the other at arm's length. Perhaps the aloneness wasn't necessary, here.

Her voice was sharp as she turned her eyes away, a crease between the eyebrows. "A weapon, I take it?" She nodded at the shotpistol that Shkai'ra still held.

"Ia," Shkai'ra said, tossing it to her. Megan caught it automatically. "You point it, pull the hook on the bottom called a trigger, and it makes holes in things. Magic, I suppose. Expensive, too; a last chance if you're cornered."

She turned and kicked her foot into a sandal, bracing the foot against the bed and winding the soft leather straps around her calf. Boots and trousers still felt more natural, but she looked alien enough as it was, and the Fehinnan clothes were more comfortable in this weather. Her back prickled slightly; it was early days, to let the little one behind her with a weapon. Still, Shkai'ra thought herself a judge of people.

As her other hand came up to support the weight of the thing, Megan looked at the Kommanza's back . . . and felt the fool. The weapon in her hands lay heavy, metal and smooth-worn wood, a means of death. Then a snide thought. *What, does she expect me to shoot her in the back? People don't kill just for no reason. . . . Well, a symbolic gesture.* A bond. So be it.

"I see. I don't think it's magical." She opened her mouth, then stopped. No, Shkai'ra needn't know everything, yet. Decision made, she continued, "You broke that door last night because you thought I needed help. I owe you a debt." *And Jaipahl never got around to telling me how Fehinnans acknowledge obligation.* She laid the shotpistol down on the desk.

"My knife is yours," she said, holding the blade out on the palm of her hand. *If she takes it, I'll steal another.* Shkai'ra blinked, her people's expression of surprise; that was a ritual they used for deep trust.

Ah, well, she thought, taking it up. She flipped it in a circle and caught the hilt. *Nice piece of steel,* she thought.

"Thank you," she said. "But you'll need one." She offered one of her own, a narrow stabbing poniard.

Megan looked at it and up into grey eyes. "If I took that, to my people, it would mean that I accepted you as kin, in a way. What does it mean to you?"

The hand holding the poniard didn't move though Shkai'ra smiled. "It basically means you'll fight for me if I need you; and I for you, of course. Not that we Kommanza need much reason to fight. . . ."

Megan nodded and took the knife. "All right." *What are you doing, woman?* she asked herself. *You can't get committed to anyone* here. *You have to get home before Habiku ruins your fish-gutted household.*

She examined the ten-inch knife. The weight of it was less than the emotions it carried. She laughed suddenly, her eyes crinkling at the corners, at Shkai'ra's expression. "How like our tools we are. *Celik Kizkardaz*, there is Steel between us." There was silence, then she stood suddenly. "So, show me this city that they are so proud of. Walking the streets as a zhaaid—Shaaid?—What does that mean?—is not the best way to see the sights. I got called that enough to fill me to the back teeth last night."

Shkai'ra turned Megan's giftblade in her hands; it was a pleasure to handle something so well made.

"Shaaid?" she said absently. "Maggot. The poorest, dockworkers, day laborers. Escaped tenants, beggars, children born without kinfast. No money, skill, or lord: a million heads in this brick warren, and two-thirds are shaaid. They die by the thousand down in Low Town; more come in every day, to find the silver bricks of Illizbuah's streets."

"Better to be a . . . gaaimun, is that the word?" They laughed and walked out into the brightness of hallway.

There were crowds along the Laneway of Impeccable Respectability; they turned to throngs as the two women turned onto the eastbound Street of Dubious Delights Tolerated But Not Approved; that was a major artery leading to the Old City that Megan had wandered the night she came in. Carts drawn by oxen, mules, horses, dogs, and humans crowded the brick pavement; folk on foot thronged among them. Naked porters bent under wicker baskets; robed upper servants; a party of off-duty soldiers in green leather tunics, hands on the hilts of their shortswords; two tall black Haytin from the Kahab Sea, feathers nodding from their fantastic sculpted manes of coiled hair.

Smells of sweat, dung, hay, smoke, hot brick dust hung around them among the creaks and clatters and babble cast back by the three-story brick walls on either side.

Not every building along Delight Street was a joy den, of course; tiny stores spilled their goods onto the raised side passages, hawkers cried, pedal-driven looms thumped from behind blank walls; a small girl in a loincloth stood and drew rude words on the stucco with a stick of charcoal until a harassed-looking woman darted out to drag her off by one ear, swatting at the child's rear energetically with her other hand.

Megan dodged around a cart loaded twice head-high with cornstalks, then avoided a priest in a soiled orange robe with stubble on her shaven skull with a whirl that brought her to rest against the counter of a wine shop. Tubs of wine, beer and fruit juices were sunken into the counter, which bore stacks of cheap clay mugs, a dipper, and the elbows of a scowling owner.

As crowded as the night street, she thought. But the nature of the crowd had changed. People spoke more loudly, and sunlight brightened them; the night folk were gone to their pallets. This city at night had a darkness more than material, tasting of smoke and incense and music. A torrent of children passed, shriek-ing with the excitement of some incomprehensible game.

She reached over to touch Shkai'ra on the elbow. "See, that one there?"

Gawking, a boy of fifteen seasons stood on the corner. Tall for his age, and big in the wrists and ankles; Shkai'ra judged him to be from the Piedmont border-lands from his long tunic and leggings and the pale skin, perhaps of a yeoman-farmer kinfast.

"An easy mark," Megan said. She slid a tiny iron slug across the counter and took a cup of pomegranate juice, cool and tart on her tongue. Briefly, she wondered at the metal's value. "In F'talezon, the child packs would leave him stripped and wondering on the DragonLord's doorstep. Not a healthy place."

"Not greatly different here," Shkai'ra said as they elbowed their way forward again. A woman in a soiled white tunic was talking to the boy. "That's Maihra, of the LowLords. They specialize in kidnapping; that one's kinfast will have to pay well for him."

Megan had noticed and avoided a number of people trained much the same way she was. Thieves had a look to them. "So. What should we be doing?"

Shkai'ra looked down at her. "You can buy anything in Illizbuah, anything that exists. But I know just the place you might be interested in."

The weapons shop was part of the Dark Creatures of the Earth Brought Forth and Transformed by Effulgent Light: one of the metalworkers' bazaars. The whole of it was covered, two stories high on arched glass-fiber-concrete; below were narrow laneways through acres of milling confusion—customers, guards, artisans, fetch-and-carry slaves, apprentices, food sellers. For all that, it was less crowded than might have been expected; access was limited, and Shkai'ra had had to show her member's sigil in the Guards', Mercenaries' and Caravaneers' Guild to enter.

"*Whulzhaitz,*" she snarled in her own language. "Sheepshit. Sometimes I think it would have been better to settle among unlettered folk. At least if they rob or kill or imprison you, it will be for a better reason than not having your papers in order."

I'd better buy papers, soon, Megan thought. *I'll probably need them to* leave *from the looks of this place.*

They plunged into the crowd. Shkai'ra's height and sword and alien looks made only a modicum of elbow work needful; she noted that surprisingly few jostled Megan, and none twice. The air was thick: smoke from the forges, despite their fuel of charcoal or city gas;

sweat, the vinegary smell of hot metal; the soapy almost-taste of quenching oil. Light was dim through the grimy skylights, and Shkai'ra found her way more by memory than sight. It played her false more than once, amid booths cobbled with board and canvas.

"Been more than a year; they shift . . . Ah, here." One alcove opened to a long narrow workshop. It was for display and a little finishing work; a lathe whirred somewhere in the background, and the teeth-jarring sound of a grindstone came, clear through the surf-roar of the crowds echoing from the pillars.

The proprietor looked up from dashing a dipper of water over his head as they turned sideways to enter. The wet glistened on his scalp, bald as an egg, and on skin as black as the soot of his trade and seamed with five decades of forge heat. He was dressed in a loin-cloth and leather apron; not a tall man, but muscle bulked huge on ape-thick arms and shoulders.

"*Hai*, Firehair!" he said, grinning hugely. He had the slightest trace of an accent; native-born, but his mother had wandered in on a ship from the Sea Islands. "No need to ask what you seek."

He waved a hand toward the walls and racks. Weapons, and things that must be weapons from the company they kept. There were swords, short double-edged cut-and-thrust blades; the long single-edged cavalry swords with basket hilts that the east coast kingdoms favored. Pensa broadswords, as tall as Shkai'ra at the hilt. Curved swords, recurved chopping blades, swords mounted on poles, swords that slid into canes and umbrellas and scribes' book stands. Knives of every description, from a main-gauche as long as a forearm, meant to do duty as a shield, to a dainty little razor-edge knife, thin and flexible enough to slip inside a belt, with the hilt shaped as a buckle. Spearheads, pike heads of metal or fiber-bound ceramic or glass. Halberd heads, knife-sharp chainlike fighting irons, throwing stars, blowpipes that slid in sections like telescopes. Behind lay bits and pieces of armor.

Megan said not one word, but the wall drew her as if the metal were magnetized. *Good work here,* she thought. *Layer-forged, from the sheen, with charcoal added.* Her eyes were caught by a blade hanging just above her eye level. *Eastern work? If I didn't know better I'd say that was one of our best. It matches our best; what a market for metal, if I could find a way to get it here.* Good iron was expensive everywhere, but east of the Lannic they did not use iron beads for currency. She turned and raised an eyebrow at the smith.

"Trade goods from oversea? Worth maybe the iron that makes it."

"Good work," he said. "As good as mine or my kinmates, but different." He lifted it down with huge spatulate fingers that were somehow delicate, and bellowed over his shoulder, "Tea!"

"See," he continued. "Layer work, yes ... but I think they used iron and steel wire, not twinned barstock. Nice! Firehair's sword is like that, but it comes from the northwest. For this, I could give you, oh, only one-twenty-fifth the weight in gold."

A boy of twelve with something of the man's build came in from the rear with a tray. The tray was grubby leather, but the flask and cups were Naiglun porcelain, delicate, simple and lovely, eggshell thin. The smith lifted one cup, the scarred and calloused hands closing on it as lightly as on a rose. "The Sun shine on you!" he said. "A pleasure to deal with someone who knows good work."

Megan gently touched the teacup with a forefinger and decided against picking up the scalding-hot utensil. "*Tschchak,* I thank you, but one can see from the color that it is oil and not blood-quenched, a less, ah, expensive way of cooling. One fiftieth."

"Brightness! The offer is an insult to the weapon.

And who needs blood quenching? Superstition! A tub of seawater with leather soaked a week does as well. For that price I could offer this." He reached over and picked out a lesser-quality dagger, still of steel; but laid beside the first the difference was obvious.

She blew gently over her cup, looked through the steam at the smith, and settled herself for a long session. "Perhaps when we speak of silver rather than gold would I consider this one, or others. The market seems to hold many smithies. Perhaps I should look around first." She raised the cup, sipped, and set it down. "I thank you for the tea. It was nicely made."

The smith scowled and signaled his kinchild to replace the cup. A horn cup of fruit juice succeeded it. "Bah. The others would cheat a foreigner on principle. I am a man without prejudice, and nothing is too good for a friend of a friend. Besides, you would care for the steel. For you . . ."

Shkai'ra laughed. "Now you've unsaddled yourself," she said. "Next to working the metal, he loves bargaining." She turned to examine a tray of arrowheads.

It went on for a while, discussing relative worth of workmanship, the smith bewailing the necessity of being generous to a friend's friend, protesting that his kin had to eat. At last, before them lay the eastern knife, three of lesser quality, and a knife harness.

"Ach, we are agreed on one-thirtieth for the one; but for the others . . ." She sighed. "The most I could agree on there would be one-seventh, silver."

"You would have my work for nothing? It pains me. Five."

Megan pondered. "Since you are *Freyat Kizkar*, Friend of Kin, I would be generous. Five and a half if the harness comes too.

He frowned deeply. "You make me cut out my heart on the altar of friendship! May the Sun see my generosity to a stranger! Agreed." They slapped hands on the bargain.

She rosed, buckling on the harness and trying various placements for the blades.

"A heavy investment," Shkai'ra said, replacing a bola with balls of stone set with bronze spikes. She hesitated as another customer came through the curtain; a blind man, old, with skin like weathered parchment. He wore a patched tunic and carried a staff and begging bowl.

"Harriso!" she said.

Megan snicked a blade back into its sheath. "Investment in the tools of the trade," she said. "Another friend?"

The man's face turned toward her, nostrils flaring. Then he smiled, his face a network of wrinkles, the smile of an ancient, wicked, merry child.

"So, you come to the City again, Red-Hand," he said in a smooth, well-modulated voice. Megan's Fehinnan was just barely good enough to recognize the accent of an aristocrat, or a scholar. "And another foreigner with you. One who smells of death-to-come, like you."

He turned to the smith. "Kermibo, my friend, today I think we must forsake our discussion of the philosophy of Annitli the Subtle."

The metalworker shrugged. "We're getting in some new barstock, anyway." He smiled sheepishly at Shkai'ra's inquiring eyebrow.

"Philosophy?" she said incredulously. "Time was your only pastimes outside the smithy were beer and sex."

"Well, a person must have something to do in their age. . . . Fare you well." As they pushed aside the curtain, he added: "And bring many more such friends; she's got more business for me than that boy acrobat you dragged along last year!"

Shkai'ra cleared her throat at Megan's look and turned her head to the beggar. "How goes the city,

Harriso?" she asked as they plunged into the crowd of the Metalworker's market.

He shrugged, and used his staff to trip a woman who had jostled him into a stack of pots. "In and out, around and about, as ever, Red-Hand."

"A philosophy you were going to study with the smith?" Megan inquired. "Written, perhaps?"

Both the others regarded her curiously. Harriso opened his mouth to answer, then shifted to a mendicant's whine.

"Alms! Alms and the Light will shine upon you! A copper buys so little, and the Beggar King must have his half of that."

A member of the Watch strolled by, eyes roving. Shkai'ra broke off a bit from a copper coil and tossed it into his bowl.

"I can smell them," Harriso said. The metal disappeared into his tunic. "You travel in learned company for a change Red-Hand. As to the City, the Sun-on-Earth, in her wisdom, has issued a proclamation doubling the taxes on bread meal, salt, and fish."

His hand tightened slightly on her elbow, and Shkai'ra choked off her reply.

"So that all may know the wisdom of this, the proclamation is to be read from the steps of the temple. Great is the wisdom of the God Among Us," he added dryly, "but I shall be content with secondhand knowledge."

The blond woman stopped at a vendor's stall and bought stewed lentils, a round of flat bread, and ground chickpeas fried in oil. Accepting the well-filled bowl, he squatted in a corner and produced a bone implement from his tunic, with a fork at one end and a spoon at the other. Eating with fastidious neatness, he continued, "Thank you, Firehair. We will speak later, in privacy, I think." The blind eyes turned to Megan. "May my fingers see your face?" The touch was feather light. "Ah, younger than the voice. Yes,"

he added gently. "If you wish to peruse the Path of
the Ten True Ways, you must follow your own way.
The printed book does me little good, in these days."

As the old hands gently took in the lines of her face,
she smiled at his compliment, but she thought of
being in darkness for the rest of her life and quelled
a shudder, feeling sudden anger for the injury done.
She could see faint marks around the ruined eyes that
spoke of deliberate blinding, yet in him she felt a
serenity lacking in most. Wisdom, she thought. Not
content but tolerance. She grasped the hand and said,
"Old books and scrolls are of interest to me. My name
is Megan, Elder." She rose and turned to Shkai'ra.
"The temple. The dome? Perhaps we should hear this
proclamation. It would, after all, be natural that
strangers go to see this place."

CHAPTER V

"What was Harriso, before?" Megan said, clinging to the arm of the pedicab. The ride was as smooth as glass-fiber springs and rubber tires could make it, but the two sweating laborers on the pedals were forced to perform a good many swerves and swift brakings in the congested street. Besides, the machine was new to her.

"A noble, and a priest," Shkai'ra said, reclining at her ease. No Kommanza liked to walk when there was an alternative, and keeping a horse in the City was beyond her means. "He fell from power, but the priests of the Sun are sacred. So they took his eyes, rather than his life. His wits are as sharp as ever, and he hears everything. I saved his life once; not much of a life, he said, but the only one available at the moment. He seems to like me well enough, 'for an illiterate heathen savage,' as he puts it."

The machine swerved among horses, carriages, wagons, and swarming pedestrians. Kilometer after kilometer of Illizbuah slid by: tall buildings and low, brick

73

and concrete and some sheathed in stucco or mosaic
or stone; streets of weavers, of lensgrinders, potters,
leatherworkers, apothecaries, chronometer-makers and
machinists; little corner temples; the blank walls that
courtyard-centered tenements turned to the streets.
The heat grew, and the crowds flowed eastward.
Ahead they could see the battlements of the wall that
separated the Old City from the New. Helmets and
spearpoints flashed from the wall; flamethrowers
snouted, and dartcasters. Five centuries ago this had
been the city's outer shell, and it served the purposes
of its masters to maintain it.

The gates were swung open and the crowd
streamed into the darkness of the tunnel, through
another set of gates enclosing a small courtyard, and
through the two dogleg jogs in the road before emerg-
ing into the Old City. Megan took in the arrow slits,
shielded slots, nozzles, and various other strange openings where the walls met the ceiling of the tunnel and
in the ceiling itself.

"A cautious people. Do they have reason to be?"
She thought of a shaaid beaten in the street, raising a
shattered no-face to the crowd, last night. The cleanliness of this city was strange, but the stink of corruption was just as strong as at home. The mood of the
crowd grated on her, raising hackles. There was trouble here, familiar trouble.

"Not usually," Shkai'ra said. "I've never seen a city
so strong, and it rules broad lands. Nobody's stormed
it since the Maleficent's time, and that doesn't count;
nothing and nobody resisted her." Shkai'ra frowned in
the tunnel gloom.

"Odd," she said. "They usually have a guard detail
here, checking papers. There are more shaaids here
than I'd expect, too. They have the money to keep
slaves for most rough work in the Old City, rather
than hire day labor."

Past the gate the roads were wider and less

crowded: a relic of previous centuries, when Illizbuah had been a garrison of administrators and absentee landlords rather than a center of trade and crafts. High walls covered in glass mosaic swept by, the tops of trees hinting at gardens within.

Megan joined Shkai'ra in glancing uneasily at the crowds around them, sweeping toward the central square. There was too much purpose here. That faded from her mind as they swept through the last blocks of offices that surrounded Temple Square. Everything did.

"Elder Brother," she breathed, with reverent awe. There had been glimpses of it, over the intervening buildings, but ... not this. The base of the temple was a block a thousand meters on a side, sheathed in white marble polished to glass brightness. Above that reared the gold-sheathed dome, two hundred meters tall; another twenty meters of flame lancing from the apex. The bright noon sun flared off it, impossible to look at without weeping eyes; a huge blazing pile that left intolerable afterimages. A monolith that must have taken years to build, and many deaths.

She had awe for the sheer daunting effect that reduced the people at its foot to less than ants, and the ages of worship, living, dying, and pain that soaked every stone in its construction. It made her homesick for the agelessness of the Goddess's steppe and mountains; as old as the world and scoured by wind and rain, not by priests. In them was no twistedness. And a small voice in the back of her mind snidely asked what all that gilding would bring. Her eyes and all her senses were fixed on the dome, and she paid little attention to the fact that they had alighted. To build such a thing, its roots must reach back into centuries of belief in their God.

"Gods!"

Shkai'ra nodded. "I didn't speak for half a day, the first time I saw it." She looked around. The crowd was dense, with little swirls of tension erupting around a fight, or a speaker, as the mass swirled to pack itself around the broad steps of the building. "Let's get a good vantage point."

A pickpurse laid a hand on her pouch. Without turning she grabbed his wrist, locked it, and wrenched the shoulder out of its socket with a twist. Looking up, she saw clouds piled over the city, hot gold towering up into the sky.

"In fact, something tells me that it would be better off this pavement," she said, with a slight tone of worry. "Let's move, kh'eeredo—I want some height." She slanted off toward a building that formed one corner of the square, making liberal use of her elbows and knees and the hilt of her sheathed saber. Megan moved in her wake, partly in the space she cleared, partly using the vicious minor tricks one of her size had perforce to learn. She looked up at Shkai'ra's back with a mixture of exasperation and amusement.

They turned into a sidestreet, edged toward a wall where it was easier to push against the squareward current, then climbed three flights of stairs past terracotta moldings to a wineshop set in the third story of the office building. Megan darted ahead, to be met by a majordomo with arrogantly raised brows.

He looked down on her in every sense of the word, then up to Shkai'ra. She stood with her head slightly to one side, regarding him with detached curiosity.

Both women were obvious outlanders, and their tunics no more than modestly rich. There was dust on their feet; he was conscious of the sweat that plastered the thin linen to the tall one's breasts, and the smell of her, like a horse that had been pulling a cart in the sun.

"This shop is full," he said, in an affected upperclass Fehinnan, using forms new to Megan's recently acquired knowledge of the dialect. "Doubtless there are those who will welcome your custom, down by the docks."

Megan bristled. Shkai'ra smiled. At least, her lips came back from her teeth as she stretched an arm over the other woman and laid a hand on the headservant's shoulder. The long fingers dug in, putting pressure on the nerve bundles; the muscles stood out in her forearm and shoulder and the thick pad around her wrist that told of daily saber drill for most of her twenty-eight years.

"My—arm!" he gasped.

"Not for long," Shkai'ra said cheerfully. With her other hand she dug a piece of silver tradewire out of her pouch. "Now, about the table? The corner one, next the window?"

The mugs of the thick, rather lumpy corn beer of Fehinna arrived quite quickly. The crowd around them were mostly robed and shaven-pated; in the white of the lay bureaucracy, or the orange of the temple. Ostentatiously, they ignored the intruders in their midst; they would have been offended to discover that these heeded them not at all.

"I *really* dislike people like that," Shkai'ra said, looking back at the door. "Something tells me . . . ah!" Shkai'ra went on, shading her eyes against the glare and staring across the vastness of the square to the knot of figures who had appeared on the temple steps. Even at this distance, the burnished steelplate armor of one was obvious. "General-Commander Smyna Caaituh's-kin, wearing the price of a thousand acres on her back. And see the ones in cloth-of-gold? Priests and high-ranking acolytes. I'd be surprised if there wasn't a riot, with the announcement they're going to make. They must want to break a few heads, chase the shaaid back to Low Town."

Out in the square the crowd was gathering, clotting into a brownish-grey mass before the steps and the main entrance. A thin line of guards knelt and faced

the crowd, their spear points a string of order across
the front of its chaos, separating them from the building and the lords. The sound of feet and voices was a
surf throb across the stone-paved expanse. Here and
there a voice raised to call on the name of the current
Avatar of the God.

"Quite a few shaaid," Megan said.

Shkai'ra thought, looked at her outstretched fingers
and glanced down at her toes in her sandals. "Perhaps
. . . five tens of thousands," she said. It was an impressive number; there were not that many adults in the
whole Kommanz of Granfor, but even so the crowd
did not fill the whole of Temple Square. A broad,
vaguely wedge-shaped blot spread out from the main
entrance to end crowded against the fringing buildings
at their feet, but to the left and right the mass thinned
into individuals.

The glittering figures on the upper tier of steps
were addressing the crowd below; a barrel-chested
herald with a megaphone relayed the speech to the
mob, who were not taking it well, from the stirring
and buzzing that rippled across the sea of heads.

Megan frowned.

Shkai'ra shrugged, sighing into the sweet beer.
This was one thing she had never learned to like
about Fehinna: her own people brewed their beer
from barley, and imported hops. "Who knows why
they're doing it exactly this way. Politicians and
priests are no less prone to making mistakes than
other folk." She finished the mug, wiped her mouth
on the back of her hand, and signaled for another;
it had been a hot day. "New taxes, that means a new
project. War, perhaps. There were rumors of it to
the south, as I worked my way up from the Kahab
Sea. But then, there always are; the neighbor states
have been staring at Fehinna like rabbits at a weasel
since the Penza stopped being a power, when the
Maleficent died."

She propped her chin on one hand. "Expensive, if they mean it. Of course, the merchant princes would have to pay for most of it, which the landowners wouldn't mind, and they dominate the Righteous Sword. Smyna's poisonous as a whipsnake, but no fool: I found that out when I was an officer in the irregulars. Not like her to let a crowd of city rabble get this big or ugly . . . sssssssa!"

The priests and generals had finished their address, and the crowd made its response, an animal noise that raised the hackles on Shkai'ra's neck with an odd, atavistic thrilling. Starvation itself makes humans passive. They creep away to die, quite quietly; once the initial hunger is done there is only an increasing lassitude. But the *fear* of famine, among those who have lived on its edge all their lives, is another matter. The crowd became a mob. Shkai'ra had seen single shaaids clubbed to death with hardly an effort to escape. But the mob poured up the steps, reaching for its tormentors with a hundred thousand arms.

"Now," Megan said calmly, closing her eyes for a long moment, "there will be a great killing. Of who depends on how clever those priests were." Her hands tightened on the cup and she looked away, unable to close her ears. She saw Shkai'ra watching, fascinated, as if it were a puppet play, and forced her eyes back to the square. She did *not* want to appear weak to the other woman.

Shkai'ra sensed the tension in her. This was altogether more serious than she had anticipated. There was no personal danger, but . . .

Around the curve of the temple came a thunder of drums, and even against the roaring of voices it rolled irresistibly. The grandees and their guards filed backward into the temple, and the doors swung shut with soundless power as counterweights levered. The two women could see the crowd recoil from the direction of the sound, or try to. Above their heads appeared a

line of bright oblongs, sun-flared: pikepoints, a block
five hundred pikes long and six deep, in perfect geo-
metrical alignment.

"This will be a massacre," Megan whispered, eyes
locked on the shining steel, a memory of a riot echoing
in her head, wondering how many parents had
brought their children to the square that day.

Shkai'ra nodded. "Not much doubt of who, either,"
she said, and grimaced slightly. "Wasteful. Watch.
About . . . now." Her curiosity was detached; unlike
most Kommanza, she cared for those close to her, but
empathy on a larger scale was not a quality one of her
breed could easily learn.

Across the square came a megaphone-amplified
voice. The phalanx had pivoted on the great building,
the outermost ranks double-timing. Now it faced the
mob like a solid bar, motionless.

"PIKEPOINTS—DOWN!"

A long smooth ripple, as the first four ranks of
eighteen-foot polearms came down and halted, staggered to present a row of points. From either side of
the rigid columns of the pikes, men and women in
light armor ran forward to kneel in ranks of their own,
under the sharp-honed protection.

The crowd surged forward, then back, eddying
along the row of foot-long metal points; the four edges
of each pile-shaped pikehead blinked, blinding bright.
Suddenly there was a flurry; a ragged figure rushed in
to chop at the heft of a pike with an ax.

The next four pikes jabbed forward and back in
vicious darts, quick as a trout's snap at a fly, drawing
free dark and wet. Megan, taking a pull at the sweet
frothy beer, gagged at the ruthless efficiency of that;
too familiar, like the full impaling poles in the Great
Market at home. The spitted body rose, passed backward over the soldiers from row to row on the polearms, limp and dangling twenty feet above the
pavement. The troopers stood motionless under the

spatter of blood and fluids from the grisly bundle, and even from here she could sense the unchanging mask of their expressions. *Like the Dragon's Guard, or Arkan Mahid; all mad. All with dead eyes.* She looked down, away from the square.

"Are they fanatics?" she asked, finally.

"Nearly," Shkai'ra replied. "Those are lifetime regulars. The Bounding Marshcats Advancing Fearless Against the Foe, Protected by the Glorious Light. Or the Bouncing Kitties, as the other regiments call them, behind their backs."

The amplified voice boomed from the square.

"DISPERSE IMMEDIATELY. TO YOUR KENNELS, SHAAIDS!" The tone was bored, the accent a peculiar lisping drawl that the mob recognized: Gaaimun speech, the dialect of the aristocracy.

The crowd snarled, a chilling basso growl. They ran forward, or the rear of the huge mass did, pushing those in front toward the line of steel, the front trying to push backward or just hold their ground. For a moment the pikes stabbed, flicking like knitting needles. The bolt-gunners knelt, stock-still.

"AIM!"

The weapons came to shoulders.

"READY!"

A thousandfold click.

"LOOSE!"

Repeating bolt-guns: they would fire as often as the triggers were pulled, with six-round magazines; those would penetrate two naked bodies before lodging in a third, or even the best armor at close range. Six thousand bolts were fired in thirty seconds, and the endless twanging of the strings was matched by a multifold thumping, like wet hands slapping fresh liver.

"ADVANCE!"

The drums spoke, the pikes moved forward. The killing machine of Fehinna walked, and nothing was left behind it but the dead. Megan's eyes flickered to Shkai'ra. The Kommanza was frowning. She swallowed and forced herself to lean back, casually.

The missile troops paused to crank the springs of their bolt-guns and collect bolts. Below, the limestone pavement was awash with red, thick trickles of it running from the long windrow of bodies where the bolts had struck, smaller streams from the thick scattering of shaaids piked as the phalanx advanced across the square. Some of those were still stirring. Under the monotonous thunder of the drums, the sound of the mob had changed. It was higher pitched now, more like the monstrous wailing of a giant child.

Around them the clerks were pasty-faced, their gaze fixed on the horror in the square. This had been unexpected, and few of them were as used to the raw salt latrine-and-blood stink of a battlefield as Megan or Shkai'ra.

The edges of the crowd below frayed as people ran for the exits to the square, pulling wounded kin with them, or trying to run carrying an inert body. Megan looked away again imagining she could see tears on those distant faces.

Over the milling slaughteryard below a trumpet spoke, high and sweet. With it came the sound of hooves. Behind the first line of pikes another row of steel points appeared, these still bright, many trailing brightly colored ribbons.

"Wasteful. But then with so many, lives are counted cheaply," Shkai'ra said. The ranks of the pikes swung open, ponderous and smooth, like some gigantic door moving on greased bearings. The lancer company sat their horses as if carved, until the order rang out.

"READY!"

The lance butts came out of their buckets and came down as the riders locked them under armpits. The remains of the mob, trapped in the open area of the square, milled and screamed and clawed the locked

portals of the temple itself. They spread away from
the death facing them, running. In the center of the
square, a child looked up and ceased pulling at one
of the bodies lying like a bundle of rags in the blood.

"Perhaps we should pay and get out of here?"
Megan said quietly, holding down her gorge.

"CHARGE!"

It began as a clattering. It built to an endless roar
of hooves as the sound echoed and reechoed on stone.
The dead and wounded were pulped under the stony
avalanche; only one or two of the war-trained destriers
balking at the uncertain footing. The lancers swept
through the bulk of the mob, then the shafts were
broken, or left jammed in bone, and the swords came
out, bright and long.

"That's a good idea, I think. This is getting completely out of hand." The Kommanza turned and
waved for the waiter, who ignored her, eyes on the
square, knuckles white as he clutched the edge of the
screen where he stood.

"You know? The priests will grind the bodies up
and feed them to the gaspits," Shkai'ra said. "Not that
I'm surprised the shaaids were ready to riot. Death so
casually handed down by decree was too much—stupid of them to riot here, rather than in their own
quarter; all it did was attract more attention." She
paused, a thought spurred by one of Harriso's comments. "Unless, of course, that was the idea."

Megan stared at her. *They're people.* She pushed
herself away from the table and the other woman.
How can you not care?

From below, over the desperate roar of the crowd,
there was a sudden thudding boom.

Shkai'ra started up. "Baiwan Thunderer hammer
me flat for a fool, there's a door from here out onto
the square!"

"We go up, then." Megan glanced out the window.
The wall was smooth stucco with no ornamentation.

"Where are the stairs?" She headed for the door. Her way was blocked by a mob of bureaucrats dropping their napkins and forks and fleeing toward the door, jamming it solidly.

"Out the door, down to the end of the corridor. The stairwell goes right out to the roof. We can— sheepshit!"

From below there was a rending crash as the doors gave way, and a long baying roar as the mob poured in, trying to escape the soldiers behind. The wineshop was three stories up, and there was a broad open stair-way from the lobby.

Press of numbers will slow them, Shkai'ra thought. *Even more so, now that they're fleeing in panic rather than attacking.* There was a chance, provided they gained the roof quickly; if they stayed here, none. They'd be trampled or taken by the soldiery as shaaid in the confusion.

She tried to force her way forward, using boots, elbows, butting head. It was useless, and even the edge of her saber failed. She slashed one man's face, broke another's collarbone with the hilt, and their neighbors hardly noticed. To the respectable of Illiz-buah, an uprising of the shaaid was an ever-present nightmare from childhood, and even the bright metal before their eyes was less terrible.

CHAPTER VI

The doorkeeper was nervous but determined. In Illizbuah, keeper-of-portals was a responsible post, and this was not the first confidential mission she had made. "My master, Milampo Terhan's-kin the Enterprising, awaits your reply," she said.

The old man bent again over the flowerbed. The yellow of the rhododendrons flared against the creamy white linen of his robe, and a single bee paused to alight on his finger. He brought it close to his eyes and studied the intricate veining of its wings for an instant. "Beautiful," he murmured. He turned to the messenger.

"Even now, people of this city are dying at the hands of the Sun-on-Earth's soldiers, because your master and his kin-in-wealth aroused them to fruitless anger. This would have been a ... disharmonious deed even if the purpose behind it had succeeded. As it is, the position of your master's enemies is even more secure. Can unwisdom ever be righteous?"

Around them the courtyard garden spread in sunlit

85

graciousness; not at all what the servant had expected of a notorious sorcerer. Birds fluted in the rich green ivy that covered the brick walls and archways; within, flower-beds, potted trees, and herbs made coolness and shade in the heat of lowland summer. The mage himself might have been any elderly patrician of scholarly bent.

She straightened her back, courteous and firm. "I am not empowered to negotiate, Honored Wisdom." She hesitated, then dropped the "Effulgent with the Sun's Light"; that might not be tactful, in the house of one the temple declared abomination. "However, my master anticipated your reply. He instructed me to point out that many more lives will be lost if the war which is planned comes to pass; directly, and by the famine and pestilence which follow the armies. Also, that the temple will not be satisfied to fleece either the city or the neighbor realms; souls, not gold, are what the Reflection desires."

Her voice dropped a register, unconsciously, as she began to quote: "'With greed I and my kinmates and colleagues can deal. For fanaticism, we require aid.'"

The magician released the bumblebee, watching its soaring with brown eyes that held a troubled serenity.

"Indeed, we of the Guild of the Wise remember the persecutions. . . . It would not be well should the current Reflection garner too much of the Sun-on-Earth's attention." He paused; it was never easy and seldom advisable to explain the workings of the Art to an outsider. "As to means, perhaps events will take a more . . . fortunate turn."

He produced a leather pouch. "The message, for your master. And for yourself, a gift."

She looked at it dubiously. "Messages can be stolen," she said. The consequences of a message from the guild falling into the hands of the temple, or even the secular authorities, were too obviously horrible to need detailing. "Best written on air. I am my master's trusted servant."

"And messengers may be taken and forced." Somehow his gesture stilled her protests. "No, I make no reflection on your honor. But none, I think, will read that message until young Yeva lifts the blocking on it; it was for such matters that we consented to her accepting . . . ah . . . hospitality with your master Milampo."

She still looked down at the bag so innocently proffered as if it concealed a poisonous insect; then her hand slowly went out to take it, twitching back as his hand moved. Its weight settled into her sweaty palm, something crinkling under her closed fingers. She tucked it away into her belt purse, then looked again at the old man. For all the drowsy, sweet-smelling peacefulness of this place, she would be glad to be back in the stink and clamor of the streets. Peace was *held* here, close and unwelcome to her.

"Honored Wisdom." She bowed and backed up a step or two. "I go." She backed further than was necessary for courtesy and left; fled, one could say, even though she only hurried and never saw the gentle amusement in the old man's eyes.

The street outside was far too quiet for this area and time of day. Normally servants stopped to gossip, dodging riders and carriages as they carried out their errands, as they ostensibly paused to rest their various bundles and parcels. It was still crowded, but only one or two carriages were out, and not a rider in sight. People walked rapidly, with their heads down as if to avoid rain, and tended to keep to the edges of the street, close under the walls and trees. Only occasionally did someone glance up for a second toward the sound coming, distantly, from Temple Square. It was like the sound of one's own blood roaring faintly in the depths of a seashell, with an odd, sharper note. The doorkeeper paused just outside the old one's gate, then carefully matched her pace to the flow of what traffic there was. It was not difficult for her to feign the hurried furtive pace of the others. As she vanished down the street, from a rooftop behind her a dark-hooded head rose over one of the ornate parapets and a hand flashed in silent signal below to a woman sitting by a shoulder yoke. She bent, lifted the yoke with a practiced twist that settled it, and followed in the doorkeeper's wake. Behind them both, a shadow flitted across the roof, followed by another.

The room had dissolved into a seething chaos: milling human meat with no direction or purpose save its own survival; no way through. Shkai'ra bounded to a tabletop.

"Follow me!" Her voice was pitched to a battlefield shout that rang over the mob noise. She leaped from table to table with a surefooted agility, riding the wobbling tables like the backs of buffalo. Megan jumped in her wake, knife flickering as panic-stricken hands clutched at them.

"I must have brains like sheepshit in shallow water trying to make it to dry land!" Shkai'ra snarled, balancing on the heaving surface of a table. "Megan, if—when we get out of this, you owe me a good kick in the arse."

The Zak leaped clear as the rocking table went over. "A commendable sentiment, but this is not the time to discuss it," she said. A hysterical figure in white clutched at her ankles. Megan slashed and felt the knife grate. A clot of bureaucrats by the door were trying to close the frail latticework barrier against the onrush of the shaaids; the basketweave portal would have been hard pressed to stop a single kick. "Fools!"

Pain stabbed through Megan's right leg. "Son of a dogsucking pig!" she shrilled, and stamped. There was a brittle snapping, more felt than heard.

"I should have thought of it, too," she continued. "Duck!"

They vaulted to the floor from the last table as a chair leg whirred through the air overhead. The folk by the door were too preoccupied to look behind; Shkai'ra slammed two knuckles into the kidney of one, grabbed a shaven head by the ear and rapped it into the brickwork, clubbed a third behind the ear with the pommel of her saber, and then shortened the blade to stab a neat handspan deep beside a spine. Out of the corner of her eye, she saw the last figure in front of Megan dropping with a slit hamstring. There was a good deal of noise.

"Right," the Kommanza breathed, wrenching at the locked door before kicking flat-footed beside the mechanism.

The women skidded out into the corridor, just as six members of the mob sprinted panting by on their way to the stairs. Below, the surf-roar intensified; this was the first spray cast before a wave that would crush. The last of the ragged figures turned; she bore a wooden club, ripped from a chair, and they could see the lice crawling amid the stubble and mange of her cropped hair.

"Gaaimuns!" she screamed. It was a curse. Her cry turned the others from escape, and hate conquered fear; they attacked.

Shkai'ra felt suddenly at ease; it would have been better in armor, on horseback, but this was a situation in which she felt completely at home. She flicked the saber forward into the two-handed grip used for work on foot without a shield, filled her lungs, and charged.

"AaaaaaiiiiiEEEEEEEEEEEEEEE!" she shrieked, a wailing falsetto that wavered up into the insane squealing of the blood trill. Her first stroke snapped up from left to right; it flickered under the cudgel and opened the woman's abdominal cavity in a diagonal line. Without pause, the sword swept up over her head; her hands shifted, the left to the end of the pommel, right on the back of the blade. It came down in a streak like a solid arc of silver to carve through the forehead of the second rioter while his obsidian knife was still slipping from its sheath. Shkai'ra's body extended effortlessly in a lunge across the falling form. The point went in under the breastbone of the next shaaid, slicing up through the lungs to lodge for a moment in the shoulderblade.

Megan stepped to one side to allow the first body to fall past her, slipping along the wall. One shaaid, stumbling over the corpse of his fellow, went down with Megan's new-bought knife in his throat; his hands fluttered up to touch the hilt as he died. As Shkai'ra lunged to skewer her third opponent, another grabbed for a blood-slippery weapon, striking from below and to the side. The gift-blade, given just that morning, spun glittering from Megan's hand under Shkai'ra's raised arm to sink itself into his eye. In the roar from behind and below, the sound of his death was lost. She leaped over the slash of the last shaaid, coming down hard on a vulnerable instep. The woman lurched and tried to grasp her broken foot. She arched back in an impossible, spine-cracking bow as the knife slid into her kidneys. As her head came back, Megan reached out, pulled her down by the hair and cut her throat, all in one motion. The knives slid out just as easily as they had gone in, and she snatched at the blade standing in the eyesocket of the one corpse. "Move!"

The bodies spilled around them in a tangle of blood and body fluids and liquid feces. Shkai'ra paused for an instant to grab a handful of rag as she stepped over them, wiping the slippery soles of her sandals.

"Let's go," she said. The corridor stretched before them, smooth stuccoed brick, to the swinging door at the end. They took it on the run, flinging themselves up the stairs in long strides; Shkai'ra checked herself to let the shorter woman keep pace. Their hands left faint red smears on the scrubbed white pine of the balustrade.

The stairwell exited on the flat central roof of the building. Five stories above the carnage of the square there was only the roar of sound and the clean breeze of the upper air; they stood on a flat courtyard of cracked grey concrete slabs, surrounded on four sides by low-pitched roofs of red tile. At the opposite end of the rectangle was another exit; beside it stood ten soldiers in heavy infantry armor, armed with shortened close-combat spears, huge oblong shields, and double-edged stabbing swords. Bright sun glinted on their harness, yellow trim on the edges of shiny green varnished plates and leather backed with fiberglass. Their officer wore the same round steel bowl helmet, but his carried a plume.

Shkai'ra traded glances with the commander. "Sheepshit," she said with slow disgust. "Glitch, godlet of Fuckups, is with me today."

The Fehinnan officer's dark face was split by a white-toothed smile. "Shkai'ra!" he said. "We *were* ordered to let most of the shaaid disperse. . . . Such a pity we'll never be able to toss the bones together again, on the other hand, I won't have to pay those thirty silvers the dice lost me, either. Kill them."

"Welcher!" Shkai'ra snapped as the squad trotted forward, at the regulation pace, just enough space between them to give support without hindering. The shields with the sun-disk blazon covered them from neck to knees; not a joint exposed. The broad heads of the spears glinted, held ready for the upward gutting stroke that would dart from behind the shields and return like the tongue of a snake. These were not gutter starvelings armed with blades of glass.

Megan wiped the stickiness from her palms onto her tunic, drew a knife, feinted, and threw. Behind the rank of his troopers, the officer ducked his head and let the blade ring off his helmet; it was too far for a reasonable throw against an alert opponent.

"Well?" she said to Shkai'ra, as they backed before the line of points. "Any plans?"

Shkai'ra bent to unclip the tags of her sandals, kicked her feet free, and tucked them into her belt.

"We have two choices," she said thoughtfully. "We can fight, or we can run." She paused. "Let's run."

She bounced backward, onto the sloping surface of the tiled roof, her toes splayed out, gripping at the slick dusty surface as she side-walked back and up, knees bent. Megan joined her; below, the squad turned and paced them. They were on the outer roof, facing the temple; they would have to cross three sides of the building's roof to climb down or gain the next.

The captain opened his mouth, then paused as the stairwell his prey had used echoed to a long howling roar.

"Aykkuka!" he snapped. The *aykkuka*, or sergeant, backed two careful paces out of the shield line before turning to face him. "Detachment. Remainder of squad, to the stairs."

The aykkuka looked up. "Shmyuta, Billibo—" she said, "shuck down, take them." Two were all she was prepared to risk, on a task peripheral to the main mission. She hefted her spear overarm and made to throw, forcing the two fugitives to keep to the roofline and circle to reach their objective. The two troopers named hit the release catches on their armor, designed to allow marines to shed their heavy harness quickly on a sinking ship. Naked but for rag loincloths, they leaped agilely to the slanted roof, spears in hand.

Megan and Shkai'ra stood to meet them. One was male and the other female, but they were alike in their taut grins, cropped hair, and brown skin rolling over muscle hard as tile.

The short spears they carried were about four feet long, a blade curving outward and broadening toward the front third. Megan could almost see the texture of the rope coiled around the handle. She backed another step, to the ridge of the roof, hearing the sounds of carnage continuing below her heels. A number of possibilities ran through her head and were dismissed. She moved forward suddenly to give herself room and saw that the one facing her did not flinch at the sudden motion. Now was a hell of a time to wish that you had trained in another weapon, she told herself. *A two-fang's length, or several feet of sword metal, between her and me would be nice.* The woman stepped forward, feinting slightly with the weapon. Megan shifted to a low stance that exposed only the narrow outline of her body to the other. She saw the blade begin to move. *That isn't a feint.*

Time seemed to pause, and she watched the gleaming edge move toward her, then past as she stepped sideways, feeling the rasping shock as she deflected it with one arm. Then she was inside the other's reach, throwing herself forward before the soldier could pull the blade back and cut through her neck from behind. Her momentum slowed as she slammed the knife in just under the rib cage. Slowly, slowly, she saw the other's hand start to move and her mouth drop open, and strained for more speed, knowing that if she'd missed she had to get past the other or it was all over. The knife twisted in her hand and then she was down on the roof, the peculiar dusty-slick feel of the tiles under her palms as they took her weight and she rolled and slid past, now unable to stop. Her mind was screaming, "GET UP, next move, GET UP. She twisted, driving her nails into the tile with an ear-punishing shriek. There was no need. The woman was down in a puddle of blood, body lying at a strange angle, held there by the hilt of the dagger that had cut heart and artery.

Shkai'ra faced her opponent with the weight on the balls of her feet, the hilt of her saber at waist height and blade slanting out. The man watched her narrow-eyed; the sword and stance were both unfamiliar, but he knew that in close combat without protection there was rarely time for a second passage. You moved, committed, and were either victorious or dead. He feinted once, low line, and halted as Shkai'ra's wrists and shoulders flexed into position. For a block, he assumed—Sun shun it, he didn't know the counters for this one! Once you were in under a straight longsword you had it, but this thing looked fit to take your hand off anywhere along the length.

The Kommanza backed her left foot a half step, breathed in, and attacked with an overarm cut to the head. The short spear spun like a propeller disk in a sweep parry, then darted out in a straight-line thrust to her midriff.

But the first move for the pear-splitter is also that for the side-downsweep. The long, slightly curved sword halted and turned ninety degrees from its angle of attack; the spear met nothing in its parry, and the cutting edge of the saber ground into the oiled hard-wood of the shaft. Even with the two-handed grip, that wasn't enough to cut it through, but the deflection knocked the man off-line, and Shkai'ra kicked, the heel of her right foot driving into his kneecap.

The man was brave and stubborn. He ignored the flash of pain from the dislocated knee, dropping the spear and trying to grapple and use the greater bulk of his arms and shoulders. Thus they were chest to chest as Shkai'ra released the saber hilt with her left hand, flip-reversed her grip with the other, and brought it out to the side, point in. That settled in just above his hip, and she ran it through his body from right to left, below the ribs. She could smell the familiar Fehinnan ranker's odor, sweat and sunflower oil and leather and metal, the smell of a tool, a thing, a trade; could watch his eyes as the cold iron slid through his stomach. For a frozen moment she held him poised, a soft sound of pleasure escaping her lips, then let the body drop and withdrew the blade with a twist to break the suction grip of muscle.

She looked up at a sudden thought, hoping that Megan hadn't seen the expression on her face; *murder-joy* her people called it. Most people didn't like Kommanza's ideas of pleasure and she, for some reason, wanted Megan to like her. She saw Megan just kicking over the woman's corpse to retrieve her knife and felt strangely relieved. Below, the aykkuka snarled, hefted her spear, then turned and ran to the stairwell, where the squad were engaged with the uprush of fleeing shaaids.

"Now," she panted, slow and deep. "Down?"

"The streets—" Megan paused to swallow dry phlegm. "The streets will not be too safe." She waved a hand; for the first time Shkai'ra noticed the rips and blood flecks on their tunics, the brown crusty stains running up her sword-hand nearly to the elbow.

"Over, then," she said. "The gaps between back alleys are narrow enough."

The pounding of their feet across the flat roof was drowned by the sounds of screams, shouts, and metal cleaving flesh and bone as they sprang to the roof of the next building, perhaps three meters away, and lower. Megan cursed under her breath as she ran. "Fishgutted, dogsucking, sons of three leprous wh—No, this way." She angled to a corner of the building and jumped. It was almost too far, over one of the more major streets, but she grabbed an ornately carved cornice and swung around to land on its other side. There were no carvings save on the corner pieces of this house, and handholds were few.

As Shkai'ra leaped, she caught a glimpse of someone in the street below staring up at them. Her long legs gave her an advantage and she didn't have to use the ornamentation for a grip. The next house was taller, and they climbed two balconies before disappearing over the peak of the roof.

"Wasted two of my good steel knives on those pigs," Megan panted. She paused by a chimney and looked down both sides. "There," she said, pointing to a stone wall below. "Does that give us a way through to a safe street, or are we still in the midst of this rat trap?"

Shkai'ra grinned and sat down to put on her sandals. "Why not?" She went over the edge, hung by her hands, and dropped to the smooth top of the wall. "Strange," she said as Megan joined her. "Usually, if there's something to protect, they stud the walls with stone splinters, angled in and out." Gripping a drain-pipe, she slid downward, landing in a crouch, sword once more ready. Around her was a formal garden, colored marble flags, fountains carved in strange shapes, bestial topiaries, potted flowers. The air heavy with sweet scents, and somewhere incense burned. This world denied that such things as bloodshed and massacre existed.

CHAPTER VII

The doorkeeper turned from the crowded thoroughfare. The street that fronted her master's estate held nothing but the residences of the rich; hence there was little traffic even in normal times, and none now when turmoil kept owner and servant in wary guard over their thresholds. She could feel a prickle of sweat, beyond what the heat of the day and a hurried pace could account for. When the market woman with her shoulder yoke of fruit turned into the street, it almost brought a sigh of relief.

Almost, but she remembered that the produce markets in the Old City were closed this day, and what vendor would have been given an order for delivery? She crossed to the other side of the street, one hand to her pouch. The sound of grit against stone under her sandals sounded loud in her ears as she hurried past glass inlaid walls.

Only one more turn, she thought. *On the grounds of my master, not even the Adders would dare follow.*

As she turned into the laneway, the market vendor

laid down her yoke and wiped her face, making a sign with her fingers. Two dark figures on the roof opposite stood; one lifted something with a metallic glitter.

Milampo's servant felt only an enormous blow beneath her shoulder blades. The huge impact threw her forward onto her face; it was when she tried to rise that the pain began. She moaned and felt a bubble of wetness break on her lips. It ran down her chin and dropped to the dusty pavement, bright red in the morning sun, one more droplet among so many shed that morning.

It was impossible to breathe. She struggled, forcing her lungs open against the wet tearing within, and crawled. One pace, two. Her hand pulled the belt pouch free from its thongs. The toss was weak, and the pouch landed a pace short of the doorkeeper's alcove.

"Hearing ... and obeying ... Master," she whispered. And there was a long night's falling into emptiness.

Megan hit the ground just behind Shkai'ra, saying, "Wait, now you should see to that hand now that we have a sec—" when she felt it. She reached out and caught Shkai'ra's wrist, in a suddenly urgent grip.

It was a tickle in the back of her mind. An elusive whiff of power coiled somewhere in this place like the delicate sound of a color or the scent of a song. "There is power here." She turned this way and that but could not pinpoint the source of disturbance. "Such power . . ." she whispered.

Shkai'ra bared her teeth and glanced around. The expression was not a smile. "Spook pushers," she said, very softly. "Oh, I don't like spook pushers. Never trust a shaman—the truest thing the Ancestors ever said." She didn't see Megan's sideways look.

They took the path to their left, breathing deep to

get their wind back. Shkai'ra sucked at the wound in the fleshy side of one hand, below the little finger.

"Should have watched the back shoulders of the spearhead—sheep-raping sharp," she muttered.

The paved way turned around a massive bush covered with thousands of tiny blue flowers moving gently in the warm, slow breeze, tapping against the stone of the statue in their midst. Megan looked up at the figure of the leaping dolphin with growing uneasiness; there was a prickling between her shoulder blades, as of approaching ... peril? Not necessarily, but something was about to happen. This feeling was one she had learned to trust.

They padded around the corner and stopped dead. Before them, a woman sat. Long black hair flowed down, over her cream-colored robe, past the cloth-of-gold cushion on which she sat, to coil slightly on the purple-and-green marble of the dais. A light wooden lattice overgrown with a green vine blossoming scarlet arched over her protectively. From a small brazier on her left, incense rose in a blue coil; to her right was a silver bowl on a tripod of bronze. She raised eyes as white as milk to meet them, from the crossed palms in her lap. Without iris or pupil; blind eyes, that saw.

"I greet you both," she said. The voice was soft, curiously hard to gauge. The face was smooth. Was the voice that of a child, or of middle age?

"I felt you in my darkness. One from afar; another from farther still. I see you in darkness, and darkness follows you: fate, but that I cannot see." Her nose wrinkled. "Blood, the smell of it; now, and in the time to come."

The woman's voice dropped like cool water into the humid stillness of the garden. Shkai'ra backed away, unconsciously, knuckles white on the grip of her saber as the tiny hairs along her spine struggled to rise against the sweat-damp cloth.

"Who ..." She cleared her throat against the

sudden roughness of her voice. "Who are you? You're no Sun priest; nor a merchant's clerk."

Megan bowed and made the gesture of respect, the clap of her hands sounding in the drowsy hum of bees from the lilac. "Lady of Power, you see much. We apologize for disturbing your, ah, meditations."

She backed up, pulling at Shkai'ra's arm, searching for a safer distance from this woman. *Shkai'ra*, she thought, *don't offend this one*. Megan felt breathless, the sensation of pressure under her lungs almost stifling.

Those eyes turned to her, and the woman laughed. "Fear me not, young-kin. I am merely a seeker of wisdom. And a prisoner, a hostage." The laugh transformed the ageless face into that of a young girl. "Or so my . . . host . . . thinks."

She raised her hands, and a faint nimbus of blue light played around the long, slender fingers.

"This moment was foreseen." Her voice was remote, the laughter faded into a cool monotone that might have come from the idol in a sanctuary carved of glacial ice.

"Now all turns on your actions. Two chance-met wanderers, and on them rests the fate of great lords, wisefolk, merchants, and priests, and common folk without number. How, I cannot see; there are too many branches of the path. On all those that go well, you fare together."

She diminished into humanity. "But it would be best if you left soon." She pointed down the avenue of topiaries behind her with a sparely elegant gesture. "There lies a gate which will not require you to traverse much of the greathouse; the household is much disturbed. Here is clean clothing."

She turned her head, and at the unspoken summons a man appeared. Middle-aged, he was near seven feet in height and corded with muscle. He picked up the white-eyed woman as an adult might a child, and it

was only then that they realized her legs hung limp
and useless.

"That way, Bors," Yeva said. The milky eyes turned
to regard the two. "Go well, I hope," she continued.
"That you go into strangeness, I can be sure of."
Megan stood, looking after them, silent.

"Come on," Shkai'ra said, waving a hand before her
face. Megan started as if coming back from a long
distance, then hesitating over the gift of the clothing.
Then she shrugged. *What else to do, wander about
bloody? For someone that powerful . . . she wouldn't
need something as simple as a gift to hold us.*

They shed their tunics, rinsed blood from their skins
in the fountain and donned the clean plain garments
that lay folded on the dais. Megan followed Shkai'ra
down the row of sculpted shrubs to the opposite wall
that encircled the garden, and to the heavy door set
into it.

Megan paused, felt in her belt, and sighed. "Another cloth gone. You'd better clean that meat cleaver
of yours." She looked about, then cleaned her daggers
with a corner of her old tunic.

Shkai'ra pulled a silk rag from her belt and wiped
the long patterned blade lovingly. The dappled patterns in the steel shone as the red-brown scum came
away.

"Ahi-a, I never leave blood on my swift-kisser here
longer than I must," she said, buffing the metal again
and sliding it back into the sheath, a practiced motion
that didn't need the guidance of eyes. "Getting good
Minztan steel this far east is near impossible. Besides,
even in Illizbuah walking the streets with a bloody
sword is a trifle conspicuous."

"What, it isn't the universal practice? I'd have
thought—" She broke off, intent. Beyond the door: a
muffled sound, perhaps a whisper, and from the other
side.

She looked at Shkai'ra; the Kommanza shrugged,

drew, the point of her saber making small neat circles in the air. "The doorkeeper, maybe. Go on."

They opened the dark mahogany panel, and met silence. Projecting walls made a U-shaped nook for the guardian, but it was empty. The liveried figure of the servant lay beyond in the street, one outstretched hand touching the threshold; a bolt-gun shaft behind one shoulder showed the reason. She was very recently dead, still bleeding in a slowing trickle, and at their feet lay a belt pouch. They both moved toward it by reflex; Megan's hand arrived first, tucking the leather bag under the hem of her tunic.

"Time to count it later," she said. "No sense waiting for whoever shot her."

Shkai'ra bent over the corpse for an instant as they passed. "Ahi-a—House of Milampo Terhan's-kin. The fattest pig among the merchant swine-princes. Fifty ships, interests in the western trade, slaves and metal and spices."

A dark figure clung to the roof above them, straining after their departing voices. Two more joined him, and they dropped softly into the street beside the body of their victim.

One knelt to run quick expert fingers over the still form. "Shadowed One, it is not here."

The leader cursed softly and flipped the body over with her toe. "Search about," she said to the others. "Our informant said this one would have it." Her head swiveled to where the two outlanders had passed. Or could they have taken it? A fine sweat broke out on her forehead. She would not envy the subordinate assigned to take *that* news to the Adderchief. "Perhaps those two should be questioned."

CHAPTER VIII

Megan and Shkai'ra strolled along the brick side-
walk, a luxury of these affluent quarters of the Old
City. Folk were about their business, seeming to
ignore what was happening only a half kilometer away.
Or perhaps not seeming, Shkai'ra thought. Old City
dwellers were not all rich, but the poor here were
mostly the servants of the wealthy; the unfree mostly
not even Fehinnans. A quiet existence, ordered,
secure; it might have been a different continent, a
world invisible from the desperate daily scramble of
the lowtown slums. Massacre did not really touch their
lives; unless they were physically involved, it was not
real to them.

The traffic of the street parted for a *laaitun* of cavalry, with bright gold-lacquered armor and ribbons
wound in the horses' manes. Shkai'ra put an arm
around Megan's shoulders and nodded to a laughing
group about the entranceway of a shop.

"Nothing stops Fehinnans when Festival is coming,"
she said. Gaily painted masks were being passed from

"I'll take a look," she said, voice low, said Megan

hand to hand: faces of *saahvyts* and *paancahs* and *waybaycs*, the devils and pranksters and house goblins that lingered still beneath the austere monotheism of the Sun. There were other goods for sale: leather wine flasks for squirting into the mouths of passersby, hand pumps for showering colored dust and strange powders, air-filled bladders for banging on heads, and feathered cloaks worked with the grapes and ears of corn that symbolized the season of growth. Even in Illizbuah the City Solstice, High Sun, was still largely a fertility rite.

"Much like *Dagde Vroi* at home," Megan said. "Days of Fools, at Year End." Her eyes narrowed speculatively at some of the powders displayed. "One of my kin," she spat, "makes things like these, but for more serious purposes and higher prices. If I'm lucky, she'll have died before I get back." Suddenly she laughed. "She would be lucky if she did!"

Shkai'ra's smile died as she looked down at her companion. "*Hoi*, you're limping? Did you take a wound?"

Megan twisted her leg to one side and looked at it with annoyed impatience. "Nothing serious—I didn't notice it at the time." Her chuckle lapsed into an almost hysterical giggle. "It must have been in the eating shop. To go through all of this and be stabbed in the leg with a table tool, with a fork! The burghers of this city are more dangerous than the soldiery. Don't worry, it's hardly visible."

Shkai'ra grunted skeptically. Megan must have good natural resistance to infection, to have lived this long; still, even a small wound could bring the green rot, or poison the blood. "Best we see to it, though," she said. They were in a district of shops, expensive goods for the Old City trade. Among them stood a small park: tessellated brick pavement with dwarf flowering shrubs in carved stone pots.

"I'll take a look," the blond woman said. Megan

leaned against one of the man-high flowerpots and extended the leg behind her; the wound was in the calf, difficult to reach.

"Remember, that fork was in a priest-bureaucrat's mouth—no telling what was on it," Shkai'ra said as she knelt to examine the puncture. Two small red dots, side by side; she ran her fingers around the affected area before applying her mouth. "Hmmm, there was something in there," she said, spitting. "Tines probably broke off."

Shkai'ra worked the wound with her fingers until the blood flowed clean, then produced a tiny bottle from a belt pouch and poured green liquid into the holes, ignoring Megan's startled twitch.

"Fishguts! What are you doing, woman, whittling it deeper with a hot needle?"

"Stings, doesn't it?" Shkai'ra replied, grinning up at the Zak, teeth white in her tanned face. "The Fehinnans make it from seaweed. Good for cuts. Now, why don't we eat, since we didn't get to, earlier."

A copper bit stirred the vendor of a nearby pushcart. A big ceramic vat bubbled in its center, sending a scent of hot peanut oil into the warm, still city air. Into it the streetseller flipped a double handful of meat chunks, onions, peppers, and pieces of yam. A few minutes later, he scooped them out with a slotted wooden ladle, rolled them in flatbread, and doused them with a hot brown sauce. Cornhusks served as platters; an extra bit brought two wooden cups of peach juice from a sweating clay jug, cool and tart.

The two women lounged back into the shade of plants and buildings, sitting at their ease on a patch of coarse grass. On the street outside a group of retainers trotted by, dressed in the livery of the Terhan's-kin. Swords were forbidden to them, but there were ceramic-headed spears in their hands, knives at belts, worried determination on their faces. Shkai'ra juggled the hot food in her hands, watching with interest from between the leaves of a potted eucalyptus tree. Happily, she inhaled the smells of warm stone, garlic, hot oil and flowers. Patterns of sunlight shifted across her face, dappling as wind shifted branches.

"Here," she said, handing Megan the second roll. "If that pouch was missed so soon, it had something in it besides the doorward's wages, or I'm a kinless sheepraping nomad." Her eyes narrowed in amusement; a Fehinnan friend had told her once that she loved strong happenings more than wine, and there were times when she saw some truth in that. And an exile with nothing to lose but her life could play such games with no regrets.

"*Rauquai!*" Megan exclaimed, blowing gingerly on her portion. "And I thought to *rest* in this city! You realize, Shkai'ra-my-friend, that since I arrived I've scarcely stopped running? Well, nothing more is likely to happen; soon I'll be able to raise passage money and sit on my butt, the fine lady passenger." Megan finished the fruit juice and peered over the rim of her cup at the Kommanza, eyes snapping. "You don't like 'spook pushers'?" Shkai'ra set her own cup down on the yellow brick, circling her arms about her knees.

"Nia. I almost got killed trusting a spook pusher, once. And the shaman who was there was supposed to be on my side."

"Don't you think you're tarring all powerful people with the same brush?"

"Well, yes, but the only part of the other world that ever touched me were my gods, and they aren't what other people would call . . . nice."

"If you even know about it firsthand, that makes *you* a spook pusher."

"Nia! Nia." Shkai'ra's eyes narrowed. "A shaman once told me that my line, the chief-kin, had as much power as your average cabbage, and it had to be like that so it wouldn't interfere with the gods talking through us."

"Ah." Megan stared down into her cup. *I obviously can't tell her—*

"How did *you* know about the spooker in the garden, anyway? You said something the minute your feet hit the dirt."

Then again . . . this morning she trusted me behind her with a weapon. But then she was safer doing that. People are less likely to kill than they are to shun . . . She shrugged mentally. She'd done well enough without friends before.

"See that fellow there?"

The Zak nodded at a man dozing in the heat. He lay on his cloak, a broad-brimmed traveler's hat over his face; beside him at waist height was a wine cup, securely planted on the rim of a tree pot. She dipped a finger into the dregs of Shkai'ra's cup and drew two lines, one around the base and another on the rim. "Watch," she said.

Very gently, she put a finger to the edge of Shkai'ra's goblet and pushed. The cup five meters away leaped in a parody of the tiny motion, and the cool liquid poured unerringly into the man's lap. He leaped to his feet with a wild, strangled yell, fist upraised. Awareness blinked back into his eyes, and the realization that there was nobody within five meters of him. His mouth worked silently; the fist fell, and his eyes with it to the purple stain on the brown cotton of his tunic. He wrapped his cloak about his middle and stole away.

The Zak picked up her cup and emptied it with a sly almost-smile. "Not everybody who can do a little magic sits under bushes and makes prophecies," she said impishly, hiding her tension. "Better to have a little fun now and then."

In a chamber overlooking gardens, beneath a dome of crystal, a robed figure, another of the Guild of the Wise, sat motionless above a brazen bowl of water.

Others had watched here before him; there would be a relief when he tired, and that would not be soon. Sensation/experience/perception drifted through the still pool of his mind, without rippling its receptivity. Leaves brushed against the brickwork of the tower; a breeze whispered through the latticework supports of the dome, laden with the scent of flowers and baking bread.

A spot of light appeared in the clear water. He rose smoothly from the cross-legged position he had kept for a hand of hours. Another figure appeared on the spiral stair below.

"It has begun," he said to the one who came. "Summon the adepts."

His gaze returned to the water. The workings of the Patterns were a never-failing source of wonder. This was the nexus of probability they had sensed; he closed his eyes and ran fingers of thought over the skein of branching alternates that ran forward from the fixed point of now he occupied. There was very delicate work ahead, a nudging at the workings of fate and chance to ensure that events fell as they willed.

Shkai'ra blinked, narrow gray eyes slitting as she turned to glance down at Megan. One eyebrow lifted. Megan waited for her to get up and walk away.

"You didn't tell me you were a witch," she said.

"Witch? Scarcely. I know a few tricks. But our people don't like to show them outside the walls of the city; it tends to get them burned."

"Hmmmm? In the Zekz Kommanz the *dhaik'tz*, the shamans, sniff out any witchcraft but their own; then eat the witches' hearts, mostly." She paused. Megan seemed to be tensed for something. *I like her, she's fought for me. So what if witchcraft gives me gooseflesh on my spirit—she's still on my side.* "Silly custom." Long fingers rested on the Zak's brow for a moment. "I trust you," she added soberly.

*   *   *

The adepts filed into the chamber and stood circled around the bowl. One touched the bowl; it rippled, cleared, and revealed the two women in the park.

The magicians waited in silence, their minds studying the scene and its implications on the planes.

"So," one said at last. "It seems that our message to the moneyhunters is a communication of more significance than we assumed, perhaps. But if we have found them, can the priests"—they all made a gesture of execration—"be far behind?"

"What matter?" another asked. "I still contend that we waste our strength here. These are all ephemera; what are their wars and quarrelings to the wise?"

"The self-christened Wise," another mind added dryly. "Still, this matter has been decided. If you wish another Council . . ."

negation.

"Yeva would be the one to deal with this matter," a woman who looked sixty years old said. "Their worldlines have already touched hers, and she does excellent work. At present, we can only see that these will somehow give an opportunity to accomplish our purpose without attracting the attention of the Undying One. With his servants we can deal; with him . . ." A collective shudder passed through the group.

"And let her not interfere more than the minimum," the first agreed. "Too much, and we may abort the seed of chance that we seek to nurture."

agreement/hope/action

CHAPTER IX

The solarium had been quickly repaired by Milampo's servants. There were new plants, and the shattered glass had been replaced; all that remained was the zigzag scorchmark, snaking its way across the paneling of the wall.

Lightning was such a showy working, and so easy when the potential-paths through the air were ready in a storm. All you had to do was . . . connect. Still, a priest would approve of retribution from the sky.

"Here, Bors," Yeva said. With infinite gentleness, the huge man set her down on the cushions and helped to arrange the unresponding legs. She looked up at the scarlet blossoms of the trumpet flowers and let them brush against her cheeks, feeling the structure of the plant, its enjoyment of sun and water, the thoughts of the gardeners as they planted and tended it. Yeva inhaled the smells of flowers and burned cedarwood, a melancholy pleasure.

Milampo, she thought with a sigh. Not all visitors were as pleasant as the two women. There had been something strange. . . .

The merchant bustled in, with the inevitable swarm of attendants. Several were members of his kinfast, along with clerks, bodyservants with pitchers of wine and juice, and four mercenary guards. Those were fitted with standard leather armor, but trimmed with bullion tassels along the fringes of the glossy varnished plates. *Their spearheads are cheap mass-produced ceramic bound with implanted fiber*, she thought with mild amusement how like the man it was to spend on show and neglect utility. But they all had steel swords, which meant a certain degree of competence, those being personal property. Not to be shown on the streets while they were in liveried service, of course. Fehinnan law frowned on private armies, particularly within the capital walls.

"Honored guest," the merchant began. He was a short man, and the afternoon sun glistened on the sweat film that covered his skin. Rolls of fat overlapped the stiffly embroidered collar of his maroon velvet tunic, and the thin vein-embossed legs beneath were trembling visibly.

"Milampo, my host," she said in a voice pitched to carry soothing tones below the conscious level. "A man of your years, unused to exercise, should not run up stairs so quickly. See, the veins in your temples are throbbing visibly; this is not good."

The merchant swelled. She was surprised that he had the courage to confront her this way, although from the smell, his nerve had been heavily reinforced with firewine.

"Slaughter!" he blurted. "Temple Square, blood—"

She raised a hand. "Need we discuss these matters with so much company?" she asked mildly.

He paled slightly and turned, with inarticulate shooing motions. The hangers-on departed, except for the guards, who stood and leaned on their spears. Members of their guild were oath-bound to their employers and could not be summoned against them even in a temple court.

Milampo breathed deeply, and when he spoke again his voice was steady. "There has been a massacre," he said.

"Which we predicted!" Yeva replied, and her tone sharpened. "Milampo Terhan's-kin, did it not occur to you that your intrigues with gold and favor could lead to real blood being shed? Or did you see it as more columns of numbers in your ledgers?"

"Enough of that," he said, waving a hand. Amethysts glowed on his fingers. "They are only shaaid; no shortage. But if the Sun-on-Earth"—his voice dropped unconsciously—"should investigate, the others *will* blame me."

"As the leader in this policy," she said. "Also as the one who proposed calling on the Wise. In which you were yourself wiser than your wont." *With suitable encouragement*, she added to herself. An inward sigh; they had hoped to prevent violence, but in matters like this, action muddied the waters of foreknowing beyond certainty. As ever, to observe was to change; to act on the knowledge gained was to change events still more. *Yet we cannot sit silent when we might save.*

"And you and your kin will go to the tables, and your wealth will be forfeit to the state," she added equably.

He wilted, then darted a glance of suspicion at her. "Never forget, if I am betrayed, none of my wealth will be yours," he said. "I also have you, as guarantee of good faith. I could order you speared this instant."

Yeva caught the glance the guards exchanged behind their master's back. One tapped a finger to her brow. These were not temple guards, or even regulars.

"Come, come, have we not agreed to aid you?" she soothed. "No need to talk of disharmonious violence."

"Agreement? Where is my message? Just now I found my faithful servant dead beside the west gate, and no such message upon her."

Yeva started, with a look of dawning interest in her uncanny eyes. Then her gaze filmed over, and Milampo shrank back with his next sentence unuttered, making the Sun sign on his breast.

information/essence/confirmation flowed through her mind. This was not speech; it was what speech imperfectly counterfeited. Ah, then her suspicions about the two were correct. The exchange of information stumbled slightly.

apologies, eldersib.

calm yourself. all who are masters were apprentice once. inform the council i have their message.

gratitude/appreciation/obedience.

She returned to the world of phenomenon that most thought real. "Be at peace, my host," she said tranquilly. It was difficult, this stumbling with words. "The message which links you to us has fallen into the proper hands."

"Whose?" he asked, paling. That message, and the circumstances of it, were enough to earn him three days of dying.

Yeva considered, and decided that it would be cruelty to inform him that the proper hands were those of two wanderers who would doubtless attempt to sell it to the highest bidder. How could she explain? Even to those with the inborn talent and long years of painful mastery, it was no more than trained intuition that those two would use their burden to bring a favorable resolution. That was merely likelihood, not certainty. It was her duty to turn the probability into fact under the bright focus of the *now*.

"That will be revealed at the appropriate conjunction of the planes," she said. A yellow bird fluttered in, to land on her outstretched finger. She slipped a feather from the sleeve of her robe and stroked the tiny creature beneath the throat, enjoying the total submergence in sensation that the bird was feeling, possible only in a creature beneath or beyond self-consciousness.

"Observe, my host; never stroke a bird with your finger, for fear of disarranging its plumage or the subtle oils thereon. Instead, use a feather in the hand."

Milampo made a choking sound and wheeled from the room, followed by his guards and a lingering smell of oily, overheated flesh, rose-scented soap and expensive musk. She smiled at the memory of his appearance, bouncing like a paper balloon filled with hot air at a child's festival. *At least he had taken his noisy mind and body away* ... She chided herself at the thought. Every human soul had its purpose, and it was no more just to despise a merchant for being a merchant than a dog for being a dog.

Still, she was heartily sick of being the trader's "guest." The only interesting conversation he had was on matters of trade, and with the laborious gentility of the second generation he avoided that as ill-bred. She glanced at the forked scorchmark the bolt from the storm had left. The stroke had been clumsy, but what did Milampo think to threaten her with, if she could block that? Would he have the gardeners beat her to death with hoes? The mercenaries would be as likely to spear him; he was not the sort of employer who would inspire devotion beyond death. He'd inspired more of his servants to loyalty when he was younger, when the memory of his kinparents lingered. As he'd grown older, his ideas had hardened along with his growing callous attitude to other people.

Calming, she settled into a light trance. The minds of the guild washed around her, and she traced the lines of force out over the city. The palace was like a beacon to her sight on this level, one she carefully avoided: minor tricks of seeing and lifting were beneath the notice of the male avatar of *Her*, but any major alteration of the webs of probability would draw attention like a wasp to sugar. For the sake of balance, she could endure the contact of those on the Left Hand of the council; the guild existed for their common interests, after all. But the God was truly mad and very dangerous; as well provoke a bull elephant in rut. Yet ... at the far edge of perception, where entropy faded the lines of might-be into a chaotic fog, there was the unmistakable presence of the Sun-on-Earth. She would have a hand in this, at the last.

She sat, tracing the possible consequences of one course of action after another. Some she might have anticipated; others were bizarre. *Yellow-skinned foreigners disembarking from ships drawn by whales?* No, that was vanishingly unlikely. Still, it had its origins. Yes, try eliminating the stranger women—*light brighter than noon, then black ruins under black sky, birds falling to lie unrotting where even death was dead.* . . . Shuddering, she pulled her consciousness back and scanned the time dimension. The future: more than a double hand of years, impossible to tell how much further. Now, nobody had ever seen that before; no force on earth could produce such effects. How could the elimination of two outland mercenaries make such a difference?

The bondservant's mind interrupted her with a blast of unconscious fear. The servant set about trimming one of the newly placed shrubs, that clearly needed no such attention. *Will Milampo never learn?* the sorceress thought. A direct lesson was necessary; next time something more important than mere free-association scrying might be lost by jostling her concentration. Sensitivity had its price; she found screening more difficult than most.

Motionless, she made a complex and completely nonphysical shifting. In a room away from the solarium, Milampo Terhan's-kin started violently as a voice spoke behind his ear. A young voice, breathless and sweet.

"Silly. Why bother, when that-self Yeva cannot walk." A silver bowl sat on a window ledge; it was a simple curve of metal, and a part-perception of the sorceress's mind admired its restraint. Gracefully, it moved away across the room and down the hall toward the solarium garden, leaving the merchant crouched on his cushions, the knuckles of one hand pressed to his lips.

The gardener dropped her shears with a clatter as the bowl carried itself into the still-scented warmth of the roof-level chamber. One blade shattered on the marble tiles, the edges of the vitrified clay glinting with silica in the sunlight. Yeva took the bowl in her hand and extended it.

"I wish this filled with water, from the spring against the south wall, the one that cannot be seen from here. Do not let the water or the bowl touch the ground. When you return, place it here and then go to your master. Tell him—again—that I do not wish to be disturbed at my work. And, that he has merely annoyed me. Have him contemplate the consequences if I become angered."

She retreated into herself, monitoring breath and heartbeat, feeling the thrill of fatigue along her nerves. Even to move a metal bowl in the physical universe was savagely tiring; magic was rarely useful for such gross manipulation, particularly without preparation or patterning.

Afraid, she thought. All of them, and of what? One without the use of her eyes or legs. But that was part of the fear; that one such as she could be a figure of power, rather than another beggar on the temple steps. She sighed. In the guild, there were few enough who could look past the surface of things; outside, almost none.

The bowl was extended toward her on trembling palms. "Young one, I thank you for this service," she murmured, taking it. There was a rapid patter of departing feet.

She placed the curve of silver in the tripod before her and waited for it to be still. She was weary, but it would be as well to be informed. The red one first . . . a pattern of thought wrapped in black, tempered. A name rose into her mind: Shkai'ra Mek Kermak'skin. The dark. Force constrained, and a place of age. Ice and iron, the sound of a waterfall, sunlight on water. Creak of rigging. Megan Whitlock.

Holding the images in her mind, she gestured at the water and spoke certain words. It rippled and smoothed, to show . . . nothing. A wry grimace crossed her mouth; she had never been very skilled at scrying in water. There was a sudden flare from the brazier at her side as she drew heat from the water and cast it into the charcoal. The silver clinged and sang as the water within it shifted from liquid to crystalline ice in much less than a heartbeat. The beads of moisture on its outer surface flashed into crystal, and the wrought metal rang in protest at the swift change in temperature.

Yeva smiled, remembering the pride she had felt at first mastering that trick. Then she spoke again, weaving the names of the two she sought into the chant. Names were a thing of power; the symbol was the thing it represented, that was the core of magic. Lesser to greater, and distance could not sunder the bonds between objects linked by similarity. . . . A complex form grew in her mind, as structured as a snowflake with inter-lattices of meaning, glowing with the color of hot steel as she pushed energy through it. To the Sight, images formed.

Ice is much better, she thought.

CHAPTER X

"You trust me?" Megan said incredulously, happily. "Who do you think I trust in showing this?" Shkai'ra inclined her head, accepting the implied rebuke.

"True. But my people . . . fear magic, wherever from."

Shkai'ra laughed suddenly. "They cast me out, so sheepshit on their customs. Why don't we go back, count our loot, and feed my cat?"

A sound echoed down the street to their left, from the direction of Temple Square. A rhythmic stamping, thousandfold, the sound of three thousand sets of ceramic hobnails striking the ground in unison. It was more a blow through the air than a sound, thudding against chest and gut. It overrode the crowd murmur, flattened clatter of hooves, creak of wood, even the slow pounding of the pace drums. And a chanting accompanied it.

> *"Earth, sky, fire, stone,*
> *Steel cuts to bone.*
> *Earth, sky, fire, stone—"*

The droning marchsong echoed back from the fronts of the buildings. The first regiment swung down the avenue, six ranks broad, pikes a perfect vertical forest of poles with the butts resting in slings braced around the neck. Behind the soldiers came a line of carts, six-wheeled and massive, grain-movers in time of peace. Now they bore another burden, one that drained in threads of red onto the paving stones, like the pressings of grapes piled high in the harvesters' baskets. Death's vintners escorted their fruits. The heavy butcher-shop smell of fresh meat hung on the air.

"I agree." Megan said. "As soon as the road is free. The cat will probably not forgive you for, oh, a day or two if you neglect him so shamefully, and somehow this place seems improper for the counting of monies."

She pulled two of her knives free, reminding herself that these people were not kin of hers, but couldn't help feeling for *their* kin, under such a tyranny—much like home. She bit off a wave of homesickness and laid the knives on the bench, searching for a polishing cloth in her pouch. "These new toys have already been tested." She scrubbed at a drying bloodstain around the hilt of one, glad that the other woman was there. With so much death around, being alone in a strange city was doubly hard.

"Hmmmm, don't forget some might have gotten in along the tang. Had a blade rust out and snap at the hilt once, that way."

"Teach your baba to suck eggs, long-legs." Megan said amiably.

Shkai'ra chuckled and looked down critically at the knives. "Good weapons, but haven't you ever wanted to put a little more steel between you and the nasty people?"

Megan nodded at Shkai'ra's long saber. "Not the weapon for someone of my height," she said.

"Ia. Nor the Fehinnan tools, either. But over the mountains, in the cities along the Ah'yia River, they use"—her hands shaped the air—"a long slim blade, with a bell guard. For the lunging thrust, and just stiff enough to slide-parry a cut—nearly got one through my lungs, once. That might be useful for you."

"I suppose it might be useful. To learn a new weapon, though . . . Show me one in the market and we'll see." She cleaned the other knife slowly, considering. "I wonder what was so important to the merchant that his servant strove to deliver it, dying." She looked up into the Kommanza's impassive face. "An interesting morning, wouldn't you say?"

"And we are doomed to live in interesting times," Shkai'ra said, "A smallsword; perhaps Kermibo would know."

Shkai'ra kicked the door of their rooms at the inn closed and dropped the bar home. With a sigh of contentment, she racked her saber and shotpistol, peeled off her sandals, and kicked her tunic into a corner.

"Summertime in Fehinna, I always feel about to sprout mushrooms from my skin," she said, stretching and yawning. Tapping a cup from the clay jug of fruit juice in a corner, she stretched out on the bed and fortified it with a small dollop of cane spirit from a bottle of twisted black glass. "Want some?"

"Yes," Megan said, following her example and setting the cup down on the floor while she pulled off her short boots. "You take a look at the pouch. How much for passage from here to the Mid-Lannic Islands?"

"That would depend," Shkai'ra said, teasing at the tightly wound, intricate knots that Fehinnans used to foil pickpockets. "I know some captains who'd sell you passage cheap. Then sell you at their next port of call; who cares if a wanderer without kin or lord disappears? The ones you can trust don't come cheap. Why hurry?"

She rolled over onto her stomach and frowned with concentration; one foot reached out absently to stroke lightly down the back of Megan's leg, who didn't move away. "Faster just to cut *tuk t'hait whulzhaits zteafakaz ... Hau!*"

Megan looked up at the exclamation of delight. Two whole coils of stamped silver tradewire had rolled out onto the coverlet: two hundred silvers, the yearly wage of a six-master's captain or the price of six fine horses. Ten gold in loose bits were underneath, half as much again.

The tall woman swung her head back and wolf-howled at the ceiling, softly. "Megan, comrade's delight, take a look at *this*."

The Zak narrowed her eyes and scraped the money together. "Ahh, precious metals buy more there. Quite a haul for a servant. And the next captain who tries to sell me off is going to dine on his own tripes."

Shkai'ra grunted and fished in the bottom of the pouch. "Something else in here." She pulled out a folded sheet of heavy paper and spread it on the yellow fabric of the sheet.

"Sheepshit!" she yelled, flinging it away and bolting upright. The caressing toes bit suddenly into the inner surface of Megan's thigh.

Shkai'ra could read Fehinnan, a little, but it was not the content of the message that made her recoil, feeling cold sweat rank on forehead and armpits. The letters ... could not be read. Not that they were in foreign script, but they moved. At the edge of vision they seemed clear, but wherever the eyes tried to rest, outlines shifted into images not-quite-seen. For a moment she thought they formed a face that looked at her—and winked.

"What the *rokatzk* is wrong with you?" Megan snapped, rubbing at the red mark on her leg and glaring. Then her eyes fell on the paper. The seal on the pouch had been sufficient symbol to shield it, but now the smell of Power drifted like unseen smoke on the still air.

"Fishgutted fool that you are, Megan," she muttered to herself as she reached cautiously for it. "I should have warded the room, even if it disturbed you. Probably too late, but—" She picked up the paper between finger and thumb, slid it neatly back into the pouch.

Then she walked to each of the doors and windows in turn, setting a hand to each and concentrating for a moment. She moved to the center of the room, or as nearly as possible with the bed in the way, and spoke a single word that rebounded against the walls, showering the air with silver that shrank to a red line around the openings and then faded altogether. Somewhere there was a shifting, as if the foundations of the room had twisted marginally out of alignment with the world. "There," the Zak said with satisfaction. "Now most people won't be able to think about this room, much less disturb us here. Of course, those with the power will see the 'hole,' and know—but only if they look very carefully."

Shkai'ra stared, shivered, then shook herself like a hound climbing out of cold water. The gooseflesh that had mottled the pale flesh of her body faded, and she unclenched fingers knotted about the hilt of a nonexistent sword and made her warding off gesture.

"*Ahkomman mitch'mi,*" she muttered. Then: "Well enough. If we're to have spookers after us, better that we know somewhat of their tricks." She considered for a moment.

"That message," she said. "That message will be wanted, and badly. Protection like that doesn't come cheap." She pulled at her lip. "We might just throw it in the jakes and make a run for it . . . No, the gates and docks will be watched, and if we were caught, nobody would believe we'd thrown it away."

She looked up at Megan. "No one will notice this room? As if it had never been?"

The small woman nodded, and Shkai'ra grinned. "Then they're going to have a problem down in the kitchens. Best we move back into my room and use this as a refuge."

Their gear was light and easily moved. "Remind me to cancel the delivered meals," Megan said. Shkai'ra nodded, laid herself out on the cool sheets, and watched the slit where furnace-hot sunlight poured through the rattan blinds.

"Glitch, godlet of Fuckups was with me this day. Not thirty hours back in the city: three fights, a pitched battle, a spook pusher—" she looked sideways at Megan "—two spook pushers and a cursed letter."

As she dropped to the round divan, Megan chuckled. Shkai'ra reached out and touched the red mark on her thigh.

"Sorry about that," she said. "I was startled." She hesitated, then slowly took her hand away from the rising bruise.

"That's all right," Megan said. And it was. She didn't want the other woman to take her hand away. Gentle fingers wakened the old feelings with a vengeance. She wanted . . . No.

After a while, Shkai'ra got up and impersonally began tracing along the muscles of the Zak's neck and back, massaging gently at the edges of the long sheaths and straps of well-defined sinew with her fingertips.

"Beautifully developed," she said softly, with her mouth next to Megan's ear. "Like metal under velvet. It's like massaging a woods-lynx." She chuckled. "Complete with claws!" She continued the slow, expert caressing with infinite patience and unfeigned quiet delight.

A black shape leaped onto the bed and swatted at Shkai'ra's bare foot with a peremptory paw. She laughed gently and pushed him away, where he settled at a far edge of the circular mattress and folded his paws under himself with an air of offended dignity.

She transferred her fingers to the area under her companion's ribs. Continuing, she looked down into Megan's half-shut eyes.

"You've not been close with anyone very often, have you?" she said. Her hair had come unbraided and hung springy and rippling, silk-fine. She let the ends touch across the Zak's face and throat and breasts, as lightly as the brush of hummingbird feathers. "Not for pleasure, I mean."

Megan sighed, and her eyes crinkled first in a somber mien that lightened rapidly. "No, and being forced is not a way to cultivate a taste for sex." One corner of her mouth quirked into a half grin. "Though, if you keep doing that, I might get to like it," she said facetiously, relaxed, leaning on one arm. "Muscle degenerated to fat is disgusting. I'm glad that you are in no way soft."

She paused a minute. "That word wasn't quite right . . . it implies no sensitivity as well." There was the droning buzz of a summer beetle on the damp air, and haze was thickening outside. "You know, I ought to go back to the market and get something to coat my claws. Something unhealthy to anyone I scratch, that is." Megan sat up and moved Ten-Knife, who had crept up to squeeze himself between them.

"Ia. Lots of places to buy that sort of thing in this city." Megan looked down at the tall one's sleepy smile and said, "You're as lazy as a steppe-tiger and twice as nasty. I think that's what I like best about you."

"Toss a dice to see who sleeps on the floor?" Shkai'ra said with a laugh. *Funny, I usually hate waiting for it*, she thought. Her skin was tight and tingling. *This time I don't.*

Puzzled, the servant looked down at the afternoon tray. "Why am I carrying this tray?" he asked of no one in particular. "Only four rooms on this floor."

Shrugging, he turned and trotted back to the stair-well, through the guest levels of the inn to the subter-ranean kitchens.

"Extra tray!" he called cheerfully across the smoky chaos of the great brick-lined chamber.

The Head cook, Glaaghi, was working over one of the ceramic stoves that lined one massive wall. She was huge, inches taller than most Fehinnans and al-most square, with muscle under enormous pads of fat. Dressed only in a loincloth and leather apron, she was a formidable figure as she turned in wrath from the vat of smoking peanut oil in front of her.

One ham-like fist rose to point at the chalkboard, and a bellow roared out. "ROOMFIVESECOND-FLOORWEST NOW!"

The servant would have turned pale if his natural complexion had allowed; as it was, he had to settle on grey. Backing out, he fled up the stairs to the second level. Of course, there were five rooms on all the lev-els in the west wing!

He stood at the door of room four, second level. "Why am I carrying this tray?" he murmured. "Better get back to the kitchens; the Sea-Cow is likely to drop me into an oil vat if I'm late about my rounds." Cheer-fully, he trotted back to the stairwell.

As he pushed through the swinging doors of the kitchen, a curious expression crossed his face, very like that of a man who, when deep in thought, realizes that a hyena is licking one of his feet.

"Why are you carrying that tray?" the cook yelled. Then, smiling gently, she crossed the room, weaving between porters carrying whole pig carcasses and sides of beef. Quietly, she laid one hand on the bondser-vant's shoulder.

"Himo," she said in a sweet tone. With an effort, he controlled his bladder. "You like to run; I should have remembered. We need"—she picked him up by the front of his tunic—"another two hundredweight of cornmeal ground, and the treadmill waits!"

In an aside, she called to another of the kitchen slaves as she carried the blubbering man toward the grain store. "You, girl! Get a fresh tray and take it to second-five west, smartly now!"

As Megan and Shkai'ra sauntered down to the exercise ground, Megan saying, ". . . you only use four knives, but . . ." they passed one of the ubiquitous inn servants as she scurried in the opposite direction. They did not see her halt by the fourth door in the corridor.

Puzzled, she looked down at the tray in her hands. "Why am I carrying this tray?" she murmured. Well, it could not be of any great importance. Best to get back to the kitchens; it wouldn't do to be caught idling. Glaaghi was not as bad as she would have been if the owners' kinfast let her, but still bad enough.

CHAPTER XI

Megan woke in the dead time of early morning, the time when old people die. It was quiet, quiet enough to hear the sounds that day tide drowned; a single set of hooves falling hollow in the distance, clap-clack against pavement; the sigh of a slow-heavy sea wind over the fluted tile roofs. Even the insistent chorus practicing their High Festival songs had stopped, perhaps because they were too drunk to remember the words. The air in the room was thick, pressing on her like hot wet towels; it smelled of sweat, wine, fruit rinds. Her bladder was full to bursting, and the heat suddenly made her skin itch. For a moment she lay still, listening to Shkai'ra's slow, even breathing, then got up off the pallet on the floor.

She relieved herself and pushed the chamberpot back under the bed, pacing restlessly. *Goddess*, she thought, *even the floor isn't any cooler on the feet under all these rugs.* She padded to the window; behind her Shkai'ra muttered for a moment and rolled over.

The window opened noiselessly, but the air outside held no hint of the breeze she sought. There was little light, and the stars were huge and bright in the cloudless sky. She sat on the deep ledge and looked out over the city, brushing back sweaty strands of hair clinging to her forehead.

The silence, she thought. *It feels as if I were the only thing in the world still living.*

Across the way a curtain twitched in its window frame—someone else sleepless? Ten-Knife landed beside her on the sill, and she petted him absently.

"You know, beast," she whispered in one ear that jerked as her lips tickled the long hairs, "I really don't need you here shedding heat on me."

The cat purred loudly, then moved its head up with a quick inquiring movement, both ears pointed forward.

It was odd, Megan thought: he seemed to be staring up the wall. Could he be hearing something from the floor above? And there was a sound from above, the sound of leather-wrapped metal on brick . . .

She pitched the cat into the darkness behind her and flicked up to crouch on the sill. Even so, she was barely ready when the dark figure dropped from above.

It was dressed from crown to cork-soled sandal in form-fitting black, eyes a slit-hole in the tight hood. One hand still held the clench-claw that had held him on the brick wall; the other clutched a glass vial that glowed dully, rotting-green. The stranger's motions were swift and very quiet, a barely audible scraping on the oak of the windowsill as he crouched for balance. But he had been expecting to be alone on it, with only the shutter between him and his sleeping prey.

Megan stayed in her crouch, pivoting on the ball of one foot. The other lashed out, the heel catching him on the side of the knee. There was a muffled sound as the cartilage gave way, and the man toppled off the windowsill to fall two stories to the concrete pavement below.

She had been reacting on reflex, her mind oddly distant from the brief explosion of violence, hearing with one corner of her mind the cat's yowled complaint at her treatment of him and the sound of the breaking joint. There had been no other noise; even then, it struck her that the man should scream. And he did, just before he hit the ground. But it seemed to Megan that it was not the ground he was staring at, but the vial in his hand. That broke, with a pop lost under the melon-on-stone impact of a human body falling thirty feet. Green vapor burst from the shattered glass, then seemed to sink into the broken form.

The corpse writhed with life, twitching and shuddering in ways that Megan knew were impossible. Suddenly, thread-like tendrils of white erupted from wounds, nose, mouth, ears, and eyes, wriggling out and puffing into dead-white pseudopods even as she watched. The black-clad body began to sag and shrink as the fungus spread.

Swallowing bile, Megan retreated from the sight of the obscene puffball mass that lay on the roadway, already no longer even vaguely human in shape.

The curtain across the way twitched again, and a small dart slammed into the wood just above her hand; the darkness and flickering lantern light having thrown the aim off. She tumbled off the ledge and felt the shutter jerk with another blowgun missile as she wrenched it home.

Shkai'ra had rolled up on her knees at the sound of Ten-Knife-Foot's yowl, the saber flowing into her hand at the sound of the assassin's breaking knee; by the time his brief scream ended on the road below, she was beginning to wake.

The corridor door burst open, the bar almost shooting back. Two figures in black came through at a run and slammed it behind them.

"Nevo!" one hissed. "Did—"

They had one glimpse of the two women, alive and hale, before Megan plunged the room into darkness. It was an absolute blackness, the color behind closed eyes under forest on a moonless night. Patterns of false light drifted before retinas deprived of all stimulation.

The assassins were well trained. To make noise would be instant death; so would staying in the same spot they had been seen in. Quiet as malice, they separated and began drifting along the walls on either side.

Megan froze as she landed and tried to control her panting. *This is what I get for relaxing my guard,* she thought. *Not a weapon in my hands and someone trying to kill us in the dark.* She rose silently and moved toward the low table by the wall, where her knives were. She heard the rope springs creak on the bed and thought, *Shkai'ra's moved.* And then: *Fishguts—now that she's moved, I won't be able to tell her from the others till it's too late.* She seized her daggers and froze again, every nerve straining to hear where their enemies were. All she could hear was the thunder of her pulse in her ears.

Shkai'ra froze as her feet touched the floor, toes splaying out like fingers to grip. Tiny puffs of air slid over her bare sweat-slick skin, illusions of coolness in the still, hot blackness of the room. Her mind calculated chances; she was taller and heavier than most Fehinnans, and so more likely to squeeze a betraying groan out of the floorboards, no matter how carefully she moved. While she was confident that no Illizbuah blackcoat was faster, reflex had sent her hand to her saber rather than the knife, which was better for this work.

Now, where had Megan been? Hmmm, best to move before Megan came out into the room and gave her that to worry about as well.

With an earsplitting screech, she jumped straight up, bounced flat-footed on the floor, and then cartwheeled silently to the left, toward the entrance. The Adderfangs would have cleared the door area: it was the last place they'd been visible.

Shkai'ra came smoothly to her feet, whirled, and lunged through the spot where she'd just stood, right foot and hand forward, left leg reclined in a tremendous line that took full advantage of her greater length of limb. Her point touched cloth, just as it reached full extension. An expert could calculate her position from that: she pivoted on the ball of her right foot, left shin sweeping around at knee height in the second half of a pirouette that would take her halfway back to the bed.

The edge of a knife touched lightly over the woodhard muscle of her outer thigh as it pushed her across the space, just parting the skin; for a moment she knew where the Adder must be, but the balance factors made a stroke impossible.

Sheepraping dung of a noseless nomad pi-dog, she thought in disgust as she landed. The bed should be just about two arm-lengths behind her, and the knifeman just beyond sword's reach back toward the door; they had traded positions twice in the last six seconds. Sweat fell into her eyes, stinging; one or two passages of real combat wrung you out worse than half an hour of practice. She gaped her mouth wide, concentrating on keeping her breath soundless. There would be no second chances here, and it could not last much longer. Not in a space this confined.

Megan considered for a long second: *if I were them, I'd concentrate one on one. If I'm right then she (he?) should be coming up the long wall.* The shriek from the middle of the room punched through her ears, and she used the unexpected sound to cover her motion around the corner of the desk, thinking irritatedly that Shkai'ra would be the only one making one hell of a noise. *Now,* she thought, carefully extending the knife before her and moving forward slowly, straining for a noise of some sort, *let us see if we can persuade this one to spit himself.* She heard a faint sound before her and dropped lower into her crouch, pulling the knife slightly closer to give her more play on the extension of the blade.

The whisper of something swinging over her head, seeking, and she felt him almost walk into the knife. A down-swinging hand couldn't stop the blade but wrenched it to one side, tearing. As the hammer blow of his arm sent her lurching off balance, she rolled forward, feeling bone smack sharply on her back muscles as he went over. She reached blindly with her other hand and slashed as he rolled to break his fall. Her claws caught and shredded something as she followed the motion that sent her skidding out into the room. She stopped on her stomach and inched to one side, the assassin choking back a cry as much of surprise as pain.

Ah, Megan thought. She. *We'll see if the attack from below works again; I don't think I hamstrung her.* She crawled back and toward the desk half a meter, spreading her weight so that no boards would creak under even her slight weight.

An easy job, they said, the assassin thought bitterly. *Just back up Nevo, they said.* She held her abdomen with one hand. *Nothing strenuous now, or the cut muscle might split and I'll spill my guts. If the dagger knicked a bowel, I'm dead meat. What did she have on her fingers? Whatever it was, it was sharp.*

The Adderfang near Shkai'ra backed toward the door, sliding each foot a careful millimeter above the boards, then bearing down with infinite patience. The big barbarian would not expect him to continue back in a straight line; his stomach muscles contracted reflexively at the memory of cold knife-sharp sword metal touching him on the ribs as she lunged. But if he backed, he could circle along the wall . . .

A sharp sound came from his right, toward the far wall and across the bed. Tahlni had made contact! He shifted his weight more rapidly, covered by the hard smacking sound of a sweep-parry hitting a forearm and—there was something soft under his foot, but he was committed now, balance shifted back. Something round and soft, with a firmer core.

ERRRRROWERREEEE!

The Adder had a moment to stand frozen by the scream of feline outrage before ten claws and a mouth fastened themselves in his calf. A cat can turn at a very acute angle and attack, even with its tail pinned to the floor; and in any case, the confining weight shifted quite rapidly. If there had been light, the others would have seen a man in black dancing in place on the ball of one foot, with a leg flailing madly in the air.

Ten-Knife-Foot was managing to produce an astonishing volume of sound, between mouthfuls. A random twist saved the Adder as a curved Kommanz sword split the place his abdomen had been a moment earlier. The same movement spun him to face the door.

The oak door slammed open. A lean, blond figure in a loincloth stood there, with a long slashing sword in one hand, peering blearily from between sandy eyelids.

"WILL YOU PEOPLE SHUTTHEFUCK UP I'M TRYING TO *SLEEP!*" he screamed, and slammed the door shut once more with a bang.

None of the combatants moved, as the sudden blaze of light speared into dilated pupils. The Adder recovered just enough to see Ten-Knife-Foot streak through the closing slit of the door as he turned, did a vault-handspring over the bed, and rolled forward in the renewed darkness to come to his feet by the outer window. He explored the wound with the fingers of his left hand, not wanting to risk wetting his knife grip. The flesh was ragged and oozing, but not enough to weaken him with blood loss in the next few minutes; he could force the ravaged muscle to operate. And afterward, he would try the taste of cat.

Megan threw herself back into a crouch as the room was again plunged into darkness, wiping streaming eyes. The sight of the room a second ago was burned into her mind, and she knew that the desk and the folding screen lay close by. The Adder had seen her on the floor, so the place to be was high. She leaped to the surface of the desk, a board cracking under her as the weight shifted. The Adder would be coming from that direction. *Let her come to me.* She toed a paperweight off the desk to keep the other coming and felt the change in air pressure as someone lunged past her at the noise. With a wrench, she pulled the light wickerwork and paper screen down on her and followed up with the dagger. She felt the blade catch on a rib, and the knife-hand, driven deep, touched cloth. Blood splashed hotly on her skin, and she sprang to the floor by the wall. *Lousy merchant,* she thought. *He swore left and right that the poison he sold for my claws was quick-acting. That one's still thrashing around.* Her fingers took stock of the knives left in the harness: three. *If Shkai'ra finishes the other one, this one will likely be alive to give us some answers . . . but how can I help her other than simply by staying out of her fight? I'd get us both killed.* She stood in the dark, feeling powerless.

Shkai'ra tried to follow the Adder's probable path, running lightly in the dark and blinking her eyes against the smarting and watering. But the confusion had thrown off her sense of distance; the hardwood rim of the round bed barked her painfully on the shins. It was a solid, substantial sound, heavy wood fiber pounding into the bone and hard rubbery muscle of her leg between knee and ankle.

That would bring the shivman. She dropped to the ground and rolled under the bed, easing herself backward until only the spread fingers of her left hand edged out from underneath, and the poised tip of her saber, slanting up.

I should have realized this earlier, she thought happily. *No mistaking who I touch: we're both still naked.*

Here, close to the floor, she discovered that she could just make out the creaking of cork-soled sandals as the Adder approached. There was a sudden crash from the corner and an involuntary grunt of pain. The stealthy footsteps approaching the bed halted, and her hand shot out, to close around a tattered trouser leg, wet with blood. Her blade flashed upward, under a knife stroke that just split the skin along her collarbone, to go in just over the pelvic arch.

Close, she thought as she felt the soft yielding resistance against her sword. If that knife had been a tenth of a handspan higher, it would have opened the vein in her throat even as she killed him. She held the thrust, up into the rib cage from below, until the point sank into a shoulderblade at a glancing angle. Then she used the leverage of his ankle to whip the blade back and forth in the massive wound; it was rare for a single sword stroke to kill immediately, but then this was an unusual angle.

Blood and fluids poured down and spattered face and shoulders and breasts; she could taste the coppery salt as she panted in the dark. The sword slid free with a wet sound, and the stink of cut bowel flooded out into the humid warmth of the room. The Adder's body slid limply to the ground.

Against the wall, Megan heard the body fall and hoped that it wasn't Shkai'ra's. *Powerless,* she thought: Then: *Power? Of course. Light we, need and light we shall have.* She set her back against the wall, pulled out the last three daggers, and concentrated. At equal distances around the room, a solid chuck sounded as a dagger vibrated in the walls. Each glowed a low, eerie red. A necessary risk.

Shkai'ra looked up, blinked. The Adder lay before her, very thoroughly dead. The odd position had meant that she'd wrenched the outer cutting edge of the blade up through his ribs, acting like a giant scissor blade. It was Minztan steel from the far northwest, the curved cutting surface forge-hardened and mirror-polished on a softer core; there was no metal that would take a better edge. This had sheared through bone, from the floating rib to the throat; he lay staring on one side, and the whole contents of his body cavity had slumped out onto the floor, a stew of organs in a bath of blood, more blood than Shkai'ra had seen from one corpse before. The body had bled out like a deer strung up on a rack. She picked herself up, her body glistening darkly from chin to hips.

"Don't worry, not much of it's mine," she said at Megan's quick glance. She raised an eyebrow at the cold flickering glow from the knives. "Interesting, but why did it take you so long?"

The fallen screen rustled as the wounded assassin stirred and groaned. A quick stride took Shkai'ra to the spot. She gripped the fallen woman by the back of the neck, searched her with swift efficiency, and dumped half a dozen assorted weapons onto the floor. Then she seized one arm and broke it over her knee.

"I don't like people who try to sneak in and kill me in my sleep," she said. Her bladed palm slammed down twice, breaking the collarbones; then she pinned the other's jaws in one hand, propped them open with her sword hilt, and probed. "Ah, poison tooth—but we want you to talk to us first. Why should we let you die before you earn your favors?" Megan came up behind and said mildly, "Treat her *too* roughly and we won't have her company for long anyway. Perhaps

if we pulled her soul out and asked questions of it?"
She had a distracted look on her face as she held the
light high enough to see by, and the woman would
never know that she was bluffing. Anything not able
to reflect the red light must be black, scarlet and darkness. She put a hand on Shkai'ra's shoulder and leaned
over to look more closely at the writhing assassin, the
scarlet light dancing in her eyes. "Well?"

Shkai'ra stiffened slightly, then forced herself to
relax. The assassin's eyes flickered wildly; her captor
brought her face up to eye level, thumbs on the shattered collarbones. There was an unpleasant grating,
grinding sound, much like that of two roughly shattered pieces of wood being forced together. Blood and
matter dripped off her onto the captive.

"I think you'd better tell us who put the engage-
ment out on us," she hissed. "Or I'll let my friend do
some interesting things to you ... and *she* doesn't
have to stop when you die." Unconsciously, Shkai'ra's
hand made the warding sign against magic and ill luck,
but she had never been the sort to reject anything
useful. As the Warmasters said, the true warrior could
make grass and sand serve as weapons.

A glow matching the color of the knives appeared,
puddled in Megan's hands. She pulled her hands
apart, drawing it into a rope-like strand that looped
and coiled in the air before the assassin's face. A hum-
ming came from it, a low deep note, eager as the
light-snake strained toward skin drawn tight with pain
and slick with blood and mucus. The Zak's voice was
cool and reasonable, dropping like the water that
wears away granite.

"Priest's ... gold," the Adderfang said at last, in a
husky whisper. She swallowed, choked, fought for air.
"Guildmasters ... Adderfang brothers ... merchant's
letter. Wi ... wizard's letter! You took ... told to
recover. Kill you." She rallied suddenly. "Kill you!"
she snarled, and spat pink foam at Megan. The racked

body went boneless, and the black eyes glazed. Her final words were almost too faint to hear.

"Curse you . . . witch."

"Ah," Megan said. "The poison was fast-acting after all."

The taut look of power faded from her face as she walked over to the bed and slumped down with a creak of the rope springs. The red light faded to ember glow.

"I'm very tired," she said. Pain shot through her head, spearing from behind her eyes to explode off the back of her skull. *Small use sorcery if it makes you feel like this*, she thought wearily.

"Shkai'ra, could you get a conventional light going? This tires me, and I'd rather explain to the innkeeper about bodies than magic." She stared down into the flickers of red that danced around her fingers. When she spoke again it was softly, in a musing tone: "I wish I could call up a gentler color than this. Green perhaps, or blue. If I had the power."

Shkai'ra looked at her for a moment, then sighed and laid the limp body on the floor, wiping her hands on the black cloth.

"It's a swamp in here," she said, pushing a lock of hair back from her forehead and clearing a pale streak in the blood on her face. Opening the shutter, she flooded the room with moonlight. The distant shouts of the watch slaves over the body of the first assassin below on the street came through it; the Kommanza whipped her head back as a tiny feathered dart flashed past her cheek, and slammed the shutter again.

"Zaik Godlord!" she said. "Blowgun, poisoned dart—that message must be important, for them to want us dead so badly. The brotherhoods don't hire cheap, and they sent four, for the two of us; they boast two of theirs are enough for four strangers."

She moved, winced, and looked down at the cut along her collarbone. It was shallow; the edge of the blade had just touched the skin, cutting only because it was honed to a thread. Still, it could infect if not cared for soon. There were streaks and patches of sticky, thickening blood over her breasts and stomach; she could feel it clotting in the ends of her long mane and the pubic triangle. She grimaced. "It will be good to be clean again." More slowly. "If it's worth this much to guard the secret, how many must be willing to pay for it?"

She picked up a lighter from the table and chuckled. "And how highly they must think of us!" The round ceramic ball that held alcohol, with the cotton wick and thumb-struck flint, sparked, and she set the flame to the fishtail methane lamp fixed to the wall by the door.

Blood pooled on the floor, bright liquid red already turning to scum at the edges, soaking darkly into the rugs. The room smelled of blood, excrement, and musky fear sweat, overpowering in the enclosed space. Shkai'ra wrinkled her nose slightly, but hers were not a fastidious people.

"Best we get someone in to clear up the mess," she said. Megan looked up, rubbing her temples, leaving a blood smear on one cheek.

"No need—hear the uproar down the hall? I think that someone finally noticed something wasn't quite right." She got up and pulled her daggers free of the wood paneling. The door opened a crack; light spilled through as the house slaves relit the lanterns in the halls. A watchslave's eye peered in, then gave place to a member of the kinfast that owned the Weary Wayfarer. A black shadow padded through and sniffed disdainfully before settling at the edge of a red-brown pool of coagulating blood and lapping.

There was a long silence. "Oh, gods!" Sarlee, one of the less likable members of the inn's kinfast, groaned, clapping her hands to the sides of her face and staring at the carnage. "Sweet Sun, Beneficent Light, *look at my floors!* The rugs are ruined!"

She shook a fist at the ceiling, as servants crowded around the doorway, peering in awe. "Protection money! Protection money!" she raved. "Ten percent before taxes we pay—to every daggerguild in the city and the Watch as well we give our hard-earned trade-metal, and look what happens! You can't even get them to protect you against *themselves.*"

She opened her mouth to continue the tirade, then hesitated and trailed off as she caught the looks everyone was giving her, even her own slaves. Shkai'ra nodded, finished cleaning the blade, and nudged her cat aside from the blood.

"Stop that—it's probably diseased," she said, picking up the animal and draping him around her neck. "Now, if we could finish our night's rest . . ." she said to the innkeeper, who bowed. The servants dragged the bodies out, after an expert search revealed a round dozen weapons, sealed vials, and instruments neither Megan nor Shkai'ra could identify.

"Sleep would be easier if this mess were cleared up," she concluded.

The innkeeper considered them, and then the Adderfangs and their reputation. "Of course," she said, rubbing her hands on her tunic. "And of course, consider the . . ." She winced. "Consider the week's rent abated, for the sake of the disturbance." A pause. "I will have bowls and towels sent, as well."

Later, Sarlee stood in the corridor, shaking her head and sighing. Perhaps the kinfast should go into something more peaceful: secret fencing of pirates' loot, for example, or counterfeiting.

Across the corridor, the slender fair-haired man closed the door of his room with a silent whistle. *And I nearly blundered into that,* he thought, stroking a small mustache with paint-stained fingers. Well, he had been lucky. That sparked a thought; he shrugged back into his tunic and began searching for his dice-box. Luck like that didn't come your way that often, and the game might still be on. . . .

As the door closed behind the servant, leaving the bowls of hot water, Megan turned on her heel and walked into the other room, kindling a light there. Shkai'ra followed curiously and found her rooting to unearth the pouch from its hiding place. She crossed to the smaller woman and took the sack, tossing it in her hands. "I think that someone wants this rather badly." Megan snagged it out of the air.

"It nearly got us killed in our sleep. I'm going to try again to find out what is of such importance. If someone wants to send me to hell, I want to know why so I can put up an argument." The headache had subsided to a dull pounding that she savagely suppressed. The anger helped. It also called to mind an earlier comment by the Kommanza. She turned on the larger woman and said, "Look, my friend, you can say what you like about my use of Power once you know the *manrauq* yourself and how long it takes to use it . . ." Her voice faded in the face of Shkai'ra's wry grin as she realized that the comment had not been meant to prick. She sighed and turned away, unknotting the pouch. "You don't have to stay and watch. Not that there will be much to see either way."

"I'll stay." Shkai'ra hung her sword on the bedstead. "We have to start somewhere, and all we have now is the Glitch-taken Adder's word. Not that I mind a fight, but even I'm not lucky enough to kill every hired sword in the city." She watched Megan with more curiosity than alarm.

The Zak took the paper from the pouch, and concentration settled like a wall between them. Nothing seemed to happen for a long moment, then Megan's hands began to tremble, slowly at first, then with increasing violence as she struggled to contain the Power hiding the message and bend it to her will; and was not successful. There was an almost audible snap as she sagged, the tension in the room gone as if swept away by a brisk wind, defeat on her face. "Whoever did this was a master. I cannot break it."

Shkai'ra leaned back against the pillow a moment, then reached over to tap Megan's hand just above the parchment, still careful not to come in contact with it. "No matter, for now. I have a thought of what we could do with that." Megan was still staring absently at the wavering, creeping letters, her brow furrowed. "Kh'eeredo, cease. I doubt that we would be attacked twice in one night, so we have at least a day in which to think on it. Tomorrow night we deal with the message, not now." She chuckled. "And you look as if you could sleep again. This magic seems to be more tiring than swordplay."

Megan thought for a moment. "I haven't much to boast of with my magic tonight," she admitted ruefully. "However good my knife work was." She looked down at the leather pouch, her face hardening. "I will break this. I don't care how long it takes; I will do it." She hurled the pouch across the room; it made an unsatisfying small *put* against the brick and fell to the floor.

Shkai'ra yawned. An overwhelming weariness was on her, and a feeling of cold. She controlled the shuddering. Violent death was no stranger to her, but this was getting to be nearly as bad as a campaign. As bad as the trail barricades in the Forest War, and that was one of her less pleasant memories. Sighing, she forced the taut nerves to relax and allow fatigue through.

"Dark One, take it," Megan said softly as she collapsed to the bed, head in her hands.

"Perhaps he, she, or it will," Shkai'ra muttered.

"He," Megan clarified absently, then shook her

head. "Ach, you're right. Last one up has to scrub the other's back, agreed? Shkai'ra?"

The tall woman turned over, murmuring, and curled into an unconscious ball. "We'll settle that in the morning."

Night was soft and deep.

CHAPTER XII

Megan had had to spend considerable time getting the brown crust out from under her fingernails; going back to sleep after a fight that messy was, she told herself sternly, nothing less than slovenly. After so long in the steamy heat of the baths, the tepid water of the plunge-pool was shockingly cold, then comforting. She forged through the thin scattering of morning bathers with a doggedly competent breaststroke and hauled herself out on the central fountain, lying back on the smooth marble and enjoying the sensation of water drying on her skin as she wrung out her long hair.

One of the few ways not to sweat in this swamp of a city, she thought luxuriously.

A figure, one of the kinfast, waved at her from the edge of the pool. She ignored his waving at first, thinking it was directed at someone else, then slid into the water with a sigh at a strangled, embarrassed shout. For a moment, she clung to the stone at his feet and watched his lips move silently before the water released its tension grip on her ears and ran down her neck in warm trickles.

". . . rry to disturb your cleansing, Brightness," he said nervously. "But one of the Shining Servants of the Glorious Light wishes to speak with you." He paused. "A prominent Servant." Devoutly, he circled his chest; perhaps the stupid outlander would take the hint. In any case, it would be his back that would feel the cane if the Weary Wayfarer attracted another temple fine.

Megan watched with cool detachment as the nervousness increased. Jumpy people said things that otherwise would stay behind their lips; it was a great advantage to be one of those undisturbed by silence.

This one is almost as afraid of offending me as he is of angering the priest, she thought. Last night's affray had improved their reputations considerably. She began drying herself, and took pity on the youth as he shifted from foot to foot and made unconscious patting motions to hurry her. It was unlikely that clerical doings were included on the inn servants' grapevine, after all.

"This priest," she said. "A high one? Rank?"

The servant searched for words. A priest was, after all, a *priest*. It was warm in here to be fully clothed, and he felt sweat trickling down his flanks. *O Sun,* he prayed. *Get me out of this, Divine Effulgence, and I'll never complain about swab-out detail or guests with strange pillow habits again.* Just for safety's sake, he added an invocation to Ribbidib, gull-headed godlet of Illizbuah the City, and to Haaichedew, the Provider of Maailun.

Megan frowned and considered her words. Her Fehinnan had improved rapidly, but somehow she doubted her mastery of the social inflections was equal to dealing with the shavepate.

"I will not see him alone," she said. "Tell him to wait until Shkai'ra, my friend with the blond hair, gets back." The servant turned grey under the natural olive brown of his skin. "My apologies, of course. Just tell him that the stupid foreigner doesn't understand a civilized language and would be a waste of his time. Use the high forms, tell him what you like," she ended with a small mocking grin, imagining the scene. "Just see that he waits until we're ready for him."

She wrung the last drops of water out of her hair and thought over the book she had found that afternoon. There were fascinating similarities to some very old inscriptions she had seen across the Lannic; even to her native Zakos. It would bear more careful examination, and her hair did need a trim at the ends. . . . She turned to go, followed by a small, hollow moan from the servant.

Shkai'ra opened the door of their room and paused for a moment. Megan lay on the bed, her chin propped on her hands, staring at the crumbling remains of a book lying open beneath her on the floor. Her hair was unbound, still slightly damp; the ends pooled beside the yellowed pages and fanned out across the linen of the coverlet, neatly trimmed. Lumpy bundles were scattered about, sagging open to show the marks of various guilds: the clothiers', the leatherworkers'. Two boxes showed the ridged ends of bound volumes through coarse brown wrapping paper. A rapier leaned against the bed, needle-pointed and double-edged, with a scrolled cup guard and long quillions. Beside it lay a severely plain leather sheath and tooled baldric.

Ten-Knife-Foot pulled an inquiring nose from a bundle and sprawled across the fragile book, twisting to present an imperious chest for scratching. The warm afternoon light slanted in through shafts of dust-flecked brightness, bringing out the deep highlights of his pelt, matched with the shining black of Megan's hair. Shkai'ra closed her eyes and sighed slightly, content.

The Zak looked up and ceased tapping her teeth with the writing quill in her hand. She smiled: it was visibly the result of conscious choice, but the expression was growing more natural.

"Did your knowledge-hunt find quarry?" she said.

"Nia—no none dares even whisper the hint of a trace of a rumor. Not a word on what the sheep-raping message might be, except that it's valuable." She shoved parcels aside to clear a spot on the bed, sat down, and began unlacing her sandals, until she could work hot and dusty feet into the pile of the carpet with a slight groan of pleasure. "Almost better in boots; the sweat keeps your toenails from splitting. . . . I see you spent every tenth-bit of our loot on the merchanters' rows."

Megan plucked at the hem of her tunic. "The tailor says that I'll have breeches again tomorrow; I shocked him with the outlandish design I wanted."

Shkai'ra slapped dust out of her own trousers, light Fehinnan cotton done to a pattern that three thousand kilometers north and west made in wool and horsehide. "Clink the metal, and even an outlander's whims are law. What's that moldy thing?"

"A *book*, ignorant one," Megan said dryly. "It seems to be an old tale, of a hero named Nixo; one who rose to high estate, then was cast down, but rose again to be a demigod of wisdom in the afterlife of Sainclem, in the Uttermost West. I'm not familiar enough with the language to be really sure; and it's been transcribed so often. The words . . . some of them sound familiar, which is strange; languages usually don't spread that far."

Shkai'ra shook her head. "I can read enough for a trade-tally," she said. "Four hundred bales of wool and thirty sacks of grain. Or 'The village of Zh'airzfurd owes service of thirty lances twice each season.' But the gods never intended me for a shaman."

Megan closed the book. "I believe someone who knows the answers to our little problem waits. Someone with a shaved head. I don't know Fehinnan well enough to talk to him—at least that's what I had the bondboy say, so the priestling is cooling his heels somewhere in the inn, if he hasn't stalked off in a huff. I told them to bring him when you arrived."

Shkai'ra stared at her for a moment, then fell back on the bed with a shout of laughter. "You told a *priest* to await my arrival? Glitch, I wish I could have seen his face when they brought that news; almost enough to be worth going under the Lens for."

Megan curled to her feet and rummaged through one of the bags. A pair of soft boots appeared. "These I found also," she said. "A good grip on the soles, perfect for my line of work. When I don't have a ship. And more of this." She produced a small flask, a tiny brush, and began very carefully to paint over the hard, metallic, knife-sharp edges of her nails.

A timid knock sounded at the door. "You deal with him," she said, waving the brush. "I won't say a thing, unless to help you keep your teeth from your knee-caps. Or unless you want him killed."

She repaired to the window ledge to complete the brushwork, taking exquisite care not to touch the clear liquid to her skin.

Shkai'ra shrugged and lay back on one elbow, facing the door. It opened to reveal the pained gaze of an inn servant and the imperturbable face of a temple priest. A third degree Spark, Shkai'ra thought, from the leaf-sign above his brow. His face was completely expressionless, but somehow conveyed an impression of bad drains and sacrificial devotion to duty.

The Kommanza scratched under her short ribs. "Will the Spark of the Shining Light, Effulgent with Truth and Justice, deign to enter?" she said. That was precisely what the codes demanded; of course, she should have delivered it on one knee, not nearly prone and tickling a cat beneath the jaw with the toes of one foot.

The priest stepped in, smiling gently. "Of course,

One Lost in Darkness," he said. "A Servant need fear no pollution." He sank slowly on the cushions near the desk, his eyes scanning automatically across the room. Not that he expected to see it in plain view, but the urgency . . .

He matched discourtesy with insult and came directly to his business. "Yet the Reflection of the Divine Light is merciful with his priests and exposes them to heresy as little as he may." Ignoring the snigger from the window ledge, he continued, "You have what is ours. We want it."

Shkai'ra began picking her teeth with a thumbnail, regarding him sidelong. "Ours, yours, someone else's . . . these are merely words. Even if we should have this item, would I say so? Indeed, I know of nothing in our possession that could interest you or your master." She paused, looking at the dirt under her nails, starting to clean under the one index finger. "We are only poor mercenaries in the Sun-on-Earth's, ah, occasional service. I hear, Shining Splinter of the Divine Light, that what the temple has is its forever, while what is ours is negotiable." She grinned at the priest, who looked as thrilled as a guest discovering rat bones in his soup. "The God's call on our services has been slim of late." And there she left it.

There was silence for a moment; the cry of a street vendor floated through the window as the Servant of the Effulgent Light forced an expression of indifference as carefully crafted as a temple mosaic, and as false.

"I—," he said, and coughed before forcing himself to complete the sentence. "—am directed to offer a certain sum for our item's return."

Shkai'ra looked at him coolly, curled one leg over the other knee, and began to strop a knife on the hard leathery callus on the sole of her foot. "I like hearing about money," she said genially. "But take pity on an ignorant barbarian, O Lightener of Shadows: be more concrete."

The priest smiled. "Ah, admission of ignorance is the first step to wisdom. One thousand."

Shkai'ra's knife continued its smooth, even movement. A great deal of money had flowed through her hands these last ten years of exile; very little of it had stuck. But this! For a thousand, you could buy a good farm, fully stocked and with half a dozen slaves to work it. Or a horse stud; or fit out three cavalry fighters; or buy a half-share in a middling merchant vessel. Greed warred with wariness; her own people did not use coined money, and her caste had little to do with trade, but she had learned never to accept the first offer.

"Not enough," she said, and smiled broadly. The priest, who had not flinched at the knife, swallowed and forced his spine to stiffen.

"It is wealth beyond your dreams," he said.

"Priest, little priest," she said, rising to her feet. The man in the orange robe was of average height for a Fehinnan; Shkai'ra topped him by four inches. "I dream more grandly than you imagine, and I am not a coastlands peasant, or a merchant, to pleasure myself with haggling. Tell me what you will give, or go."

The priest flushed. *Peace through contemplation of the Light,* he chanted silently. *Peace through contemplation of the Light. Peace* . . . Presently, he won back enough self-control to speak.

"I am a Servant of the Effulgent light," he hissed.

"And I am Mek Kermak, godkin, descended from the Ztrateke *ahkomman,*" she said. "*How much, priest?*"

"Two thousand; and passage money to anywhere, so it be four hundred *kaahlicks* from Fehinna's boundaries. Death if you return."

"Nice place," Megan said. "They pay you to leave. Shows their bad taste in people."

"Disobedience to the God's will can lead to—"

"Sunburn?" Megan said.

Astonishingly, the priest smiled. "Oh, yes," he said. "A very severe case. Think on it."

He swept from the room; Ten-Knife followed, sniffed suspiciously after him, then turned and made a burying motion with his forepaws.

"He looked as if he was sitting on a caltrop," Megan said, "when he didn't look as if he was imagining us less our skins. But was it necessary to offend him? A certain barbarian of my acquaintance said that was dangerous."

Shkai'ra looked past the closed door, teeth showing between slightly parted lips. "You'd already offended him, kh'eeredo," she said. "I wanted him so angry he couldn't think straight. As the Warmasters said, the only time it's safe to lose your temper with an enemy is when they're tied and under your knife. But I think in the end our existence angered that one; the priests of the Sun don't like outlanders."

"Two thousand," she continued. "They must want it very badly. With that much, I could . . . But that offer of passage money! I'd risk Baiwun's hammer if that doesn't mean a rope around the ankles, and a rock tied to it over the side."

She sighed happily. "What would you wager that isn't the last offer? Troubles follow each other like packhorses today."

The sun moved its slitted bars across the floor, through the blinds. Megan returned to the crumbling pages, puzzling slowly over the ancient words. Shkai'ra lay, her hands laced behind her head, happily running over uses for that much silver, and ways of staying alive with it. Less than a tenth-day passed before the next knock.

The tall woman turned to her companion. "Do you want to insult this one while I watch?"

"No, no," Megan said graciously. "Merely offending through ignorance cannot hope to equal the effects of deliberate provocation."

The door opened. This man came unescorted; a tall, lean figure in a green undress tunic that had as much embroidery at neck and hem as the regulations allowed, or rather more; he wore a fox-faced festival mask that left only his mouth visible, curled in a smile that matched that of the animal above it.

Bowing slightly, he swept off the mask and tucked it under one arm. His dark-brown hair was foppishly curled and waved, with a slightly tousled air that owed nothing to chance; jewels glinted on fingers and the hilt of his shortsword, and in one ear—some of them were genuine. He smiled engagingly out of a face paler than most lowland Fehinnans', and in a pleasant way remarkably ugly.

"Shkai'ra!" he said, rolling the glottal stop off his tongue with an ease few of his countrymen could have matched. "Won't you invite an old friend in? Surely you're not still sulking because of the dice god's partiality to me?"

Shkai'ra glanced at him sidelong. "Odd, how Rib-bidib always smiled on you when you used your own dice." She grinned, and the man relaxed fractionally. "Come in, Sammibo, and consider it payment for that little ... accident, when I taught you to play bannock."

Curled on the bed, the Zak saw him flush; his sword-hand twitched, and she noticed that the little finger was missing a joint.

"I'm sure it must have been a very little accident," she said, slyly thickening her accent and dropping into the superior-to-inferior inflection as if by accident.

He turned to her with an eyebrow lifted in aristocratic disdain, which turned to a stare of frank interest; he suppressed a jest about cradle-robbing that sprang to mind. Shkai'ra would take it in good part, but the little one . . . Snakes didn't have to be big.

"Sammibo Haadfayul's-kin," he said curtly. For a moment he struggled to keep the pose, then sank down laughing on the bed between the two women, dumping the cat onto his lap. After a moment, they joined him.

"Ahi-a, the gods make jesters of us all," Shkai'ra gasped at last. "Still running errands for that tight-arse Smyna, or are you full-time Intelligence Staff now, Sammibo?" She lifted a hand as he began to speak. "Bid high, you're not the first, and I—" she glanced at Megan "—we intend to squeeze this melon dry."

He looked down, ruffling Ten-Knife-Foot's ears. The animal bore this with a pretense of aloof dignity, sniffed at his hands to prompt memory, then began to rumble.

"Shkai'ra," he began, and looked across at Megan. She touched a finger to her hair.

"Megan, called Whitlock," she said.

"—and Gaaimun Whitelock's-kin," he continued. "Seriously, you've wandered into deep waters this time. This goes all the way up to the Iron House, on the military side, and you've seen the flame-ringers are in it up to their shining pates. I'm authorized to offer seven thousand silvers, an estate near Shaarlosvayl, and reserve commissions in the irregulars—"

"Sheepshit, Sammibo," Shkai'ra said easily. "I know the border country; the 'estate' has probably been bare since the tribes broke over the border in the Five Nations War, about the time my mother was born. Seven thousand would put it back in operation—and we could then spend the rest of our days fighting hill folk raiding parties, saving the regulars the expense.

"You'd not be this stupid. Iron House? Anus of a diseased packmule, you say: this has Smyna's grubby pawprints on it. I don't mind that she's greedy as a fish, or treacherous as a crocodile, but she's *cheap* to boot; she's trying to get the High Command with the methods of a New City joyhouse grifter. Now, tell me something serious."

"Something portable," Megan said. She spread the fingers of one hand before her. For a moment, out of the corner of his eyes, Sammibo thought he saw a reddish glow outlining them; when startled eyes swiveled around, it was gone. "I prefer travel and clean fingernails; growing cabbages was never my ambition. And to be sure, we are not ignorant of the *complexities* of this situation, good Zav'mibo . . . Sammibo? Talk to us as among the . . . wise." She laid a slight, significant emphasis on the last word.

Sammibo ran his hands through his hair, a spontaneous gesture that left the fashionable coiffure disarranged not one whit. "You'll regret this," he sighed. "Always did think you could raise to a three-quarter-five hand, Shkai'ra."

She nodded. "And you always thought you could bluff your way out of a wolftrap, Sammibo," she replied affably. "Go back and use your golden tongue on Smyna—get authorization to raise the offer." She smiled lazily, leaning back with fingers laced about a knee. "Use it to talk. Some things I wouldn't wish on my worst enemies."

He looked from one woman to the other. Shkai'ra relaxed, friendly and lynx-ruthless; she would probably wade into a tavern fight to save him for acquaintance's sake, and just as easily leave him holding a double handful of intestine if it suited her, then make some heathen offering for his ghost: He had never pretended to understand her. The other—he struggled to pronounce the foreign name in his mind—Megan. She was sitting cross-legged, black hair fountaining to the sheets, one strand startling foam-white against its darkness. Her nails tapped on an expensive metal belt buckle. He frowned inwardly: why were her fingernails making that clinking sound?

The Fehinnan officer rose to his feet, shaking his head. "Well, if you think better of it, you know where to reach me," he said. "If not . . ." He shrugged. "I'll pour a bottle of brandy at the cremation."

His bow was elegant, a slight incline of the back that managed to take in both of them. At the door, he paused for a parting shot: "Wizards and priests—Smyna backstabs for advantage, but they do it for the treachery's own sake."

The door shut behind him with a sough of air. Megan turned to her companion; her lips had opened when they heard laughter behind them. Reflex brought them to their feet, the Zak blinking incredulously as she realized it was coming from the second room, the one protected by her wards.

Standing just past the locked door between the rooms was a girl-child, no more than seven years by her height and face. She gathered long silver-white hair in her hands and danced a few steps, holding the silky curtain about her like a veil. She laughed again.

"He was pretty, wasn't he?" she said in a singsong voice, skipping past Shkai'ra.

"You don't care right now, but you—" she said, flitting past Megan, touching one finger to the tip of her nose. "You noticed how pretty he was."

Ten-Knife-Foot ignored her until, with a light, butterfly motion of one hand, she stroked across his ears; there was a momentary expression of startlement, a hiss, and the cat disappeared beneath the bed. The child began to hum as she moved, her audience locked in staring silence as she darted about the room.

"The other man I didn't like at all. No, he looked nasty. Don't give it to him; they'll just kill you anyway. Oh, before I forget, you will sell it, but still give it back to us, too. I know, Yeva knows, I know."

Megan shook off some part of the feeling of strangeness and leaned forward with her questions. Some part of her noticed a coolness and the scent of jasmine.

"Little one . . . child . . ." she began.

"Child? Not child, I think. Look. This is the 'not-me' that goes out. You have seeing enough to know that." For a moment, she ceased the darting grace of her movements, standing before Megan. "Look and see who I *am.*"

Her eyes were dark from corner to corner, as black as her hair was impossibly white; they seemed to drink light as the mane threw it back in blinding fragments. Yet there was a familiarity.

She began to whirl around them, faster and faster, her silver hair swirling out in lines of brightness. "Learn from the mistakes you will make," she said. And pirouetted, spun between them, laughter fading into distance. Silence.

Shkai'ra scanned the room with slow care, as if to make sure that the child was truly gone, licked fear-sweat off her lips, spat.

"I. Don't. Like. Spook pushers," she said. And jumped at the hand on her arm, half drawing her saber before she realized it was Megan. The Zak looked up at her.

"I did know her. That was Yeva." Her voice was utterly without levity. She turned and looked around the room as if seeing a strange place. "The astounding amount of power that woman has." Her eyes followed something unseen about the room a moment as the cat cautiously emerged from under the bed. His eyes also followed the movement of nothing to the corner of the wall; then he fell to washing himself.

Shkai'ra snorted. "Nomad shit. Yeva's adult, black-haired, white-eyed, blind, and can't walk." She paused. "Oh, the 'not-me that goes out.' " She shivered. "Oh, I don't like spook pushers."

She propped her head on the heels of her hands and cocked an eye at the window, where the light of the westering sun was reddening. She tossed the pouch in her hand.

"Whoever we decide to sell this to," she said, "we ought to get it out of our hands. I can live without more visitors of the sort we had last night; in fact, we'd be much more likely to ... Best we drop it off, then let it be known that it's not here."

Megan looked dubiously at the leather sack with its cryptic contents. "Yes ... but somehow I can't imagine asking the innkeepers to put it in their fastbox for us."

"Harriso." The Kommanza replied.

"Harriso?" Megan echoed in surprise. "But ... anyone can kill a blind beggar."

"Yes, but no one has, and Harriso's been working the alleys for many a year. Most beggars don't live long; but somehow when it comes Harriso's time, he doesn't go. Anyway, who would suspect a blind beggar of having the treasure that's set all Illizbuah on its ear? If you want to hide something, put it where folk won't look. Best we go after dark, to keep it discreet."

Megan shrugged. "Well, you know this city better than I. But it's still two hours to sunset, and we've slept, bathed, and eaten. What shall we do until it's time to leave?"

I've learned a few things among strangers, and one of them is that sometimes the best thing to do is wait, rather than take, the Kommanza thought, and gave Megan a slow smile, reclining back on the round bed, running a finger down from chin to hip. Megan flushed, quite unlike her usual pale merchant's mask.

"I think I'll have another long bath." She left abruptly, leaving Shkai'ra lying on the bed looking at the closed door thinking thoughts alien to her training. *I'd like to get her in bed, but that would be ... empty, somehow. I could kill our friendship with the wrong word right now.* She dropped her head on her crossed arms and smiled ruefully at Ten-Knife, then stopped with alarm.

"Do you think this is what outlanders call falling in love, cat?"

Ten-Knife stuck his rear leg in the air and groomed.

CHAPTER XIII

The Alley of the Long-Dead Dog glistened slimily in the dim light of the fading sun. It was never bright here, where the decaying buildings slumped toward each other above the uneven pavement of broken brick. One end of the alley was blocked by the blackened hulk of a burned-out tenement, and in the exposed, rubble-choked pit a hut had been built of timber scraps, old paving, and shattered marble facing. The little structure leaned tiredly into the rubble, always seeming on the point of losing its frail identity in the chaos of decay around it.

Megan and Shkai'ra slid down one wall of the alley, cautiously. Not that the sort of blade who could find no better territory than this was anything to fear, but predators who do not learn wariness seldom live to any great age.

The Zak looked down at the hovel with distaste; it was the perfect setting for the King of the Rats to hold court in filth and squalor; she could feel the soles of her soft boots slipping greasily in the moisture beneath.

Shkai'ra looked sidelong, reading the other's face and keeping her own carefully mask-like.

"Odd," she said, tapping the roof below them. "He should be in; in this part of Illizbuah a beggar walks soft at night. The meat on their bones is valuable, if nothing else." She leaped softly down to the overlapping stone shards of the roof, crouching. Her face turned up, dark in the shadow save for eyes and firecoal-bright hair. "Come down, see if you can get this door open."

"Hmmm? Ah, I see." Megan landed, ran fingers featherlight over the surface, and began to probe delicately with a small tool that had been part of her belt buckle a second before. "This lock is beautiful work . . . there!" There was a click, and a meter-square section of the roof lifted fractionally.

She turned to look at Shkai'ra, one hand still on the door. "Now why does he have a lock that would do justice to a Gaaimun's home? And on the roof?"

The Kommanza lifted the square. "You should see his alternate door," she said, dropping through the opening like a long-limbed shadow. Megan followed; head and shoulders first, then a backflip that landed her on her feet. A knife disappeared back into its sheath.

The interior of the hut had a spare, scrubbed cleanliness that made bare stone and wood elegant. A hearth was built into one wall; beside it in a niche was a vase that held a branch and two half-open buds. Three closed cupboards were built into the walls; a woven mat of creamy wool served as hearthrug and sleeping pallet, with a small carved chest for storage and pillow.

"How does he do this?" Megan asked, settling herself where she could see the *tabana* and admiring the clean curve of the branch. "And why . . ."

". . . does he trouble himself with the creation of beauty that he cannot see?" The dry voice came from the street door. Harriso strode in with a confident step, leaned his staff against the door frame, and slid a bar across the plank barrier. The ruined eyesockets turned to Megan, the lecturing voice so much like her teachers' that she had to smile.

"Observe, young one," he said. "Observe, and all the worlds and Otherworlds are open, even if your eyes are blind. A blind beggar is what the world sees; this does not mean that I must live or think to match my role. Surface appearance is seen; the assumptions follow. Blindness increases one's perceptions in other regards, not least by revealing how much of what the sighted think they see is the reflection of their expectations."

Harriso stirred the fire and used a splint to light a lamp of courtesy; the tea service moved through his hands with the familiarity of many years.

"As for this place, there are those who would hear the teachings of the elder days; better students than I had in the temple, many of them. If they have little trademetal, there is the skill of their hands. . . ."

Shkai'ra motioned with her eyes, drawing Megan's attention to the location of the staff, within easy reach of the blind man. "I *thought* I would have heard your stick on the street," she said admiringly. "I still can't see where your bolt hole is, in here."

Harriso's brows rose. "One is supposed to stay within, if hooves thunder on the roof above? In the Alley of the Long-Dead Dog?" He reached over, and the dark wood of his staff prodded one wall. "Also, notice that if the roof moves, the walls do also." The staff went back into its corner, and he turned back to the fire, lowering himself carefully onto the other end of the mat. "Hai, old bones are brittle."

Megan, noting the ease with which he still moved, snorted slightly. "Elder, at the smith's you mentioned a book, words of someone called the Subtle? If you would indulge my interest, I'm sure that we can be persuaded to fetch your shawl and a nice warm brick for your old feet."

"Child, I began my study of the Precepts of Annitli when . . . I had considerably fewer Sun-turnings than you do now. By all means, every journey begins with the first step, but . . ." The unexpected smile flashed again, and there was a glimpse of the boy who had sat big-eyed beneath the weight of his scroll. "At that, you would be a better student than Shhhcaair' here, who remains convinced that the best way to study eggs is to open them with a saber."

"Ah, one must make allowances for the savage, Harriso, if I can be so free with your name; but I am trying to train her to speak and wear somewhat besides goatskins." She winked at Shkai'ra's mimed outrage.

He served the tea and sank back to the rug. "It does this ancient one good to sense the children at play; but what is it that you want of me?"

"Ahi-a, the pleasure of your company and the sweetness of your smile, Har'hzo," Shkai'ra said.

"True, just as all priests are naturally bald," he said, throwing back his crisp grey mane. "For the pleasure of company you are well provided, since you returned to us, Red-Hand. Strong happenings, of late: you escape the great killing in the square, strange events at the Weary Wayfarer, of which I have heard surpassing little . . ."

"We thought you might hold something for us, Elder," Megan said quietly.

There was silence for a moment, save for the soft crackling of the fire. The little room smelled of lamp oil and incense and tea; the blind man's nostrils expanded as if to catch a scent beyond.

"I am not a banker," he said at last. "Besides, the pawnbroker tells me that you have not quite enough to redeem your second-best suit of armor." He held up a hand to forestall Shkai'ra's response. "I know. It's not that you have no money—"

"It's just that I never have money for *long*," she finished. "Besides, I hate to waste good money on paying bills; when I need it badly, I'll steal it back." Her manner became serious. "There is some risk involved. The Adderfangs tried to take it from us; on temple commission, we think. Or military."

An old fury tightened the wrinkled face. For a moment, they could see what he had been like in the day of his power, a cold pale anger.

"The Reflection should be as a shepherd to his flock; instead he is a ravening wolf." The remains of eyes swung to Shkai'ra. "You are not of this land; you have no obligations here, and your nature is as it is. But his . . ." Control clamped down. "Why the God Among Us permits this . . .

"Yes, I will hide your . . . treasure. Nor seek to know what it is."

Megan laid the pouch before his knees where he sat easily on callused heels. His fingers touched it lightly and drew back for the merest instant. "Yes, I will hide this for you. But more is involved here than swords, or than the Right Hand of the God Incarnate dreams, I think." He noticed the boiling water.

"For now we will speak of other things. Maaigan, Annitli said: 'Consider the serenity that may be found in the most commonplace of actions. For example, the brewing of tea, and its pouring.'"

CHAPTER XIV

"Your sword, O soldier," the Adderfang said with patient courtesy. Jaahdnni Layee's-kin, Squadron Commander in the Triumphant Steeds Silhouetted Against the Morning Sun, detached from her cavalry regiment for intelligence duties, glanced around the antechamber. Her escort stood stolidly; six troopers from the special-forces section of the city garrison. There were only two blackcoat Adders present, that she could see, but ...

"By all means," she said from between tight-clenched teeth. *Control*, she thought. *Let the city rabble see how a Layee's-kin behaves under stress*. The assassin took the long basket-hilted blade with a bow; was there a smirk behind his facemask? The door of the sanctum swung inward.

The interior was a surprise. This was the fifth head-quarters the Adderfangs had established, a mere seven hundred years old. Once it had been a suburban retreat, a place of privacy and relaxation for a kinfast of wealthy wine merchants. The city had grown around it; the level of the land rose; when the time came to pave the streets of the New City, the new avenue ran past the first-story windows of the older structure. The maps that moldered in the archives of the muncipium showed only fill and sewage pipes; considerable gold and a sharp-curved knife had ensured that. More gold had emptied the extensive cellars and raised supports for the tenement above; the sewer pipes had proved useful for carrying away the dirt, and later the bodies.

Jaahdnni had expected new-rich showiness. Instead, there was dark paneling, flamewood shining with oil and polish. Scroll racks and modern bookcases covered two walls; a terrestrial globe stood in one corner, an ancient thing—she could see the differences, how ice had waxed and seas waned since it was made. A low desk piled with neat stacks of correspondence occupied one end of the rectangular room. Behind it . . .

She swallowed nausea at the obscenity. Shamelessly portrayed in mosaic of crystal and onyx, *a solar eclipse*.

The soldier dropped her eyes down to the desk's occupant. The Adderfang was so ordinary, reclining easily on her cushions in a neat dark civilian tunic. The marks of childhood malnutrition still showed around her eyes, along the darkened fingers; perhaps also the memory of hunger prompted the open box of sweetmeats and the pug-jowls of the Adderlord's face. She smiled, showing bad teeth.

"Jahlini, of no kin." she said. A hand twitched, and servants appeared. Twins, a boy and girl of perhaps fourteen. Jaahdnni was impressed; matched blonds of that comeliness were not easy to find. They bore trays of tea and small seedcakes, setting them before the two women with fluid grace and retiring silently.

The soldier introduced herself, consciously avoiding the superior-to-inferior inflection, then drew papers from her waist sash.

"General-Commander Smyna is most displeased at the commission accepted from . . . shall we say . . .

another faction—the House with a Golden Roof?" she continued. Carefully polite, she sipped the tea. After all, it was better to be within the sacred bonds of hospitality that protected a guest. Especially if you were dealing with city scum—lowlife city scum at that. She leafed through the papers by one corner. Only under orders would she lose face like this, to actually speak to one of these. "And I have been told that your *latest* commission, for the Iron House, is quite late. We had hoped that your organization would have been more . . . adept, shall we say, in carrying out so small a project as a retrieval." She looked up, her face blank, asking innocently, "After all, your artists are said to be much better than any outlander. Was I mistaken?"

Jahlini sighed mournfully. "Alas, recovering the message from the two barbarians proved to be somewhat more difficult than at first imagined." She ran a casual finger down into the interior of her cup before pouring; good, it was smooth. The kitchen staff were loyal, but one never knew. "Perhaps we have become somewhat oversubtle in the pursuit of our art; after all, for the most part we deal with persons of refinement, residents of Illizbuah, the City, who appreciate subtlety. Not barbarians or country bumpkins. . . . Ah, you shame me as your host; do drink." She poured herself a cup from the common pot between them and drank; the soldier followed suit.

Jaahdnni held the cup just below her chin and regarded the Adderchief through the gentle steam. Suddenly she realized one thing that had bothered her: the wet smell of stone and concrete that lay under the scents of wood and linseed oil. The scent of the herbal tea was pleasing, and she sipped again; perhaps dealing with this one, city though she was, wouldn't be that difficult. *I am so far removed from her that there's really no point in taking her tone as an insult, and demanding her sword. That was for nobles.*

"A lovely blend of tea." She inclined her head to

the other. "You do your guest honor." She sighed. "I fear, however, that I must return to necessity. If the little item is not returned to us, then I fear we will have to ask for the return of the fee—oh, very politely, of course. My commander is most concerned that this trifle not fall into the, ah, wrong hands, shall we say." *Namely yours*, she thought, and pasted a smile on her face. Strange, the room that had been so cool was becoming stuffy.

"Yes, indeed. I have prepared a letter of apology which will be delivered to the General-Commander. Now, what—ah, complexity. I fear we are too given to it. Take the use of *dhilmaan*, for example. Honey?" she added, holding a spoon above the pot. The soldier hesitated, noted that the Adder was taking none, and shook her head.

"No, thank you. Dhilmaan?" The word was curious; in city dialect, it meant "loving twin."

"A poison. Two-stage; one part is administered as a solid, the other as a liquid or in crystalline form. One is insoluble in stomach juices; the other dissolves and activates it. Any systemic poison will do."

Jaahdnni looked down at her cup. "But . . . you drank from the same pot," she said weakly. Her breath caught; that might be fear. Pain shot down her left arm, then lanced into her chest as she toppled and arched, straining for breath. Air rasped into her throat, past muscles locking and contracting on the yielding cartilage of the windpipe.

"Oh, the activator was deposited in a thin film on your cup," Jahlini said, nibbling delicately at a seed-cake and picking up a sheaf of papers. "Hmmm, fortunate that the temple won't allow really potent aphrodisiacs to be legally sold for festival use—that would cut into our profit margins severely. . . . Where was—ah, yes, the poison in the tea. From beyond the Kahab Sea; HammerHeart, they call it. The doctors say it brings the most intense pain that a human being can feel; no doubt an experience rich in fascinating sensations." She glanced over her file of documents.

"You seem to be short of breath. Perhaps if you lay down for moment, my good gaaimun? Yes, like that." The soldier was lying on her back, only the crown of her head and her heels touching the floor. The lean body arched like a bow, thrumming with muscle spasm; veins swelled in her throat as she strove to scream, a pressure so intense that a fine red mist burst from the capillaries behind one eye. "Now, as I said, General-Commander Smyna will be receiving the letter of apologies tomorrow. Also a regretful notification that we cannot allow outsiders to dictate the time or manner by which we execute a commission. . . .

"But enough of these social pleasantries," she concluded, when the twisting figure in army green was still.

From the antechamber came scraping noises; the door was too thick to let through the hiss of blowguns, but an armored corpse made a good deal of noise. At the last, Jahlini clapped her hands.

"Niecibo," she said. Her secretary picked his way into the room, stepping over the emissary's body with an incurious glance.

"That letter of apology," she continued. The thick folded paper slid across the desk. "See that it arrives tomorrow, at her bedchamber's threshold. With the heads, of course. To remind her not to instruct us in our business." She finished the tea. "And send me the new Overseer of Terminations; perhaps he will prove more competent than his predecessor." She looked down at the body. Dhilmaan was such a tidy method; it prevented the sphincters from giving way on death.

CHAPTER XV

Megan touched the crown of her head and winced; the thick coil of braids was almost too hot to touch, and trickles of sweat ran down the flushed skin of her face and neck. It was hard not to give an audible sigh of relief as they passed into the shadow of the colonnade that fronted this side of the temple's bulk. Peering around one of the thick stone columns, she studied the work gang toiling to remove the last bloodstains from the pale limestone flags of the square. The aqueducts had been opened to flush most of the residue away; looking out over the bright scene, it was difficult to remember the sights and sounds of so many dying, only days ago. But flies still buzzed around the thick brown crusts on the storm drains, and faint under water and carbolic came the sweetish smell of rotting blood.

She shifted uneasily, very conscious of the looming bulk of the temple. It seemed to crouch, despite its height; crouch above the city like a beast on the body of its prey. Firmly, she took control of her imagination.

When she spoke, it was without glancing back at Shkai'ra.

"It is past the time agreed," she said, scanning constantly. "And if all these so-high wish what we have, why haven't they arrested us?"

"They believed our story about a cut-out," she said. A third party holding the goods, in a place neither of them knew, under instruction not to release it unless the two women were alive and free.

There were uniformed figures aplenty on the great expanse of the square, but they were patrols or functionaries, going about their business; and many priests, of every degree. For the rest, traffic was sparse and furtive; it would be some time before the center of Illizbuah's life bustled once more. Megan felt curiously naked; she was unused to having ten acres of open space about her in the center of a city.

"Still no sign of them. I still don't like the idea of selling it to the General-Commander. You said she had reason to dislike you."

"And I, her," Shkai'ra said with a shrug. "But I'm willing to deal. And the Reflection probably likes me even less, on principle. Our best chance; nobody would believe we haven't sold it *somewhere.*" Her lips pursed. "From the way things have befallen, I'd say it's some interesting piece of dirt. Factions want it to discredit others, but quietly, no open seizure. I wonder if any of these so-friendly parties know the details of the others' offers."

Megan snorted. "Wouldn't it put a weasel in the henhouse if they didn't, and we told them?" She stepped back another pace, unconsciously shunning the bright expanse of openness before them. "Although my life would not be worth the satisfaction; besides, I am not in the habit of giving information to anyone." She leaned against the cool stone of a pillar and looked over at Shkai'ra, concealed by the bulk of the next. "If you were they, would you pick this spot to trade it in? Coming here was like bending over and inviting the world in general to kick you in the arse."

Listen to yourself, she thought, forcing stillness. Blathering. *Voice or body; it seems one or the other must be moving.* The feeling of wrongness grew, and she had not survived to adulthood by ignoring such warnings.

Shkai'ra spread a hand; Megan could see the fingertips protrude from behind the column. "So long as they pay, why not? Even now, there's a good deal of coming and going here; two more are unlikely to be noticed. And who would expect them to make deals on their rival's doorstep? It makes sense."

"Ha."

Two figures in dull-green uniform tunics with short-swords at their belts separated themselves from the guards around a work detail and sauntered casually in their direction. The two women straightened to meet them, maintaining their careful positioning on opposite sides of adjacent pillars.

One of the army officers smiled, yellow teeth against the sallow olive of his face; the skin was sheened with sweat, but that was natural enough in this weather. He loosened a pouch from his belt and hefted it encouragingly. Megan stepped forward, and felt a crinkling sensation on the back of her neck.

"This smells like the DragonLord's compassion," Megan muttered. The feeling of tension grew; she half turned.

Shkai'ra stiffened as she walked, keeping a smiling face. Behind them there was the faintest clink of metal on stone; from behind and to their right, down the arcade. The sort of sound an overeager archer might make, the bolt-gun sounding as she twitched at a target's motion toward escape.

"Shields," Shkai'ra said, in any easy, conversational tone.

"What?" the Fehinnan soldier on the left replied, the smile slipping away from his face.

"You don't bring shields to a parlay," she continued, and launched herself forward from a standing start, body horizontal to the ground and one hand outstretched before her, stiffening into a blade.

The spearpoint of her fingers slammed into the vulnerable soft spot just below the breastbone, and the man halted as if flung at speed into a stone wall, his face purpling as shocked heart and lungs struggled to function. The Kommanza landed cat-stanced, feet braced; her crossed hands gripped the man by the belt and swung his passive body around the pivot of her heels, to stand between her and the side of the temple. The pulse thuttered in her ears, and the sudden coppery taste of combat excitement was on her tongue.

This is what I was born to do, she thought briefly.

Megan only had a flash of what Shkai'ra did as she ran. The man was too big for her to hold. He went for his sword, his weight going forward. One step, two, and her body left the ground in a kick. He never had time to drag the sword free, as his elbow broke under the impact of her foot. His body caved in toward the agony flaming through his arm, and Megan landed, taking the single step that put him between her and the others, one hand grabbing for the broken limb. As her hands closed on a forearm, solid and almost too big to get a good grip on, she was reminded of the sensation of deboning chicken. She twisted a little to hold the man's attention and shifted her hold to the wrist. She wasn't sure, but the slamming of the arm against the swordhilt might have broken some of the small bones in it. The soldier was rigid and sweating with pain, a muffled whine trailing from his throat as he fought to keep from crying out. She dug the claws of her other hand into the opposite side of his tunic, feeling cotton give under her tense hands and smelling the rank sweat that had broken out on him. She looked over his back toward the temple, very conscious of the immense open space behind her.

"What now, O master tactician?" Megan snarled. "They evidently didn't think as highly of our preparations as you did!"

Before the other woman could reply, a voice called out from the arcade. "Shoot!"

There was the barest second before the bolt-guns spoke. Megan felt the tense body between her hands quiver and jerk as three solid blows hammered it back against her grip. A four-bladed quarrel punched through breastbone and spine to spatter blood and bone chips stinging into her eyes; she tasted the hot salt of it through opened lips.

Shkai'ra drove backward the six paces to the pillars, holding her once-living shield between her and the squad of bolt-guns that fanned out from the row of columns. It would not be long before a lucky shot whipped through soft tissue and struck her with killing force; even armor of proof would not stop a bolt at less than a hundred paces. From the corner of her eye, she saw Megan shed her protection and dive scrambling for the same cover; the dead man had twice her bulk or more.

No words were necessary as they dashed down the line of pillars, ducking and weaving with rabbit-like randomness, spending the minimum amount of time on the vulnerable outside arcs of their flight. Bolts snapped and skittered around them, knocking chips from the stone sheathing of the concrete pillars. The soldiers did not take the time to fan out into the square and gain a better vantage for their fire, trying to keep on their quarry's heels, and exhausted the six rounds in their magazines.

Megan clutched at a line of red on her thigh as they rounded the corner. "Nothing, scratch," she gasped at

Shkai'ra's unspoken question. They looked out across
the open expanse of the square, with its scattered parties of guards. Their eyes met.

The blond woman jerked her thumb down to their
left, along the front face of the temple itself, to where
the great double doors stood open. "Only place they
won't expect. No time—now!"

They pounded down the frontage, past startled
groups of worshippers, and up the broad shallow steps.
There was no guard on the door; they plunged into
shadow nightdark after the blazing sun of noon. A
corridor lay before them, twice forty feet high, and
nearly as broad, the main avenue to the interior of
the dome. There was no succor there. Shkai'ra turned
toward a secondary door on their left, with a quick fist
to the throat of the robed guard and a swinging kick
to the latch that held it. The rending tear of wood was
loud in the scented gloom. Choking, the underpriest
barely noticed the smaller figure's trampling feet.

The soldiers poured through the door. An upperpriest glanced at them, then returned his attention
to the prostrate door guard. His hands moved with
swift skill, examining the injury; the larynx had folded
back on itself, rather than simply crushing. Now, if he
was skilled, and she was lucky. . . .

He placed his thumbs on either side of the prostrate
figure's throat and pushed. There was a subdued pop
and the cyanic blue of the underpriest's face began to
fade. Her superior rose and folded his hands in the
sleeves of his robe.

"What is this?" he said evenly. "Weapons and violence in the house of Her?"

"ShiningRadianceoftheDivineLight," the captain
gabbled. He jittered from foot to foot, and even in
the temple the troopers behind strained forward like
hounds on the leash. "We pursue two, ah, heretics.
Unbelievers! Yes, profaning the temple, offering violence to a Holy Servant. Please, let us pass."

The upperpriest became utterly still. A slight sign sent one of his attendants noiselessly down the corridor; the rest ranked themselves behind their master, faces as blank as their shaven skulls.

"What manner of persons were these, Child of Light?" he asked.

The officer strained in an agony of frustration. Failure was not going to enhance his record; besides, one of the dead outside was a friend. "Ah, females, two, one tall and fair, one short and dark, ah . . ."

He stopped, appalled. The priest nodded, once. "So, you too know of this," he said somberly. "Even among the Righteous Sword, true God-respecting obedience is seldom to be found." He sighed. "Return to your lord, and assure her that these miscreants will be found and their secrets plumbed." He paused. "All their secrets."

CHAPTER XVI

The corridor was long and narrow, lantern lit, tunneling deeper into the massive outer wall of the temple, lined with grey stone. Panting slightly, Megan and Shkai'ra paused at a junction.

Shkai'ra rose lightly on her toes, peering about, the tip of her saber making small precise arcs through the incense-laden air. It was close and still and absolutely quiet, even more silent than the steppe or deep forest, for there was no movement of air.

"Well?" Megan demanded.

"Well, what?" Shkai'ra asked.

"Where are we?"

Shkai'ra shrugged eloquently.

The Zak snorted. "Up or down?"

"Up, I think. We may see the dungeons soon enough."

Ghost-silent, they slid along the upward-tending corridor to their right. Deep-recessed niches held doors every ten paces or so; for minutes they passed locked doors, skyshafts, silence and bittersweet sandalwood smell and unpeopled immensity.

"Where are the priests?" the Zak asked.

Shkai'ra snarled wordlessly. This was worse than being shrunk to hand-height and lost in a prairie-dog warren; cities were bad enough, but this . . .

"Zailo Unseen knows," she said. "This stone dungheap has as many rooms as half the City; the priests swarm in it like maggots in a greenrot wound, but they can't fill it. Most must be at the noon service, anyway; still, only a matter of time until we run into one."

Faintly, a hum had made itself felt, working its way into bone and thought; not until the sounds were almost separate words did they consciously notice it. Directionless, it seemed to thrum through the thick, poured stone around them.

"Perhaps we should find the source of the chant," Megan said.

Shkai'ra paused with one hand on the slick stone lining of the hallway. "I wish . . . demonshit, I don't even know which compass point we're facing, or how high we've come! All right, then. But quietly."

Megan lifted a silent eyebrow and moved forward, hugging the inner, right-hand wall. There was little sound, save for the soft scuffle of her moccasin-like boots and the harder click of the rigid leather on Shkai'ra's feet. The upward tilt of the corridor grew stronger, ending in a staircase.

The Kommanza took the treads two at a time, her feet touching lightly to push her upward; once the polished wooden tip of her saber scabbard went clack against the wall, and she swallowed a curse past bared teeth. The smell of incense grew stronger. At the top was a landing; another flight of stairs above, another corridor on either side of them. Directly before the stairs was a portal of thick green glass with the light of an open space glowing through. Shkai'ra dropped down at the last step and crawled forward at floor level to peer through the pebbly glass, Megan beside her. Before them was the open vastness of the temple interior; a few steps below was a broad balustraded terrace that ran a hundred meters above the floor-level altar, just where the dome rested on the square bulk of its support. Shafts of light stabbed down from the lenses in the dome ceiling, hundreds of meters above, diffusing softly over the vacant altar block. Ordered ranks of priests stood in the stalls, their endless chant rumbling through echoing space, relays of replacements slipping in as others left for food or rest.

The two women slithered backward, their eyes fixed on the door so far below. Shkai'ra put her lips next to her companion's ear. "We've come around to the north side," she breathed. "If we can get straight down, there should be an exit and an unsecured passageway for worshippers."

They rose, turned, and froze. A priest stood below them on the steps. Shkai'ra's mind struggled briefly to reject the evidence of her eyes; it meant an untrained city dweller had walked to within a body's length of her without enough sound to alert her.

"I fear you will have to postpone your departure," the priest said, her face and voice calm. "My mentor would speak with you."

She stepped forward, beginning a gesture that commenced with the raising of a hand. There was an utter confidence in it; the priests of the Sun were inviolate, and she had other reasons for unconcern. The two outlanders felt a tightening of their skins.

But Shkai'ra's reaction had begun even as her mind blurred in bewilderment, guided by reflexes encoded at a level that knew neither doubt nor hesitation. The rough-dimpled bone of her sword hilt rutched against her calluses as the left hand flicked along it, looped thumb and forefinger under the pommel. The blade came free from its sheath of leatherbound wood with a hiss of metal on oak greased with neat's-foot oil. Her right palm slapped home on the long grip just below the circular guard, and her foot stamped forward as she lunged with a guttural grunt of effort.

There was a moment's coldness, and a smell of wet salt. The Kommanza found herself kneeling, shaking her head to clear it of a lingering musical tone. Megan gripped her by the back of her tunic and hauled her backward.

"The image is gone. I don't know how or where, but I do know we'd better go as well."

The copper-haired woman looked down dumbly at the sword. The curve of the cutting edge glittered cold and clean in the lamplight. A swelling clamor broke out below as she sheathed it and Megan pulled her toward the upward stair.

The tumult rose to a dull, muffled throbbing, like the sound of the sea through thick forest, then faded as they trotted down the corridors. They took the left-hand turnings, trying to work their way back toward the outer shell of the temple, but found themselves forced to climb, ramps and staircases turning up and inward. The concrete of the building's substance was sheathed everywhere with stone, polished granite and marble kept immaculately clean but faintly greasy to the touch like all rock in a humid climate. The air was as cool as a cellar; the Sun Temple was large enough that most of its bulk kept to the ambient temperature of the foundations, and smelled of incense and damp and the faint indefinable odor of age.

The corridors began to narrow and curve more sharply. "We must be inside the dome itself now," Megan said, between long deep breaths. She was making two steps to her long-limbed comrade's one, only the trickling sweat marking exertion as they wolf-paced up the steepening slopes, trotting a hundred paces, then walking the same.

"Ia," Shkai'ra said. "Best . . . we . . . stop . . . and rest, soon. We may need our wind."

They reached the end of the ascending passage, passing through a hole-like exit in the floor of a horizontal corridor that stretched off to either side, curving gently inward to the right and left. Shkai'ra stood blinking for a moment; the lanterns were more closely placed here. She paused to examine one.

"Getting on for empty," she said. "They can't keep all this up without much coming and going. We've been too lucky for it to last." She made the averting sign with her sword-hand.

Megan tried a door to their right. It swung open easily; she ghosted it wide with a finger and stood back, before venturing within. A four-meter alcove stood revealed; a knee-high jade balustrade was all that separated it from the huge lambent yellow cavern of the inner dome. They edged through and swung the door home behind them; from this vantage three-quarters of the way to the top, they could see that the alcove was one of a ring that circled the dome, disguised in the ornate inner carvings. From below there would be only a pattern of light and shadow.

A tube-like machine was bolted to the balustrade, pointed at the floor hundreds of meters below. Megan touched it gingerly and bent a look at Shkai'ra.

"A toy for keeping watch on the faithful," she said. "A farlooker." The Kommanza put an eye to the upper end and adjusted the focusing screw. "Hmmmm, and a strong one: you could almost read someone's lips." She paused. "Why, the sheep-raping crow eaters," she said with reluctant admiration. "So *that's* why they tell folk to make their confessions with their faces to the Sun!"

Megan stepped casually up to the balustrade and looked down past her boot tips to the tiny figures below. The hunt seemed scattered, disorganized, groups of yellow robes and knots of bewildered worshippers on the acre-broad pavement. She leaned over to the telescope and appropriated the eyepiece. "But this is blurred," she said. "Is there a magic to it?"

The Kommanza grinned. "No, try turning that, there."

"So." She fiddled a moment with the knob and scanned the mob below. A second later, she stiffened and started cursing in a number of languages. "Lady of Winter! I've never seen that before, but I don't want a closer acquaintance. Look and tell me. I want to know what I'm fighting."

Shkai'ra squinted downward. "Oh, Glitch of the Inspired Perverse! They've brought out a Mind-Sniffer. It can follow us anywhere—and turn our brains into worked-over oxturds inside our skulls if it gets close enough." She spat on the marble floor. "I think it's time we left; they don't take those out of the temple, not in daylight, and there aren't many, or so I've heard. Thank Zailo Protector."

Megan had backed up from the edge and was running her fingers over her knives. *Fishguts!* she thought. *Magic is what I—we need . . . and don't have. Nothing I know would fight something like that.* She opened her mouth to call Shkai'ra on. No sense in waiting for it to find them.

"What are you doing here? I have done nothing wrong to be replaced. This is my post." Megan swung around. Did they all creep around silently? The old man's eyes were unblurred but vague. "You are . . . not of the Sun. I really should do something. Yes, maybe I should call someone. Yes, yes." He mumbled on and turned as if to do just that.

She lunged, caught a wrist, and pulled sharply, twisting as she did so. He staggered off balance, his free arm flailing as his knees struck the balustrade. She pulled back, trying to keep him from going over, but had to let go; his weight would have dragged her over, too. She doubted he was conscious when he hit; he had only screamed once on the way down. The

floor below was suddenly bright red. "I didn't mean
to do that. Now I've really announced our presence."
She looked over her shoulder and thought of the warren behind the door. She stepped up and stood on
the railing the priest had just fallen over. "We can't
risk getting caught in that maze again. This railing is
unbroken by the walls."

Shkai'ra looked down at the confusion so far below.
"And you're a thief," she muttered to Megan. "Who
did you steal from, the blind?"

Megan snorted and tapped a foot against the slick
oily smoothness of the balustrade as her companion
struggled to remove her tight riding boots. Grumbling,
the Kommanza slung her footgear around her neck
and stepped up, her toes curling to grip the jade. She
looked to her right.

"A long way down," she said quietly. "All the gods
curse these people; mountains are bad enough, but
they have to build them. Earth should be flat."

Megan shrugged. "It wouldn't kill you any deader
than falling thirty feet."

"But you'd have longer to think about it. . . . Lead
on."

Swiftly, almost running, they trotted around the
inner surface of the dome, passing chamber after
chamber opening into the dark corridors. The top of
the balustrade was less than half a meter thick; thinner, where it passed the partition walls between
chambers.

"Hai, about here," Shkai'ra called when they had
reached a point across from their starting place. "The
main downshaft should be around here."

They skipped down to the floor, Megan waiting for
Shkai'ra to replace her footgear. A risk, but being
lamed was a worse one; and they might have to move
without care for their feet.

Shkai'ra unclenched her teeth and looked resentfully over her shoulder; it was unfair, that cities should

be where the best loot was. Especially when you couldn't just burn and sack the accursed places; too bad Eh'mex, the hammer of Baiwun, hadn't come down on this rat's nest long ago.

They moved out into the corridor; this was broader, and it ran directly away from the inner chamber of the dome. Shkai'ra put out her hand. "Wait," she said thoughtfully.

Megan raised a brow. "Priest killers should wait to be discovered?"

"No . . . I've heard of this. This corridor must lead directly to the main buttress, then down to the underlevels."

"Good!" Megan answered. It would take a while for search parties to climb up to them, but much less time to block off the possible escape routes.

Shkai'ra looked at her. "This is the fast way down."

They ran forward. The temple was too big to be disturbed by one small altercation, the chant of the choirs continuing as they would until the building fell. The sound of their breath and footfalls gradually became the loudest thing in a world of stone-rimmed narrowness.

At last they came to an alcove more brightly lit than most of the warren. Stacked along one wall were wood and wicker containers, much like openwork coffins, with a greased oak runner down each long edge, and on the other wall a dark, narrow square hole left the corridor; they could see that it ran just under the surface of the dome, in a huge curve to their left around the surface and down.

"Don't tell me this is your fast way down!"

Shkai'ra laughed silently. "I've only heard of this; it's not well known." She examined one of the coffin-sleds. "Some mystic thing, supposed to symbolize the descent of the Sunless Soul—the priests use it in their rituals. Yes, it slides down . . . Ah, this must be the brake: see how you can press it with your foot." She paused. "There may be someone waiting at the other end, or death along the way." She lifted one of the vehicles to the flat stone launching stage and climbed in; Megan waited behind her. "It's been . . . a good time, knowing you."

She winked, latched the cover of the sled, and jerked her body forward. The sled moved, slowly, then beginning to gather speed even as it carried her into the blackness of the hole, feet first.

Megan stood stunned for a moment, shocked by the strength of her own emotion. There had been so many years of solitude. So many years since her parents died, and everything she cared for had died; the risk, the risk . . .

Abruptly, she unfroze; cursing herself mechanically, she followed. The hinged wicker framework of the capsule swung shut over her face; it was more solid than she had imagined, a hot musty smell of reeds catching at nose and throat. She felt the runners catch, then begin to slide as the wicker bullet moved forward under the impetus of her weight. The first sensation was speed, pushing head and shoulders back against the padded rest. Then she was floating, hair bristling over her back at the strange weightless sensation.

Suddenly she had a wild urge to shriek in exultation; suppressing it in the shuddering, bucking darkness, she grinned at the black pressing down on her eyes. There was a wild lurch as the sled turned a corner, frame groaning under the strain, runners screaming protest at occasional greaseless spots. Acceleration threw her against the side of the sled, back again, and around until up and down were lost in plunging chaos.

Suddenly a scene that could not be was. . . .

Something turned from the straight trail and lunged at the wall, straining against its leash and drooling a curious hunger. The hot claws of its attack lifted the top of Megan's head and scraped behind her eyes.

She threw the image of a wall at it; a *kreml*, a fastness, keeping her mind safe while it mewed outside the gate. It became an oozing thing that worked in, and around, and under, and through her defenses, smelling of battlefields and rivers thick with decaying fish and flies. Desperately, she thought of clean water, sea and ocean, as her muscles locked into an unconscious spasm, rigid and clawing into the wickerwork. It plucked at nerve centers, scrambling for access. Pain. Her hands began to move without her volition, her defenses beginning to crumble, as it began to force her mind to its mold. Then she was again aware of the sled, wickerwork splintered under her claws, and her blood pounding in her ears.

Shkai'ra plunged through darkness, the speed picking up until the sled bucked and vibrated with the slight irregularities of the stone. The smells of hot oil and scorching wood flew up at her; she touched her foot to the brake on the curves, just enough to keep control. And still the speed increased.

Faster than a good horse, she thought. *Faster than the Great River in spate.* Then with a sudden realization: this is *wonderful!* She threw back her head and screamed, the high, exultant, falsetto screech of the Kommanz warcry.

Then the rattling banks turned into a prolonged hissing as the curve flattened out and the sled barreled into a long flat stretch an inch deep in water. The sled braked to a stop, and an attendant scurried forward to guide it to the landing and throw open the cover.

He paused for a moment, paralyzed, at the exceedingly unpriestly occupant. Still laughing with the thrill of the ride, she shot up one hand to grip him by the throat. The other, fisted, flashed up to land under his nose. She tossed the corpse to one side and rose in a crouch, eyes darting around the cavernous underground chamber.

An instant later, the second sled rocketed around the corner and slowed to a stop. As the rush of the disturbed water died, there was no motion for a long moment. Finally, the cover swung open slowly and Megan stepped out, pale as snow, licking a trickle of blood from a bitten lip.

Shkai'ra caught her by the shoulders, hugged her soundly, and deposited her on the dry surface of the landing stage.

"That was fun," she said, "kh'eeredo. Let's get out of here before they bring on their tame spook." She jerked a thumb at the exit, a barred wooden door set in plain oozing concrete; they were far below the level of marble sheathing. "There'll be an exit to the sewers—risky, but better than breaking for the surface." She sobered, the exhilaration of the ride fading. "It's that damned monster of theirs that bothers me."

Megan's answer was harsh laughter. "It bothers you!" She pulled the memory of the hug close around her, against the thought of the Sniffer. They hurried down a corridor chosen at random. Megan felt along under her jawbone to the spot behind the ear where the carotid pulsed and wondered if she would be quick enough once the Sniffer got close again. *I will not become a beast of theirs,* she thought, and concentrated on running.

When they paused for breath, Shkai'ra pressed her shoulders back against the weeping concrete, feeling the slow drops soaking through the linen of her tunic and mingling with the clammy sweat on her flanks. The priests were close now, no more than two corridors away . . . it was so difficult to estimate distance in this stone warren! She bared her teeth. There must be weirdwork on the tracking; hounds would have given themselves away with their noise by now.

"Where are we?" Megan whispered.

"Lost. Back to the turn and right this time." They padded back and took the other turning, straining to sense the downward slope they sought. The lanterns were few and far between here, hurtful to eyes night-adapted by hours beneath the earth. The sad smell of wet stone had been with them so long they scarcely noticed it; despite the underground chill the air was sticky. They came to a crossway in the low tunnels, and Shkai'ra eyed the arch above her head with hatred. She could stand erect only in the center, which put her feet in the drainway, a wet cold chafing inside her boots. This level was all beneath the water table, kept open by drainage to the sewer tunnels and the pumping system.

Behind them the noise of the temple search party grew. Then it was answered from the right, downslope. Megan turned toward the rising left fork of the T-shaped junction.

"No!" Shkai'ra said. "Death that way; too many of them on the middle level above, the tunnels are too wide. Better we chance a fight, try to break."

Just then the sound began behind them. It was a whining, saw-edged shrilling along the nerves. And there was something else behind it, something that drove needles into her ears and blurred the darkened scene before her eyes.

Baiwun, be with me now, Shkai'ra thought desperately. She invoked the mental disciplines of the Warrior's Way, then slapped herself savagely across the face. Weakness swam in her, leaving her barely conscious of falling to her knees. A metallic sound came to her from a vast distance; she knew it was her saber clattering on the floor, but somehow it was too distant to matter.

The sound leaped into Megan's mind, forcing its way in through channels burned with pain from the last time. She stumbled and almost cried out. Acid seared its way into her, and the vague sound of metal

on metal did nothing to shatter the hold the Sniffer
had on her. She brought up her hands, crooked into
talons with the effort, as she felt her mind start to
crumble. Her teeth were being driven through rusty
metal; she was smothering in broken glass; it hurt to
breathe, it hurt to think, it hurt . . .

*No. I am. I think. Megan is my name. Megan.
Megan.* She was down on her hands and knees, striving to rise. *I decide. I. I.* It became an anchor. A
fragile thread that grew thinner moment by moment.
From somewhere nearby Yeva's power joined her own
frail defense, a blue-violet surge of power that drew
shield over them.

The pressure eased. Awareness returned. Shkai'ra
shook her head and groped for the familiar bone grip
of her sword, staggering back to her feet. The taste of
blood was in her mouth, and she felt the pain of the
wound her teeth had made. Vision cleared—

She started backward a step. She and Megan stood
in the rising arm of the T; the two parties of priests
had met before them. She could have reached out her
blade and touched the foremost of them, or the . . .
creature held on a straining leash, and none so much
as glanced at her.

"They must be here!" the foremost priest said.
"They were seen! The beast says they're near, very
near, near enough for us to see with the eyes that see
light." The priest gave a savage jerk at the leash.

"Someone must be feeding it shit, then, because
that's all it's got left for brains. About time to make a
new Sniffer; you must have let them slip by you,
somehow. His Radiance is not going to like this. Or
us."

There was stone under her hands. The Zak raised
her head and opened her eyes, blood trickling out of
one corner of her mouth. The first thing she saw was
the Sniffer's stare. The bulging eyes had once been
human; now they were distorted, oozing and blood-

shot. It was hairless, limbs stretched to gauntness, pallid white. Skin hung in loose folds under its chin, and it crouched, beastlike, staring at her and drooling greenish spittle on itself, mouth working as it chewed the air. For a second, she thought that the priests had them. Then her ears started working again. She moved to brace herself as the priests argued, unseeing. The motion sent the monster—she could not call it anything else—into a frenzy, twisting and backing to be free of the chain. The one priest cuffed it, and it snapped at him, then cringed. It began its mental howl again.

"Stop it!" the priest said sharply, cuffing it again. "*I don't need a headache either. They are not here.*"

"Bring your pet worm," said another, who seemed to be in authority, running a hand over his shaven scalp. "They can't have gotten past us downslope; you must have lost them back in the cross passages. Quickly!"

They trotted off down the two women's backtrail, leaving the downward slope free. Shkai'ra looked after them, suppressing a hysterical giggle.

I saw that, she thought. *We were standing in plain sight and they didn't see us. I won't think about it. Not now.*

Megan pulled herself to her knees. "We . . . ha . . . have to get out now." She braced herself against the wall. *We can't expect her help again,* she thought. *What it cost her to get into the temple and help us, I don't want to think about.*

They took the downslope, slowly recovering from the battering their minds had taken, picking up speed. Then, like a nagging tooth, Megan was aware of the Sniffer, at first fading, then growing stronger, trying to settle a hook into her brain. "They'll find us if they follow the Sniffer. It just tore the chain from its keeper's hand and hunts us alone. *Na Koru, rozhum.*"

CHAPTER XVII

The mildewed lattice, swollen and heavy with dampness, took the two of them to wrench loose. As it swung back with a crash and the raw, sharp smell of urine and rotting garbage welled up, Megan looked at Shkai'ra.

"So, these are the sewers. Why aren't I glad that we've reached them?" She eased the grating down and followed Shkai'ra into the rough brick shaft. The stream of water from the drainage channel fanned out in the cracks in the wall, running cold over one hand and trailing down her forearm. The way was closed behind them, even if the priests delayed in following their monster.

Shkai'ra was moving down the wooden handholds as quickly as caution allowed. "Hurry. They group around the waste chutes."

"They?"

"Come on!"

A rung gave way under her foot, loosened by the heavier woman's weight; Shkai'ra had just set her feet

on solid stone when Megan's cry of "Look out!" came
down the shaft.

Megan followed, coiling out of a ball to land on her
feet. Her legs absorbed the impact of her weight, but
the force of her landing was still enough to drive a
small sound from her lungs.

As she rose from her crouch, Shkai'ra's eyes and
teeth gleamed in the darkness. "Who do you steal
from—the deaf?" she whispered. Her voice scurried
around the tunnel, sibilant and cut by the drip of
water and a rustling noise in the distance.

"We have time for jokes, *heavy one*?"

"No—follow me."

They edged along the narrow path barely wide
enough to stand on, the sluggish flow of water only
inches from where they stood. The darkness was not
quite black; enough reflected light filtered through to
suggest an oily sheen on the rippling surface but not
enough to guide the feet.

"Do we have to swim through this?" Megan choked.
The stench was heavy, palpable, not raw as it had been
in the shaft, but oily and rancid, clinging to the inside
of nose and throat like the scent of overripe bananas.
She twitched as something multilegged and slimy
dropped from the ceiling and crawled down her
cheek.

"Nai," Shkai'ra said, dropping back into her native
language. The slow drip and splash of the water had
changed slightly, sounding against something other
than stone or water, a hollower sound. "There are
canoes for the repair crews," she continued, guiding
Megan's hand to the side of a small dugout. "Quick,
we're not safe yet."

"This is so difficult to see that you have to tell me?"
They pushed off into the current. Shkai'ra set a relent-
less pace, pushing the paddle deep into the thick fluid.
"Paddle hard," she gasped. "But don't let your hands
touch the water." Megan labored to match the taller

woman's stroke. "Stop making ... dark ... hints ... and tell," she breathed, matching word to effort.

At that moment, a heavy crunching twitch struck at her paddle; the sensation reminded her of a fish striking at a hook. She raised the suddenly heavy paddle, twitching and jerking in her hands. Straining through the dimness, she could make out a small wiggling shape. An alligator only twice a handwidth long, the twin of the voracious little pests that she'd seen in the swamps. Perhaps a trifle smaller. Behind them the rustling was growing louder and the water began to seethe.

"Why have you ..." Shkai'ra snapped over her shoulder. "Oh, kill it. Quick, the pack will be here soon."

Megan had shaken the paddle as Shkai'ra spoke, then, realizing that it would never let go, crushed it against the body of the canoe, feeling it pop and break like a grape with bones. The others were close enough now to snatch at the remains as she used the paddle again. Faintly, in the fetid darkness, she could see that there were only teeth left still clamped deep into the wood of the blade.

They had slowed, and the rest of the pack had converged on them.

"Koru, Guardian of Lives, give us strength! Shkai'ra, paddle faster!" She tasted the cold salt of sweat on her upper lip. "I've no will to be eaten alive." She paused an instant to beat off two of the beasts clinging to the side of the canoe. Behind, a sliding, scraping noise was building. "And in such small bites!"

"Can't go faster," was the panted reply. The boiling sound of foul water whipped into froth was close now; the outriders of the horde jerked upward along the gunwales, and the Kommanza smashed the handle of her paddle across their bodies as she switched the blade from one side to the other. "There is one differ-

ence between these and the swamp breed," Shkai'ra
panted.

"What?"

"These . . . their bite is septic."

"Wonderful! Move, woman—we're clear of most of
them."

I could scream, Shkai'ra thought. *Or vomit.* Her
eyes probed the darkness overhead. "There should be
an access here . . . ah!" A movement in the air and a
hollowness in the darkness marked the way out.

A thrust with the paddle against brickwork stopped
the canoe. "Hold. There must be a service ladder here
in the shaft. . . . Sheepshit!" The relief in her voice
shifted to disgust colored with urgency. "It's broken
off." Her fingers traced old brick, crumbling in the
wet; a trickle of oily liquid fell on her upturned face.

Megan rammed down a surge of panic. "If we can't
get out here, can we reach the next one?"

The canoe thudded against the wall and rebounded.
Shkai'ra had not answered; there was a dim flash of
metal as she jammed her dagger into the ancient mortar of the access shaft and hammered it home with
the butt of her paddle. "Climb over me, quick," she
husked.

Megan reached up to the Kommanza's shoulders,
her fingers sinking into the hard deltoids. Careful not
to shoot the uncertain footing of the boat out from
beneath the other woman's feet, she moved to a pre-
carious balance on Shkai'ra's hips, then climbed lightly
to place her feet on the shoulders. Reaching up, she
wove her hands through the lowest secure rung and
braced a foot on the dagger hilt. Arching her back in
anticipation of the strain, she looked down into a
deeper blackness. "Climb," she said.

There was an instant of joint-cracking tension as the
Zak felt her companion's full weight; she bore the
brunt of it on her arms, not daring to throw strain on
the sodden mortar and eroded brick imprisoning the

Kommanza's blade. Hands clamped her ankles; an arm reached up to circle her thighs, tightened to bear weight, and the other hand reached for her belt. The long body slid over hers, and she gave a grunt of relief as Shkai'ra's hands reached the rung above hers. Her feet gripped the hilt of the dagger, worked it free, and brought it up for gripping as she hung one-handed. Below, she could hear the canoe capsize under the scrambling impact of the gator herd; the slow current bore it away.

Megan tossed the knife upward. "Here," she said. "The walls curve inward to the ceiling; can they reach the access hole?"

Shkai'ra caught the hilt, more sensed than felt, and paused to hawk gummy phlegm into her mouth and spit into the water below. "Yes," she said. "There's growth on the brick lining, and the surface is rough. Take a little time, but they won't stop on a hot trail. At least there's no blood to drive them into frenzy. Couldn't you do that glowing-knife trick? We could use some light."

"True, but do you want to wait for them while I concentrate?" Megan replied. Below, the thick viscous liquid at the sides of the tunnel was being whipped into froth as the caimans scrabbled at the slick growth that covered the bricks. Soon it would be stripped away, and the claws would grip.

Unseen in the darkness, Shkai'ra spat in the direction of the noise. "No," she snarled. "Only one way to go."

"Let me go first."

"Why?"

"If those shoulders of yours get stuck, I don't want to be behind you, like beer behind the bung, and if I get stuck . . . well, you will just have to use those stilt legs and push." She paused a moment. "Hard," she added, and squeezed past.

Shkai'ra stared up into the darkness, and knew that

it would need all a warrior's sense of shame to make her follow into the narrow lightless filthy smallness of it. She gritted her teeth and began to pull herself up; just then a small shape thudded into one leg. White-hot needles punched into a calf just above her boot.

"Sheepshit!" she yelled. "Glitch take all vermin."

Twisting into a U, she hung by one hand and reached down with the other as the four-inch alligator thrashed wildly, trying to tear a mouthful of her flesh free and drop clear. She snapped its neck, then broke the jaw to force the cartilage-locked teeth out of her flesh. Grimly, she scrambled to follow Megan. The shaft still loomed like a mouth waiting to swallow; but there were too many real mouths below. *At least this one is toothless*, she thought with a wild inward laughter.

"All praise to the Mighty Ones," she muttered, in her people's standard response to bad luck. "Now they've got a blood trail to follow." The noise below rose to a frenzy as the warm red drops spattered their maddening scent into the water. A few lucky ones took bites from their dead cousin; the others drove forward in a slithering hill against the walls of the tunnel, their combined thrashings raising the mound out of the water.

"Faster—they're climbing the walls after us." An endless scuttling of claw on brick underlaid her words.

The shaft climbed vertically, then angled over toward the level. The darkness was absolute now, pressing wetly on the eyes. The only sound was their own hoarse breathing, falling muffled and dead into the still, confined air of the drainage shaft.

Shkai'ra could feel the weight of city-sour earth above her; it pressed on her chest, made each breath a labored effort. Instinct fought reason, told her to draw knife and smash, tear her way clear to air and light before the walls shifted and crushed her into darkness forever. Not even a soul could escape from here; it would be trapped with the rotting body, eternally unfreed by cleansing fire, never to be reborn.

The training of the Warmasters saved her. The true killer should hate all that lives, and that hate would make one strong.

"I hate," she whispered, harsh and hoarse in the meter-high roundness of the shaft. "I hate you all. I hate . . ."

Megan heard the grating whisper begin behind her in a language that she did not understand; hate and fear and lostness beating through the alien tongue, powerful enough to carry meaning. She could almost see the red flare of rage around her, and every sense cringed from the terror in the sound.

". . . the miserable spook pushers and their ratshit message, and I hate the bungling incompetence that got us into this, and . . ."

It was the last, desperate grasp of someone falling into hell, blaming everyone else. *This is hell*, Megan thought. *Darkness and that sound will be with me forever and this tunnel will not end.*

". . . and I hate the priests and everybody breathing free above. And I hate . . ." Shkai'ra hissed, her voice shrinking into a singsong chant. Memories opened and bled; it was the voice of a child alone in the dark with pain and fear.

No way out, Megan thought. No opening. In a cold sweat, she imagined her groping hand suddenly finding a wall in the dark. In the blackness. To be eaten alive.

". . . but I live, you die. You go, not me. I'm strong now, not weak . . ."

The hair rose on Megan's back, and she fought down the trembling fits that threatened to lock her here, unable to move either forward or back.

". . . no one will hurt me again; I'll live and kill, until the gods come to eat the world. And *I'll dance in the flames* . . ." The Kommanza's face worked into a rictus of hate, but her body moved forward, its movements guided with a preternatural calmness even as threads of spittle drooled down from her lips. In her mind, the ancient Litany of Hate continued.

The force of Shkai'ra's fear clawed at Megan's mind, but there was no way for the Zak to stop, to perhaps ease the fear. Megan opened her mouth dazedly and shook her head. Sweat ran down her temples and under her hair as she fought off Shkai'ra's emotions. She gasped again, aware that the air no longer moved at all. From somewhere inside herself she pulled a defense against the other. *Fishguts,* she thought. *That might be helping her, but it's not helping me at all.* She pretended that it was a challenge, issued in the childpack; one to perform or lose *zight,* her face and position. She crawled on.

In the blackness before her, suddenly there was no floor. She stopped and felt around the edges, fingers sliding in slimy softness. Her breathing was reflected back to her with an odd metallic ring—cold, and shifting slightly. *So that's why the air is dead.* She clamped her teeth on her lip a moment.

Shkai'ra ran into her feet. The sudden interruption of the steady mechanical crawling shocked her consciousness back into control.

"Move!" she rasped, then realized that the command had been given in Kommanzanu. "Get going," she repeated in Fehinnan, uncertain this time whether it was a command or a plea.

"Shkai'ra, we, ah, have a bit of a problem." The Zak's voice was oddly muffled, carefully calm.

"*Now* this is revealed unto you?" Shkai'ra said, the rhythms of her cradle-speech rubbing through the tongue she had learned. The effort of talking helped to bring her back to herself a little.

"The passage ahead of us—it goes almost straight down. And there's water at the bottom."

Shkai'ra choked off a sound that might have been

a whimper. Turning her head, she sank teeth into one arm hard enough to draw blood, then clenched a fist and slammed it across the three inches of space available into the side of the tunnel.

The pain overrode fear; to a Kommanza, pain was deeply linked to discipline and mastery. "The . . ." She hawked and spat. "The kinless cowget turd-eating Fehinnans build these tunnels shaped like a *shuh* rune. Down and then up again, farther up on the other side and out to the cellar levels."

The Zak felt sudden shock as if solidly stopping a blow and began to realize how close the tie between them was. *I. Am. Not. Afraid. Of small. Spaces.* She put her head down a moment, her forehead on the weeping concrete. Sympathy so close would not aid them. "The bottom of an S-curve?" Already she imagined the icy feel of scummy water forcing its way into her lungs. "We don't know how deep, either, after that fishgutted storm." She drew a deep breath. "We'll have to turn on our backs and go down head first, to bend around the curve." She froze a second, then with a hurried scramble she edged around and started down the shaft, frantically forcing her body to do what was necessary. *If I stop I'll never make myself do this,* she thought as the water oozed through her hair and touched the top of her scalp, rising only as fast as she could get purchase in the slime.

The sick, tight feeling in her chest got worse as she forced her way under and something squirmed away from under one hand. It was as cold as the Dark One's breath. She thought of breathing. The blood rushed to her head and pounded in her temples, the darkness behind her eyes pulsed red. There was no air. She scrambled and shoved through sludge. Her nails caught at projections and gave her purchase as she realized the curve was scraping past her knees. Fighting painful constriction, she lunged upward, striving for air, and life.

Shkai'ra waited long moments before turning. Even so, it was not until the skittering from behind grew close that she drew a quick dozen deep breaths and pushed herself forward and down.

If I'm going to be eaten alive, I want to drown first, she thought as the oily water closed over her face.

She jackknifed her body to bend around the down-curve, braced her feet against the ceiling, and pushed with all the strength of her long thigh muscles. The impetus carried her to the bottom of the straight section, to where the shaft curved level once more at the bottom of the U. And there she stopped; the tunnel was partly blocked by sediment, and the buoyancy of the air in her lungs kept trying to drag her up and back. Her face scraped against the concrete of the tunnel's roof, her shoulders jammed and sank into the slippery softness of the bottom. Outstretched before her, there was no room for her arms to gain leverage; only the strength in her fingers and wrists was in play against the slick-slimy surface. Her boot toes scrabbled, but her shins were still braced against the curve of the shaft, and it held her feet flailing almost uselessly in the water.

She ignored the overwhelming urge to exhale, knowing that the burning in her lungs would be tenfold worse if she gave in.

In the end, it was the mushy resilience of the fermenting waste along the floor that saved her; bone could not give way, nor concrete, but the thick organic mud flowed away from beneath her straining shoulders.

Zaik, godlord, bad enough to drown, but to drown in shit.... An insane giggle at the thought almost killed her, filling her mouth with cold rancid water as she pulled herself along the bottom stretch. Little strength was left as she broke free and floated up the vertical rise; she might have drowned on the surface

itself if fingers had not wound in her hair and held
her mouth above water as she retched and coughed.

Megan's voice came from above her head, harsh
and strained but with a note of relief. "Just think. If
I hadn't had you as a guide, I would have missed these
glorious sights of this wonderful city. Do you take all
newcomers through the best parts?"

She was braced in the vertical upshaft, knees and
back preventing her from sliding back down onto
Shkai'ra. She looked up as the Kommanza braced herself. Faintly above, she could see a dim light that
seemed brighter than the glowing slime rubbing off
the walls. The comment drew nothing from Shkai'ra
save a strangled "OUT. Get *out* of here."

They resumed the climb, the phosphorescence fading as they climbed higher. They had reached bare
concrete when the shaft grew slightly wider. After the
first few feet, Megan felt one hand slide again and
knew that the dull ache spreading through her hands
and knees was more than just the pressure of climbing
straight up. A slight projection in the wall gouged into
one kneecap, and she wished that she had her own
leather breeches rather than this useless shift. The Zak
levered herself up another foot on flayed knees and
realized that she could see the wall in front of her.

Another foot, and another. The light was strong
enough for her to see the damp patches where her
hands had touched the roughness of the concrete; a
little brighter, and she would be able to make out the
redness. She was cold and sweating with effort. Her
hand hit the wooden grill covering a side passage and
clung to the hard smooth bars as to the promise of
salvation.

"Zailo Unseen, don't stop," Shkai'ra panted behind
her. Leather saddle-trousers had left her knees at least
in better condition than her comrade's, but the need
for escape was a physical hunger now. Below she
could hear a plopping and splashing as the first tiny

fanged heads broke the surface of the water; soon claws would scrabble at the walls. The gators were still following.

"There's a grating," Megan explained as her fingers ran over it. Woven tightly, it would pass water and air but nothing living larger than a flea. The surface of the wood was oddly slick under her hands, treated somehow to shed the damp and resist rot.

"Of course there's a grating! You think folk want to wake up with the little crawlers sharing their straw? Open it!"

Megan braced herself and strained; her face was pressed to the unyielding surface, and she could see dimly up a sloping square tunnel. "I can't . . . budge it," she gasped.

Shkai'ra made a sound, mostly a groan but with the hint of a whimper in it. "It's meant to keep things out and let offal through—there's a spring holding it closed; it hinges in. Pull."

Megan cursed herself silently. Anger made her wrench sharply on the grille; there was a rending pop as the laminated wooden spring gave way.

"Just a few feet, and then into a lighted room," she whispered back to Shkai'ra. *Goddess, to be clean . . .*

CHAPTER XVIII

The Adderchief slammed a palm down on the polished surface of the table. The sound fell into a silence that filled the cellar room among stolen finery and bare, dew-weeping walls.

Around the table, the aristocracy of the Adderfangs sat, their eyes lost in the shadows of their hood-masks. They were the elite of their kind; aristocrats among thieves, assassins, alley bravos; overlords of protection rings, banks, the houses that satisfied tastes so curious that even Fehinnan law looked askance. Their organization was ancient by Illizbuah reckoning, which stretched back to times when the shape of the continents themselves had changed. There were rules, laws, a tradition of decorum. This display of emotion was unseemly. Behind the masks, certain calculations of power began to shift.

"Two of our best dead," the Adderchief continued. "On a standard mission, with only two clients—" she used the antiseptic terminology of the trade "—and those sleeping. An Adderfang killed in plain view—with his own fungus grenade!"

They winced at the humiliation. Face was important; their reputation was their livelihood. The Northside Serpentchief spoke, greatly daring:

"The red-haired barbarian . . ." He let the phrase trail off, no need to remind the Adderchief of the fiasco at Raisak Staaiun last year; no doubt the reference would not be lost on those considering new leadership, either.

The Adderchief's voice was much calmer when she answered, and for the first time that evening the man was frightened.

"That," she said in carefully measured tones, "is not spoken of in my presence. Not more than once."

The gathering tension was broken by a voice, but not from any of the six darklords. They rose to their feet and spread out with smooth economy; any observer would have noticed that they had lost little of the alley skills in their years of mastery.

The sound came from the garbage chute, in the wall against which their council table had been pushed. ". . . hinges in," they heard. "Pull."

There was the click of a miniature bolt-gun being cocked, and the first bolt slid from the magazine into the groove, its point black and tarry.

It was a shock to be free of the confining tunnel. Megan lay for a moment, panting, under the table before turning to help Shkai'ra. It was then that she heard the small sound. She froze. That had been a weapon, a weapon like . . . She looked up and stared along the shaft of a bolt into the eyes of a crouching figure in a black hood. From beneath the table, she could see the legs of five more.

Shkai'ra followed her, staggering as she crawled with the aftershock of adrenaline exhaustion. Slowly, she looked up and sighed.

"Oh, sheepshit."

*   *   *

The Adder kicked the last of their clothes into a corner and turned to finish tying Shkai'ra. Megan's breath hissed between her teeth as she pulled on the bindings. Her arms were strained behind her back, hands tied to feet and thumbs to toes. Lying on her back, her full weight lay on her wrists, sending sharp, random pain shooting up her arms. One Adderfang inspected the shot-pistol he'd taken from Shkai'ra.

"We go to pick grapes and the rivers run wine." The Adderchief laughed softly. "Five thousand gold we will get from the General Staff. Three thousand from the tight-arse priests." Her voice caressed. "Revenge best of all." She leaned forward and began heating a knife blade in the glass chimney of the alcohol lamp on the table before her. "A shame to spoil the temper of a good blade, but guests are always dropping in before the facilities are ready. Thoughtless of you, Red-hair . . . and for the love of the Sun's shadow, throw some water over them; meeting over a sewer is bad enough, without it crawling in with us."

The one had finished with Shkai'ra and rolled her on her back, her knees spreading in an uncontrollable reflex to ease the pain of unnaturally strained limbs. He gripped her above the hips and looked up at the leader.

"Not yet," that one laughed, muffled behind the black hood. "Later, when she needs cheering up."

Megan felt hate and rage flare up in her. She strained again, gasped as the icy water splashed over her, shook her head, and spat at the figure before her. "*Kouritz H'Rokatsk!* Your mother died of leprosy before you were conceived!"

The Adder backhanded Megan casually as she turned to watch their chief. A green light flared in Megan's eyes, and she fell silent, seeking something, anything, to fix her power on. The Adderchief knelt by Shkai'ra, considering. The others gathered closer. Shkai'ra's face was expressionless as the metal touched and sizzled briefly on the upper curve of one breast. The Adder gave a deep sound of satisfaction. "Don't talk too soon," she said happily.

Megan pulled harder on the twine securing her thumbs, as the sizzle filled her ears and the scent of scorched meat drifted out into the humid closeness of the room. She could feel the stiff, harsh fiber cutting into the skin, but if only she could pull . . .

She sagged a second; then what? A roomful of armed assassins against her. She strained again, and her nails grated on the stone beneath her. At the harsh sound everything went still. *Pull?* she thought. The directionless fury cooled suddenly to an icy knot within her, and her mind stopped its fruitless thrashing. By straining her hand, she could just use her nails . . . so. She ignored the cramping in her hand and felt the threads stretch and snap as she snicked through the first few. Not allowing her hands to fall free, she turned her gaze around the room and assessed her chances. *We are going to die*, she thought, but which one goes with us? The one tormenting Shkai'ra was just too far away, with others between. She turned her head to look at the one who had struck her and slowly began to shift her weight.

One of the black-clad figures glanced up uneasily. "Ah, Darkness," he said. The Adderchief looked up. "I think I can hear the little crawlers in the waste chute."

There was a barely perceptible stirring motion, quickly checked. The Adders spent much of their working lives below the surface, in the huge network of tunnels, sewers, and blind basements that spider-webbed beneath the streets, pumped free by the giant windmills along the walls. The labor of generations had pushed through new connections; there were chambers down below that had no direct connection with the light, and many a householder lived unknow-ing above. There were boundaries and territories in the sunless roads, and wars fought in darkness. The crawlers were the fear that never left those who passed their time below; no menace when you could shut a barrier on them, or run, but to be trapped with no way to block an entranceway . . .

Irritated, the Adderchief lifted the knife blade and studied it for a moment before reheating. "The grate is closed, and the spring is new," she said.

Shkai'ra's eyes snapped back from the infinitely remote place within her where they had been focused. Consciousness returned, and there was a hard, delighted malice in the carrying tone she used.

"Not since we broke it climbing in," she said.

The Adderchief hesitated as the others wheeled to stare at the opening in the wall. The first of the crawlers dropped with a click to the flagstones of the floor and scuttled, seeking the blood-scent from Shkai'ra's leg wound. Her hand wound in Shkai'ra's hair, and she tensed to draw the other woman forward onto the glowing iron. That moment, frozen between fear and hate, was her undoing. The Kommanza's head snapped sideways and her teeth sank into flesh; she could feel tendon and artery beginning to yield as she gripped and worried, heedless of the pain in her bound hands. The assassin lord shrieked, as much in surprise as in pain; it took her long moments to free herself, and blood trickled thickly from the ugly wound on her knife hand.

At the assassin's cry, Megan leaped, her hands arching out in a swift slash that tore through her target's face from brow to chin. She felt fluid spray across her fingers and her claws catch, slowed by the muscles but sinking to the bone as fatty tissue shredded away.

The woman staggered back screaming, hands clasping the ruins of her face. "My eyes! My eyes!" The black hood showed ragged, sodden edges through her fingers, and bright blood splattered her hands—blood and other fluids.

More crawlers had dropped from the hole, lashing in the feeding frenzy brought by the scent of blood. The assassins were moving with the speed that was their safety. Megan's cramped limbs failed her as she tried to finish the one, and she staggered. She never saw the blow that felled her; she only felt the stunning pain that blossomed in her back, a spinning kick knocking her into the wall. The world blacked out for a second.

The Adderchief alone paused at the door. "Remember me: Jahlini Buhhfud's-kin," she taunted. "As long as the crawlers give you time. They won't eat your hair; the priests will pay us for that, at least. Hearty appetite!"

The door slammed on the sound of her laughter, leaving them in the darkness and the sound of scales on stone. Below, the grate hung loosely against its moorings; each scrambling push of crawlers forced it open long enough for a few to pass, before the weight of the others dropped it back again. Soon the press passing through would float it wide open on a sea of backs; for a moment, only a hand of the tiny reptiles could pass at a time.

Shkai'ra twisted to crush one of the crawlers that had found her in the dark. "Megan! Megan!" she called, then, "Yie! Cowget bastards! Megan!"

"No . . . no need to shout," Megan gasped, desperately trying to regain the wind that had been knocked out of her as she levered herself up, first on her forearms, then knees, finally staggering to her feet.

Shkai'ra heard the table go over with a crash and a sliding, scrunching noise as it was pushed against the wall. "Say something, so I can find you," Megan said. "*Get me loose!*"

It was an instant's work to free Shkai'ra, and a bit longer to relight a lamp. They spent a hurried moment bracing the table; the tunnel was narrow, and there would not be enough of the reptiles pushing on the

surface of the wood blocking the entrance to shift it.
The crawlers already in the room were easy enough
to deal with; a hard quick stamp and a sound halfway
between a crunch and the bursting of a ripe tomato.
Even this close to the sewers, the smell was heavy;
the ruptured digestive tracts were foul with the food
the crawlers scavenged from the city's wastes.

At last they paused, silent except for deep panting
breaths. Shkai'ra leaned back against the wall, wincing
but accepting the pain for the support. Her eyes
strayed to the door, and a meditative look came into
them. Slowly, a smile flashed among the bruises and
drying blood, and she shared it with Megan.

The guards outside the council door were bored. It
was a high honor to guard such a meeting; common
shivpushers could not dream of it, and there had been
excitement enough, when all the dark ones had come
boiling out. The Southside Serpentchief had been badly
wounded by someone or something. But the cryptic
command to guard the prisoners while the crawlers
finished them had been baffling. What prisoners?

Still, they knew better than to question an order
from Adderchief Jahlini herself, especially with one of
her supporters removed from power so suddenly.

A scream came through the door—weak, exhausted.
The guards nodded at each other and crouched down
expectantly.

Surprisingly, words followed. "Oh, please . . . the
grate, it must have closed—there aren't any more
coming, but—ah, no! I'm tied—"

One of the guards rose to his feet and laid a hand
on the handle of the thick plank door. His companion
stopped him.

"Yo' out yo' taany ratfuck maahnd?" she drawled in
thick New City patois.

"Why shoul' the dark ones gi' all tha fun?" he said

petulantly. " 'Sides, order was to let crawlers gnaw 'em. No mo' crawlers, we goin' do it."

She nodded reluctantly. He approached the door with caution, pressing his ear to the wood and hearing nothing but a low moaning and a sudden cry of pain. Satisfied, he opened the door a tiny crack, standing well back; the other Adderfang poised to kick it shut and slide back the bar. He saw only Megan lying, apparently bound, on her back, knees spread, sobbing slightly. Behind the hood, his grin spread.

"Naace," he said. "Ev'n all bash' up. No need to kill fast . . ." Together, they strolled into the room. They never saw the Kommanza at all.

When they woke moments later they had been roughly bound with the fragments of the prisoners' ruined clothes.

"Naace," was Megan's comment.

Shkai'ra grinned down at them. "Sorry we can't stay and entertain you," she said, "but like thoughtful hosts, you've already provided that." She kicked the table away from the hole, and they bolted the door behind them.

The screams did begin soon.

"Now what? We've our weapons, assorted wounds and blood, and not much else. Once we find a way out, you think we can walk the streets like this?" Megan asked.

Shkai'ra shrugged. "Well, with those manacle scars and the battering, you could always claim to be an escaped slave."

A long search later, Megan spat, "Well, what can you see? Darkness take it! I want out of this warren. Is that the way out?"

Shkai'ra turned from the peephole, light falling in a thin shaft into the darkness of the cramped corridor. She turned to her companion, a half grin showing white in the gloom of the corridor. "There's a room out there, all right . . . from the decorations, I'd say a joyhouse on the Street of Dubious Delights."

"Better than the sewers."

Shkai'ra felt carefully around the edges of the panel; there was a sharp click and it swung inward. Before them was a sea of garishly colored pillows, broken here and there by waist-high padded platforms of varying shape. It was L-shaped, and a chorus of moaning and slapping sounds came from around the bend. "Door's probably that way," Shkai'ra said.

"Shall we interrupt?"

The customer was a woman in her middle years, on her knees amid a pile of pillows. Several of those were needed to support the lithe young boy crouched behind her, his hands clenched in rolls of tissue as he thrust with steady metronomic regularity. There was little chance of the woman seeing the two naked and bloody figures, as her eyes were closed and her face buried between the legs of the girl who lay before her. That one did see them, and raised startled brows at the sight of the edged metal in their hands.

Shkai'ra raised a finger to her lips and pointed toward the door with the tip of her saber. The girl nodded, leaned back into her nest of pillows, and resumed a series of artful moans, interrupted by bites at a peach she selected from a nearby bowl. Shkai'ra speared another with her sword as they padded by, Megan quirked up one corner of her mouth as they slipped by. *So what did you expect in a joyhouse?* she asked herself. She slipped out the door behind Shkai'ra and closed it softly. The mosaic was cool on her feet as they passed a number of closed doors. She nudged Shkai'ra. "Do they keep a tally of who enters? If not, then two more customers who had been, ah, a trifle enthusiastic, in the baths wouldn't be noticed, would they?"

The taller woman pursed her mouth. "Hmmm," she mused. Her eye lit on a cool blue hanging of light cotton. She ripped it down with a jerk of her wrist and began wrapping their weapons in it.

She threw an arm around Megan's shoulders, practicing a slight stagger. "I guess we're drunk. Sing in the shower, and if we complain about our clothing being stolen, we can probably get a couple of tunics. I know the management in places like these; I did a stint as a bouncer in one when I was down on my luck, once."

"Sing? I have a voice like a raven!"

"So be an *inconsiderate* drunk."

CHAPTER XIX

The Street of Dubious Delights roared around them as they staggered from the joyhouse doorway. Lamplight and window glow ran across the busy pavements; after the close incense-scented silence of the inner rooms, the smells of sweat and dung and garlic struck like a fist at taut nerves. They both knew that a crowd was the best hiding place, but something old and blind within urged them to seek out silence and darkness.

The two women leaned against each other, feet weaving and voices raised in discordant snatches of song. Two more foreign sailors would attract little notice, except from the pickpockets and slavers; scars and weapons would persuade them that these were best left alone, even with a small keg split between them. They passed the darkened mouth of an alley between two bright shop fronts, and reeled in among the fruit rinds and the smell of stale urine.

Megan tugged at the cheap cotton of the whorehouse tunic, brightly printed with what a Fehinnan would consider erotic patterns. "I'd like to get out of this wiperag," she began, then swayed to one side and began quietly vomiting against a wall. There was a limit; across half this huge and alien city, to kill and kill, and running in sewers like a hunted rabbit . . .

The sudden image of a murderous bunny turning at bay with a dagger in its teeth brought a half-hysterical chuckle that turned to a curse as she spat the taste of bile from her mouth.

"Fortunate that we didn't eat before this began," she said. Wordlessly, Shkai'ra laid her hand for a moment on the back of the Zak's neck; Megan didn't even begin to twitch away, accepting comfort.

"Now," Megan continued, "I want to hole up some-where. And shake for a sennight." She looked up at the brightening stars with mild amazement. "Only a little after sunset!" she said.

Shkai'ra nodded. "Warrior's time," she mused. A shake of the shoulders. "Best we go."

"Shkai'ra?" Megan said quietly.

"Hmmm?"

"Don't you think it might be a good idea not to go back to the Wayfarer? Even if they haven't picked up on the fact that we've gotten out and had us followed, they will be watching the inn and each other." They were still a few blocks away from the Weary Wayfarer, near the docks, having swung around to approach the inn from another direction than that of the New City. The streets down here were narrower and the poured-stone light posts fewer. The taste of bile was still raw in the back of her throat, as if she had scoured the membranes with sand, and she could smell the foul-ness when she inhaled.

The blond woman was silent for a moment, eyes scanning the road and rooftops. "Best we do," she said. "If possible. It's a big city, but hard to hide in if the right people are looking for you. Anywhere else, I'd not know the ways in—more chance of being caught off guard.

"They won't just try to kill us again," Shkai'ra continued, musing, ticking off points on her fingers. "*Eh*, they'll assume we've stashed the message and it'll come out if we die or vanish. *Ka*, too open an attack would reveal things to the Sun-on-Earth, and this must be a faction fight below that level, or we'd already be on the flaying tables. So they have to snatch us, for torture, without creating too much of a fuss. Not easy. Better if we got in unseen, yes, but what really worries me is the priests setting spooks on us."

"How good are the wizard-priests?"

Shkai'ra snorted. "At what, mounted archery? I couldn't tell a spook pusher from a spavined pimp—you'll have to handle that."

"I'm just a red witch with a few tricks," Megan said, casting a look back over her shoulder where drag marks from a mugging showed dark in the damp of the street, and checked her dagger in its sheath. "Foolery with wine cups, twistings of light and shadow ..." Her voice trailed into silence. "Could you get in unseen, alone?" They stopped in a puddle of dark in an alcove where one building jutted out. Megan sneezed at the odor of cat piss and almost missed Shkai'ra's snort.

"Can the Sun rise? What do you have in that small mind of yours?"

"Keep an eye out for trouble while I think."

At this, Shkai'ra shrugged and turned to peer down the street. "Don't think too long."

"*Cohrse nahht, gaaimun.*" At the rumbling bass at her back, Shkai'ra shied violently and whirled, sword already arcing out. The tall, burly, scarred Fehinnan porter made no move to dodge as the edge swept horizontally through his neck nearly two meters above the pavement, and said, in Megan's voice, from considerably closer to the ground, "Will this pass, in the dark?"

"Well, I'll be a sheep-raping offspring of a nomad

leper," Shkai'ra swore, peering more closely. The
edges of the figure seemed a little blurred; she
squinted and saw her companion's figure beneath, as
through muddy water.

The illusion vanished. Megan stood before her, wiping sweat from her forehead. "That's tiring. Especially
in warm weather. But there will be less effort when
the image is what people expect to see."

"Ahi-a," Shkai'ra said, tapping her chin. A cold
smile bent the wide, thin-lipped mouth. "Do you know
what an oxgoad is?"

The pile of wicker cages reached the full five-meter
height of the main kitchens. Below stretched the
orderly chaos of tiled floor, stretches of wooden
counter, and the great multiple brick hearths; the hen
pheasants clucked and circled wearily, as if resigned
to their fate. A violent squawking brought the attention of an undercook.

He saw the black-furred figure crouched in the second tier. "It's him!" he cried, through the hiss of fires
and thudding of cleavers. "The demon!" He reached
out, grabbed and threw the first object that came to
hand. As this chanced to be a stuffed and roasted
salmon fresh from the bake oven, a shrill scream followed the fish as it whirled through the oil-smoke
haze.

The salmon smacked flatly into the brick wall behind Ten-Knife-Foot. This alone might not have distracted him; a paw outstretched through the lattice of
a cage was only a hairbreadth from the cowering and
hysterical form of a quail in the far corner. The shower
of scalding oily droplets was sufficient to attract his
attention.

The cat streaked for the top of the pile. An
equally unthinking reflex drove the undercook with
a burned palm to attempt to climb the pile after the
four-footed nemesis of the Wayfarer's kitchen staff.

Even braced against a wall, the thin withes were inadequate to support his weight, and the pile exploded outward.

Most of the cages were secured only by straw. The oddly muffled sound of four and sixty woven cages thudding down over table and hearth and vat was lost under the noise of near twice as many birds freed and driven frantic in the same moment. A large turkey, with the wit of its farm-bred race, made a perfect ballistic trajectory into one of the great ceramic vats lining the opposite wall. A few brief flailing strokes of its wings distributed enough smoking-hot peanut oil on the near-naked skins of the kitchen slaves to send half a dozen screaming and leaping into the center of the floor. Turkeys of the four-footed breed scampered up the walls, their two sets of claws grappling at the bricks. Chickens landed and scurried, clucking. The quail and pheasants circled above, bedewing the trampled food and leaping servants below with guano. One with more presence of mind than the rest fluttered in to perch on the highest object available.

Unfortunately, this was the centerpiece of the kitchens this evening, an elaborate confection of spun sugar, crystallized caramel, ginger, and flake pastry, all adorning a centerpiece of froth-whipped cream and brandied sliced gooseberries. The bird landed, clutched, was entrapped, and sank layer by layer to lie thrashing amid the berries and cream, until its claws scrabbled through the pastry shell and spilled the fruit on the bare feet of Glaaghi, the head cook. There it formed a complement to much of the superstructure clinging to her face and shoulders.

She scraped the sticky goo out of her eyes just in time to see a fleeting black shadow, hampered by the hysterical quail in his mouth, dart between the legs of one of the burned kitchen slaves. The slave staggered as the cat hit him and tried to lift his other leg into the air as well, as a flailing wing hammered him across the shin. He fell into another servant, and both tumbled back to hit the edge of the trestle table holding that evening's late dinners out of the way until they could be delivered to the common room. The table arced like a released catapult, plastering the entire results of an evening of careful work against the opposite wall.

With a bellow that almost silenced the pandemonium, Glaaghi snatched a cleaver from the block just behind her and, skidding in fruit, feathers, pheasant dung, and sugar, went after Ten-Knife-Foot.

"Killing's too good for you, you scraping of a whore's scabs! I'll make cat soup without doing you the good of cutting that verminous, mange-ridden throat! I'll . . ." The tirade became a wordless roar.

The head cook was heavy, but capable of a good turn of speed once started, and unlike the cat, she saw no necessity to weave among feet and tables. Through the shrieking ruins of what had, not sixty seconds before, been a busy but well-ordered kitchen, she plowed with the ponderous inevitability of a knight's destrier. Ten-Knife-Foot had been making for the main stairs to the upper levels. Glaaghi's course made that impossible, and the cat turned and ran for the ladder-stair that descended to the storage level below. Most traffic to the bins was by the counterweighted lift in the far corner of the great room, or by the steep ramp from the rear laneway.

Ten-Knife had the quail gripped closely, at the base of the throat; there had been no time to attend to killing it, and the frenzied battering of its wings forced the cat to keep his head high as he weaved his way through the milling feet and down the rough wooden treads. It also slowed him enough to keep Glaaghi only a little beyond a cleaver-swing behind.

Good practice, Megan thought. She was trembling with the effort of keeping up the image, reaching to

prod the slow oxen walking to her left. *But I should
have hidden with Shkai'ra.* As the cart of new linen
rumbled around the corner and down the incline to
the door of the undercellar of the Weary Wayfarer,
she could just make out the flicker of movement marking the drawing back of one of the watchers who
waited for a small dark woman. Or a tall red-blond;
together or apart. A Fehinnan porter and his laundry
interested him not at all. "All right?" she muttered as
the cart creaked to a stop, below.

"... hot!" Shkai'ra's answer was muffled by the
bales of linen bedding, but Megan caught the last
word. With a grunt, she swung open the door that
would block them from outside view and dropped the
image, shaking hands and shoulders to loosen muscles
tense and fatigued by concentration. There was a surf-
roar of noise from somewhere in the bowels of the
inn; she wondered vaguely what it might be as she
turned to help Shkai'ra move the bales and get out.

The undercellar was dim. Little could be seen of
Ten-Knife-Foot save for the flutter of quail wings as
he raced across the littered floor and bounded to the
top of the oxcart. There he paused, glanced over one
shoulder at the looming figure of Glaaghi, and began
throwing sheeting aside with flying paws, mroewling
around a mawful of feathers.

Tense and made sensitive by the stain of maintaining an image for much longer than she'd ever done
before, Megan caught a blast of cat-thought ... *big-
one, safe, help big smelly big big watch-out, help
feather spit, eat-good, help big bright-sharp, hide, run,
hide, here safe, hide-with, help run, angry, SNEEZE
feathers, HELP* ... Shkai'ra's hand snaked out between the bales, snapped the quail's neck, and pitched
the cat to the other side of the cart over Megan's
head. "Stupid beast, go away!" she said.

Glaaghi thundered past Megan who was leaning
casually on the cart, and beyond, no longer able to

track the cat by the sound of the shrieking bird, still chasing shadows.

Shkai'ra heaved a bale of sheets off her shoulders and rose to stand.

"Something tells me," Megan said, looking down at her claws to hide her tired smile, "that there's going to be another itemized bill." Shkai'ra giggled almost hysterically and climbed out of the cart. Leaning on each other, they staggered upstairs to bed.

In a comfortable corner of the roof, far above, Ten-Knife-Foot settled down to rid his quail of the irritating feathers

CHAPTER XX

As the door closed behind them, Megan headed reflexively for the bed, tired and aching in every limb, but forcing herself to stop and check the warding on the room. She regarded the ward sign, the thread-thin band of silver outlined in red, both now bracketed in a thicker band of *blue*. Someone much more powerful than she was reinforcing her spell, subtly and with care. Someone she had felt before. Yeva. Megan looked over at Shkai'ra and said nothing. None but the most powerful would even think of checking for these wards; perhaps only their God-King could see them, should he be interested—at least from what everyone's reaction was when the Avatar was mentioned.

Every pillow, from both beds, was piled against the framework between two of the posts, forming a nest just below where Shkai'ra's sword hung. In the middle of this Megan sat curled, with the sheet pulled up close. She frowned at her nails and resumed rasping at one of them, not satisfied with the edge. Shkai'ra looked up from a cushion where she had been painting her scratches and abrasions with the brown liquid from the bottle in her hand, almost flinching as it stung in each wound. "You'll wear them away if you keep that up."

"Hmm." Megan's reply was an affirmative mumble that showed she wasn't really listening. "I'm sick of this. This is not my idea of a restful stop on my journey home."

"Hah," Shkai'ra snorted. "You'll rest when you're a withered ancient of forty or fifty snows. If we live that long, I'll join you by the fire!" Megan glanced at her, nodded absently, tossing the pouch they had retrieved from Harriso, when the army's offer had seemed to be the best.

"There is only one person that we could possibly give this message to without getting our arms and legs pulled off before having our throats cut."

"But she'd turn us into frogs . . . or those slimy worms that live under rocks. I don't want to live the rest of my life catching flies!" Shkai'ra said, only half in jest.

"Look," Megan said shortly, dangling the pouch by one string. "This I cannot—understand?—cannot break. The priests, the army faction and the Lowlords have had a good shot at killing us. Every time they lose face, they'll try harder next time. They have to, from what you tell me."

A baffled voice drifted in from the corridor rather plaintively. "Why am I carrying this tray?"

Megan sat up sharply. "Oh shit, I forgot to cancel the meals!" Shkai'ra, got up and jerked the door open. Her frustration showed plainly by the way she snapped at the servant. "Room four!" She grabbed the tray and slammed the door shut.

The servant stood looking at the door and then at her hands, counting slowly on the fingers; she looked up and down the corridor, counted again, turned the hand over to count a third time, and finally shrugged and went downstairs.

Shkai'ra stood a second by the door, then put the tray down and wrenched the cork out of the bottle. "Well, then. The priests won't stay bought, nor the General-Commander, and we can't buy the Adderfangs in the first place; we just have to be better than they are for a while."

She chuckled again and poured the cups full. "Life won't be so bad with webbed feet." She laughed, as she drank the red wine. "I'll pick out my lilypad. Hard on Ten-Knife; quail are scarce in the swamps."

The cat looked up from the bed, then closed his eyes again. He was lying on his back, paws splayed, stomach comfortably rounded. A pink and reminiscent tongue lapped once at his jowls.

Shkai'ra tore the leg off the barbecued duck. "Not enough alcohol here to slow us down; only one bottle," she said mildly. Finishing with a comfortable belch, she crossed to her room and returned dragging a chest. Licking grease off her fingers, she flicked the latch open. "But this time I'm taking some precautions."

She lifted the lid with a toe. Inside, neatly wrapped in waterproof bindings, was a set of Kommanz cavalry armor, the gear worn by horse archer-lancers on the prairies of the Red River Valley: flared helmet with a long nasal, back and breast of four-ply lacquered bisonhide on fiberglass, laminated thigh and arm-guards of the same, greaves and round shield.

"With all that? The clatter will wake next century's dead. And if we have to climb . . . best cross your warhorse with a cat. Or a fly."

Ten-Knife came to nose hopefully at the box, sniffing at the familiar scents of leather and oil and varnish. "Mrrrrffeoooow?" he said.

"No, lazy one, you don't get to see the countryside from horseback," Shkai'ra said. To Megan: "I'm quite nimble in this, but you're right. This is what I wanted, since that sheep-raper stole my shotpistol."

She pulled a rosewood case from its clip along one side of the box. Inside was a curving shape of wood and horn and fiberglass, a little over a meter long. The central grip of the bow was hardwood, carved and shaped, with a cutout to allow shafts to pass through the centerline of the weapon. The thick laminated arms ended in offset bronze wheels; the string passed over them, adding pulley and camming action to the power of the draw. Four long arrows snapped into a quickdraw quiver along the grip, and thirty more were in the round leather tube she slung around the small of her back.

The weapon turned in her hands, dark and shining and lovely, coming alive as she strung it with a complex tool of bronze and bone. From the box, she strapped on the armguards of her armor and slipped a bone ring over her right thumb. Then she drew to the ear, thumb lapped over the cord and hand locked around it.

"Kill at a thousand paces with this," she said. "Penetrate armor at half that; the drawstrength is two-thirds my bodyweight. Up close, the shaft will go right through a horse and kill you on the other side."

Megan padded over and tested the string. "Nice to be able to knock them out farther away. If we see them first." She turned to the window, easing it open. The warding should keep anyone from looking; it would take a light shining out in darkness to break that. Across the way . . .

"Shkai'ra, the ones with the blowguns are still waiting across the way, I think," she said.

The tall woman slung the bow across her back. "Six gets you one they're still dogging the back, too."

"Then how will we get to Yeva?"

"And you the acrobatic one," Shkai'ra said, raising

a finger until it pointed at the ceiling. "Until we get a few blocks away, then catch a pedicab."

Megan snorted lightly. "If you can overcome your fear of heights," she said.

Megan moved silently over the hard, slick tile of the roof, faint moonlight melding her dark clothing into a colorless wash. Above, the huge soft stars glowed in a sky of scattered cloud. This was Low Town, the tenements of the poor, smelling of bad drainage and fever and slum. Mingled in among the tenements were the occasional mansions of wealthy kinfasts whose trades fattened on the swarming humanity crowded here; those were well guarded.

Shkai'ra followed, almost as agile, but with an occasional clatter of boot on baked clay. *More heights, and never a big enough lead to get down,* she thought. Her face was set; in the Zekz Kommanz, the highest thing was a warrior's lancepoint, and she did not like the roof road.

"Is this ... really needful?" she whispered. "I haven't heard them for a while, and the streets would be much faster."

Megan motioned her to silence and poised, her eyes closed. It had rained recently, and the tile was dusty/damp, smelling of earth. She strained her hearing: a squeak. *Cork, squeaking on a wet surface.*

An image flashed into her memory, the Adderfang dropping down onto the window ledge beside her. The cork-soled sandals and the sound of him shifting his weight as he struggled for balance, in the instant before she swept him to his death.

"No, it isn't really necessary," she whispered. "If you don't mind having them above you."

The red-maned head flashed around. Lips skinned back; she sank down beside her comrade. They lay and peered back across the roof, only their eyes and the tops of their heads showing over the ridge.

Coolly, their gaze swept over acre upon acre of jumbled roof, like a relief map of the mountains, broken here and there by the dimly lighted trench of a road.

Moonlight and knife-edge shadow flattened the cityscape into a pattern treacherous to the eye. They both waited with the hunter's patience, taking slow deep breaths, their attention traveling steadily from the farthest to the nearest point in smooth arcs.

Megan saw the figures a fraction of a second earlier, black-clad, stealing noiseless from one puddle of deep shadow to darker ones. There flashed before her eyes the basement room and the sizzle of her friend's flesh, and the intense desire to watch them all die shook her. Her hand clenched reflexively, driving nails to grate on the tiles, then loosening to fall to her knife hilt. The shadowy figures vanished, reappeared, flitting.

The Kommanza laid her hand on Megan's, where it was drawing forth the knife. "Don't want to let them get that close," she mouthed, as Megan's attention snapped to her; she tapped the bowcase slung across her back. "Let's fight *and* run," she said, defusing the rage shining in the Zak's eyes. Her words even drew a smile as Megan nodded.

It would be well to cut the odds a little, and the pursuers were on their trail anyway. Vindictiveness would make them more careless. *I never liked running,* Megan thought.

Shkai'ra squirmed farther down the roof and touched the wheelbow in its leather case, running knowing fingers over the familiar weapon. The pulley wheels at either end responded smoothly to her gentle tug, spinning silently on well-oiled bearings. Shooting from a solid roof would be easy after a galloping horse.

She drew the one and a half meters of bowstave from its case with a convulsive move that sent her sliding two armlengths down the low-pitched rooftop.

Swearing softly, she wormed her way back to the roof-tree. Megan was on her back, staring along the long edge of the roof and the broader street that had blocked their way, thinking. "Don't take too long," she said.

"Then tell 'em not to move around," Shkai'ra answered sardonically, taking a quick look over the ridge. The pursuers were closer now, about two hundred yards. The first had paused on a rooftop, risking exposure for a better chance at spotting the quarry.

Shkai'ra edged back, far enough that she would be hidden kneeling, and nocked a shaft. She rose, taking a deep breath and emptying her mind. Practiced from birth, the art cut channels in the synapses; all you had to do was get out of the way. She knew the smooth arc of the arrow, the target, the sudden jolt as the two met. The nock of the arrow drew to her ear. The point came up, elevated for the arching shot. There was a rattle and clack as she loosed and the long string of the wheelbow hummed through the pulleys.

The sound must have carried to the target; he came up from his crouch, head darting this way and that as he sought the unfamiliar sound. He was still seeking a second later when the shaft sliced down vertically out of the night. Sound carried well, here above the muffling walls and streets; they could clearly hear the crunch as the three-bladed hunting head slammed into his neck just inside the collarbone, and the single muffled grunt. That was all, before the body collapsed loosely and slid out of sight along the reverse slope of the distant roof. The Adders were determined to capture them, with Jahlini's anger to face if they failed. Over that ridge boiled a dozen of them, running openly now that their quarry had revealed itself.

Shkai'ra's hands moved with blurring speed; the second shaft pinned an Adder as she leaped from one roof to the next. The massive power of the heavy bow stopped her leap, a focused jump losing direction, turning into a loose tumble three stories to the pavement. The third arrow drilled through the back of a knee as the nightstalkers took cover; the fourth knocked chips of tile into the eyes of an incautious one who had turned to peer from behind a roof ridge.

"Not bad, at that distance and in darkness, without good footing," Shkai'ra mused happily. She had never been judged more than a passable archer among her own people; the saber was her favorite weapon.

"Stop singing your own praises and come on," Megan hissed, her voice harsh. The knife was a good weapon, but it lacked reach. "I've spotted a route that will give us some time."

She slid down the roof, caught at an ornament, and landed cat-footed on the high courtyard wall below. The Zak teetered a moment, standing in the slant of the V of obsidian knives laced along the wall's top, and glanced at Shkai'ra.

"Come on," she continued impatiently. The razor flakes of stone were angled to prevent searching hands from climbing over the boundary, not to stop a walker from traveling along it. Carefully, steadily, she paced along it, then halted. Her eyes flicked left. The courtyard gaped, a high building beyond it, joining at right angles to the low corner-block they would climb to from this wall. An agile pursuer might well . . . would use that building, and leap to the one she and the Kommanza sought. She looked back at her companion and flashed a single smile before running nimbly along the remainder of the route. She would need a place to rest and concentrate.

Shkai'ra blinked at the expression on the Zak's face, shrugged, and dropped to the wall. Her larger feet were more awkward in the narrow slot of footing; one glass blade broke and clattered to the courtyard. She looked down to see a dozen tiny hairy dogs dance out beneath. Their eyes were bright black buttons as they yapped and squealed at the figures above.

Like noisy mops with legs, Shkai'ra thought. So, the Slinkers should be right behind, drawn by the noise.

Just then there was a crunch and one of the dogs fell silent, its final yipe astonishing from an animal so small. *Slinkers*, Shkai'ra thought, concentrating grimly on maintaining her balance. She had never liked the two-stage alarm system favored by Illizbuah's richer merchants and vicelords. The nails-on-slate squealing of the dogs was bad enough, but the giant weasels gave her a spider-on-skin distaste that had little to do with their deadliness. A tiger was more dangerous, but somehow cleaner; and she would not care to be the slave assigned to the kennels, soundless enchanted whistle or no. *It's wasteful of dogs*, she thought. *Even if they do order the little fuzzballs in job lots.*

Reaching the roof, she hauled herself up beside Megan, ducking her head to wipe her face on the short sleeve of her tunic.

"I thought you were in a hurry," she said in a whisper. "Why delay now?" Her hand went out, then was snatched back as if from live coals. Megan had traced a figure into the tile with the point of her dagger and slashed the palm of her hand. With an emphatic gesture, her bloody hand descended into the rune as a low hum began, a note that shuddered on the edge of hearing, impossibly deep for one so small.

The Adders were coming across the diagonal with frightening speed, like human spiders, each hand and foot placed with finicky delicacy. Their final leap down from the higher building was a marvel of fluid authority. So much so, that for a moment Shkai'ra too seemed to see a carven ledge where their grasping fingers reached.

Unfortunately for the assassins, there was no ledge. They were close enough for the women to see a paired expression of disbelief on their faces, mouths straining under the black masks. The confident skill of their movements turned to a frenzied scrabbling for nonexistent finger holds as they fell into the Slinker pack below.

The third scrambled on the tiles, flailing to shed momentum before it carried her over the edge of the courtyard. Alert brown muzzles and bright red eyes followed with disappointment as she teetered on the eave, then catwalked back over the roof ridge.

Shkai'ra looked down, to see a long shadow disengage from the pack and run with humping swiftness back toward the kennel. The moonlight was treacherous, but the Kommanza was fairly certain there was a leg in the creature's mouth. "Hunger's the best sauce," she murmured, and turned to the Zak. "Useful trick. Now, I think, they will be annoyed."

The remark passed unheard. Megan's breath slowed, and her eyes focused again. The hum spiraled up into silence; she jerked at her hand, and it came free of the tile with a slight hesitation, as if stuck to the clay. Yet there was no sign of a wound on her hand or mark on the roof. . . .

"Hmmm?" she said, and gestured vaguely behind her in the direction of the New City market square. "That's the way, from here."

The Zak looked down into the courtyard. Chitterings and ripping sounds told of a quarrel over the Adderfangs, and all the dogs were silent, even the last, as it moved in a straight line across the flagstones, desperate speed in its leg-blurring scamper. The form that undulated smoothly behind it gave every appearance of leisurely disinterest as it gained.

CHAPTER XXI

Kilometers of roofs later, Megan dropped from the limb of a chestnut tree onto the creaking shingles of a tall building. She wiped bark from her hands; they crouched, looking back along their track from the vantage of the fourth-story height.

Shkai'ra rubbed gingerly at one buttock. "Hope the Glitch-damned thing thing wasn't poisoned," she said.

"Don't worry," Megan replied. "That was streets ago; you would have stiffened and fallen if it was." Her casual tone hid her worry. She paused and touched one raw-scraped cheek, wincing. "Dogsucking offspring of darkness, but I feel as if I've been beaten all over with a club!" She paused again, an expression of disgust creeping over her features. "What on earth is that stink?"

"Zaik knows. Burning sugar, maybe?" Shkai'ra's eyes scanned backward. "Those last three are persistent, considering how we've whittled them down this night; if we could only be sure of enough lead, we could take to the streets and outrun them—"

She froze. Slowly, her head turned to face Megan's. They sank down on the rough, splintery surface of the shingles. Even over the cloying thick sweetness in the air, they could smell the dusty, sharp odor of dry rot.

"Three?" Shkai'ra said.

"Then why are we running?" Megan replied.

Shkai'ra raised herself on one elbow, until her eyes were just level with the rooftree. "It's taking them a long time," she whispered.

Behind them a power windmill turned idly, disengaged, its eggbeater blades a figure-eight curve against the bright southern stars. Shkai'ra's eyes narrowed in thought.

A knife burst up through the thin sun-warped shingles, exactly in the spot her throat had been a moment before. At full extension the point of the blade kissed the skin under her chin, enough to start a tiny trickle of blood. The black-clad arm withdrew, too swiftly for her to seize and break it.

She sprang erect; her saber snapped out and down through the papery squares of cedar below her. No result; they must have had a quick escape planned. Arrows would be useless.

"Come on, down and in," she called, turning and half running, half sliding toward the eaves of the low-pitched roof. "There'll be an opening under the roof. We can't let them get out into the darkness."

The Zak followed, feather-light and soundless where Shkai'ra's boots brought muffled crunching. The overhang of the roof was slight, and beneath it louvered vents gave out into the night. There was light from within; belike the owners of this place kept that and a night-watcher on hand. Neither would have accomplished much against an Adderfang.

They gripped the eaves, backflipped onto the sloping surface of the ventboards that opened in a half-V to the outer air, and paused, surveying what lay within. The place might have been a tenement or mansion four centuries ago when the New City had been first enclosed. Now it had been converted to a manufactory for making the cheap hard candy Illizbuah's lower classes loved. A huge circular vat filled one end of the floor, four stories below; others of smaller size were grouped down the walls, two sets of three separated by a raised plankwalk. The interior had been gutted, save for structural timbers bracing the concrete-block walls and a few for cranes and hoists.

At their feet lay a sparse network of such rafters. A ladder led down to the second floor, where there was a skeletal tracing around the central opening, and a decked timber floor along one wall where a hoist door stood open beside a swing-out crane. The three Adderfangs turned from the platform.

"I'll take the ladder," Shkai'ra said. Her quiver was empty, and that was her only distance weapon. Megan nodded, and headed purposefully toward a dangling pulley and hook arrangement that swung out over the center of the building's interior.

The ladder was simply an upright timber that had had crosspieces pegged on, leading down to a foot-wide horizontal beam. Shkai'ra took the inside, putting the wood between her and the Adderfangs, and made speed by dropping straight down with an occasional grab to slow herself. It was only twice man-height, and she wanted to have sound footing on that beam before the blackcoat was within striking distance. After that, she did not await much trouble; the assassin would be more at home fighting here where one step to the side would end fifteen meters down on flagstones, but long knife against a Kommanz cavalry saber was no contest.

The assassin had the same thought. As he ran cat-certain along the narrow beams toward the ladder, he unlimbered a weapon quite unlike a knife. It was a chain, two meters in length; the last half of the links had outer edges honed to a razor edge, and the tip ended in a ball of spikes. A fighting-iron, and deadly if well used.

The end curled around the ladder and came within a hairbreadth of taking the Kommanza's face with it when it withdrew. Shkai'ra saved herself with an astonishing sideways leap onto the horizontal beam; she landed off balance, and beat a shuffling retreat to keep the whistling length of metal out of reach. The figure in black handled the strange killing-tool like a master, keeping it whirling in a great fan of figure eights that put moving metal between every inch of his body and Shkai'ra's long curved sword.

She backed, feet groping for balance, right foot forward, poised to lunge. This was like the standard foot-fighting without shield stance, using the menace of the point to substitute for a defensive weapon, but the need to remember the gap on both sides of her was a continual nagging distraction, and the chain was the natural enemy of the sword; it could be thrown hard against the edge and used to drag the blade wielder off balance. Once balance was gone half the fight was lost; and this thing could curve right around a parry and cripple you. On flat ground, or in armor, or with a shield, she would have felt confident enough. As it was . . .

No shadow of doubt showed in face or stance or poise. Her mouth was slightly open, breath even, eyes slitted and wary. The blade poised, then flashed out at the vulnerable spot where the hands whirled the chain. He jerked back, but used the same motion to pivot the swing of the fighting-iron down toward her feet. It would slice them open above the boots, or wrap around her ankles and throw her off. She leaped straight up and cut, but there was no force behind it when a good landing was so crucial, nor time to draw the slash. A line of red opened on his upper arm; the eyes behind the hood widened slightly. She gave ground, feet still moving in a fast light shuffle. He followed and raised the chain at an angle; the death-circle of his swing now centered at eye level, angling out toward her.

Megan had run along the beam to the spot opposite the loading doors. Her position was too exposed and vulnerable for wisdom, but she hoped that the sheer outrageousness of that would throw them off. Apparently it did. She dodged a shuriken as if it were a thrown knife in a *cniffta* game and reached the center of the beam. The sheave pulley was locked at the top by a friction block, rope coiled on the wood and dangling down. She seized the coil and looked to see one assassin heading for another ladder. The other watched them all coolly, and directed. Megan's hands had gathered the right amount of rope . . . she hoped. She leaped straight back, allowing the beam itself to pull her into the correct arc to knock the one straight out the doors, or crush her against the crane. Neither worked.

As she swung, the younger assassin spun around and brought up a blowgun, while the other leaped out of her way. She was just too close to change direction and arched past. As she missed, she felt the jar as a dart sprouted in the rope by her arm; her other hand swept around with the trailing end of the rope. The hook on the end of it took the young Adderfang under the chin. Her weight dragged him across the floor to fall toward the vats below, but the snapping of his neck prevented the jawbone from tearing out entirely. The body hung somewhere between the second and third floors, twitching spasmodically as nerves died in the already-dead body.

Megan landed in a roll on the loading bay platform and came to her feet, knife in hand, to confront the leader of this group. She stared into eyes gone black with hate and thought, *Of course, I've killed her guildkin . . . as I will kill her*. Her boots grated on the dust and grit that had collected; it smelled of ragweed and dust, drowning in burned sugar. It was furnace-hot up under the roof, and she could feel the sweat prickling on her lip and running down her face as she watched the assassin before her. *Let her think it's fear-sweat.* Above the mask, dark eyes glinted. To the side, she heard the struggle between Shkai'ra and her opponent, harsh gusts of breath and the scuff of leather on wood, but she couldn't shift attention from the death that threatened. Here, with feet of space echoing below, the speed and quickness that could compensate for the other's reach would be nearly useless.

An outsider would have seen nothing fearful in the figures of the two women facing one another save the knives gleaming in their hands. The only moves they made, at first, were slight shiftings of the feet and hands. Eyes locked on her opponent's, Megan raised her dagger a fraction of an inch, playing through the possible sequence that would end with the knife buried in the Adder's guts, and found it instantly countered. Play and counterplay . . . every move, even to the constriction of eyes, vital to the death of the other. Not showy, but the one who failed first would die.

Testing, Megan twitched the hand farthest away from the other, another knife suddenly appearing in it to spin toward her opponent. The Adder leaned aside and countered, her blade tearing the cloth over Megan's thigh as she retreated. All of ten seconds had passed, feint and counter; both were breathing hard. The hollow sound of the thin floor warned Megan that she couldn't retreat much more; the edge was too near, just a few feet behind her.

The Adderfang allowed herself to be distracted for a fraction of a second by the clang of steel on steel on the beams across the building. That was enough. As her eyes flickered back to Megan, the Zak feinted again. The Adder lunged to counter and committed herself. A flurry of movement and the assassin sprang back out of range. A tearing sound had marked contact, and the cloth of the assassin's hood gaped open at throat height, though Megan's blade still showed clean.

Dogsucker! Megan thought. *That one should have done it. This one is as fast as I am. A trick is what I need . . . and a good one.* Again the game had begun, the Fehinnan determined not to be taken in a second time.

The edge was a body-length behind Megan, and she could hear the thick plopping sounds below as the sugar boiled. Her idea was dangerous. She began to drop her guard as though tiring. She allowed her eyes to shift and made her breathing harsh. She licked her lips and began to edge back, showing classic signs of fear and tiredness. Her counters to the other's moves slowed, and she let fear show on her features. Behind the mask of her face, she watched the assassin accept the messages she was sending. When the Adder was sure enough to begin forcing her toward the edge, she backed and flung the dagger at the assassin as if her nerve had broken.

As her hand shifted to the throwing position, the other lunged and came in for the kill. Megan fell back, trying to avoid the knife, but taking it in the shoulder rather than the throat; she locked crossed hands around the assassin's arm, then rolled. The Adderfang was moving forward already, couldn't stop, and she flew over Megan's head, assisted by a boot in the belly. Shock just had time to dawn in her eyes, changing to panic, as she realized that she was not going to land on this level.

Megan followed through, feeling the edge of the floor hit her at chest height. She threw herself forward and hung, held by the leverage of her outstretched arms and her claws dug into the wood, the grating shock of the knife in the bones of her shoulder greying the room out. The assassin fell, spiraling down, reach-

ing to catch something, anything. She landed in the
main vat, the force of her fall driving her under. She
flailed to the surface, screaming horribly as the boiling
sugar pulled her down again. She thrashed as if to
climb the air, flesh already loosening from the heat.
A last clenching of a grey-cooked hand and she was
gone. Megan swung one leg up onto the edge and lay
there a moment on her belly, panting. She watched a
drop of her blood follow the Adderfang, then her head
snapped up to Shkai'ra's fight.

Dark One take the knife! She pulled herself up and
dragged the thing in her shoulder loose, stuffing cloth
into the wound to stanch it. The knife was bent where
it had turned on the bone; useless. She pushed the
pain to the back of her mind and ran through the
maze of beams to help her friend.

Shkai'ra had been backing steadily before the whir-
ring menace of the chain. They had edged around the
corner and were on one of the slanting diagonals that
angled back toward the long walls of the factory; soon
the concrete blocks would be at her back.

Zaik eat him, Shkai'ra thought. *That thing has too
much reach, and he's too good. Stalemate, but only as
long as I can retreat.*

She hawked a thick glob of phlegm from her dust-
dry mouth—and cut backhand for his throat. He
struck: the chain wrapped itself around the blade in a
shrinking circle of blur. With a wrench, he hauled
forward to throw her off the beam.

Shkai'ra had been waiting for that; she spat into his
face, used the pull to leap forward into the corps-a-
corps, and the sudden slack on her sword gave space
to strike savagely inward with the eaglehead pommel.

Blinded, off balance, the Adderfang then showed he
was a combat master, not merely skilled. There was
only one possible move that would restore the tension-
grip of his weapon on her sword; he took it, and
leaped backward and down for the next level and the

longitudinal beam that ran nearly beneath them. The chain sprang taut as his weight plummeted downward, and he used the inertia of Shkai'ra's body to swing himself to a secure landing.

The Kommanza did not even have the option of dropping her blade; it was secured to her wrist by a hide loop. She fell from the beam, twisting in midair as her fall once more brought slack into the chain. The long steel slid free with a slithering rasp, but there was no time to bring her feet back beneath her. With a monstrous, flesh-straining effort she caught the first-story beam as she fell, the sword dangling loose from its strap, her body hanging beneath the timber balks.

Her opponent's face was hidden behind the mask, but she could detect his grin from the set of the narrow strip across his eyes. Her mind still functioned, smoothly turning over alternatives; would keep doing so until the heart ceased. From below came waves of sticky, unbearably sweet fumes, stifling hot. Ahead of her, behind the Adderfang pacing forward under cover of whirling iron, a black shape hurtled downward to the great vat at the head of the factory; there was a single hideous scream.

She ignored it. *Maybe I can bring my legs up and kick at his ankle,* she thought. It would mean enduring at least one bone-shattering strike from the knife-edged chain, but if she could override the pain . . .

Splinters drove into face and arms as she hugged the wood, jackknifed, poised a boot. There was little chance she could hold on with a broken arm, still less with her skull laid open, but the alternative was to let go. Below, the smaller overflow vat bubbled.

Megan took in the scene even as she began to sprint for the ladder, realizing there would be no time for that. The assassin's chain clinked as he shook it to assure free play; Shkai'ra tensed for the ultimate move.

There seemed to be a great deal of thought as Megan's body moved. A memory of the Adder leader's scream as she struck the boiling sugar. A knife laid hilt first in her hand. Her own voice: *Celik Kizkardaz, there is Steel between us*.

There was only one possible move; half a dozen steps along the central beam gave her momentum, and she leaped out and down. An extra story's height gave her arc the distance needed across the open space; the assassin took the full force of her body in the moment before his upflung metal whip could slash down on Shkai'ra's hands. Her bootsoles shocked into bone, halting her in midair as the energy of her falling body was transferred to the man's heavier frame. The assassin fell sideways; the flailing chain wrapped itself around his neck as he plunged. A crack of breaking bone sounded as he landed on his back across the edge of the vat.

Megan fell, straight down. Her hands reached out for the beam under which Shkai'ra hung; claws scraping wood in passing as her eyes locked with the Kommanza's.

Oh, shit, Shkai'ra thought. She twisted her head to see Megan land in the soft, syrupy goo of the smaller holding vat, and lie for a second before sinking.

The frozen instant seemed to last forever. The Zak had not sunk at once, the sugar could not be fully liquid. Bubbles broke the surface, and even as a hand groped through into the air, Shkai'ra heaved herself to the beam and knotting a dangling rope around her waist. With an almost physical effort, she thrust away the thought of scalding, treacly liquid candy forcing its sluggish way past nose and mouth.

Not time to sing her deathsong yet, she thought desperately. *But if she can't remember to keep her mouth closed, I'm going to kick her next incarnation's arse.*

She pushed herself off the beam, swooping down

to halt with a jerk that left her heart in her mouth; or it might not have been solely that. Heat lay on her skin like liquid; she gritted teeth and thrust her arms into the vat of hardening caramel.

"Ai!" she gasped, groping. Not hot enough to scald the skin off, but . . .

She thrust the sensation away, along with the thought of what it might do to her hands.

The hot candy burned, flowing thickly into Megan's eyes and nose and ears, weighing every limb with pain, heat that clung and seeped. Megan pushed the blackness aside and wondered why she was not dead; reflex blew air past her teeth and then clamped lips shut. She struggled and thrashed to reach the surface as the candy forced its way into the corners of her mouth. Burning, burning. Instinct turned her face down into the cooler lower strata. Air exploded from stressed lungs, and for a moment her mouth and nose were clear. She remembered hearing that drowning was a gentle death—*who told them so?* Her hand broke the surface for a moment, then it was lost, and the knife wound weakened her. Nausea overwhelmed her; the hands in her hair seemed like the first dream of death.

Shkai'ra filled her lungs, gripped; her whole body arched in a steady, controlled convulsion as she pulled Megan from the syrup's embrace. Eyes stared blindly, rims white. The air came out in a long *hugggggggn* of effort, as the muscle stood out on arms and shoulders and back, hard as tile under the skin. The Zak's shoulders broke the surface, and Shkai'ra transferred her grip to the belt, hands scrabbling for purchase in the soft slickness of hardening candy. The legs came free; the larger woman twisted against the rope around her waist, turned the other over her arm, and jerked her under the diaphragm to force any blockage clear of the breathing passages. The pulse under her hand beat quick but strong.

Shkai'ra looked up once she was sure that the limp weight in her arms was not dying. Suddenly, she realized that she was hanging straight as a plumbline over the center of the vat, all sides equally out of reach.

This, she mused, *is going to take some thought.*

Megan's eyes lost their glaze as full consciousness returned. Shkai'ra knelt beside her, sponging the gummy contents of the vat away from her face with a dampened cloth; the expression on the hawk features was amused and almost tender.

"You're undersized," she said with a slow smile, laying a hand on the other's cheek. "Maybe I should throw you back?" Then, more seriously, "If you do something like that to me again, I might get really angry."

Megan grasped the hand, and felt some of the small hairs behind her ears pull out by the roots as they stuck. Irritation, relief, and a crazed amusement at living roused her more than the blessed feeling of cool air on her skin.

"Do to *you?* As if it wasn't bad enough to nearly get me drowned in *sewage water* . . ."

Slowly she sat up in the circle of Shkai'ra's arm and realized that they were leaning against the overseer's walkway. She turned to her companion and made mock threatening hitting motions.

"And if you ever make me risk my skin like that again, I'll refuse to cry your name to the wind for your funeral." The sweet stench had a strange undertone now, and the body of the young Adderfang overhead jerked slightly lower as tissue slowly tore. Megan began to pry hard caramel from her fingers. "*Versht za?* Do you understand?" She caught her lip between her teeth as the burns under the candy became painfully obvious. "I'd better not try to pull this off . . .

my skin would come with it." She began to laugh, leaning into the circle of Shkai'ra's arm. "In . . . in . . . candy! What a gruesome joke."

Shkai'ra grinned in response. "You can't be too bad, then." She looked around at the scattered bodies. "Gods and demons, the candy is going to taste odd this month—and we both look like we've been through the tiger once already. Let's get going; but from now on we walk to see your tame spook pusher. On solid ground, and leave the rooftops to the pigeons."

Megan tried to stand, staggered in a wave of dizziness. Shkai'ra threw a supporting arm around her shoulders and clamped a hand under the opposite armpit.

The Zak tried to shrug off the arm, staggered again and gripped at the back of her comrade's tunic. "Thank you," she said.

Shkai'ra grunted noncommittally, wincing at the pain of a pulled leg muscle as she took the first step toward the door. She set the pace carefully; they could both ignore pain if they must, but the body did not give its warning lightly, and there was little danger of pursuit in the immediate future.

The street outside was dark; the lanterns did not survive long in this part of the New City, and the merchant princes of the municipium were stingy about their replacement. They cut an odd figure, both bloody and torn, powdered with dust and woodchips and new scabs that cracked across as they moved. Megan was spitting to clear her mouth and dragging at bits of hard candy on her eyelids; Shkai'ra walked with the saber naked in her hand, and the sleeve of her tunic was sodden and flopping to the elbow, more than enough to deter any predators attracted by their wounds and weariness.

As she hung on to Shkai'ra's arm, Megan felt very strange. She dismissed it as the aftereffects of the fight and the close brush with death. She set herself to keeping up to the slow pace that Shkai'ra set, thinking that the hot, pulsing feeling in the wound in her shoulder would fade now that a bandage was on.

Outside, the cooler air was a relief; the moon had finally risen to light their way. The burning sensation and shortness of breath didn't fade but spread in slow waves centering on the wound. The night swam in front of her eyes and grew darker, shot with patches of colors that couldn't be there. Megan set her teeth and ignored it. If it was what she thought, then resting wouldn't help; only the sorceress could. It was growing harder and harder to force herself to breathe.

They were almost to the Old City gates before Megan staggered again; her knees buckled, and Shkai'ra swayed as her friend's weight came fully on her arm.

"Ahi-a, what is it?" she inquired.

"My—shoulder," the smaller woman gasped.

Shkai'ra leaned her back in a puddle of light to examine it. The injury was a typical puncture wound, deep and narrow; the wadded cloth and the hardening syrup had prevented much bleeding. It had begun to close by the time she had put a temporary pressure bandage on it, back at the factory. Painful and bone-deep, but it should not be giving her this much trouble, not without having hit a major artery. There had been no nerve damage; Megan moved the arm too well for that. The Kommanza had been dealing with wound trauma most of her life; she was puzzled, until she saw the faint bluish discoloration around the edges of the wound and convinced herself that it was not a trick of the pale uncertain flame of the lantern. She rocked back on her heels, gone white about the mouth, and let out a shuddering breath. The smell of the sudden fresh sweat that broke out on face and flanks and armpits was rank in her nostrils.

"Poison," she said quietly. "I thought . . . it usually acts so fast, but the cloth, and then the sugar . . .

probably got most of it." She paused, then added with startling intensity, "We've *got* to get to the spook pusher! Can you walk, kh'eeredo?" To herself she added: *And when we get there, she's going to help or learn the look of her own liver.*

"Walk? Of course not," Megan murmured. The thin ghost of a smile strayed across her mouth. "But I can crawl, if I have to."

Shkai'ra bent to pick her up; not that she could carry the Zak far in her present condition, but . . .

The sound of rubber-shod wheels on the brick pavement brought her head up with a snap. A three-shaaid gang-pedicab, the pedalers approached, pumping with predawn weariness.

"Ahi-a, halt!" she cried, then cursed vilely as she realized she had spoken Kommanza. Fatigue pressed on her, burning in her joints; her mind seemed to be moving like sheets of glass separated by wet sand. She repeated the call in Fehinnan, waving the meter-long length of steel for emphasis.

The pedicab was typical of its type, a four-seater carriage of light wood and leather on spindly wheels, pulled by a pyramid of toilers standing over pedals geared with ceramic and hardwood that powered back to the rear axle. It was a cumbersome vehicle, and the human engine was tired; still, they moved with remarkable speed. The whole clumsy apparatus seemed to circle in its own length and begin to accelerate back the way it had come. But for a moment inertia held it, straining.

Shkai'ra moved. Faster than was natural; almost faster than could be believed: she had called on the last reserve against extremity, nearly gone *ahrappan,* berserk, body powered by a hysterical strength that might have pulled muscle loose from bone. With an effort that cost almost the last shreds of sanity, she forced herself not to plunge the saber between the rear pedaler's shoulder blades. Instead, she laid the crusted edge against his throat. "No."

He looked around, and screamed. Millimeters from his eyes was . . . not a face, a mask. Lips thinned to vanishing peeled back from teeth bared almost to the angle of the jaw. Foam spattered, hot and rank; eyes showed the whites around the entire edge. And even in his terror, he knew astonishment that a human voice could speak from that frightfulness, in syllables of grating ash.

"New City-House of Terhan's-kin now or *die, get of a nomad pig. Pick her up and go!*" The voice almost spiraled up into a falsetto shriek, almost but not quite into the blood trill of the Kommanza *zh'uldaz;* Shkai'ra's neck quivered with the effort of denying the killing squeal.

Shkai'ra stood before Yeva, representative of the Guild of the Wise, and stared into the blind white eyes. She was without fear, not even truly conscious. The disciplines of the Warrior's Way had stood her in good stead, and the training of the Warmasters that many did not survive; it allowed her to call on reserves down to the cellular level, and keep drawing until the last were exhausted. She was using them recklessly; in this state, she could continue until the blood vessels in heart and brain burst loose from their moorings.

Megan lay very quietly. The bluish discoloration had spread, and she was having trouble breathing. For the last two kilometers Shkai'ra had been holding her, forcing air into and out of her lungs with pressure under the diaphragm.

She said nothing to the magician. No words were necessary, and she was beyond words. Silence. Yeva leaned forward from her nest of cushions and laid a hand on Megan's forehead.

*   *   *

In the darkness somewhere a newly familiar voice called and faded. The blackness was shot with blue and flashes of stars. Out of the pit of her mind, Megan rose on the fog in a whirlpool of ghosts and dead things. She floundered, lost in the night, and called for her father. He came, but only as he had died, in the *Va Zalstva*, the arena. He raised a flayed hand to her and was swept past her to disappear into the black. She followed, falling endlessly screaming into the depths of her mind, surrounded by the hated and the loved things in her life; and still she fell. And fell. And fell.

A hand touched her in the darkness. She turned and saw the shadowy figure of the sorceress Yeva beckoning. Sure that this was another of the misty shadows that offered false assistance, she almost ignored it. Then the voice called her name again and spoke.

"Young-kin. Your time of growth is not yet on you. There is one who calls, one who still needs. You should not pass this way, for I bar it to you. There lies your way." She pointed into the mist, then her image swelled and pulsed, as it blocked the way out of the bottom of Megan's mind, whirling into an intense bloom of light. Megan threw her hands before her face and thought, *One who still needs me?* A bright sword danced before her eyes, light gleaming off its curve, pointing the way that Yeva's image had indicated. Faint as a curlew's cry on the wind came the sound of her name, shredded and tattered but still hers. She gathered the shards of herself together and called back.

"I come." She stood now in darkness and realized that she stood only in her mind. Vaguely she could feel something beneath her; for a dizzying moment she was both standing and lying, then with a wrench she pulled another name from the dark, hurled it before her and followed it like a slung spearshaft out of the night.

"*SSSHHHHKAAAAAIIIIRAAAAAA!*"

*   *   *

For a long moment little seemed to happen and the sorceress held her pose as Shkai'ra waited. Then the Zak's chest heaved, paused, settled into a more normal rhythm. The bluish tinge began to leave lips and fingers; not quickly, but the normal pink began to creep back, and the angry red of burns somehow looked more superficial, as if only the upper layer of the skin had been parboiled, and not the layers of subcutaneous fat and muscle beneath.

Yeva withdrew her hand, "So," she whispered. "The body knows the secrets of its own healing. We merely show it the way." Though the downward spiral of the cosmos was to death and dissolution, life was as strong a force. She could feel the minute particles in the blood seeking out and neutralizing the toxin that had been spreading, clogging the tiny flashes of nerve transmission; felt the fluids moving and isolating heat-damaged tissues. She urged the process forward; warmth and breath and life flowing to fill the dark places, the damaged places, healing.

Shkai'ra's gaze stayed fixed and inhuman, until the signs were unmistakable. Then the process of release began, the implanted commands loosening their hold on heart and glands and organs. As she began to crumple toward the floor, she could feel the Warmaster's voice, echoing down the decades: *For everything there is a price.*

What a headache coming, she thought with a last flicker of rationality before her arms and head struck marble—and heard Megan murmur her name, softly.

CHAPTER XXII

When Megan woke, she lay a moment savoring the languid feel of lying on a soft surface, still feeling a bone-deep tiredness in every limb. Her thought drifted as lazily as the drowsy buzz of a cicada that she heard in the distance. Until last night's events replayed themselves for her.

She sat up abruptly, clutching the edge of the divan as dizziness swept over her. Her knife harness lay under her hands, tangled in the light sheet that had covered her. A light robe that had apparently lain by her feet now lay on a patterned stone floor. This was definitely not the Weary Wayfarer.

Shkai'ra lay to her right, snoring slightly, her hands grasping the strap of her scabbard, on another divan similar to the one Megan now sat on. Plants filled the room, growing toward the skylight, moving gently in the green-smelling breeze blowing from the open windows to the double doors at one end of the room. They also stood partly open, revealing a glimpse of a garden outside. A waterfall cascaded down the wall at that end of the room, filling it with a trickle of sound. Sunlight slanted into the room, and as the plants moved, they cast cool green shadows across the low table that stood before her, bearing a red glass decanter and three goblets.

She felt as if her tongue were wrapped in dusty wool, and her breath rasped her throat dry. The decanter, condensation sliding down the glass, drew her like a lodestone. Her legs were shaky, and she stumbled once before she sank down by the table and seized the pitcher. Then she hesitated. So many people had tried to kill them lately—even if they would have been easy to kill while unconscious. . . . She shrugged, and though every sinew protested, poured the pitcher into the plants. At the waterfall, she looked down at the fish swimming placidly in the water. *Seems safe enough.* She scrubbed the goblets and the pitcher before filling them from the water falling into the pool.

Water flowed down her throat in a cool rush, and it took an effort of will to stop before she made herself sick with drinking.

Ach, she thought, wobbling back to the table, *that is the closest I've ever been to Death and still cheated him.* Her skin was still burned, but only as if she had fallen asleep in the sun in late afternoon, while the dagger wound gave off faint twinges of a weeks-old injury. Her head ached, but the water soaking into dehydrated tissues would ease that soon. She refilled the goblet and sipped again, looking over at Shkai'ra, who slept on, oblivious.

Megan's legs trembled less as she bent over the Kommanza and reached a hand toward her shoulder. Then she reflected on the tight grip the sleeper kept on her sword hilt, stepped back a pace, and called her name.

The Zak looked down at the bladetip poised

beneath her chin, then at Shkai'ra. "A little jumpy, are
we?" she asked.

The Kommanza brushed sleep out of her eyes and
laughed softly. She looked around for the delight of
seeing—"I know we're not dead or I wouldn't feel so
terrible." The sword slid back into the sheath with a
slithery rasp, and Shkai'ra gingerly felt her head.

"Yes, it's still there. Do you think a goblet of water
would help?" Megan asked innocently.

"Now why would I want to wash? Wine is what
one drinks." Shkai'ra swung her legs to the floor and
shuddered, holding her temples. "On second thought,
water would be better." At Megan's chuckle, she pretended a glare that dissolved into a grin.

Megan handed her a goblet of cool water, sat down
next to her as she drank it, trickles escaping the sides
of the cup, trailing down her neck and breasts.

Megan put out one hand and rested it gently on
Shkai'ra's arm. "I . . . realized something, finally."

Shkai'ra bent to put the cup on the floor and covered Megan's hand with her own when she straightened, the touch carefully casual. "Oh? Anything I
should know?"

"I think—I think . . ." she paused. *How big a fool
am I going to look if I say this? She's probably just
interested in making love to me, because I'm exotic in
this part of the world.* "Why were you so upset?" She
changed her mind at the last moment, retreating to a
safer topic.

"What, at you getting poisoned and nearly croaking
on me?" Shkai'ra opened her mouth to make a flippant
answer and paused as she caught the intensity of Megan's stare. She looked down at the smaller woman and
then closed her eyes, sighing. "I don't know how to
explain it," she said at last. "My people don't have
words to describe what I'm feeling. . . ." She scuffed
the tile floor with the ball of her foot. "I can hardly
say I 'love' you. That's something I can't say to a

person. In my tongue, the closest I can get is, *A-moi lei-ehuk naigz!* 'I suffer a state of affection for my horse!' "

She sighed and scrubbed her hands through her hair. "I could say *fa'hr*—respect, or *lawkup*—admire, but the words are only approximate to what I *feel!*" She pulled her legs up to sit cross-legged, her brow furrowed as she went on.

"I'd miss you. I've always liked you, ever since you went over the rail of that boat rather than just give in and be a slave. I've ... gotten used to having you around and ... well ..." She raised her hand as if to touch Megan's face, stopped it, hovering. "I've been attracted to you, too, as the Fehinnans say. But I wanted you too much to push it—you'd have hurt me if I tried to force things. I feel, I guess, what Fehinnans call gratitude and I'd call obligation. You've saved my life—"

"—as you've saved mine," Megan broke in. But at the interruption, Shkai'ra didn't continue but shrugged helplessly.

"We shared steel," Megan prompted.

"Ia. But ... well, I'm not stupid enough to think that most other races like my people. We aren't *nice*, we aren't *likable*, and we don't care as long as other people fear us."

"You care. Are you afraid I won't like you because you're too Kommanza?" Shkai'ra's answer was a reluctant half nod. "I already do like you; and what you're describing of your feelings sounds an awful lot like love to me. Or at least the beginnings of love."

"I don't know *how!*" Shkai'ra said, throwing her hands up. "I was never taught to love the way Fehinnans, Pensa, or anyone *else* seems to!" Her voice spiraled up in frustration and anger.

"These emotions! They're like great *rocks* grinding around in my head! I was *content* with the way I was before, why do I have to change to fit what everyone

else, every *ekafrek* in the world, thinks is right? I'm
what I was taught to be. Why go through the bother,
the trouble, the discomfort of changing?" She
slammed a fist on the divan, winced and cradled her
head.

"You already have changed as far as I can see,"
Megan said gently. "If your people are so brutal, they
couldn't have friends. You've introduced me to three
friends of yours and talked of others; friends in the
Fehinnan meaning of the word."

"Well, I could hardly get along in this city without
following *some* customs!" Shkai'ra answered tartly.

Megan smiled. "You've changed, then. You've
changed enough to feel something you don't have
birth-tongue words for. Do you trust me?" she asked.

Shkai'ra nodded, a little puzzled. "But what does
that have to do with love?"

Megan raised her face to the other woman. "You've
been very careful how you touch me ... *akribhan*. I
trust you not to frighten me."

The puzzled look in Shkai'ra's eyes faded as she
understood. The foreign word sounded like "kh'eeredo,"
which she'd already been applying to Megan, without comment. Kh'eeredo—one who covers my
back—in most contexts. It was the only word for
anyone close.

She leaned down slowly, hesitantly and touched
Megan's lips with hers; felt her tremble. Holding herself back, in a way she never had before, she touched
Megan's face, gently, and ran her hands down to her
breasts. *She says I've changed, but have I changed
enough for her?*

Megan caught her hands there and faltered for a
long moment before pressing them to her, shaking as
if terrified, her breath coming in long gasps. "I ...
I'm afraid. Even if you think less of me for it."

"It's all right, kh'eeredo, it's all right." Shkai'ra

murmured, and somehow it was. She didn't feel contempt for the admission.

"You're beautiful," Megan whispered. "I'd be lonely here, without you." Shkai'ra kissed her, slid her arms around her. Megan clung to the taller woman as if drowning, as long forgotten sensation woke in her body. "Ach! Akribhan, my Steel-kin! Gently, please. I'll give myself to you, but please, gently."

Shkai'ra's answer was feather-light kisses as she lay Megan back on the divan, red-blond hair mingling with black. "Ah, Shkai'ra. I *l-love* you."

"I need you, Megan. I love you, too." Shkai'ra's answer was a low whisper, as if ashamed of her admission, but the words were there, with her hands and her lips; almost new, a seed planted long ago by a woman long dead, this idea of love. That much Shkai'ra had changed; her family would have said softened, gone weak. The Kommanza taught themselves that they were strong, that they didn't need, however false that was.

As the afternoon sun slid down the sky, Megan and Shkai'ra made love in the shifting shadows of the plants.

When she woke the second time, Megan looked up into the rustling green above them. Shkai'ra's arm was across her middle and they were crowded onto the one divan.

The Zak smiled and slid out from under, stretching. She padded over to the table and poured herself another cup of water before settling on the cushion there. It was twilight outside, a cool breeze blowing off the garden.

Now. Someone must have seen to putting us to bed and cleaning us up, she thought wryly. *The last one I remember is Shkai'ra, but she was in no shape to help herself, much less me. That leaves the sorceress, which means this is the merchant's guest house. Not really a good place to stay long. So. Yeva is the one to speak with.*

Megan got up, swayed, and sat down just as rapidly. *Later.*

"A good thought, young-kin. A healing depletes all the reserves," Yeva said quietly. At the now familiar chuckle so close by her, Megan flinched reflexively, then sheepishly put her knife back in its place.

"Your pardon, *Teik*—Lady. I'm sure you understand my unease."

The sorceress nodded. "My name is Yeva—please use it. Formality ill becomes kin-in-power." She sat on one of the cushions, the second goblet already by her hand, but empty. She smiled at Megan and continued, "And if we are of alike power then would you drink with me?"

"Gladly—but alike power? As an eating knife compares to a longsword!" Megan's caution was already falling before her curiosity, but she continued using the formal tone. Her training as a merchant demanded she be very polite with an acquaintance, especially if the person had earned respect. "If I might ask, how do you do the appearing-out-of-nowhere trick?"

"Trick indeed. It's much like your warding. A 'turning away of the mind,' a 'don't look here' message—very simple, really. Has no one taught you these things?"

"Simple." Megan looked down at her hands, turning them over as if she had never seen them before. "Often, simple things are the hardest to do." She gripped the edge of the table and was up on one knee, raising her hands to shield her eyes. "Knowing that there is no Blood or Steel between us, the thing that yet binds is Power. So do I, called Whitlock, answer the debt I owe you and freely give . . ."

"No." Yeva's voice rang sharp, all the warmth gone out of it as she rejected Megan's oath. "I do not accept this debt, for it does not exist in my eyes. I own no one, by no intent. The binding of friendship is all that I take from you."

Megan had rocked back on her heels at Yeva's abrupt interruption. "In honor I can't do anything else! I owe you my life!"

"No, you healed yourself. I merely assisted you. I cannot teach you." Yeva held her hands to the smaller woman, palm up. "Come. Freely. And 'see' with me. Leave the anger and try to understand."

Bluish-white light played gently around the hands she held out to Megan. For a moment there was silence as the Zak looked down into the light flowing in the long-fingered hands. Slowly she reached out to cover Yeva's hands with her own. As they came into contact, the scarlet light flared in Megan's hands, brightening minute by minute to an orange glow. They sat, surrounded by a soap-bubble swirl of light, blue and red, as they warily shared what they knew, colors deepening as trust grew.

Megan could not or would not remember what passed between them. Her mind, still reeling from the close brush with death, felt, for an instant, the inquiring murmur of the others in the guild as they became aware of the rapport, but the alienness of the way they thought and felt and believed rang through her mind. The pool of power that Megan was familiar with—her people's life—jangled against the power here, slowly at first, like a file on metal or biting through rust; shrieking on brain and bone, faster and faster, a harp-string pulled tighter and tighter sawed through bone—

Megan wrenched her hands free, snatching them close to her chest, trembling, white showing around her eyes, as Yeva sat back slowly. "You see?" the magician asked. "Your power and ours does not mesh easily."

Megan nodded mutely. All chance of learning from these witches had been shattered by the tide of information she could not seem to place in any framework in her head; facts with no meaning or context to keep or use them. All seemingly useless.

A moment passed, enough for a ray of sunlight to shift and warm them both. Megan shook herself as if shaking off an idea, even a cherished one. "I've always depended on steel, anyway."

Yeva smiled, at once cool and compassionate. "I have found a weapon with an edge sharper than any steel. Yourselves."

Megan shrugged trying to be casual. "Only death has the sharpest edge, they say."

The sorceress's voice became brisk. "You will need to turn it, then. After defending that scrap of paper you found by . . . chance . . . the factions will not believe you could surrender it. Each seeks the credit of using it to ruin their mutual enemies." Her fingers tapped the base of her goblet. "Best awaken your lover, before we speak further of this. A night and a day and a night again of sleep should be sufficient."

A moment later Shkai'ra stretched and sat up, yawning. She smiled at Megan and winked.

"If I may interrupt," Yeva's voice broke in, dryly. "There is still a slight problem to be discussed." One hand gestured gracefully to the cushions. "Sit. I have called for more water. As your 'healer' I suggest you eat something light. Fruit, perhaps." Her voice brooked no thought of objection, and Shkai'ra moved slowly to the table to sink down next to Megan.

She opened her mouth but was forestalled. "Since you owe me her life and yours, I suggest that you watch what you say to me." Laugh lines crinkled around Yeva's eyes. "Your feelings toward the, ah, spookers, as you put it, are known to us."

A servant padded in bearing a tray with another pitcher and a bowl of fruit. She set it down on the table, looked around, and clicked her tongue in disgust at the rumpled sheet on the floor. Yeva reached out to forestall Megan's comment and spoke. "I thank you, but you may leave the bedding until later." The woman started and stared around, obviously not seeing them. "Leave me," Yeva continued.

The servant bunched her tunic under nervous hands. "Lady, my master asks if all is to your liking and . . ." She backed toward the door as she spoke, her eyes scanning the interior.

Yeva's voice was impatient. "Yes. I need nothing else. Now go!" With that the woman bowed and was gone.

"He never learns. Never. He still tries to force his bondlings into spying on me. That should only be another strange tale to tell about me, and they are not aware of your presence, Only Bors knows, since he cleaned you up and put you to bed; him I trust." She cocked her head and laid one finger to her cheek, "looking" at Shkai'ra. "You were about to say?"

"Just that I never quarrel with someone I owe a debt to, at least not for the first day." Shkai'ra reached to fill the goblets with the new pitcher, felt it, and snorted. "Phagh. Not only is it water but warm as well." As she poured, the cups clouded as ice formed on them. Shkai'ra looked up to catch the glance passing between Megan and Yeva. "More tricks. For something that angers so many people, you two are pretty free with it." She rinsed her mouth and swallowed. "So. A problem?" She leaned back and waited while Megan sipped and watched the other two.

Yeva looked down at the goblet before her, so casually filled, and at the women who would drink with one called an Abomination by the Sun priests. She smiled to herself. Bright souls these two had, outlanders though they were. That much she had seen in the scrying-ice a sennight ago.

"We had decided that a message of some sort was necessary, to deliver to *someone*, for your safety."

Shkai'ra threw her head back, poured the contents

of the goblet down her throat and wiped her mouth
with the back of her hand.

"True enough. Nobody believes that something they
want that badly doesn't exist anymore. Ever hear of a
mercenary believing a farmer who swore there wasn't
silver buried under the hearth?" She glanced across
at Megan. "You still have it?"

For answer, the Zak produced the stained, sticky
piece of parchment. "What *does* it say?"

Yeva passed her hand over the shifting script as it
lay on the rosewood of the table. There was a curious
sensation, as of a click a finger's breadth behind the
eyes. Megan picked up the much-folded slip and read.
Her face lost all expression; after a moment, her
shoulders began to shake. Shkai'ra took it from her
fingers and read the common Fehinnan lettering.

"*Yes?*" she said. "For one word—'Yes'—we've been
chased, knifed, nearly eaten alive, tortured, soaked in
shit, dropped in candy . . ." Her voice trailed off, hesitating between fury and laughter.

Yeva spread her hands and smiled with an impish
glee. "Well, the Merchants' Guild asked us if we
would take a hand in matters; we decided to, so . . .
yes."

The Kommanza dropped her head into her hands
and began to laugh; then she fell over on the pillows
and beat hands and feet against the fabric, gasping as
helpless tears ran down her face.

"Ai, ai!" she wheezed. "I haven't seen anything so
good since the drunken nomad drowned in a mead
vat at Solstice Fair, the year I left Stonefort. Heroes
we were, leaping from roof to roof like eagles, slaying
all in our path—for a treasure of great price: a parchment saying 'Yes'! 'Yes'!"

Megan sank back on the cushion, almost lying
down, laughing so hard that she almost couldn't
breathe. "Would it . . . have been any better . . . if it

had ... had been 'No'?" And she wiped tears away
from the corners of her eyes.

Through gasps Shkai'ra managed to say, "Or even
'Maybe'?" She fell over again at the idea, wheezing.

Megan smoothed wisps of hair away from her face,
straightening the cushions she sat on. "Ach, a story to
tell children ... but not one that priests or army
would believe." She picked a slice of melon from the
bowl and bit into it, catching a fragment at the corner
of her mouth. "Now, what are we to do to pull them
off our trail?"

Shkai'ra rose, pulled out her saber, and began polishing the already bright steel carefully. "We've
thought of leaving the city, but ..." She put the sword
down across her knees and began ticking off points on
her fingers. "*Eh*, the ports are watched and we would
have to travel by horse or foot, both slower than river
or sea. *Ka*, if the army succeeds in starting this war
of theirs, then the countryside will be mobilized and
not very healthy for outlanders, even mercenaries. I,
for one, do not care to be a conscript in their Glitch-
taken holy war. *Sh'ra*, they've already tried to kill us;
even if they catch us elsewhere, that wouldn't stop
them from doing it then." She looked up. "Enough
points?"

"Too many," Megan said. She looked up from
where her nails tapped on the tabletop. "We can't stay
in hiding forever, and I cannot stay here. It's too bad
that we couldn't just give them *all* the message. After
all, what good would it do them?"

"But none of them would believe that the message
was just one word," Yeva broke in. "It wouldn't be
convincing enough...." She thought a moment, sightless eyes looking off into the far distance. "I have an
idea that might be your answer!" She looked over their
heads, smiling. "If they *all* got what they *expected*,
then they would be convinced, wouldn't they?" Her
gaze lowered to the other two. "Do you think you

could see that all three factions got a glimpse of the message?"

Megan suddenly felt as if her mind had started working properly again. The pieces of this plot fell into place, and she began a slow smile at the thought. "Give them a lie they will believe, rather than the truth they cannot." She slapped the table. "I'm sick of being the quarry; let us turn the tables."

"Put a weasel in the henhouse, with the right message," Shkai'ra said enthusiastically. "Hmmm, but each will need a different emphasis—what if they compare notes?"

Yeva tapped a long finger on her chin. "Shoes from a leatherworker, steel from a blacksmith—and for the impossible, a magician."

Simple enough, she thought. *The material is already sensitized. Now, what is it that the powerful of this city fear most of all? Ah, of course . . .*

She arched her hands over the parchment and raised the patterns in her mind. They hung before her thought in an intricate knot of light strands. Now, this corresponded to the basic human mind—all the recipients would be human, of sorts. Here, the common character elements: a line of suspicion, a loop of treachery. She had known a gull-taker once, in her youth as a hedge-wizard, a man who made his living from fraud; he had told her that it was nearly impossible to run a successful scam on the honest, although such were fortunately rare. This would apply the same principle; she inserted the last of the subliminal clues, tapped energy from her environment, and sent her mind plunging through the matrix of the spell. Possibility warped, and *might* became *is*.

The two adventurers felt a momentary clenching and a sudden chill. Megan felt the surge of energy spiraling into the focus and almost, almost saw what was happening. A glimmer of something not quite there, caught out of the corner of an eye. She wanted power so badly that she could taste it; then cast the idea away. *Yeva cannot teach me,* she thought. *I am a red-witch and will remain one. Living on the edge of a knife is good enough, and I've done well enough without more power.*

"There," Yeva said. "Take it and read, remembering the lie." Shkai'ra scanned the now lengthy message, pursing her lips and raising a brow.

Megan took it in turn. "Fascinating," she said. "You, apparently, have been corresponding with Habiku—though you couldn't know who he is—to sell me to slavers again. The man has no imagination."

"And you are taking the priests gold, for me," Shkai'ra added, turning to the sorceress. "This is a *fangaz'i whul pukkut,*" she said. "A sheep-bitten wolf—unbelievable."

"For you," Yeva replied, "not for those whose nourishment is treachery. We call them 'mind-that-sees-lurkers'—paahnit. They will believe."

Shkai'ra's teeth drew back from her teeth in an expression that bore no relation to a smile. "The Fehinnans like a circus," she said. "Now they'll have one."

Yeva turned her eyes to Megan's smile, if it could be called that, and nodded. "Perhaps you could use some assistance? I believe that your rooms at the inn are still being watched by everyone, and I cannot shield you here much longer. It takes as much power to keep up your invisibility over a long period as it does reaching out over a distance ... or into the temple—I did that once, only with assistance. Take counsel between you—I will not really be here for a moment." With that, it was as if she withdrew into her mind and was ... gone though her body still sat with them, one of its hands lightly clasped around the base of the cup.

Megan turned a thoughtful eye on Shkai'ra. "I find myself with a strange appetite for more discussions of philosophy with a certain ex-priest. . . ." She trailed off and raised a questioning eyebrow at the Kommanza.

"Probably the safest place in this stone warren," she mused. "When?"

Megan poked a finger into her hair: it crackled. She mumbled under her breath, picking at patches of congealed sugar still sticking to her abraded skin. "Not until I've had a bath. Even after being cleaned up and you finding sugar in the damndest places I'm not clean yet. Many baths."

"Just a little candy, and nibbling it *was* fun; the sooner the . . ." Shkai'ra sat up, stood, gripped her head in shaking hands, and sat down again. "On the other hand, perhaps we should rest a little," she continued, gritting her teeth against the heaving of a rebellious stomach. The reserve against extremity was not tapped without a price. She sank back resentfully, closing her eyes.

"Although I'd like it better if the resting were a different place," she said softly after a moment's pause. The magician seemed . . . otherwhere, at present, but she remained cautious. "Not that this one hasn't dealt well with us, but I don't—"

"—like spook pushers," Megan finished with weary humor. "And I don't particularly like to swim, but we'll both do what we hate if we have to." She rose, wincing, and stood beside the blond woman's side. "Me to the hot water, if I can wake our hostess; you, back to sleep, akribhan."

Shkai'ra rolled onto her side and sighed, curling into the crisp cool surface of the linen sheets. Her breathing evened out, and she was asleep in moments. Sleep relaxed the hard, wary lines of her face; for a moment it was possible to see her as she might be at peace, unthreatened. Megan stood in silence, just looking, then put out a hand to hover just over Shkai'ra's shoulder. She felt the heat radiating from her, and as a sound came from behind them, snatched the hand back.

"You care much for this one." Yeva's comment was quietly spoken, and not a question. "A good person to have at your back."

"So I thought."

"Well, then. As a guest, as my mentor reminded me, I also can have guests." She paused, color tingling her pale cheeks. "I should have realized it before. No matter. The servant can show you the way." She clapped. "I don't think I have to tell you to move slowly."

"Ach, moving at all is the problem." Megan bowed slightly. "I still would like to speak with you, once I cease feeling like a smashed clockwork toy." Yeva's cool amusement followed her out of the sunny room, like the scent of lavender.

Like a great sperm whale rising from the depths, the Weary Wayfarer's head cook lumbered up the stairs. Servants shrank against the walls as she passed, gawking at the afternoon tea tray in her hands. It had been many years since Glaaghi had carried anything heavier than a ladle.

She slowed as the bare concrete and stone of the working quarters gave way to paneling and tile; that aspect of the old manor had needed little change when the Weary Wayfarer had become a business as well as a home to its owners. One of the upper-slaves stopped her.

"The owners wouldn't appreciate this," he said apprehensively. Old highlander tattoos showed on his cheeks, but years in captivity had worn the soft dialect of coastal Fehinna into his tongue.

Glaaghi grunted. She was a free employee and highly valued; the kinfast might own her kitchen, but it was *hers*. She waved the tray slightly.

"Trouble in two-west-five," she said. "Not taking trays, and the lazy fishbrains can't tell me why." She plodded stolidly on, uneasy in her feast-day tunic, conscious that it diminished her. In leather apron and clout she was a figure of terror; with blue cotton on her shoulders she was a fat, middle-aged servant woman. "I will find out what's going on. Even if they prefer that only the younger, comelier servants wait directly on guests and are offended by me." Still, she was careful not to tread too heavily and not to knock against anything.

The stairs creaked under her weight, and she remembered why she'd stopped coming up to this level. If someone had been standing down the hall, he would have seen Glaaghi's head and shoulders emerge from the stairwell, Titanlike. Even out of her realm, the head cook was impressive. Not for nothing did the under-servants call her the Sea-Cow behind her back, being very careful to be out of earshot.

She stopped in front of second-west-four and looked down at the tray in her hands. "Two-west-four has their tray. Only four rooms on this floor. Why am I carrying this tray?" She shifted the tray to one meaty hand and scratched her head, counting. "One, yes. Two, yes. Three, no breakfast tray today. Four has theirs." She looked down at herself and her puzzled frown deepened. "Now why would I dig out my festival tunic and do something strange like come upstairs?" She lumbered back down the stairs still muttering. "Festival? Maybe that's it. A festival trick. But why am I carrying this tray?" The slave was still where she had left him.

"Here. You take this. This isn't my job." He looked puzzled as well.

"What?" he said, trailing in her wake as she headed back downstairs. "Didn't they take it?"

"Didn't who take it?" Glaaghi asked.

"Why, second-five-west," he said.

The head cook stopped on the stairs, one hand on the balustrade. "I, I don't remember," she said. "I must have spoken to someone. Yes. I must have." She sounded more confident. "That is an extra tray. Take it downstairs. I have work to do, and good tunics don't mate well with grease."

CHAPTER XXIII

Megan gnawed on the end of her pen, then carefully drew in another line. "There," she said. "Hmmm, it still isn't very complete."

Shkai'ra scowled. "You'll need more information than that, if you're to get our little scrap of paper into the temple," she said. "Not just floor plans; the organization, and what approaches would work."

"At least you've agreed I'm the one to deal with the priests," she answered.

"Little people are better at hiding, and neither of us could pass for a local, but you're closer. Agreed: you for the temple, me for the Iron House. But how are we going to do an in-and-out with the Adderfangs? With the contract, both of us are kill-on-sight blade fodder." She prodded a finger at the paper. "And we don't even know enough for *this*."

There was a dry cough from the hearth. Harriso looked up from his teapot. "Although elderly, I am not quite on my pyre," he said. "For the temple, recall what I was: guidance I can give, and the Beggar King has often sent me to deal with the Adderfangs."

He crossed the little room and gently lifted a stone from the irregular wall. The niche within was dank, but the documents were safely enclosed in a greased leather bag, tightly sealed. "Now, with your help, Red-Hair—"

"Now wait a minute, Harriso," Megan cut in sharply. "Granted that all you say is true ... I, for one, don't wish to expose anyone else to the risk. Besides, even if we succeed in pulling the hairs from these skunks' tails without getting stinking, we can always leave. This is not our home, though perhaps it is becoming yours," she said in an aside to Shkai'ra. "Afterward, the survivors are likely to have long memories and come looking for you." She paused. "I won't do that by involving you more."

Harriso's ruined eyes swung toward her. "Child," he said in a voice soft with power, "I have lived eighty turnings of the Sun. Many more than most. All that I loved died long ago; memories and words are left, memories and words."

He paused. They might almost have thought him asleep, but for the schooled stillness of his cross-legged stance. "Because I have bent with my fate, do not presume to believe that I welcome it. Two things remain to my hand. Those chance-met friends I have made, here in this second world, my second life." His voice dropped, caressingly. "And my enemies. While they are, I am. We are bound closer than kinmates or parents. This—" he touched the message "—puts me within reach of them again. Those who cast me down and oppress my people. Let me bring us to our ending and give a fitting farewell gift to those who saw more than a blind beggar."

Megan's lips parted slightly, then closed in silence. Shkai'ra dropped a hand lightly on her shoulder. *Death pride,* she thought.

Harriso poured the tea and set the cups out with the quiet gestures of ritual. The three sat, glittering firelight casting highlights from below on the harsh cheekbones of the Kommanz steppe, glistening on curtains of raven's wing hair. They drank.

"So. Now that you infants have listened to the voice of wisdom—" the wrinkled face lost its inhuman serenity in a smile of friendly mockery "—consider the coming Purification in the temple. All of Illizbuah will be there, or that part that can cover its nakedness and contribute to the Servants' treasury. A small, agile person might do well."

"I suppose that a warhorse plunging around in the crowd would be rather obvious," Megan said. "A Purification? If the crowd is that big, it might be my best chance. When?"

"Three days from now. Enough time for me to pay . . . a visit to the ones the current Reflection of the Effulgent Light finds useful tools. Yes, by all means, the Silent Knives first. That will clear the way for you, Red-Hand, to drop the pomegranate of discord among the warriors, to scatter its seeds. Then, before any but vague rumors of turmoil spread, we send the message of disharmony to the Reflection and watch the results among them allfifi. It will be some time before the survivors have the leisure to seek out the authors of their troubles."

Shkai'ra blinked and choked on the last sip of her tea. "Harriso, you were wasted on these dwellers-in-stone-warrens," she said. "You should have been a Granfor Warmaster; you have just the devious, nasty mind. When I asked for your aid, I wasn't expecting you to set our strategy."

The fire had died by the time they were done, and even several pots of the tea were not enough to keep hoarseness from their throats. Harriso stood, moving unerringly in the semi-darkness, and began to sling a blanket curtain across the middle of the hut. Megan paused in fluffing a pallet.

"Harriso," she said in a thoughtful tone, "it seizes me that one thing is lacking in your plan."

The blind man inclined his head toward her. "Can it be found on such short notice?"

"If I know anything at all of the underside of cities, yes," Megan said, her eyes focused unseeingly on the dim shape of Shkai'ra pulling off her tunic. "A small, swift, inventive, and very, very greedy child."

"Excuse me again, young one, but is the Shadowed One still busy?" The Adderfang apprentice looked up sourly from the records spread on the low table at the stooped figure of the beggar leaning on his staff. The small boy who had led him here hadn't ceased moving *once* since they had arrived, and had contributed greatly to his decision that the Beggars' Guild could wait, for a change.

Sunstruck, blind old fool, he thought. *Three times I've lost my place. Adventure in the Assassins' Guild, hah! Might as well be a priest.* He prodded again at an aching molar with his tongue and broke his silence.

"Yes! My Shadowed, Luko, is very busy today and is likely to be so for another finger-width of the candle, so could you kindly sit down? And keep the boy quiet." As if on cue, the urchin spoke up again.

"Grandfather, I hafta go to the jakes, the latrine, I mean. I hafta, now!" He tugged at the beggar's cloak and set up a whine that carried around the room.

"Why, Dahv, you know your kin-mother told you . . ."

The old one's maundering died away as the two were escorted down the hall by another apprentice, who looked just as thrilled as Luko's.

By the Sun's shadow, the two are enough to drive you mad, he thought. And what could be so important that he wouldn't even mention the insult of being kept waiting? Harriso, yes, that was the blind one's name. Not a frequent contact, but logical. After all, who better to deal with dwellers in shadow than one blind? It showed the Beggar King's understanding of his place. He turned back to his papers and wondered if Luko would be in a better mood now that the madam had been in to pay her protection. When they got back maybe he ought to risk disturbing him. How many throwing stars could he have in his office, anyway?

Officious child, Harriso thought, as they were led back to the waiting area. Luko was normally much easier to see during the evening hours than this.

He felt Dahvo's hand on his arm and thought that the boy played his part well. If they believed a clan or kinfast stood behind them, perhaps it would make them hesitate a little before killing them. *Ai*, he sighed mentally, the Adders were too fond of killing these days. Subtlety was what they lacked. It had been otherwise in his youth.

Harriso felt the sour expression on the apprentice's face; not at all unlike an acolyte serving in the outer chambers of the temple, even to the petty pleasure he took in keeping a supplicant waiting. At last he sighed, laid down his pen, and scratched at the door of the sanctum before entering. The blind man strained hearing honed in darkness; there was a muffled bellow and a sharp thunk of steel on wood.

". . . and if you won't stand still for it, bring it back!" the voice said, and bellowed again: laughter this time. The heavy door swung open and the apprentice waved them through; his hands shook slightly as he did, and a fresh scar showed white against the pitted inner surface of the door, at neck height.

Harriso walked in slowly, more slowly than necessary, with a hand on Dahvo's shoulder. Rooms were largely a matter of smell to him; this one was . . . stale sweat, cane spirit . . . yes, and perfume overlying sexmusk. The Adderfang's voice sounded, round and thick and heavy; there was an impression of meaty forearms thick with hair and wet jowls. The tone was still shark-jovial from the lethal baiting a moment ago.

"Well, old no-eyes, does the Beggar King complain of our tax again? Or have freelances been at the bowls once more?"

Dahvo shifted under his hand; Harriso could tell that he was glancing around, impressed. The garishness must be truly hideous. The old man spoke softly.

"Perhaps my business should remain confidential, One in Darkness," he said. The Adderfang snorted heavily and leaned on the wicker backrest behind his cushions. It creaked heavily.

"Then why bring the boy? Unless as a present for me."

"He is my eyes and ears," Harriso said absently. Then: "There was a commission for ... those-who-remove, recently. Concerning the recovery of a missing object?"

The backrest creaked again and stopped. Harriso could hear the man's breathing catch and pant; the sharper scent of fear was in his sweat. Silently, the blind man produced the folded paper from his robe; at a warning squeeze, Dahvo took it gingerly between thumb and finger to deposit it on the Adderfang's desk. The boy returned to his position. The rustle of stiff paper unfolding was plain to sensitive ears, but Harriso squeezed again.

"He's unfolded it now, Grandfather. Now he's started to read."

"Porpoiseshit!" the Adder gasped, and slammed the paper face down on the desk; a fact which was noted in Dahvo's clear treble. He had always been one of Jahlini's supporters; that had gotten him this sinecure in Guild Liaison, when he grew too heavy for active commissions. But if she heard he had read this ... whatever it was ...

From the Servants of the Effulgent Light ... Thank

That Which Coiled in Darkness he'd stopped reading more.

"How did—" He stopped, took several quick breaths, and a long pull at a bottle of cane brandy hidden beneath a cushion. A moment later he regretted that; it was happening too often these days. Decision crystallized.

He yanked at a cord. The door opened, and the apprentice side-flipped through, landing in guard stance and looking astonished as nothing edged flew in his direction.

"Get the Adderchief," Luko began, his voice an octave higher than usual. "Tell her that Luko will pay with his liver and lights if it isn't more important than anything she's doing now. No, you fool, leave the door open!" It would be hard enough to convince her that he hadn't heard, done, or read anything as it was.

They sat for long minutes of echoing silence, Luko sweating still more, jamming thick hands against each other to still the urge to reach for the black glass bottle; Dahvo fidgeting; Harriso serenely motionless. Very faintly, he smiled; the taste of intrigue and danger and great events was not one he'd thought to enjoy again, and he found that the appetite had not vanished so thoroughly as he had imagined. *Like most cravings*, he thought, *it grows with the feeding.*

The apprentice did not reappear. Instead, Adderchief Jahlini herself eased through the door. Harriso knew the smell, dry and old and somehow reminding him of wet metal and rat fur. She stayed silent as she crossed to the desk and flipped the paper over.

Luko burbled, a safe three paces away, with his face carefully averted. "I didn't read a word, not a word, Darkest!" he stuttered. "As soon as I knew, believe me . . ."

"Oh, I believe that, Luko," she said softly, smoothing the parchment down with one hand. The other curled fingers toward the slit under the right armpit of her tunic. "Not even you would be fool enough to bring me to this, when your name is at the top of the list."

The knife she drew was small—a handspan and a half, slightly curved, with a hilt of dimpled bone. Luko's black jacket parted soundlessly; the point slid in just under the floating rib and drew down and across, finishing with a twist.

He fell, and she stove in his larynx with a sandaled heel. "No dying words from you," she said coldly.

Her eyes moved to Harriso and the child, and even in his darkness he felt them. His reply was cool and dry. "Consider, Commander of Silent Knives, that I at least cannot read the product of any pen; nor can this child of the streets. And further, will sources of information be forthcoming if your reward is a journey to the sewers to dine with the crawlers?"

She stood silent. Suddenly, Dahvo ran forward, kicking at her shins and pounding at her waist with small fists.

"You leave Granther alone!" he cried. "I don't like you! You smell!"

There was a hard smack as she backhanded the child into a sobbing huddle on the floor.

Not worth my time, she thought as the grey face of Luko's apprentice peered through the door. "Get me the . . . no, the Assistant Master of Terminations, and my guards! Who would have thought so many?" she muttered, ignoring the old man as he helped Dahvo to his feet, leaning on the desk. He sidled out the door as black-masked figures began to pour through it.

Harriso went to hush Dahvo and found him already quiet. The boy sniggered slightly. "She didn't even hit me as hard as Ma does. Did that bit good, din't I?"

"Yes, Dahvo. Now come—this place is too close for my liking."

"How? They blindfolded me on the way in and led us both. I'm lost."

"This way." Harriso turned around a corner, hearing the *fttt* of blowguns behind them, coming closer. He pulled Dahvo into a doorway and listened to the sounds of Jahlini's housecleaning. It sounded as if many were going to die in this.

Blindfolds worked well with those dependent on sight. Everyone forgot that the blind remember. Out of darkness then, the blind man led the boy.

The heavy smell of frying food told him that they were near the exit . . . or entrance, as the case might be. The latch clicked and the small door swung open.

"Now, Dahvo, be my eyes for a short time again. Has anyone moved the box from below or disturbed anything?"

"No, but I think the fight's following us." He sounded a little nervous.

Harriso smiled and stepped to the box below, to the small barrel, and then to the floor. "We have time. Close the door." He could hear the muted rustle of conversation and the clatter in the kitchens on the other side of the door.

A thump and Dahvo was down as well. "Come along. You shall have your reward for playing my grandson. You shouldn't get hit for not making your quota today. Maybe even tomorrow, if you're careful."

They moved through the kitchen and the restaurant, weaving between seated patrons, cushions and low tables. As they got to the door, Harriso squeezed Dahvo's shoulder and pressed the bit into his hand that Megan had given him to pay the boy.

There was an unkitchenly clatter from the kitchen, and a figure fell through the fishbone curtain, black-clad, rigid, with a small dart pinning the hood to the throat. The restaurant cleared with lightning speed as panicky diners realized the Adders were fighting among themselves. Some nearly stumbled over an old beggar who sat by the corner of the building, shaking his bowl, crying, "Alms! Give and the Light shine on You! Alms ..."

CHAPTER XXIV

Sammibo could hear the gate lieutenant's nasal voice echoing down the entrance corridor of the Iron House long before the portals came in sight. There wasn't much traffic here after sunset, and discipline enforced silence. *For most,* the staff officer thought. *That youngker is making enough racket for himself and twenty other fools.*

"It's obvious, little Rahlini; the great red cow doesn't understand the high speech. She didn't even look up after that last insult—graciously delivered as it was."

Sammibo softened his step as he paced past the faded stains around the side entrance, smiling. He caught Shkai'ra's eye over the shoulder of the lieutenant and the hapless private who was a forced witness to his baiting of the outlander. Shkai'ra leaned at her ease against one of the doorposts, ignoring the light drizzle soaking her tunic; her back rested against time-blackened brass-strapped, oak, towering four body-lengths above her. The gate under-officer turned to her again.

"How long will you wait for the officer?" he said, in labored city patois. Under his breath he added: "Offspring of a sow and a shark," in the formal tongue, but very softly; the foreigner's passivity had made him bold, but there was something about the scarred hands thrust into her belt that contradicted it.

Shkai'ra jerked her head slightly to indicate Sammibo and cleared her throat. "I see," she said, in officer-class Fehinnan with a slight burr, "that you're still using lapdogs and imbeciles for guard duty, Sam."

The lieutenant abruptly became a model soldier. "Ah, sir," he began.

"And still stuffing pikeshafts up their ass to make 'em stand straight," the Kommanza continued.

"So, do you take him out on the practice field, or shall I?" Sammibo said, with a gesture halfway between a salute and a wave.

"Nia, pillow-soldier, he's not worth the trouble. Vultures might puke on his shadow; I can't be bothered." She cast a wink at the private, who clutched her pike and stared solemnly ahead as bright spots appeared on her cheeks. The barracks would be amused tonight.

Shkai'ra flipped a ball of hard rubber from her belt and began squeezing it, tossing it to the other hand every tenth contraction. Pushing past the rigid lieutenant, she leered and whispered; his braced attention quivered.

Her grin faded as they entered the hall. Lanterns and reflectors barely touched the dimness; around them the great pile of stone and brick and glassbound concrete hunched in on itself, hugging its darkness. The Iron House was not the oldest building in Illizbuah; the foundations of the Sun Temple went back before the Godwar, before the world was changed and broken. But it was the only structure of its era that had not been rebuilt out of all recognition. Long years had passed since its builders piked cannibal bands back from the four-story walls; the crumbled concrete of another cycle had been dragged from ruins to make its mortar. It had always been a fortress; the smells of sweat, oil, polish, and musty stone made a cold aura.

"You're laughing in the shark's mouth," Sammibo said. "Insisting on giving it to the High Commander personally. She bears no overwhelming love for you." All the while, they had been passing through the thickness of the outer wall. At the first cross corridor of the warren, a guard detail fell in about them, fully armored.

Shkai'ra shrugged. All that stood between her and a spearpoint between the shoulder blades was her appraisal of her opponent's cast of mind. That, and luck. She made the gesture with her sword-hand out of habit, but uneasily. There had been too much luck about of late, both good and bad; the gods must be taking a close interest in this fight. Gods, or . . .

"You mean, she has the malice of a viper," the Kommanza replied, snapping her attention back to the matter at hand.

Sammibo winced and glanced around, the reflex of years on the fringes of the High Command. One of the guards had twitched; that might be a trick of the eye, and body language was difficult to pick out under a leather-and-fiberglass suit stretching from pate to foot. Sammibo decided that Smyna trusted him exactly as he did her.

"She also . . ." Shkai'ra let the comment trail away. Baiting the Fehinnan was amusing, but she had no desire to ruin him. "She gives me the money, she gets—" she tapped her belt "—this."

Sammibo stroked a satin-gloved finger down his mustache and adjusted the fine green linen of his dress tunic. "Well, at least let me hand the message to her," he said unhappily. "No need to remind her of your presence more than necessary."

They paused at a colonnade to watch a group of mercenaries; from the equipment, Shkai'ra judged

them to be the headquarters company of a Kaalyn
light cavalry regiment. The fifty meters of airwell
above them was misty with the light rain, soaking the
troops with javelins slung in hide buckets across their
backs. A company of regular Fehinnan infantry
watched, drawn up in what the manuals called an
honor guard formation; the troops knew it as "suspicion guard."

"Hiring, I see," she said. Silently, she extended a
hand with the parchment.

Sammibo took it with a sigh of relief, tucking it
behind the sky-blue of his sash, under the tache of his
broad-bladed infantry shortsword.

"Don't try to read it, Sammibo," she said.

"It's eyes only." He shrugged.

"Sammibo, when they carry you to the pyre, you'll
pick the pallbearer's pockets, just to see what's there.
But this was written by spookers."

There was a slight check in the staff officer's stride
before he said smoothly, "Duty forbids, in any case."

"But you would have tried."

"Well . . . perhaps. Good intelligence is the heart of
military science."

Toward the centrum of the fortress some effort had
been made to modernize the interior: murals and colored marble floors clashed jarringly with door frames
graven in demon faces. Incense fought with mold;
guards stood at four-meter intervals, unmoving; the air
had a greasy, cold soup chill. It was familiar from her
days as a commander of irregulars. *We Kommanz have
a name for treachery*, she thought. *But we don't have
to look to our backs in battle.* She made to spit on
the flagstones, then reconsidered.

They halted for a moment at the ancient, inner
doors. There was a line of discoloration at about chest
height, very faint, where the guard had made its last
stand centuries ago, when the Maleficent's troops had
become the only hostile army ever to set foot in the

Iron House. On either side sentries stood, statue-like; Shkai'ra watched with interest as a fly crawled across one's face and over a motionless eyeball.

Sammibo darted a glance at her as the door swung open, its twice man-height moving soundlessly on oil-wood bearings. She was too calm, he thought; but it was hard to be sure.

The chamber within was vaulted, a wedge-shaped segment of a circle two tiers in from one of the outer towers. Soft indirect light came from panels in the roof. Shkai'ra noted the narrow decorative slits rimming the ceiling. More than decorative; she would have wagered an eye that there were winch-wound siege crossbows up there, covering every movement in the room.

Smyna sat at on a low padded bench, overlooking the massive map table that was the centerpiece of the huge headquarters chamber. Around stood a clutch of staff officers and senior unit commanders, moving counters with long-handled rakes. Since her own people used a similar system, the Kommanza took in the dispositions with a glance.

Odd, she thought. *Most of the foot concentrated around the city. Easier to supply on navigable water, of course, but why not farther up the Iamz Valley, if they're planning a campaign in the south?*

The commander of Fehinna's capital garrison looked up with a slight, cool smile. Shkai'ra could feel Sammibo tensing at her side; she did not delude herself that he would lift a finger if the general ordered her cut down on the spot, but it might cause a little regret.

Not that Smyna would. The Kommanza had never been a real threat to the General-Commander; nobody in her position could be. Chance had given her the opportunity to cause her some trouble and embarrassment . . .

Smyna's eyes staring from the mask of mud and

blood as bright arterial blood pulsed from the leg wound, her fist stained red on the pressure point. Shkai'ra pushed aside the memory.

No, Smyna would never grant her the dignity of ordering the sort of hasty execution others would; that would imply real fear and hence respect. It would be far more to her taste to see the outlander groveling for a minor scrap, ignore her with lordly disdain. And not even notice her sword. Grey eyes met black for a moment, and then the westerner looked away, casually. It would not do to let Smyna see her lack of regret, and no Fehinnan aristocrat gained or held this much power by being a fool.

The General-Commander turned to Sammibo, ignoring the barbarian commoner, raising a slim brow. Shkai'ra noted sardonically that for all her calm, she was the only one present wearing even partial harness—chain gorget and steel breast-and-back, part of the priceless suit that was one badge of her office.

The staff officer wordlessly extended the parchment. Smyna waved it toward her chief aide, a stocky, bouncy figure hovering at her right.

"Such trouble," she said. "For a trifle." She reached for a cup of chilled pomegranate juice on a tray held by the nearest soldier-servant. Her attention strayed from the map table to a file folder in her lap.

Shkai'ra was acutely conscious of the staff officer standing with the message in hand; she could feel the sweat trickling down from her armpits over her flanks, chilling in the cool air that fans brought up from the basement, the dankness carving faintly through the incense. The dim, rich colors of the room seemed intolerably bright. Her breathing remained calm and even, and the grey eyes traveled casually across the room, noting the position of each human and object. Soldiers; she was a warrior, and the next few minutes would show the difference.

The aide unfolded the parchment and read, casually at first. Then he stopped with a deep hoarse grunt, the sound a mailed cestus driving into the pit of his stomach might have brought forth.

"Why!" he shouted, raw disbelief in his voice. "I was the only one you could trust—"

He stumbled backward. Rage replaced fear on the heavy features, and his hand went to the hilt of his blade.

Smyna had scooped the parchment from the floor. The cool, regular detachment of her features became very ugly as she scanned the short lines. The reflex that drove her into a fighting crouch saved her life as her aide's sword skittered over her shoulder-piece and plowed across her upper arm in a blow that would have ended in her neckbones if she hadn't moved.

"So, Fehinna needs a General-Commander more 'pious and reverent to the Servants of the Light,'" she said in a deadly whisper, as the long cavalry sword slid free in her good hand. The voice rose to an insane shriek. "Kill him!"

The room tensed, but the expected bolt did not flash. The aide laughed and drove forward in a lunging thrust that she stopped only with a desperate twisting leap.

"Did you forget who sets your guard?" he inquired nastily. There was a deep bass throb from the hidden gallery that ran around the council chamber, and a heavy bolt plowed chips from the floor inches from his foot. A moment later, there was a wet crunching sound, and an arm thrust limply through the slit. It hung, and dripped red slowly on the priceless carpets. Confused shouts and the clash of metal followed through the arrowslits.

The staff officers had frozen at the clash of steel, immobilized by total incredulity. The field commanders were less hesitant and more used to sudden emergencies.

Forming a knot, they backed toward the portals, raising a shout.

"Treason!" they cried. "Guard, guard!"

They had reckoned without the atmosphere of headquarters. Sudden disciplined action, here, suggested foreknowledge of the plot. The crossbows hummed.

Prudently, Shkai'ra had dropped behind a wooden map chest, dragging Sammibo with her for additional cover. She grinned into features gone liquid with dazzlement; beyond him she saw one grey-haired staff officer doggedly crushing the throat of another with her map pointer, oblivious of the dress dagger buried in her midriff.

"Such madness!" she laughed, the sudden shrill wild giggle of her folk. He shrank from the blaze of orgiastic pleasure in her face as she looked out over the scene. "Such chaos!"

She suddenly grew calm. One of the dying field officers had swung the doors open, leaving a glistening trail as he slid down the mottled ebony. "I'm for the outside, Sammibo," she said, in snarl. "Glitch godlet of fuckups be with you—this is his realm—and for the sake of some good times, hide under the table!"

A darting rush brought her to where Smyna and her second-in-command dueled among the ruins of their hopes. She stooped, swept up the parchment, whirled, and ran for the door, the impetus of the back-kick she snapped at Smyna's knee speeding her on her way. Deliberately, she did not draw steel; that would force potential obstacles to keep their blades for their opponents, when the sight of a bright edge out of the corner of their eye might have drawn a blow. She whirled through the fight in an almost dance, cleared the last half-dozen paces with a striding run, and dove headfirst through the open portals, confusing both the bolt-gunners behind and the halberdiers before. Landing on crossed fore-arms, she bounced to her feet and ran; no time now to pick directions, but it would be best to be on the expanding outside edge of the sphere of chaos she had exploded.

CHAPTER XXV

There was no problem blending with the crowd. Megan's problem was moving against it; the Avenue of Triumphal Arrogance was blocked for two kilometers back from the square, and the mass of humans and vehicles moved in slow inchworm jerks. The subtropical sun beat down with a pitiless white light that threw the scanty shade black and knife-sharp at the edges. Megan could feel it soaking into her skin, as palpable as the sweat that stuck the tunic to her back and turned her loincloth to a sodden raw-chafing rag; body heat joined it; marble-faced concrete radiated its share back into the throng. The heavy smell of massed sweat was thick in the humid air, and hot white dust stirred by thousands of feet.

She could feel hotter air puff up from her collar with every halting step. The press was worse than a theater or arena crowd in F'talezon, and these were aliens. Any close contact brought a slight overfall of emotion and thought, unshielded; there was the constant soft pressure of bodies and minds forcing their way into her own sphere of selfness. With an effort, she forced her attention on details—a small boy being berated for coming to the ceremony unwashed; someone nearby who had been eating strong onions.

With a skill learned in the childpacks, she wriggled forward and nudged against the back of a knee. The man staggered. "Apologies," she muttered, slipping past. "I stumbled." A narrow space between two goldsmiths let her through; there were advantages to small size, whatever the big redhair thought. She imagined Shkai'ra in this oilpress, and her lips quirked slightly as she ran a wet hand over a slick forehead.

She stopped again in a knot where two litters jostled for position. The wayservants jostled and strove to outshout each other, vainly; for all their curses and thumpings, the litters were jammed. Some of the crowd ahead were beginning to look and mutter, clutching resentfully at bruises. Even with meek clerks and law-fearing storekeepers, there were limits to what could be done with a hot, irritated Illizbuah mob.

The litters were placed down with a thump, and one noble leaned out from the shade of her awning to talk to her neighbor. She looked maddeningly cool in a tunic of multicolored silk ribbons tacked together every handspan; even the lapdog that panted beside her heightened the contrast. Beside the litter the bearers crouched, necks bent to keep their wooden fetters from pulling on galled throats.

Megan glanced down. There were many things missed by simple failure to pay attention to what was underfoot; being closer to the ground than most, she was less prone to that error. The litters were nearly a meter off the pavement on their legs, most of that showing as an inviting black gap between stone and the underside of the padded couch with the wayservants all ahead.

The shade was welcome. Megan relaxed into the comparative coolness and watched the ankle's-eye view of the crowd. There seemed to be too many here of equal rank for the shouts of "Way, way for the Brightness Iaasac's-kin" to have much effect, however many upperservants flourished the ivory batons of their status.

Most of the respectable part of Illizbuah was here; all those with guild or kin, and some of the less respectable as well. Shouts of "Stop, thief! She has my pouch!" rose above the dull surf-roar of the crowd. The sharp clear sound was a shock through that pounding of white noise; she thought warily that this would be the perfect place for an assassination, where no small betraying sound would be heard before the blade struck. The better thieves must be having a fine day of it. She suppressed the sudden crawling feeling along her spine. *I'm going into the temple to slap the cobra on the nose,* she thought irritably. *What are a few assassins to that? Besides, they've had chances enough to slay me.* Although that last was part bravado, she admitted to herself that she had been very lucky. Or . . . had it been luck? A shrug: she would never know what Power had been at her side.

Snatches of conversation drifted through the slats overhead. "The market for hides is booming, and we cannot get supplies."

". . . but Kinmother!"

". . . a new sheersilk tunic from Chin for the next festival."

The gaaimun in the next litter leaned over, tugging pettishly at the fringe of his striped awning. Megan wrinkled her nose at a wave of too-sweet scent, and felt the boards creak above her head as the woman there shifted backward. *Something we agree upon, at the least,* the Zak thought.

"Don't you think it's just a trifle too hot to really enjoy a Purification? One feels as if one's burning oneself. Although this is supposed to be a particularly disgusting heretic."

"Oh?" the woman above drawled with studied disinterest.

"Oh yes! She tried to teach that the Divine Effulgence was nothing more than a ball of glowing rock—and that it went around the earth, rather than the Ineffable Truth's teaching, that we circle about the God."

"Oh," came the reply. The Zak could feel both the gaaimun shift as they drew the suncircle on their breasts.

Ignorant foreigners, Megan thought impatiently. *Koru, Guardian of Lives, makes the sun shine and we do circle it. If it were glowing rock, the Dark One would have put it out. Silly thing to get burned for.*

She craned her head out from under the litter and looked ahead. The road broadened before her, fanning out in a delta shape as it joined the square.

"Ah, Jaabno, run over to that vendor and get me a cup of . . . What's this under your litter, Maahgli? A new pet?"

Glancing out, Megan met the gaze of her shade's occupant, their faces inches apart but reversed; she noted how the Fehinnan's silver-wound hair trailed in the dust as she knelt on the cushions and peered with bafflement under her conveyance.

"What," she said in outraged tones, "are you doing under there, taking . . ." She groped for a word. "Taking my shade without permission?"

She really looks very much like a sheep, Megan thought. *If sheep wore silk ribbons and jewelry. Nice piece of silver and turquoise.*

"Enjoying my road," the Zak replied. "If you must come and put your litter on it."

The Fehinna's puzzlement was giving way to real anger. Megan reached out and tweaked her nose sharply, then scuttled out crouched, weaving through the crowd at knee height. Given nimbleness, small size, and a ruthless willingness to hurt, it was possible to move with some speed, much faster than a search party of tall standing officials, even with the weight of authority behind them.

Behind her, outraged shrieks told of disorganization spreading. That had been childish, but then a childhood spent stealing buckles in the River Quarter was far from the worst training you could have for a time like this. *It will give that dull person something to entertain her tedious friends and relations with.*

The interior of the temple was almost as bright as the square, where the gilded dome had left phantom afterimages dancing across her eyes. The contrast with the darkness of the entrance tunnel was dazzling, and calculated. All four of the great lenses in the dome were uncovered, sending beams stabbing down through four hundred meters of air blue with incense to break blindingly off the circular gold-and-crystal sunburst Holy of Holies atop the central altar. A hand bell silenced the congregation as they crowded to the barrier, keeping the central dome free. There was no sound but the sighing of their breath and the deep, rapid chanting of the choir grouped around the balcony that girdled the dome one hundred meters above their heads.

The great jeweled sun-shape began to turn, smoothly, soundlessly, on jeweled bearings. The fierce light was thrown back in huge swirling patterns, through the hazy air, dappling the stern faces of the onlookers and the glossy interior of the vast building. A long-drawn AAAAHHHHHHHHH broke from twenty thousand throats.

From the eastern door, the entrance of the rising Sun, came the procession of the priests. The Reflection of the Beneficent Light himself was there, about him the gold-colored robes of the Inner Circle, each with a globe of purest crystal in one hand. They moved into the clear space about the altar, their sandals whispering in a swaying rhythm on the yellow marble, their left hands flashing up to stretch toward the sun, their right hands reaching to the floor.

The sound of their chanting rose, clear and deep: "Continuance of life! Continuance of Life! On High, on High, the Sun grants Continuance of Life!"

Behind followed younger priests, whirling about the procession. There were a thousand of them; half gripped hand bells of brass in their right palms; half rang bells of crystal and silver, an eerie tinkling resonance under the deeper tone of the metal. Their left hands swept tall unlit candles of deepest red through the air as they danced; the young faces were blank, ecstatic, as they traced an intricate pattern across the floor around their seniors.

Behind came red-robed priests, men and women who walked with a long measured stride alive with the consciousness of power: they were the Hands of the Effulgent Light, the ones asking the Question; they wrung answers out of heretics. In their midst, they carried the recanted heretic among them, roped under the arms and suspended on long poles to twist above the heads of the crowd. She wore a white robe with a stylized pattern of flames rising toward her face. The victim was unmarked; Megan could even see that all the finger and toenails were intact. But she was . . . not unconscious, for her eyes were open, and she moved. It was the pattern of movements that was strange—odd jerks and twitchings as if the human's limbs were trying to flex in directions not allowed for in their design. The priests set her down before the altar with a jar, and she gave a single scream.

Megan felt the overflow from the woman's mind and recoiled, even before the knowledge of what she felt seeped through. There was familiarity to the touch, like the Sniffer. Once, as a child, she had seen the ants at a nestful of hatchlings; a swarm cutting apart everything that had made her human.

The sacrifice writhed against her bonds as the red

robes fastened her to the central spine of the altar's disk. That rose, now, from the spinning gold, and showed itself to be plain, hard steel, black and smooth. The robe was ripped away, and the crowd fell to their knees, heads bowing like a ricefield in the evening breeze. Megan did not glance down; she had full opportunity to see the changes that had begun in the other's body. The victim's head rolled back, and she howled. Not a scream, but a thin screeching keen, and the skin bulged out in the beginning of a sack beneath her jaw as the spike bearing her rose.

A ripple went through the crowd. The Zak raised her eyes with theirs to the apex of the dome, smelling the fear-sharpness of her own sweat over the sickly musk of the incense. Half an hour ago, she might have convinced herself that she played a dangerous game. That was then; here, there was no escaping truth.

It took a moment for the significance of the shapes she saw to snap into a picture behind her eyes. Slowly, slowly, a massive lens was lowering from its niche at the very summit of the dome. Gilded chains thicker than a man's arm supported it, as it dropped with fluid precision to the center of the great space, then it intersected the four beams from the fixed lenses, and a fireburst of light sprang into being below it. Brighter than the sun; Megan's eyes averted themselves by reflex to the corona of trembling air that surrounded the point of focus. The chanting of the priests slowed; the young acolytes stood quietly in their ranks, swaying, their bells chiming with infinite softness, like leaves in a glass forest. The chanting rose and fell in harmony with the unhuman cries of the heretic as she was raised gradually into the region of fire.

Megan wrenched herself free of the growing swell of fascination and dread washing at the edges of her mind. *This was not what I came to do*, she reminded herself grimly. But there could be no better time.

She sidled over to one of the junior priests stationed

at the barricade between populace and hierophants. She tugged at his sleeve, gently, then more forcefully, as his rapt face remained locked on the scene above their heads. "Elder Brother—"

"Pay heed and do not disturb the Light!"

"But, Elder Brother, I feel the need to bare my sinful thoughts . . ."

"Not now," he said, his voice still vague with the blankness of the drugged. His hands made small fluttering gestures, but he did not look away from the rising pillar. It was far from the spot of incandescence, but there was a new note in the screams, and the bells of the acolytes rose to complement it. What the priests had strapped to the altar might not be human any longer, but it could feel pain.

Megan seized a hand, dug her thumb into a nerve cluster, and pressed the scrap of paper into his palm. The man started violently. The Zak was amazed; with that grip he ought to be twisting paralyzed on the floor.

"Outlander, if this is not important . . ." he began, glancing down at the writing. His eyes snapped wide; Megan could see the pupils swell and shrink to dots as a twitch of fear ran through his body. Screwing up his eyes, he averted them from the script as if to deny they had ever lain there.

"Stay here!" he gasped, panting, and blundered off across the floor of the altar space. At any other moment, swift murmurings would have followed swifter action from his superior. Now there was no reaction, even when he nearly blundered into a bellringer in panicky haste.

Megan showed a shark's grin as she watched the young priest repeat, more diplomatically, her efforts to arouse attention. The upperpriest responded well, once his junior waved the message before his eyes. He staggered, and would have fallen but for a strong young arm to hold him upright. The Zak was tempted to stay and watch the progress up the table of ranks; there should be increasing terror with every step upward, as those who might be genuinely feared if they knew too much were reached.

She turned and began her rapid squirm through the crowd. Resolutely, she kept her face turned from the point above. The screams of agony were shriller now, and on each the upper choir came in faultlessly, one octave below, the deeper tone prolonging and carrying the sound of pain across the echoing chamber. Woman and trembling light met; there was a moment of silence, then a steam-driven *fuff* as the moisture exploded out of the body. The pure carbon that remained burst into flame, and the pillar sank back toward the altar. The acolytes chimed their bells in a relaxing dissonance and danced forward to light their candles from the body, before sweeping out in a flower pattern to hand them to the waiting congregation.

Megan could feel the huge tension release the crowd, letting them sink back into themselves. Still, she reached the doors before the crowd itself could begin to move. Even slowed by shock, the temple security forces should be moving soon.

But by then I'll be in the alleys, she thought. *And the Reflection will have troubles of his own.*

The Second Priest, Kayhri, mounted the steps to the High Priest's level with the strangest mixture of haste and reluctance. The chancellor had finished the major ceremony and had left for his apartments before the Sunforsaken message had reached her. The great doors of the temple had already been ordered open to allow the minor ceremonies of the Seven Nights of Exultation Unhindered by All Tedious Ordinance to continue.

Great Light, she thought, *I would be the one to have to bring it to him. The faster I do so the safer*

. . . and also more dangerous. Divine Sun guide me.
Her thought trailed off as she tapped on the first door
of the Inner Sanctum, nodding to the young orange-
robe who opened the door. *That idiot Ehlvaio didn't
even think to have the bearer of this detained. Perhaps
he could see the justice in being kitchen staff again. . . .*
She stood on the mat before the door, genuflected to
the image of the Sun at eye level, and entered quietly.

This was not the audience chamber, but one that
had a balcony looking out into the dome itself. Below
the main platform ran another walkway that the guard-
priests alone had access to. Cubilano sat at the exact
center of the opening in the wall, surveying the crowd
that drifted to the doors not yet open.

She bowed at his back and waited, then cleared
her throat nervously. Cubilano did not turn from his
contemplation of the scene below the balcony, but his
voice was chilling. "You disturb my Communion with
the Sun after such an occasion?"

"Reflection of the Divine Light, forgive this one that
is less than the shadow that creeps . . ."

"Enough! Forgiveness is given to those who come
to the point!" Very slowly, he turned his gaze on the
hapless replacement of his chosen successor.

Fascinated, the Second Priest stretched forth the
hand with the scrap of paper in it, her eyes locked on
her superior's. "Brightness . . . the message of the
Guild of the Da—"

Struck speechless by the sudden motion, she froze
as the paper was snatched from her. He scanned it
and his face, which had been still before, hardened to
stone. "So, treachery. Where is the purveyor of this?"

Kayhri swallowed and thought of the condition of
her soul. "She was not . . . not detained, Brightness."
The rest of the words came in a rush that died away
awkwardly. "I will see personally to the lower one's
discipline, Brightness; he really should have . . ." Her
words lay in the thick silence on the floor. Dimly she

could hear the counterweights creak as the great doors began to swing open in the temple below, and the renewed crowd mutter as it shifted forward toward the outside. She braced herself for what was coming. She had never seen the High Priest move so fast, without the deliberation that was normally his, as when he had snatched the message from her.

There was the small sound of paper crumpling. She opened her eyes and saw that his were no longer fixed on her. He leaned forward over the edge of the enclosure and signaled to one of the red-robes.

"Younger Brother, there is another heretic in the temple. I trust that you will do much better than the last time." His voice rose just a fraction, and the icy edge was enough to make the guard-priest blanch. "Less than two days ago ... No, Kayhri, stay." He turned back to the red-robe. "Send another of the Hands to me. Go! And stop the doors, now." The crushed message was cast down without a second look. He knew what it said, and that was enough. Kayhri was not going to like her penance.

Megan looked out from behind one of the pillars by the doors. They were just starting to swing open, and she had to restrain herself from being among the first to leave. That would have silhouetted her between two groups of Fehinnans, the worshippers leaving and the next batch awaiting their turn.

Fishguts, she thought with disgust as the uproar began behind her. Not altogether surprising, but she had hoped for a longer period of disorganization. Someone in this pile must be competent.

Priests were trying to herd the congregation into order as they streamed toward the opening portals; they stopped midway through their arc, and murmurs of irritation broke out, almost loud enough to drown the amplified call from the corridor roof above their heads.

"Hearkening and Obedience!" The traditional shout of a temple herald brought slow silence. "Hearkening and Obedience! The Divine Light has revealed to Her Reflection that among our faithful ones lies a Shadow, an outcast of the Dark. This one takes the form of an outland woman, smaller than most, black of hair but fair of skin. All faithful, look about you! Examine your neighbor! If it is the one in need of Purification, draw apart from her. Touch her not! Point to the Darkness, that we may restrain it!"

Fresh tumult broke out. Megan drew deeper into the shadow of her pillar and watched the crowd break up into circles in the corridor and down the temple steps. Any short woman with fair skin seemed a fair target; she saw one blond ringed, and several men. Megan was not surprised, being familiar with the ways of crowds. Her eyes darted about.

A thin trickle of worshippers was still threading out the door, the heedless and impatient. There were not enough to provoke more than a quick scanning glance from the Hands who had begun to fan out through the mass of humanity. One was a prosperous merchant, spare and thin; his wayservant held a priest in argument as the master halted briefly before sweeping out. A young girl held the trailing end of his feather cloak from the floor, just in front of the pillar. Megan was careful to keep the razor-tipped ends of her nails clear as she clamped the carotids.

The servant woke a few minutes later, sitting propped against a temple pillar, with a splitting headache, wondering what the commotion was.

Megan busied herself arranging the fall of the cloak quite carefully as they passed the ring of priests into the heat of the square. The merchant had not noticed his change of servant, except for an irritable growl when Megan had jerked the cloth as the servant fell. They proceeded down the steps to his litter. Megan's neck prickled, and she expected to hear the shout of discovery any second. She kept her pace slow, matched to the dignity of the merchant, who turned to step into his conveyance.

"What? You're not . . ." he sputtered.

"Did you know that several threads are loose here?" Megan said. She leaped forward from the steps above, going right over his head as he ducked reflexively, the cloak flung completely over his head. "See for yourself," she said, and burst through the litter, scattering cushions into the crowd. She heard laughter begin as the man struggled to right his clothing, waving his arms in the air, hindering the attempts of his entourage to help him.

She reached the center of the crowd, and rather than continue running and drawing attention to herself, stopped and edged around, craning her neck and asking taller folk what was happening, all the while unobtrusively moving them forward while she moved back. Now . . . the alley should be around here somewhere. . . .

The Hands of the Effulgent Light surged out of the temple. The slow, steady surge of purposeful movement in the crowd was giving way to eddies of disquiet; the security priests clubbed and pushed their way toward the center of disturbance, hindered by the clumsy help of the pious crowd. The square locked tight into a straining mass of flesh, grilling in the heat, misted by white dust. Noise rose to a shrill, bewildered roar. Over it rose the slithering multiple crash of shod hooves on slick stone pavement as a squadron of lancers cantered into the square from the southeast entrance.

The horses were nervous, with a contagion caught from their riders. An expert might have seen a slight raggedness in their ranks, but the priests were not experts and busy besides. One broke free of the press and ran to grasp the bridle of the commander.

"Fellow Servant of the Light," he began. "We have to seal off—"

The lancepoint from the second rank took him high in the chest with a hard snapping sound as the four-sided pyramid-shaped head punched through a rib. The priest looked down incredulously, then staggered back off the point. He was still staring at the spreading stream of blood down his chest when the squadron commander spurred close and cut twice. The second drawing cut was across the back of his neck; the sword caught between two vertebrae, and the body hung for a moment until the weight pulled it free. The crowd, seeing a repetition of massacre, tried to burst away from the troopers crushing itself against the walls.

"Sun and General Commander Smyna! Sun and General Commander Smyna!" she called, and the troopers took it up raggedly. *"Treason! Treason in the temple!"* The squadron spurred forward, one or two horses stumbling and sliding over the body of the priest.

Another section of troops double-timed into the square from the eastern exit; infantry this time, with bolt-guns and the close-quarter stabbing spears of the marine detachments. The cavalry commander wheeled her mount to watch as the crowd poured away on either side like water cleaving before a ship's prow; the square would be empty soon, which suited her well. Cavalry needed room to maneuver, and a sitting horse was an easy target. Around her, brief combat flared; the Hands were not trained or equipped for open combat, and the citizens who had joined them were worse than useless. Screams drowned the battle shouts.

She spurred forward to greet the marines and take command. There was just time for her to realize her mistake before the bolt-gun shaft slammed under the nose guard of her helmet; it punched through bone and brain to bury itself in the sponge-and-cork backing on the other side.

"Treason! *Rebellion in the Iron House!*" the leader of the infantry called. His troopers swept forward, firing from the hip and then closing on the riders, whose mounts spun in caracole among the crowding bodies. Most of the Hands were down, and only a fraction of the crowd turned to join the temple loyalists. But a fraction of that crowd was thousands, and their hands moved for the lancers. Behind them, the last of the priests retreated up the broad stairs of the temple, stave and chain striking on lance shafts and swords; they stood, and fought, and died so that the great bronze doors might swing shut on the battle. And the cavalry retreated before the mob and the marines, their backs to the closed portals.

Even the horses went down under the weight of the mob, screaming in fear over the crowd roar. People fled the renewed bloodshed, clutching children and weaker kin, their festival finery spattered red. Elaborate masks crunched underfoot, blood oozing through empty eyesockets.

In the alley, Megan almost couldn't distinguish festival sound from the fight noise rising behind her. She blinked back a sudden memory of her own, stepping aside to allow a troop of dancers with torches and ribbons past her. They were laughing, and a few were singing and staggering slightly already in their dance, clutching at each other. Megan thought that they should encounter the new riot just around the corner of the square. "Hai! Hai, don't go . . . Hai!" Ignoring her, they went on. "Shit!" She felt a sudden choking. "They aren't kin of *mine!*" she told herself, hating what was happening. *I've my part in it. I can't ignore that. I'll just think about it later, when I can.*

She cut through a small park, almost stumbling over the couples in the grass. The crowd here was closer, and she stopped by a fountain to look for a rapid way through. She stepped to the rim and leaped for one of the dryer ornaments higher up. The stone under her hands was slick. As she went from fountain to low balcony, then up the side of the building, she noted that the color of the water was changing from blue to green. *Festival*, she thought. *We've given them some festival.*

CHAPTER XXVI

Megan lay at her ease on the tiles, chin resting on cupped palms. Shkai'ra leaned back against the shallow slope of the roof, sipping from the iron-glass flask. The red baked clay of the roofing was gritty beneath them; the warm-earth smell of it mingled with the rank smell from columns of smoke that rose like pillars into the late afternoon sky. From the fourth-story roof they could see a dozen major fires, and the clamor of the fire fighting squads mingled with the sounds of combat and riot—and even of celebration; this was a large city, and most of the citizenry were reluctant to sacrifice their festival.

The chaos in the streets was abating, as squads of the Elite Guard sallied from the palace quarter. Yet the faction fights still ran through the city, along street and alley, in chambers and close places beneath the earth. It would be days before the Sun-on-Earth's troops flushed the last hold-outs into the light; much that was done this sennight would never be known.

The two women lolled above; they had an excellent

view of the roads about, and their high perch made it unlikely that those who fought or fled would pass by.

Cat-content, Shkai'ra stretched. "Like nobles at the cage fights," she said, handing her companion the flask.

Megan didn't reply at first, sipping and replacing the cork. "Too many people striking at random. If someone kills me, I don't want it to be by accident."

Shkai'ra bent a casual eye on the scrimmage below. They could see figures dodging among the planters and shrubs, tree trunks and curbstones of a small public garden. Brief glimpses of black cloth, street tunics, the mottled green of camouflage paint on army leather armor. Harsh breathing of humans in desperate effort and fear of death; rutching of hobnails on brick.

"On the whole," she said, "I'm glad it worked out this way. Not just for us—there would have been a lot more damage if that war Smyna wanted came off." She frowned at herself. "Must be getting attached to this place . . . oh, well. At least this way it's mostly people who took up the sword themselves. 'Take up the sword, take up death: your enemies', and your own,' as the Warmasters say."

Megan looked at her. *She's surprised me*, she thought. Aloud, in a reflective tone: "I think that message is still dangerous—dangerous as a plague carrier—and it is still floating around somewhere in the temple." Her eyes dipped to the pavement.

This is not my city, she reminded herself. *These are not my kin . . . but I'm glad Jaipahl didn't live to see this. Fehinna is a beautiful place, if only the so-called government would just let it alone and not keep coating it in blood.*

"Where was I?" she asked, trying to match Shkai'ra's casual tone. "If any of them should start putting the facts together and realize who planted it . . ." She peered into the gathering dusk between the buildings.

"Amazing how long someone can live with the intestines hanging out, isn't it?" Shkai'ra chuckled and called out softly, "Stop trying to stuff them back in, man." She shook her head. "Still, they always try, don't they?"

"Perhaps Yeva has that answer as well," Megan said after a moment. "After all, some magics can be released from a distance."

"You and that spooker with the funny eyes." Shkai'ra looked down at Megan. "I have a spooker as a lover, and she wants to talk to the other shaman. Ahi."

Below, a priest stole furtively behind the knot of soldiers who stood panting and bleeding over the dead assassins. Her hand scattered a fine mist of powder; seconds later one soldier shook her head and another staggered, his features contorting. With shrieks of insane fury they fell on each other, striking blindly. A shortsword sheered off most of the priest's face as she turned to run, quite by accident.

"Not a bad sort, as shamans go," Shkai'ra concluded grudgingly. She swiveled herself over the rooftree and slid down the opposite side on her stomach, dropping lightly over the edge and landing, with springy resilience, on a small balcony.

"Coming?" she called softly.

Almost at that moment, Megan landed lithely on the balcony railing, which put her eyes nearly on a level with her comrade's.

"You bellowed?" she said, and was scrambling down the side of the building before the Kommanza could answer. Shkai'ra looked after her, cursed, and paused to thrust her sandals through her belt.

They were level as Megan leaped across to the lower roof of the next building. Shkai'ra grinned as she began to skirt the central courtyard, stepping quickly and lightly along the eaves just above the terra-cotta rain gutters. The smaller woman sped ahead again, down into the courtyard and along the top of a board fence.

"If you will take the wide road . . ." she called from a story higher on the roof of the next house.

Their speed grew, and with it a wild and reckless exultation. Shkai'ra leaped, and the rest of the journey was scattered fragments: a cat staring at her disdainfully from a ledge she traveled along hand-over-hand. a shred of vine tearing loose from under her hand, and a pot crashing down from its windowsill to shatter on the roadway.

They outdistanced the Elite Guard squads and the quiet they brought. That moved out in a wave from the palace of the Sun-on-Earth, making little distinction between revelers and rioters, except that the latter were more prone to stand and fight, and therefore die; the celebrants of the festival scattered with a drug-bright uncaring, to resume their play elsewhere. The streets were slick with blood and wine, bodies knotted together in love or death. And at the last, there was only the quiet of the richer sections of the New City, where celebrations were private and guards kept the peace.

Milampo's estate fronted on the Street of Sweet-Scented Shade Nourished by the Gold of the Sun. Chestnut trees lined the courtyard walls along it, meeting to mesh their leaves together over the pavement. The long green tunnel rustled softly in the light evening breeze, full of shadows and the smell of leaves. They slid down a wall, fingers and toes gripping, and dropped to the concrete.

"We've been—" Shkai'ra began, then pulled Megan back into the shelter of the doorhouse. A group of assassins flitted down the street, moving from tree to tree; they were in place for an assault on the merchant's house just as a squad of soldiers rounded the corner.

"Nasty weather lately," the Kommanza whispered,

as a shortsword flashed by their refuge. The flying point swung a trail of red that hung in a perfect arc before spattering on the whitewash above their heads; in the darkening light the blood was black against the glimmering paleness. Shkai'ra slid the latticed door closed: a risk, but it was unlikely that the preoccupied fighters would notice the slight movement. "It's raining sharp objects. Best we let these good folk finish their business before we knock."

Megan leaned into her companion's shoulder and sighed. *So nice to see a fight and not be involved,* she thought. Then: *Goddess, I must be more tired than I thought!*

The combat settled; in the last purple dusk of twilight, they could barely see flies settling. Shkai'ra opened the door, and they stepped over a lax arm that lay before it, a throwing star slipping languidly from relaxing fingers into a pool of blood.

"Ahi-a, we've been lucky." Shkai'ra mused. "Or the hand of a god has been on us, or a spirit, or . . ." She nodded toward the merchant's house, still reluctant to name the occupant. Names gave power. "You like that one, don't you?"

Megan's hand idly traced the graffiti scratched into the courtyard wall—"Hail profit"—and a crude picture of the Reflection involved with a mule.

"*Dah* . . . if matters had been different. I might have been her student . . . disciple, perhaps."

But we think too differently, a stubborn inward honesty said. Illizbuah and F'talezon are months' sailing apart, but the Guild of the Wise and the Lake Quarter were farther still.

"Give me steel anytime," Shkai'ra grumbled, hammering on the portal with the hilt of her dagger. "Killing people by . . . thinking . . . is, ah, sloppy, somehow."

The door-slit at eye level opened, and a frightened child's face peered through.

"Boy! Send to your master's guest, the Wisdom Yeva, and tell her that the message bearers have returned. Quick now! She might be angered if you keep her waiting."

There was the sound of a stool overturning and the patter of bare feet on flagstones. Shkai'ra nodded. "Easy enough to seize which name brings the fear-sweat in that household, and it isn't the master's." She snickered.

"You are quick enough to use the name of power, when it suits you," Megan said, bringing a rueful shrug from the Kommanza.

They waited. A bee wandered sleepily in the flowers of a vine that overgrew the walls; garden-scent blew to them, overriding the street odors of dung and death. Megan pushed herself upright and listened, head to one side. "Hola, he returns, and with one even smaller than himself. The merchant must have found grown folk too expensive to keep replacing."

The child led them through the half-familiar strangeness of the garden and into the main wing of the house. Guards and servants were absent, perhaps hiding in their quarters, or gone to find richer pickings than a trader's pay in the chaos of the streets. But the interior was almost painfully bright, with lanterns and a spendthrift's hoard of wax tapers.

Megan shuddered at some of the colors and decided that she much preferred the Weary Wayfarer's more subdued taste. Suddenly, she was sick of the inlay on inlay and over-ornamentation. Simple, clean-cut stone, beautiful for its own sake, was better. *Like home*, she thought.

Milampo Terhan's-kin was hopping from one foot to another—an interesting sight for one of his bulk. His round brown face was flushed and shiny with sweat as he waved small, beringed fists in the air. The color of his face almost matched the thick varicose veins writhing across spindly legs; they in turn set off the bright orange silk ribbons wound upward to his knees, securing his sandals. A purple tunic from Chin hung stiff with argent embroidery, cinched by an acid-green velvet sash. The costume was considerably crumpled, by both figure and unaccustomed exercise.

"Peace!" he shouted to the mage beside him. "Peace! Trade will be ruined for a year; my kin will be levied twice over for damage repair and municipal service—the reconstruction taxes will be worse than a war, with our competitors left to steal markets! And you—"

Yeva moved her fingers slightly, and Bors stepped forward. With no trace of effort, he lifted her out of her chair; in her white gown of linen she seemed a child, cradled against his breast. The disquieting white eyes turned on the merchant with the amused toler-ance of an adult for a relative's spoiled and noisy offspring.

"Peace," she said. "Your more moral trade-kin went to the flaying tables, arrested for their direct approach to the Reflection, for protesting his cherished Holy War. They sacrificed their lives; what have you sacri-ficed other than shaaid you don't care about and money?" She raised a hand, cutting off his bellowed interruption, to indicate the two warriors. "Here are those who carried our message with such skill and daring. Do they not deserve praise and reward?"

The merchant turned and regarded the two women. His first reaction was a drawing back and a glance about for his guards. What he saw was not reassuring: a tall scarred blond outlander, with the worn hilt of her saber under one palm and a small swift darkling, less obviously foreign but with a cold amusement on her face. They smelled of sweat and smoke, of things the Terhan's-kin had labored long generations to force out of their lives. He set his shoulders and was somehow more than an overdressed fat man squealing at fate.

"Magician you may be," he continued quietly. "But you have no right to make a jest of my life and the lives of my kin and guildsibs. Are we playthings to you?"

Yeva paused, surprised. Her eyes closed for a moment of thought, then strayed to the two who waited with an alert, wolfish patience. The merchant was a man without justice, but his accusation bit a little.

"Yet you asked our aid," she said gently. "You cannot cavil at the manner of it; we warned that it might not be to your liking. These two—"

"—probably tried to sell my life to the biggest bidder on a scrap of paper!" Milampo said.

"Certainly," Shkai'ra said. "But they wouldn't stay bought." Megan kept a considering silence, her eyes roving the surface of the room.

Yeva sighed imperceptibly. "There are things here which you cannot know," she said. "I may not tell, nor could you understand if you heard." She turned to the two. "And for the paper you left on the temple floor, do not concern yourself. That has been attended to."

Shkai'ra nodded stiffly. She did not relish the feeling of an unseen hand behind her striving, but there was little to be done.

"Out of my house!" Milampo stormed. It was an act of considerable courage, and his hand shook as it pointed to the door. "And take your greasy thugs with you!"

Yeva signed to Bors. "I go," she said. "And warriors of such . . . perception and resource will doubtless find their own recompense."

As Bors strode from the room, Milampo suddenly realized that his means of leverage was leaving. He waved a languid hand at Megan and Shkai'ra. "I'll have the porter give you a copper or two for your

trouble," he said, and started after the servant and the
magician, calling something about compensation. Shkai'ra
looked after the merchant and the mage with interest;
Milampo was sweating and trotting to keep pace with
Bors's long strides, his yapping complaints reminding her
forcefully of the dogs he bought for his watch system.

He seemed to have forgotten their presence completely: natural, or perhaps Yeva's last gift. Her eyes
followed the three out into the corridor; this led naturally to a cool, appraising examination of the interior
of the room.

It was interesting. The floor of this entry hall was
glowing, pearly Baihma marble, except for a twelve-
meter oval in the center, which was clear heavy glass
over a pool of fantastically colored fish. The walls were
hung with Pensa tapestries and hex signs, where they
were not crowded with shelves full of knickknacks.
Milampo's taste seemed to run to solid gold yoni with
emerald centerpieces, along with carved jade jaguars,
figures of swans and leaping dolphins done in a blue
glaze, crystal goblets tastefully inlaid with his name in
tiny rubies, and other items less restrained. A granite
plinth bore a silver statue of the merchant himself in
one-quarter scale; quite accurate, except that the artist
had left out twenty years and about a hundred pounds.
A scent of costly incense drifted on the air, overpowering
the smoke and stench from the festival and riot-torn
city. Cool air gusted up through ducts from the chamber
below, where slaves pedaled endlessly to power the fans.

Shkai'ra tapped a fingernail against her teeth.
Megan hefted an alabaster vase that held a white powder and several silver straws. A moment, and she
turned to find her motion echoed by the other woman.
Their eyes met, and Shkai'ra's mouth stretched in a
slow grin. "We'll need a sack," Megan said.

—"No, no, that's too heavy. Just pry out the gems."

"What, and ruin this thing of deathless beauty?" was the snide reply.

"You—yes, you, the greasy one with the double chins. Pick that up and . . ."

"A pity we don't own a horse."

"Oh, we will."

The guard had been doubled at the gate of the Weary Wayfarer's Hope of Comfort and Delight; no more was necessary. Here along the harborfront, sensible rioters, arsonists, looters, and celebrants knew better, even in a drug-fogged state. Even if one got past the guards, there were the guests to deal with.

Megan halted and stared fixedly at the pikeshaft that swung down to bar her way: it was at about chest-height for most, which put it on level with her eyes. She could see clearly the nicks of brighter wood in the heft where a blade had stuck. She turned her eyes to the door guard, the gaze flowing slow and gelid up the length of the weapon to rest on those of the pikeman. A spark of red flickered in the black of her pupils. "I'm a *guest* here."

His face flushed hot, then cold. The shaft swung up. Wordless, Megan stalked on through into the busy courtyard.

Shkai'ra followed, leading the burdened horse with a slow, ratcheting clatter of hooves on brick. Smiling, she rested a hand on the guard's shoulder.

"Smart man," she said, and laughed.

CHAPTER XXVII

"God Among Us, the prisoners have arrived."

Aygah the Forty-first, a young male Avatar of Her, rose from the chair. That was one of several low shell-shapes slung in frames of tubular steel. There were no Fehinnan sitting cushions here in the private audience chamber; the furniture was solid, waist-height, of plain blond ashwood polished to a silky finish; the only touch of luxury was a throw rug over a couch—north-western snowtiger, pale and silky and beautiful. The room itself was cool smooth stone on three sides, the fourth open to a view of terraced gardens and the Iamz, flowing molten beneath the dawn sun. The morning breeze blew through the open wall and its low balustrade, smelling of flowers and the brackish water of the tidal estuary.

Aygah sighed and slowly finished his cup of tea as Smyna and Cubilano were thrown down on the hard-wood boards at his feet. They lay prone, unbound; the guards stepped back to the walls and stood at an easy parade rest. Neither prisoner would dream of moving;

the God's presence pinned them more thoroughly than any spearpoint.

The petulant adolescent face of the Sun-on-Earth turned to the wall. A print hung there, strange to Feh-innan eyes: a grassy slope and a two-story house of wood; on the lawn a dark-haired woman, face turned away from the viewer.

"Damn," he muttered, in a language no human being had spoken in a hundred generations. "Almost got it right that time." He transferred his attention to the figures at his feet, and suddenly ... changed. Stance, the tension of hands and body, expression, all underwent a subtle transformation. In a corner, the crouching scribe wrote steadily: no word of the God was insignificant. All must be recorded, for the temple to plumb their oracular meaning.

He walked over to the two lying on the floor, his face somehow contriving to look much older; his voice changed, straining for a baritone that the body could not reproduce. "Riots," he said. "During the holy festival. My holy festival." He began pacing around the room, apparently arguing with himself over the two failed conspirators, the voice and stance changing as he spoke, often with dizzying speed.

"As the Sun-on-Earth ... no, you fool, I'm the Sun-on-Earth, and I say ... no, both of you are wrong. We are the God—STOP IT! All of you! This is confusing the issue! Riots, disruption. Remember that. All of us, remember and stick to the point! Well, if we insist ... I suppose.

"Oh, you have been a very naughty girl."

A senile voice won out and the God stood looking down at Smyna. "You ... lost the war? No, that was that awful woman a few centuries ago.... Ah, the riots—yes, riots!" Mumbling, the God paced across the two of them, paying them no more heed than rolled-up rugs on the floor. With a sudden fluid move, the God turned. "You wanted to start a holy war.

Without my—our! ... Go away and leave me alone. This is important—express permission. As well as causing discord in the Iron House—wasn't that her grandfather? No. No. This is today; now. Not four hundred years ago. Pay attention, can't you?—" The God-King slapped himself on the head, his right hand darting across to stop the left from striking again. "—Stop that!—Also killing many of the hands that I need to carry out my plans for Fehinna." The decisive voice faded again into the argument of many, and Aygah continued pacing.

"Got to find a better way to edit," he muttered. "Maybe use amnesiacs? No, too risky, might get stuck in a brain-damaged hulk." His voice was abstracted, turned inward. The body jerked, turned, strode briskly to the clerk in the corner and took paper and pen.

"Why don't you write something useful?" a new voice said—a woman's voice, with an archaic lilt to the spacing of the syllables. She dashed off a line and handed it back; the slow, inhumanly graceful pacing resumed.

The priest-scribe looked down. She was a scholar, of sorts, and recognized the cursive script in use before the Maleficent's time, before Fehinnan received an overlay of Pensa loan-words. *The Sunne-Suyr-Grawnd bai Truly madde*. She paled, looked up to be certain those eyes were no longer on her, and scratched the offending line out. Had not the God once said: "I am large: I contain multitudes"?

The God-King came to rest near Smyna, standing on one of her outstretched hands without noticing. There was a crackle, and beads of cold sweat broke out above Smyna's upper lip. She made no sound.

"*Look at me, woman,*" the Voice said. She knew that Voice; it was that aspect of the God called Must-Obey. She looked up into the eyes and felt herself falling, whirling away into a blast of contending voices; an image formed in her mind of huge dusty storehouses heaped with treasures and trash, glittering in decay. There was no resistance in her; three thousand years of submission lay behind her, generation on generation.

"Oh, I see. Yes, overenthusiastic. What *was* it that you did? Oh, yes—killed the shaahayds. No, they say shaaid now, don't they? And all those fires, and the soldiers fighting each other. Bad girl."

Aygah's face turned to the door. "General," he said crisply. A figure in green stepped in and saluted, bowing low and going to one knee with his face to the floor.

"Are those . . . hillbillies . . . tribesfolk, whatever, still being troublesome up in the Blue Ridge country?"

"Yes, God Among Us," he replied evenly.

"I really must do something about that," Aygah muttered, abstracted once more. "Poison gas? No, I already did that, and it didn't work. Plenty of time." The tone became crisp once more. "This one," he said, resuming his pacing and kicking Smyna absently in the ribs as he passed. "Send her out there, have her kill them. All of them, and don't let her back until it's done. Now go away, you foolish woman." Smyna crawled backward from the room, leaving faint blood marks where her injured hand pressed the boards. A silent servant appeared, buffed the spots with a cloth, and slid away.

"A shepherd," Aygah said. "That's what I intended the High Priest to be—Chancellor, my Right Hand— when I created the office." He looked down at the man. "Thousands dead, then a Purification disrupted by one woman, priests; *My Hands* killing soldiers and being killed. Raising taxes on staples to finance this little dream of yours? This is shepherding my flock? Perhaps I should give you to our enemies. You'd help them right into surrender. Bad boy. Bad, bad, bad."

A harsh bark of laughter, and he circled Cubilano slowly. "Why did we start that? The shaven heads?

Oh, you don't remember, either. Well, it was a long time ago ... you were the God only two hundred years before I was. Back to business." The boy sighed and tapped Cubilano's head with one foot. "Look at us, fool. We decide when the world is ready for Our benevolent rule. The Fehinnans as my chosen will be enough, for now." The voice darkened. "And you have the presumption to tell me what to do, with your little schemes? There is very little I can do to you that you haven't done or seen done. ... Ah." The God lifted his head as if listening to an internal dialogue. "Yes. Good that you reminded us. It was religious fervor that drove you to this. Commendable, in small quantities. The cannibals of the islands and south coast need to hear the word of the Sun. I think you are just the person to do the job. I never want to see your face again. If I do, Right *Hand*"—sarcasm rang heavy in his tone—"I'll have it removed."

He turned to the general who knelt by the door. "Advice. This one was supposed to give us good advice. We'll need a new adviser, new Reflection of the Effulgent Light, new Right Hand, new Chancellor, new everything. Wasn't—" He looked down at Cubilano. "I said I didn't want to *see* you again, tiresome fellow!" The man who had been High Priest crawled from the room; Aygah reflected that the man had seldom felt more genuine fear. "Didn't I tell you to fetch the old one—the one before that one ... what was his name, Arhis, no Harriz, something like that? I'll see him in a few hours, or whatever."

Absently, the God turned back to the table and turned a paintbrush in his slim fingers, his eyes straying back to the painting on the wall. "Next time I'll get it right," he said. "I may not have Andy's talent, but I've got lots of time."

In the corridor outside, Cubilano stumbled to his feet. Perfect humiliation had burned his face to a certain purity; the dark eyes looked inward, blind. Blinder than the ruined eyes of the figure who leaned on his staff among the line of those waiting for audience; Cubilano might have passed him by if the staff had not reached out to tap him on the chest.

The blind man's aquiline nose flared slightly. "Didn't recognize your old fellow student, then, Cubi?" he said, very softly. Cubilano jerked; nobody had used that nickname since the training classes in the temple, forty years gone. Forty years of struggle and effort. "We were friends once. Remember how I used to protect you from the well-born, who didn't like a scholarship boy studying in the elite school?

"But I recognized you," the blind man went on. "By smell. I have to recognize people that way, since you ordered my blinding. Even that I would let be, if you had been a good shepherd to the people; instead you burned them on the altar of your pride—sacrifices to yourself, not to the Divine Sun. Now go—" He paused, remembering what the other boys had taunted Cubilano with. "Go *scrape the chickenshit off your clumsy feet, serfkin!*"

The taunt lanced home, through all the years of mastery: a child's cruelty, to a small boy lost and friendless among the children of the great ones. Cubilano had spoken scarcely a word in all the time since the guard came. Now he cried out and raised a hand to strike. The spearhead dipped down and touched delicately at the base of his throat; he looked up along it into bored, cool young eyes under the helmet brim. His shoulders slumped and shuffled off down the corridor, and for the first time his walk was an old man's.

The soldiers of the Elite Guard were not too rough with Smyna: fanatics they might be, but soldiers were soldiers. The officer of the detail was almost friendly, in a distant way. The guard did not need to fear that her treason would prove contagious; he sent for the palace garrison surgeon, to splint the hand, and waited patiently while it was done.

"So, it's the border for you," he said.

Once the hand's healed, a fast horse and over the mountains, she thought. Not much of a chance; the Painted People of the mountains had little love for her breed, but a better path than a lifetime of raid and patrol work, and once over the mountains in Kaina; well, there was always a market for swords. *General-Commander of the Righteous Sword, then a mercenary at two bits the month,* she thought. Bitterness was acid at the back of her throat.

"Do me a last favor?" she said, putting down the winecup and watching unmoved as her fingers were forced back into their rightful positions.

"Depends," he said warily.

She flashed a bright smile that gave him a brief flicker of disquiet. *Lucky this one's going,* he thought. *Truly, the God is wise.*

"Just pass on to my kinfast: 'It was the red-hair's doing.' We've a previous debt with her. This makes it worth following up."

He shrugged incomprehension. "It seems little enough," he said, and hitched at his belt. "Time we were going; it's a long ride to Shaarlosvayal."

Jahlini wrenched the long knife free from between her opponent's ribs and came erect, shaking tension out of her shoulders. The dim flickering light cast shadows across the interior of the disused warehouse; the ranks sitting quietly on their heels beyond the fighting circle were motionless, patches of deeper black.

Usually there was a certain formality to meetings of the Adderfang Dark Council. Today that had been dispensed with. There were too many empty seats and too many wounded; the Southside Serpentchief sat propped between henchfolk, one eye gleaming fever-bright from the white bandages that covered her face. Patches showed redly wet, rimmed with dirty yellow discharge; her breath came in a rhythmic bubbling. The two supporting her shifted uneasily as that brought a faint hint of corruption, sweet and cloying. Who would have expected a human to have claws? They were uneasily conscious that their overlord was now in a minority; Jahlini had few supporters among the sector lords, now.

The chief of the Adderfangs rose from the body, gasping. *Too old,* she thought, conscious of the burning cut along one arm. *Too old, if only one passage leaves me winded.*

"That settles it," she said hoarsely, scanning the black-masked shadows-within-shadows. This was even more poorly lit than tradition demanded, and it smelled of the docks, coffee and molasses and timber-balk. The usual meeting place had proved to be known to the Intelligence Section; ten globes of lungrot had gone down the ventilators, followed by commando squads in gasmasks. *But they wouldn't follow us into the tunnels,* she thought with a flicker of triumph. *We can rebuild.*

"We can rebuild. We go to the cellars, fight off the other brotherhoods, then we rebuild—"

The Southserpent made a wet noise of assent. Jahlini looked in her direction and flinched mentally at the hate in the single eye, though it was not directed at her. There was little left of her face; Jahlini would have sworn it was impossible to live a day with those wounds, much less a week. The claws that had torn her face off newly come out of the sewers; the rot, Dark Shining One, the rot. . . . *But the red-hair is mine,* she thought. *When we have the time. The gates are watched, they can't get out.*

"Rebuild?" a man's voice snarled. "When the others have taken our protection circuits?"

"The smuggling?" another continued.

"Two of our joyhouses have been torched—and we don't have enough blades to protect them!"

Another figure stepped up to the edge of the circle, knelt to touch her knife to the line, and sprang in, fresh, tossing the blade from hand to hand. Behind her, there was a rustling as others moved to stand in line.

"Rebuild, with a new Adderchief," the challenger said. "Must be, oh, a dozen here with knife right."

Jahlini sank into a crouch. *But how many would try it, after I kill this one?* she thought. Her lungs burned, and the blood from her arm turned the sleeve sodden on her arm.

CHAPTER XXVIII

The jeweled message egg spun across the floor, trailing a length of silver chain and a large black tomcat providing momentum. Megan felt it bounce sharply off one ankle, then whirl under the bed; from beneath the mattress came rattling bangs and the cat's satisfied whuffling as he picked the toy up and moved it to a new spot by the door. Ten-Knife-Foot settled himself carefully, adjusting all four paws, then batted the sphere of diamond-studded silver against the oak panel. There was a hollow boom, and the ornament rebounded; the cat gave a small jump of delight and retrieved it to begin the process again.

The Zak turned a ruby idly in one hand, flipping it gently over each knuckle, holding it up to admire the tawny crimson reflections in its depths. *Pity I couldn't take the setting*, she thought. *I wonder where Milampo got the idol.* It was an even greater pity it had been one-eyed. A jingle drew her attention to the center of the bed. Shkai'ra had just upended another counting-house bag over her head, and a spray of tradewire and foreign coins tumbled down, slivers of red-gold lost in her mane of hair.

"I've always wanted to do that," Shkai'ra said, a little sheepishly, glancing sidelong at Megan sitting cross-legged on the window ledge. Bouncing off the bed, she crossed to where a mass of rainbow-colored silks lay tossed about. The tunic she was wearing was bright green with orange fringes; she pulled it over her head, rummaged in the pile, and held up another critically. Stretching, she rose to her toes and let the heavy dense-woven silk fall into place, sighing at the feel of the smooth fabric on bare skin. This one was a blue just short of black, the sleeves flaring to end above her wrists, the knee-length hem sewn with small bullion medallions that kept the drape smooth along the long taut curves of her body.

"How do you like this one?" she asked, buckling on a broad leather belt, tooled with vine leaves picked out in gold.

Megan looked up and smiled. "I like that. Much better than the red one before that. It clashed with you. That one shows you off."

She cast a critical eye on the pattern of gems on the white stone ledge before her and carefully placed the ruby into the design. "You want to see something funny? Come on."

She went into the warded room, picking through the minted bits for the silver, opening one of the windows. "Watch." She carefully aimed and tossed a bit into the midst of a group of revelers who were hitting each other over the head with bladders, elaborate festival costumes suffering under the wobbling blows. A second's pause as they realized what had hit the pavement; then a frantic scramble to grab the silver. Megan chuckled and tossed another bit into a group about twenty feet from the first. "Even without warding, if you're careful, no one *ever* thinks of looking up!"

The Kommanza laughed. "Godlike beneficence," she said. "More so—all the gods I've met are stingy as starving coyotes." She picked up a heavy, round Pensa coin, chiseled into fretwork, sighted, and flicked it off the head of a staggering reveler two stories below. The man in the fishmask staggered still more, looked down at his feet, and fell to his knees. He picked up the coin and gripped it between his thighs; puzzling, until they saw him raise both hands in the Fehinnan attitude of prayer.

Back in her room, Shkai'ra leaned back against the opposite end of the window opening and tucked her feet beneath her. "That dark brown looks good—a little drab for festival clothes, but good."

Megan looked down at her tunic and adjusted the sleeve, tugging at the small red embroidery. "Festival? It's comfortable, and dark. What do I want with anything more?" She was honestly puzzled.

"Well," Shkai'ra bent and seized a handful of fabric, "you might try this or this or this—" Laughing, she pitched one tunic after another over Megan's head, the folds of thick smooth cloth settling over her like huge orchids.

"Hey! Ach. Stop!" Megan sat down suddenly, overburdened with cloth, and pulled away the one lodged over her head. "I suppose they are nice. Like this one." The silks and satins slid to the floor, pulled by their own weight, except for the honey-colored one across Megan's lap. She ran her hand over it as if it were a cat and said thoughtfully, to the air, "This one reminds me of Shyll . . . in winter before the summer sun washes the hair color away. . . ." Her voice trailed off as she stared down at the cloth, her hand mechanically continuing the slow stroking motion.

Shkai'ra's grin faded. "Megan," she began, almost shyly. "There's . . . I've been an exile for a long time. I'm twenty-and-six snows; five years since I left the Zekz Kommanz, a long time to wander without a roof.

There's an estate. Not far from here; good pasture, and the pomegranates are sold by name. Back aways, I put a, hmmm, down payment on it. The owner lives elsewhere and owes me a favor. The manor is nice; not large, but, well—room enough for two, and to spare. More later, but . . ."

"The harvest festival will be beginning soon," Megan said. "And the river will be slowly starting to grow its skin of ice. The north wind will blow from the steppe, carrying winter in its teeth . . . I have a revenge. And kin."

She looked up at Shkai'ra. "Come with me. Only for a short time. I want to show you my home." She half reached out a hand to Shkai'ra, who had gone very still.

The Kommanza started to speak, then leaned her head against the windowsill for a moment. "Mine are a homefast folk," she said softly. "I have *do* have friends here . . . even though none so close as you, who I've known only this tennight. I know this place; the wounds of my homeroots are only now scarring. Must I cut them again?" She looked up, and astonishingly the cold eyes glimmered in the afternoon light. She held out a hand, palm upward. "Stay?" she asked, a plea without hope.

It was late. Megan raised her head from her knees and stared blindly into the darkness. Across the alley, on a ledge, two gleaming coals glinted; the eyes of a cat. She scrubbed angrily at the corners of her eyes. Water lapped quietly at ships and docks and pilings below the niche she had found on this rooftop. It smelled like home. The quiet call of the shipwatch drifted up to her ears.

I cannot stay. I cannot stay and I cannot demand that she come with me. This is her place, and I am as strange here as she would be there. I cannot stay. Goddess, weaver of lives . . . curse you.

She was perched where she could just see the four-master that had arrived yesterday. The ship looked sound enough, and the general air on board was quiet and calm: a timber run up the north coast, then across through the islands of the Great Sea. She would be on it when it left.

I want to scream and smash things . . . kill someone, hurt someone as much as I hurt. But I found out a long time ago that that doesn't work. She stood up and started back to the Weary Wayfarer, using difficult and dangerous ways across the roofs so she wouldn't have time to think. The new guard on the roof just nodded as she slipped past him. His silence had been bought with one of Milampo's gemstones.

She walked along the quiet corridors, her boots noiseless on the rugs, feeling sleep soaking the building. Every other lamp was lit, reflecting warmly on the wood-mosaic walls.

She curled into the warm curve of Shkai'ra's back a short time later, careful not to wake her. As she drifted to sleep, her thought was sorrow for leaving, along with joy at going home—strange and bitter-sweet. A tear slid down one temple and was lost in her hair.

CHAPTER XXIX

The wineshop was half sunk into rubble. Not ground—there was little in the harbor district of the Old City—this was the ruins of past cycles. It was dark inside, cool, musty and heady with the smell from the vats lining the back wall. Shkai'ra ducked her head beneath the low beams, staggered slightly, swayed back erect.

"Wine," she said to the proprietor. "Wine, strong an' cold." Her voice was slurred, and the staccato gutturals of Kommanzanu heavy in it.

The owner peered at the big foreigner. Most customers here ordered wholesale and knew their vintages. This one? "One-twenty-fifth silver for a liter crock," he said. That was outrageous, but the disturbances had raised prices generally.

Bloodshot grey eyes flickered over him; he could sense that they used him only as a resting point, focused on some inward thing. A hand tossed a minted bit on the table. A *gold* bit. A *whole* gold bit. Enough for a tun of Aahngnaak that would need four horses

324

to pull it. The shopkeeper felt a sudden chill; nobody treated money they had earned that casually, and this was no aristocrat. He whispered sharply to a kinchild.

"A stone jug: the Maanticell, quickly." That was a frontier vintage, respectable but not distinguished, the sort of wine a magnate would serve at a banquet.

Minutes stretched, and he watched the impassive hawk face. She had plainly already seen the bottom of the goblet more than once, but there was little of the slackness of wine; merely a cold grimness that settled like a mantle around her shoulders. The sleeves of her fine blue-black silk tunic fell back, and he looked at the thin white scars on forearms that rippled as her fingers moved on the worn bone hilt of a curved sword.

There was a clatter from the street door, and a ragged urchin slipped through the screen of wooden beads at the foot of the stairs, the door ward panting behind him.

"Pardon, Kinelder, he—" She swiped at the boy with her staff. "Come here, little limb of darkness!"

The child dropped flat under the swing, rolled across the flagstones, under a barrel raised on timber slats, and tugged at the red-haired foreigner's tunic hem, grubby fingers closing on the round gold-thread mandrels that hemmed it. The shopkeeper closed his eyes and winced; he was a kindly man and would not wish serious harm even to a shaaid cub doubtless come to see what he could pilfer. A clip across the ear would have been enough.

Astonishingly, there was no blow or cry of pain. He peered, and saw the bright head bent as the woman in the blue tunic went down on one knee. The boy grinned and shifted from foot to foot, reveling in his importance.

". . . more trouble than an ape, Dahvo," she said.

"No," the boy whispered, in a clear carrying tone.

"Said you'd want to know: 't old blind gimp bowl-shaker, tha know? Big one now. He . . ."

The woman grabbed him sharply by the forelock; the words dropped to a murmur. When she straightened again, her face had changed. She smiled, and the shopkeeper recoiled as she vaulted the vat with a smooth raking stride, landing easily. The wine arrived; she swept it up, weighed the stoneware jug thoughtfully, then tucked it under her left arm. "No use wasting good liquor," she muttered thoughtfully. "Or letting it get in the way." Her eyes rested appraisingly on the stairs.

The boy scurried up and tugged at her again, at the tooled leather of her weapons belt this time. She started from her tactician's reverie and grabbed him by the scruff of his neck.

"What, pest?" she asked, with what was almost a chuckle in her voice.

"Ol' bowl-shaker, he say tha'd give me a bit," he said hopefully, wide-eyed, with a look of total trust. The woman's eyes flicked back to the granite risers of the staircase, each worn almost to a U by sandaled feet.

"And you came without being paid in advance?" she asked. "No, here's your bit." She fished blindly in her pouch and pressed the result into his small, hot palm. He stared down at it and for once had no words.

She took the scabbard of her saber in her left hand, holding it horizontal to the ground for a fast draw-and-strike. "Stay here," she said. "Not much chance they're in place, but it could start raining hurt," she said, and was gone, taking the steps in a bounding run that left only a faint *tap-tap* of sandal leather on stone behind it. There was a blare of light and noise from the street as the door swung open, and a smell of dust; then the cool, fruity darkness of the cellar-store returned.

"Sun in Her Glory!" the owner of the store muttered. His gaze fell to the boy, who started, tucked the gleaming sliver of metal in a loincloth that looked to have started its career as a dishrag, and began to edge toward the exit.

"You can keep your reward, child of the streets," the shopkeeper said. The slum boy looked unconvinced, but there was nobody between him and escape. "It must have been mighty good fortune you brought."

Dahvo scratched his head, examined the result, and cracked it between thumbnail and forefinger. "Dunno," he said, puzzled. "The message—'Fear the revenge of the defeated, and take ship for your life.' Na much good about that, izzit?"

"Twenty?" The head supply clerk arched his brows. "Twenty breakfast and afternoon trays returned unused from second-five-west?" He pursed thin lips and rolled the cork-covered surface of his pen between ink-stained fingers.

Glaaghi scowled. The tiny attic office crowded around her, smelling of paper and dust, lit by a single skylight bright with morning through its coating of grime. The occupant fitted easily into the room; barely thirty, she knew, but looking older. He was pale, a legacy of his Nefaai father; thin brown hair receded from his forehead over pinched features.

"Do you realize," he continued, "just what the cost of—" He paused to examine a list. "The cost of ten times ten double eggs, corncakes, syrup, tea, coffee, lemonade . . ."

"Which you use for blood—I can see it boiling in your veins," she sneered heavily. "I tell you—" She hesitated. "I tell you there's something strange about second-five-west. I sent Ehaago there; he came back with the tray. A day in the sweatbox, and he 'forgot' again."

The clerk sniffed and steepled his fingers. "The fact

remains, with the disturbances, prices have risen. The Weary Wayfarer's Hope of Comfort and Delight is not a charitable organization, and we must all pull together to control costs. Prices have risen steeply. Now, a deduction from your very generous stipend—awk!"

Glaaghi closed a hand on his shoulder and another on his elbow, big work-roughened hands sinking into the flesh of a small man who had spent many years squatting behind his table. That overturned, and she led him to the door on tiptoe.

"So, I'll show you," she said.

"But, but—put me down, woman!" His attempt to free himself was futile.

"It's not polite to talk back to your mother," she said and thumped him down on the second floor.

He looked about the corridor. "Why deliver *five* trays to a four-room floor?"

"You can say that to—" They both started. The clerk passed a hand over the back of his neck in unconscious reflex at a feeling of cold wind touching his skin. The world blurred and shifted, as a pressure they had not felt lifted from their perceptions.

The cook looked down at the clerk. "Didn't you just say, four rooms?"

He nodded again. "Of course, I—" He stopped, with a mental sensation of running into a concrete wall. "But . . . there are five rooms here! There are five on all the floors. I . . . forgot. And *I remember forgetting.*"

They both drew the circle of the Sun on their breasts. For a long minute they stood and stared at each other, implications running through their minds like rabbits before the hounds.

"There's always a certain amount of wastage," the clerk said thoughtfully.

Glaaghi nodded. "Not waste! The servants get it, and the hogs what they won't eat!" She nodded again, with enthusiasm.

He tapped at his chin. "In any case, the room fee covered it."

Glaaghi waited through a musing silence.

"Well, we need to order the new rugs and arrange protection from the new Dark chiefs."

"And no mystery here, eh?"

"Mystery?" the clerk said, arching his brows once more. "Of course not. And now, Mother, I think we both have business to attend to." He minced decisively down the corridor.

CHAPTER XXX

Megan tilted her head back against the mast and looked up, up to the dizzying height where the sails were being released from the port bindings; quick-release knots were tied at the reef points of the smaller sails, and the larger ones loose-hauled. The rigging swarmed with crewfolk, seemingly as tiny as the gulls wheeling raucous above. The breeze was off-shore, running with the beginning of an ebb tide, but still the air bore a hint of open sea.

She looked down at her hands, lying on her crossed legs, warm in the sunlight. *Why so cold and empty?* she thought. *I'm going home to fix Habiku.* Her goods were stowed, with a minor ward to make sure that no straying hands discovered reason for them to disappear. The ship was making ready to cast off on the shipmaster's word, and the pilot stood by the wheel.

So why the tight feeling under the breastbone? It was absurd; even Shkai'ra would laugh. Shkai'ra. *You did say goodbye,* she reminded herself. *You did leave the kin-gift knife with her, so there's still a link. It isn't as if she died; life will continue. . . . So why do you feel so alone?* she asked herself sardonically.

There was the usual last-minute confusion at the boarding plank; a kinfast of fur traders was late, and their folks were dashing up with bundles in their arms. The sailors avoided them with practiced nimbleness, until a brace hauling on a line chanty-walked backward into a servant scooping spilled beads off the deck; there was a curse from the petty officer, and the sound of a rope's end encouraging the landsman to mind his step. The shipmaster shouted over the side as the row tug bobbed alongside, looking woodchip-small beside the great windjammer.

Tide at full flood soon, Megan thought. *We'll be underway in twenty minutes, with the favoring wind, and more easily than the mankiller lanteen rigs common at home.*

The Zak surged to her feet and strode to the rail, as if to leave hollowness behind. Leaning on the teak, she looked out over the docks. Alien. All strange, even the smells, too warm and spicy beside the cold riverports of her memory. She wanted to be home; not going home, but being there. She drove one nail into the hard wood and watched the teak splinter up around it, oblivious to the clatter of low-geared winches behind her raising a spar.

I told her I'd miss her. It's not even a couple of hours yet. Damn. Going nowhere in circles if I don't stop.

She forced herself to concentrate on the ship; there should be useful hints, here. *Let's see.* Square rig above, fore-and-aft below, staysails . . . A young crewwoman skipped nimbly along a spar, far above.

Wouldn't Shkai'ra have just cringed at being that high, she thought with the beginning of a smile. *And done it anyway—damn!* Wistfully: *But I wish I could have shown her a Ri.*

* * *

The horse shied. *Bastard kinless cowturd,* Shkai'ra thought savagely. There had been no time to saddle, barely enough to throw the frame for the heavy saddlebags over the restive animal.

Just the sort of handless cow that a merchant would buy, she thought as she edged it, snorting and rolling its eyes, through the gate and into the street. *All looks and nerves, no stamina or sense.* This was the sort of beast that shied at a blowing leaf or a shadow, Zailo Unseen alone knew what—

The horse did a standing jump, all four of its slim legs shooting out in an equine starfish. It landed, bucked hugely, and bolted. Shkai'ra's legs clamped home effortlessly; she had ridden from the age of three, and nothing short of a warhammer could throw her, even bareback. The saddlebags pounded against the horse's shoulders: from one came an enraged ERR-EHRO-HWAW- ERRRR as Ten-Knife had the air squeezed out of his lungs in midhowl. Chickens, children, and pedestrians bolted from her path; she retained enough control to swerve around a cart laden with early-season watermelons and baskets of peaches. That prompted a thought; the curved sword slipped into her hand, rose and fell with a solid *tchik* of steel into pine as she slashed the ropes holding the rear gate in place. Behind her there was a roar of falling fruit, the wet sounds of melons striking stone, a wail of peasant anguish; twelve span of oxen tossed their heads and lowed plaintively as she dashed by. Then she was around the corner and onto Delight Street; it would not be wise to gallop here, with the Watch so thick. She reined in and risked a glance behind.

There was no obvious pursuit; the remnants of fallen factions would not dare to operate in the open, not yet, not while there was a chance of catching her in the streets. She used the point of her saber to twitch a blowgun dart out of her mount's haunch, then reined it in sharply with one hand. Behind her, down

the Laneway of Impeccable Respectability, came the
joyous screaming of the street children as they
swarmed over smashed melons. The Kommanza
looked up through heat-haze to the morning sun; she
had a little time, and there would be few faster than
a rider to follow. The main gates would be watched,
of course, but there were too many ships and too
much harbor, if she did not linger to haggle for
passage.

Swing south to the harbor, she thought. *Then west.
Sure as there's pus under a scab, they'll be after me
soon.* She heeled the merchant's show-beast into a
slow canter, threading her way among wagons and carriages and pedicabs. The dart had probably been poisoned, but horses had more mass than humans; it
should last. Then whoever ate it was welcome to the
bellyache.

And I feel godsdamned wonderful, she thought. *I'm
doing what I really wanted. What's Illizbuah to me?
You were taking counsel of your fears, stupid bitch.*

The docks and warehouses of the Northern Adventurers were crowded; half a dozen sizable craft were
leaving on this tide, and twice that number of coasters
were making ready to beat north from Port to Port.
The sea wall gate was opening as the tide matched
the water in the basin, letting the first of the coasters
through.

The air was pungent with the smells of sugar and
wine, dried fruit and heavy cheap rum; bales of cotton
cloth and crates of tools and weapons stood by. Mus-
cle-powered cranes ratcheted; carts rumbled by on
ironwood rails, coasting down inclines from the upper
stories of the warehouses. Porters trotted up gang-
planks, bent double under their burdens, naked skins
shining; an overseer stood by with her whip's jagged
ceramic beads dangling against one leg. There were
carts and wagons aplenty; few looked up at another

rider, even one forcing her way through the throng with unmannerly haste.

Wish I could use my saber, Shkai'ra thought. But that would be madness; not only was there the Watch to think of, but sailors were not as meek as most city Fehinnans. It would have been more useful to unlimber her bow, in a running fight like this. These easterners did not understand horse archery. . . .

The weight of the animal forced a way for her among the crowd. It was winded now, favoring the right foreleg, muzzle low and trailing streaks of foam. There was more on the front of her tunic, spattering it where it wasn't dark with horse sweat. That brought an absurd pang; she had *liked* that dark silk . . . because Megan had.

The beast lurched and staggered sideways. *Poison,* she thought. Horsewoman's reflex brought her legs up and she vaulted off. The animal splayed its hooves, attempting to recover; one knee buckled, and it went over on its side, kicking wildly. The bystanders scattered from the hooves. Shkai'ra darted in, swearing, thankful that it had collapsed on the gold and armor rather than her cat. She seized the leather strap connecting the bags, waited for a heave, and pulled it free.

"You," she snarled, catching a bystander by the collar. "Where's the *Gullwinged Gainsnatcher?*"

"There" the man choked, pointing. "Just casting off—leggo."

Shkai'ra threw the saddlebags over one shoulder with a grunt of effort and added the dufflebag as she looked behind her. There were half a dozen figures pushing their way through the crowd; hard-faced, looking uneasy in their civilian tunics of unbleached cotton. Two carried bundles wrapped in rags, and the shape suggested bolt-guns. She craned, using her height recklessly; yes, others with hats on heads that might be shaved. She did not bother to check for Adderfangs; if they wanted to be unseen, they would be.

One of the first party spotted her copper-blond hair over the dark crowd. She could see yellow teeth bared in a pockmarked brown face.

She turned, kicked a man behind the knee, forced her way into the space he left, and shoved. *It should be easier for one than a group*, she thought. *I'll gain some distance on them.*

There was a weary *errowr?* of protest from one saddlebag.

The gunwale under Megan's hands was starting to take on the appearance of worm-eaten barnboard, splinters sticking up in random directions. One of the crew had ventured to protest, pausing in her way along the deck, and was greeted with an icy stare and the slow, reflexive crooking of one hand. The crewman decided the gunwale could always be sanded smooth later, and took his eyes elsewhere while he still had them.

Megan looked out over the crowd and vaguely wondered what could be blocking the way down the road, just in sight around the edge of the oil jars and livestock cages being loaded on the next ship. Something was disturbing the flow of the crowd; heads were starting to turn.

The third and fourth mooring ropes were just rattling on deck when an outraged shout rose from the spot where the traffic was blocked. *More interesting things going on*, Megan thought. *That's one thing I won't be sorry to leave behind.* A snide voice in the back of her mind commented that she would probably go mad very shortly of boredom. She sighed and looked down at the scratchings on the rail.

The crowd thinned out toward the water's edge, where the piers projected out from the dock like the teeth of a comb; there were too many carts for toes to be jammed so closely together. The *Gullwinged Gainsnatcher* was two piers west; the Kommanza could see her masts and stays, swaying as the tug pulled her head out into the basin, but she had not cast completely free, not yet. A pile of cotton cloth stood before her, twice head-height; cheap stuff printed in the bright patterns the northern forest and sea-land tribes of Newfaai and Naiskat loved. She went straight at it, not even slowing her run, up and over the steep-sided pyramid of cloth. As she reached the summit, there was a deep musical throb, and something half-visible went *thrup* by her shoulder.

She slipped down, braking with her heels; another bolt slammed through the space her spine and breast-bone had occupied a moment earlier; the skin between her shoulders roughened. Then she was flashing along the clear space beside the departing ship, toward the great cable still stretched from a concrete bollard to the stern. It was the last, holding the three thousand tons steady while the tug brought the ship's stem into the current. The longshore crew stood ready to hit the release catches; tension pulled the meter-thick sisal taut, squeezing water in a steady flow out of the fibers.

Shkai'ra felt the breath panting deep and swift into her lungs. There was no time, not with a repeating bolt-gun behind her; eight meters of water between her and the deck . . . and she was carrying nearly her own body-weight in gear.

Her teeth grated painfully as she leaped from dock to bollard and out along the cable; the thick hawser seemed suddenly thread-thin as it stretched ahead to weave through timber balk below the rail. Below, the morning tide sucked hungrily at the oaken piles of the dock.

At the scream and thrum of weapons, Megan's head snapped up, just in time to see bright copper hair flash, then Shkai'ra pelted through a clear spot. *Running as if she could outrun bolt-guns,* the Zak thought. A bolt skittered by, shattering on a stone column, and the Kommanza was up on the rope connecting the ship and the dock. The scene froze with the longshoremen standing, mouths agape, staring at this madwoman.

"Move!" Megan cried. "If you freeze you'll fall!" Her voice was lost in the noise. "Move!" she screamed. And other running figures were now visible. One stopped to kneel and take careful aim.

Shkai'ra's feet gripped at the rough surface of the sisal through the thin leather of her sandals. Natural balance and warrior training took her out above the hungry water, foot curving swiftly before foot in a walk that was half a skip. *Got to keep going—fast,* she thought. Like tumbling or a sword-hand throw. Faster you move, easier to balance.

She was halfway between dock and ships, and even the weight of the hull could not deny the hawser a slight curve. There was a massive sudden impact below her right shoulder, the blow of a sledge swung overarm. She felt a sharp prickling as the point of the bolt touched her skin, a tip of metal through the saddlebag and the steel helmet it contained. With a monstrous wrenching effort she seemed to leap, twisting in midair, coming down straddle-stanced along the rope, crouching. Her balance was saved, but the position immobilized her for a crucial brace of seconds. She looked back, to see the bolt-gunman kneel and sight; looked at her own death.

Something snapped in Megan's mind. The lost, cold feelings surged up, becoming raging flames, forge-heat. Living elsewhere with Shkai'ra alive was bearable. Her akribhan dead?

"NO!" Her hands leaped forward almost of their own volition, one pointing to the bolt-gunman, the other raised to sky where the Sun shone. For an instant, she forced the pool of Fehinnan Power to her thought, bearing the shrieking pain as she called for fire. A red glow outlined her whole body, rapidly brightening to orange, like glowing coals, drawing a line from the sun, through her, to the bolt-gunman on the dock.

He threw back his head and howled, flinging the weapon from him, tearing his clothes and hair, screaming that he was on fire; his skin blistered, turning black, cracking open, though no flames were visible. He threw himself into the harbor, still screaming.

Steam rose.

Shkai'ra darted the last ten steps to the railing. Behind, there were screams and frantic prayers and a sickeningly appetizing smell of roast pork; the crowds exploded away from the place of magic like quicksilver on glass. But not many had seen, and it would take time to spread word. The Kommanza cleared the rail, tossed her burden to the planks, and dove, pulling the slight figure of the Zak down with her. Another bolt buzzed by overhead and sank a handspan deep in the rearmast; others followed, and a blowgun dart. Then the whole great fabric of the ship lurched as the longshore crew slammed their mallets into the releases of the bollard. There was a sudden alteration in the movement as the *Gullwinged Gainsnatcher* slid out into the harbor basin and swung toward the open gate; above, canvas crackled as the crew unrove the topgallants to put steerage way on her.

Through the gates, the twenty oars of the tug flashing. They cast off and reeled in their towline as the offshore breeze and the making tide caught at the long hull. The ship heeled, and the keel bit water as she headed for open river and the sea beyond.

Megan lay limp beneath Shkai'ra as the Kommanza raised herself on one elbow. Her eyelids fluttered, and a small sound escaped her.

Shkai'ra slowed her breathing with an effort. "I

changed my mind," she said. The thin mouth moved in a half smile. "Sea voyages are so healthy. . . . You said something about revenge on someone?"

One of the bosuns strode near, a belaying pin tapping at the hilt of his knife. The blond woman jingled her pouch, flashing a gold bit between thumb and forefinger, and the bosun smiled. Beyond, Ten-Knife's small black head poked free of a saddlebag, glanced about, then retreated to lie glaring in the sheltering darkness, eyes darting from side to side.

Megan's eyes snapped open, and she tried to raise herself on one elbow. "A . . . sloppy . . . way . . . to kill someone, hey?" she gasped, and smiled.

"It'll do," Shkai'ra said, returning the smile; it lit her harsh features. "It'll do very well, love."

APPENDIX A

Glossary

All terms are Fehinnan unless specified.

A-moi lei-ehuk naigz—Kommanzanu, "I love my horse" (literally, I endure a state of fondness for my horse)

Aahngnaak—a wine

Ah'yia—a river

Ahkomman—Kommanzanu, the kinfast (marriage) of the gods—the High Kommanz

Ahrappan—Kommanzanu, berserk

Akribhan—Zak, an endearment

Almerkun—northern of the two continents on the west shore of the Lannic Ocean

Aykkuka—sergeant

Baiwun—Kommanzanu, a god, Baiwun Thunderer

Baihma—a southern sea island

Byeliy-skayishka—Zak, white-lock

Cayspec—a river and bay

Celik Kizkardaz—Zak, "There is steel between us"

Dhaik'tz—Kommanzanu, shaman, wise person, scholar

Dhilmaan—loving-twin, a two-stage poison

D'waah—a country just northeast of Fehinna

Ekafrek—Kommanzanu, slave, contemptible, scum

Eassho—eastern principality on the shores of the Kayspec

Eh, Ka, Sh'ra—Kommanzanu, one, two, three

Eh'mex—Kommanzanu—the god Baiwun's hammer

Eh'mex mekagro nai—Kommanzanu, "Eh'mex be far from me"

Fa'hr—Kommanzanu, respect

Fangaz'i whul pukkut—Kommanzanu, "a sheep-bitten wolf," unbelievable

Fehinna—a country on the east coast of Almerkun, on the Lannic Sea

Freyat Kiskar—Zak, friend of kin

Gaaimun—the highest class

Gawhud—a northern god

Glitch—Kommanzanu, godlet of fuckups, trickster figure

Granfor—Kommanzanu, as in "the fortress of Granfor"

Haaichedew—goddess

Haytin—southern islanders

Iamz—the river where Illizbuah is located

Illizbuah—capital of Fehinna

Jayskri—a northern god

Kaahlicks—a distance

Kaailun—a southern country

Kaina—a country across the Palach mountains in the west

Kommanz—a people living in the far northwest (see *Ztrateke ah'Komman* and *Zekz Kommanza*)

Kommanza—a native of the tribe, Shkai'ra's people

Kommanzanu—the language

Kouritz h'rokatsk—Zak, "Conceived on a leprous corpse"

Kyuba—an island in the Southern Sea

Laaitun—small military unit, 20–30

Lakaz—a northern country

Lannic—the sea between continents of Almerkun and Hirop

Lawkup—admire

Maailun—a country north of Fehinna

Maanticell—a Fehinnan wine

Minztan—forest-dwelling people of the northwest, near the Kommanza

Mitch'mi—Kommanzanu, "Be with me"

Mo'kta moi-trutka azhyt—Kommanzanu, "Well, dip me in dung"

Mofoar—Fehinnan for slave, slavish

NaZak—Zak, foreigner

Naiglun—northeastern coasts of Almerkun

Newfai—a northern country

Olsaytn—a northern god

Payalach—a pale-skinned tribes of the western mountains, barbarians

Paancah—a goblin or devil

Penza—a northern people divided into many city-states

Poquay—fortified slave trading post

Raisak Staaiun—the compound where the God-King is renewed

Rauquai—Zak, an exclamation of either mild pain or pleasure

Ribbidib—Illizbuah, the gull-headed, six armed god of luck

Rokatzk—Zak, a curse (see *Kouritz h'rokatzk*)

Rozhum—Zak, so be it

Saahvyts—a goblin

Sainclem—a paradise in the uttermost west

Shaahayds—an archaic term for shaaid (five hundred years or so)

Shaaid—lowest free class

Shaarlosvayl—a small city in Fehinna

Tabana—a flower arrangement

Tecktahate—kingdom, state (lit. "overlordship")

Tecktahs—nobles, lords

Tuk—Kommanzanu, take, sieze

T'hait—Kommanzanu, that, those objects

Uraccano—hurricane

Ussay—a northern god

Versht za—Zak, "Do you understand"

Waybecs—a goblin

Whulzhaitz—Kommanzanu, sheepshit

Yawac—a northern country

Zailo—Kommanzanu, a god, Zailo Unseen

Zaik—Kommanzanu, the supreme god

Zak—a country east of the Lannic and the Mitvald sea, Megan's people

Zekz Kommanz—the six realms that make up the country of the Kommanza

Zh'airzfurd—a town in the Zekz Kommanza

Zh'uldaz—Kommanzanu, warrior (or killer, murderer)

Zoweitz—Kommanzanu, a curse

Zteafakaz—Kommanzanu, steerfucker

Ztrateke a'Kommahn—full name of the Kommanza pantheon, the gods

APPENDIX B

Fifth Millennium Notes
(with files from Karen Wehrstein)

LANGUAGES

General Note: The spoken languages of the Fifth Millennium generally arose from small groups—often only a few hundred people—of post-Fire survivors who remained isolated for many generations after the fall of global civilization in the 2040s. The population of Earth remained below 100 million total for nearly a thousand years after the disaster, and by the end of the Fifth Millennium (c. 5000 AD) had risen to no more than approximately 600 million.

LANGUAGES OF ALMERKUN
(N. AMERICA)

General Note: The area between the Arctic and (very roughly) the old U.S.-Mexican border spoke languages derived from pre-Fire English. By 5000 AD, this could mean little more than the present-day common origin of, say, English, Hindi, and Armenian in Proto-Indo-European of 2500 BC.

KOMMANZANU

Origin: English, some influence from Lakotah, Cree. Earliest written form: runic syllabic script in use for ritual purposes from c. 3200 AD.

History:

Proto-Kommanzanu was formed in the 2044–2800 AD period. Linguistic change was rapid, as the core group of speakers moved repeatedly into new environments and underwent very rapid cultural change. Characteristics were loss of vocabulary items (e.g., literate and technological terms) and radical simplification of word-stems.

Old Kommanzanu arose 2800–3000 AD, once the original speakers settled in the central Red River valley. An inflectional grammar using both prefix and suffixional modifiers developed. Vocabulary developed several specializations, e.g., many words for different states of grass, and a very extensive set of terms for combat and war.

Modern Kommanzanu—a fairly arbitrary term—dates from the period of expansion, as the Kommanz peoples gradually pushed north and west through the tall-grass prairie zone between the High Plains and the boreal forests, eventually (c. 4200 AD) reaching the Westwall (Rocky) mountains. Significant developments included the development of a positional syntax requiring both inflection and position with the sentence to agree; also a glottal stop and a "click" sound similar to that of the ancient and unrelated Khoisan languages of southern Africa. Tone also became more important.

Contact with the substratum languages of the expansion zone produced dialect growth, as did continous contact with the steppe nomad (graizuh) tongues and the Minztan language group to the east and north. Also, the original "Granfor" dialect was the main source of innovation, and the western and northern versions are more archaic.

Dialects: All the *Zekz Kommanz*, the Six Realms, speak mutually comprehensible dialects of Kommanzanu. The northwesterly dialects are "old-fashioned" to the ear of someone from eastern core area. E.g., Granfor (Red River) *mitch'mi*, "with/for me," is pronounced hard *m—eht—ch* (as in *child*), *then '* (*glottal stop combined with "click" sound*) and "*mi*"— *with a nasal sound. Kai-Gara equivalent, whitch-me*.)

Area: Northern tall-grass prairie zone of Almerkun (N. America) in an arc from roughly northwestern Iowa through south-central Alberta.

Description: To outsiders, Kommanzanu sounds choppy and guttural, with the hard "click" sounds breaking up the flow. Stress rises rapidly at the beginning of a sentence and falls slowly; stress accent is used to indicate mood and voice (e.g., interrogative).

Sample Vocabulary:

naik	horse
zteaz	cow
zhiv	knife
bannaf	sword
s'tyka	lance
whul	sheep
gakk	stranger/enemy/slave/spy
moi	to me, mine
mi	I, self
yoi	to/toward/concerning you (singular)
a	prefix, to/toward/concerning
fut	castle, keep
ztun	stone
ahrappan	berserk, mad with anger
ahKomman	High Gods
kh'utz	axe
zhop	cut

Number of Speakers: c. 1,500,000

FEHINNAN

Origin: English, Tidewater Virginia, nuclear area between Iamaz and Hannosc rivers.

Earliest written form: Old Fehinnan, c. 3000 AD.

History:

Old Fehinnan, roughly from the origins of the language through its first thousand years. At this stage the language (always very conservative) was closely similar to English, differing mainly in developing a five-case declension system for nouns and an inflected verb, combined with a noun-adjective-verb word order.

Old Fehinnan (probably originally spoken by no more than 10,000 to 20,000 people) spread through developing trade contacts to much of the old coastal plain and piedmont areas of the eastern seaboard, from the Delaware south to Georgia. The northerly areas remained in fairly close contact with the central dialect, but the southern—Kai-Lun as they came to be called—diverged, under the influence of the Palach highlands tongues. Fehinna at this time was a loose, mainly religious confederation of tiny village republics, feudal estates and fishing/trading towns, centered on Willzburh (later Illizbuah). Large areas of wilderness separated the inhabited areas, and there were probably wide divergences of dialect. Little knowledge of these has survived. The Willizburh dialect was used for ritual purposes.

Middle Fehinnan (or the High Speech) emerged as the urban and upper-class language of the First Tecktahate (First Kingdom) of Fehinna, established in roughly 3100 AD and enduring, gradually declining, until 3800 AD, centered on Illizbuah. At its height the First Tecktahate absorbed most of the eastern coast of the continent, but it was loosely organized, feudal in its core and surrounded by lightly governed vassal states, some still tribal. Characteristic features were the acquisition of a tonal (sung) accent system to accompany the already elaborate inflections, and absorption of vocabulary elements from other languages. The written language was gradually modified to accommodate changes, especially by the development of diacritical marks to indicate tone.

Modern Fehinnan emerged after the 100-year interregnum following the Penza conquest of Fehinna during the lifetime of the Malificent (fl. 4000 AD). At the same time, much of western Fehinna was overrun and occupied by tribal peoples from the Palach highlands. The establishment of the Second Tecktahate and the gradual reconquest of the piedmont zone saw also the gradual establishment of a new literary standard, based on the speech of Illizbuah and the surrounding area. This incorporated further syntactic changes, primarily the development of differential inflections based on social status. (For an unrelated but analagous development, see *Arkan.*) In addition, there was a massive influx of loan-words from the Penza language, particularly with regard to commerce, administration and war. A more conservative dialect, closer to Middle Fehinnan, remained in use for liturgical purposes. Modern Fehinnan is very stable, due to the spread of literacy and printing; there is an "accepted" dialect and pronunciation, common to the upper and middle classes throughout the realm.

Dialects: There are perceptible differences of accent between the Tidewater and Piedmont dialects of Fehinna proper, but few in grammar. The speech of the northern kingdoms—Mai-Lun and the others—differs more strongly, particularly in the greater Penza influence; a 20th-century analogue would be the difference between, say, Scottish and Texan English—without a unified written form. The Kai-Lun areas have no single uniform speech, and are related to Modern

Fehinnan roughly as French is to Latin, having been much influenced by the Palach languages but not by Penza. Modern Fehinnan is having an increasing influence through trade and cultural prestige among the literate classes.

Trade-Fehinnan—a simplified pidgin—is used as a contact language throughout the eastern coastal area of Almerkun, the Carribean, and increasingly throughout the Lannic basin wherever Fehinnan traders have penetrated.

Area: Fehinna, Mai-Lun, Essho, D'wah, parts of Kai-Lun. Recently (4900s) colonies on eastern shores of Lannic, southern continent.

Description: Modern Fehinnan is a soft, musical language, half-sung. Note: Equals or superiors refer to themselves as "I" and speak in first person to equals or subordinates. Inferiors one caste removed speak of themselves in the third person (s/he) and refer to superiors in the impersonal tense (e.g., "She petitions the lord" for "I (inferior) ask you (superior)"—from a bourgeois to a noble.). Inferiors more than one caste removed, or anyone to the God-King, refer to themselves in the third person impersonal (it) but use the intimate tense (e.g., "It petitions thou for I (very inferior) asks you (exalted superior).")

Sample Vocabulary:

meh	I, me, mine
yaw	you (singular), yours
yawl	you (plural), yours
y'tem	them, theirs
slaveshaaid	poor, lower caste
olboi	yeoman
illiz-olboi	merchant, bourgeois (literally, city-yeoman)
raatah	bureaucrat, civil servant
raadha	gentlefolk, upper caste
sarchah	scholar
gawshowta	priest

bayid	soldier/warrior
vakar	herder
gofo	servant
maysil	bodyguard, retainer, vassal
fechta	employee
momah	mother (legal term)
feeda	mother (biological)
sucah	child (infant)
runnah	child (preadolescent)
kinin	youth, preadult
pa	father (either legal or biological)
sis	sibling (either sex)
bro	relative
labro	friend, comrade
getha	family (spouses and children), kinfast
aytatin	foreigner (savage, barbarian)
palachah	barbarian (specific, highlander, mountaineer, westerner)
cosoka	sycophant, flatterer
sahah	spy
ahlina	lover
sowba	hero (implies braving of danger)
ayup	north
sayth	south
ays	east
ways	west
yip	up
daahn	down
waasht	white
nayga	black
iyp	wages
kukas	enslavement, domination
brotaaht	friendship, comradeship
crawch	genitals (both sexes)
fayn	sex (activity)
clama	kiss
maacin	sexual intercourse (reproductive)
ahlin	love
hain	hand
aid	head
ipul	breast

braad	hair
thayng	tongue
chompa	teeth
ted	foot
rigglah	finger(s)
chayc	buttock
buah	city, town
shaaic	house, building
gwin	door
winna	window
covrin	roof
taals	floor
showah	bath
payle	pool
shaishaaic	latrine
shai	excrement
critah	animal
owse	horse
baahtah	cow
swaitah	sheep
clucah	chicken
wayb	duck
waing	bird
plashah	fish
craicah	shellfish
gawsyn	Sun (god)
olsaytn	devil, demon
tennet	angel
nif	knife
cain	quarterstaff
chayte	sword
stucah	spear
wacah	mace, club
holof	pike (long)
chopah	axe
kowayt	armor
dow	shield
shonirn	crossbow
plincah	bow
tic	arrow/bolt
hahayt	helmet

maysh	paper
macah	pen
smowk	ink
cawn	maize
baid	wheat
tawtah	potato
plaic	farm, estate
tunurun	mill, machinery
awda	liquid, water
es	is, state of being
bo	good, fine
chaint	wonderful
facsit	bravery
wai	road
bowai	highway
maarl	cement
raise	grass
tawn	stone
lai	brick
claar	glass
duhut	ceramic, clay
doma	false, fake, fraud
laycin	lick
sain	give, bestow
swap	sell
dayl	buy
pomo	insult, denigrate
gaw	go
insh	do
cayt	kill

Number of Speakers: c. 20,000,000

LANGUAGES OF THE MITVALD ZEE AREA

IYESIAN (LAENCHAIS)

Spoken circa 3000–4000 AD.
Origin: French (Alpine dialects); analytical, unin-

flected language. Spoken as administrative tongue throughout Empire of Iyesi (3100–4000 AD). Extensively used as diplomatic, cultural and religious language in subsequent periods.

Languages derived from Enchian are spoken by many of the tribal peoples of northwestern Europe. Note: Even at its height the Iyesian Empire was thinly populated, with major centers separated by wide areas very thinly settled. Small pockets of unrelated ethnic and linguistic groups persisted throughout the Imperial period, especially away from seacoasts and major trade routes.

Sample Vocabulary:

Genhomm	freeman/woman
Peutr'npeau	perhaps a bit
Paral	speak
doi	you

ENCHIAN

Direct descendent of Old Iyesian spoken in eastern kingdom of Tor Ench, related roughly as modern Italian is to Latin, although the written form has archaizing tendencies and many Tor Enchian aristocrats would deny that the two are separate languages. More inflections, loan-words from neighboring languages.

Number of Speakers: c. 6,000,000

LAKAN

Indo-European language derived from Sinhalese with Dravidian elements; originated in a series of seaborn folk-migrations from roughly Sri Lanka and southern India to southeastern Europe in the period following the breakup of the Iyesian Empire (c. 4000 AD); the proto-Lakans were formally allies and mercenaries of the Empire—in fact forced their way in. The original language was rapidly modified, and the present tongue is derived from a contact-creole between the tongue of the invaders and local languages—Enchian, and descendants of Albanian.

Number of Speakers: c. 5,000,000

YEOLI

Origin: Old Iyesian. Spoken in Yeola-e and (after c. 5000) parts of the former Arkan empire; a closely related language is spoken in the Demarchy of Roskat. Related to Iyesian much as modern English is to Anglo-Saxon.

Number of Speakers: c. 4,000,000 (Roskati c. 1,000,000)

ARKAN

Origin: American English. After landing of Ark Corporation (orbital habitat) in 3200 AD the original language underwent little change, as the Arkans remained a small, isolated group (like many in the contemporary Iyesian Empire) but, very unusually, had a written language of their own. After the fall of Iyesi, Arkan expanded as the nascent Arkan Empire did, overruning and replacing the previous tongues of the Italian peninsula and adjacent areas. (Mostly Enchian, but with numerous small relict groups speaking Italian or Arabic-derived languages.)

At the Arkan Empire's peak in the late 4900s various Arkan dialects were spoken throughout the north-central Mitvald area. Regional accents arose, but the highly centralized Imperial apparatus confined these to lower-class use and the written speech remained very uniform.

Description: The most conservative of all the English-based languages of the Fifth Millennium, Arkan remained an uninflected, positional language. Modifications included sound-groups derived from the "substratum" languages of the central Empire, and vocabulary borrowed from Enchian; there was also a system of class-based pronouns and verb cases governing speech between different castes. A 20th-century English speaker might be able to puzzle out simple phrases in Arkan if the script were Latinized, although the spoken language would be totally incomprehensible.

Number of Speakers: c. 15,000,000

ZAK

Origin: Slavic (Russian), Germanic and Turkic influences. Originally spoken along much of Brezhan river; now confined to F'talezon and adjacent areas as a first language, with settlement enclaves in areas downriver to Bravhniki on the Mitvald. A simplified form is widely used as a trade lingua franca on the Brezhan and in adjacent areas.

Number of Speakers: c. 500,000

BRAHVNIKIAN

Origin: Old Zak. A much-simplified tongue (related to Zak roughly as English is to German) spoken in Brahvniki City and environs. Brahvnikian and the Zak trade-patois are mutually comprehensible when confined to simple phrases.

Number of Speakers: c. 300,000

AENIR

Origin: Slavic (Ukrainian, East Russian), Turkic influences. Much influenced in early stages by Old Zak. Many regional dialects. Spoken throughout middle and lower Brezhan and areas to the east; written, but no official dialect.

Number of Speakers: c. 6,000,000

RYADN

Origin: Lithuanian, heavy Finnish influence, later in contact with Old Brezhanian dialects. (Proto-Zak, Proto-Aenir). Spoken in open steppe country east of the Brezhan by nomadic (Ryadn) and semi-nomadic (te-Ryadn) groups, stretching far into Central Asia.

Number of Speakers: Unknown

MOGH-IUR

Origin: Magyar (Finno-Ugrian). Spoken in Mogh-iur kingdoms tributary to Arko until the Yeoli War, northeastern Imperial provinces.

HYERNIC

Origin: Tigrinya (Semitic language spoken in Eritrea, northern Ethiopia). Some influence of substratum languages (Enchian, Greek and Albanian-derived). Not generally a written tongue.

Number of Speakers: c. 800,000

SRIAN

Origin: Central Sudanic languages (principally Bornu). Some influence from substratum language (Arabic). Result of folk-migration across the former Sahara desert as climatic changes increased rainfall c. 3000 AD. Modern form reduced to writing during Iyesian period. Spoken on northern African coast.

ANGLUN

Origin: English. Spoken by isolated but advanced kingdom in northwestern Europe. Complicated tonal inflection system, with extreme shortening of word-elements to single syllables. Some loan-words from Enchian.

Number of Speakers: c. 900,000

MORYAVSKAN

Origin: West Slavic (Slovak), extremely conservative, some borrowing from Iyesian and more recently from Mogh-iur.

Number of Speakers: Unknown; widespread through central Europe

SOLDENKOR

Origin: Swedish. Positional grammar, few inflections. Has recently spread widely due to folk-migrations.

Number of Speakers: Unknown; widespread through north-central Europe

Notes on Fehinna

4970 AD (871st year of the Second Tecktahate, Sun Year 2930)

Area: 125,000 sq. m. (most of Virginia, parts of West Virginia, Maryland and North Carolina)

Climate: Slightly warmer than at present, particularly in coastal areas

Population: 12,753,000

  Rural: 10,552,000

  Urban: 2,201,000, which consists of:

    Nobility: 120,000

    Middle classes: 300,000 (includes yeomanry, merchants, artisans, priests, civil servants, all other intermediate classes)

    Foreigners: 50,000 (legal residents)

Free poor: 8,500,000 (includes nominally free
tenants, shaaid)
Slaves: 3,733,000 (includes native and foreign)

Birth rate: 22 per 1,000
Death rate: 18 per 1,000
Demographics: Roughly 1 in 5 children do not live
to reproduce. Average age of death for those who
do is in the mid-60s for men and late 60s for women,
with the lower classes dying younger than the
higher.

(Upper classes have a slightly higher birth rate than
lower; slave birth rate is slightly below replacement;
urban death rate slightly higher than rural. Main
causes of death are degenerative diseases (e.g., heart
failure), cancer, infectious disease.)

Physical type: Predominantly a long-established
local race, a stabilized Caucasian-Negroid mixture
characterized by medium to short stature, olive to
light-brown skin, dark wiry to wavy hair, brown or
black eyes. Slightly lighter skin color and straighter
hair in the inland districts, particularly near the border
with the Palach highland tribes.

The slave population was traditionally largely
derived from the mountain peoples to the west. These
vary widely (with substantial Fehinnan admixture near
the border) but have more Caucasian genes. Other
sources include the Kai-Lun areas to the south (similar
to Fehinnans but with more Palach mixture) and the
areas from Joisi on the coast north (Caucasians). In
the last two centuries, the Middle Sea (Carribean),
Zarzil Continent (south America) and, most recently,
the areas across the Lannic (Mitvald Zee, Africa) have
been tapped.

The Fehinnan ideal is medium to tall by local
standards (c. 5′5 to 5′9), compactly built, muscular,
with broad shoulders and (in females) broad hips; a
toast-brown color is most esteemed. Oval faces with

regular features are most favored. Both white and black skins are regarded as mildly repulsive. People with fair hair and light eyes are regarded with some suspicion, and stereotyped as violent, highly sexed and mentally primitive. Blacks are regarded as intelligent but effete.

Costume: Standard Fehinnan dress is a cotton loincloth (a 3-ft. strip of cloth tied around the waist and drawn up between the legs), a halter for most women, and a knee-length tunic often worn with a cloth or leather belt; commonly, a pouch and knife are worn on the belt, although the tunic will have pockets. Sleeves may be short or long. Footwear is most commonly sandals, cross-strapped to the knee. Hats of various types (leather, straw, felt) and caps are commonly worn out of doors.

Prepubescent children usually go nude or wear only a loincloth in warm weather; otherwise, children's clothing is much like adults. The lower classes, particularly in the country, may go barefoot in summer, as do many children, and may strip nude or to the loincloth for work.

The tunic may be modified to suit occupational needs; leather for manual workers, blacksmiths, or hunters, for example. Cotton is the most common fabric, but linen, wool and mixtures are also worn. In colder weather, the tunic will be of wool—often a knitted overtunic pulled on over the usual woven cotton, linen or linsey-woolsey garment. Leggings of cloth or knitted wool may also be worn, and fitted shoes (or clogs for the lower classes). Scarves, pull-on wool hats, and gloves are also known.

Upperclass persons, particularly rural gentry and the military aristocracy, may wear tight trousers, boots and a shortened tunic for hunting and other outdoor work.

Middle-aged to elderly members of the upper classes wear ankle-length, long-sleeved robes of various types, often with a broad sash around the waist or over the shoulder; all members of the upper classes do so on formal or ceremonial occasions. (These resemble a caftan, and may have a hood). Such robes are usually brightly colored, and may be heavily embroidered, and are accompanied by curl-toed slippers as footwear. Conical cloth hats accompany formal wear.

Uniforms: Members of the army wear a dull-red tunic with badges of rank on the shoulder. The tunic is worn under armor when in the field, with additional padded undergarments.

Priests wear formal robes of a bright saffron color, with hemming and cuff embroidery to indicate rank.

Civil servants wear a white tunic, with a script-case slung over the shoulder to carry documents, slide-rule and writing implements.

Only soldiers, nobles, and accredited members of the Guards, Caravaneers and Mercenaries' Guild may wear weapons (knives longer than four inches, spears, swords, etc.), although exceptions are made for some sailors, merchants and border-dwellers. Nobles in the country generally wear a dagger and long straight single-edged sword.

Conventions and Taboos: Fehinnans have no nudity taboo as such, but do have certain customs as to appropriate dress. Going nude in public is acceptable for children, or when swimming or bathing (both usually done communally), or at private entertainments, or for athletics. Generally, public nudity is otherwise considered more appropriate for members of the lower classes—vulgar for the middle castes, and for an aristocrat a sign of contempt for the viewers. Stripping to the loincloth is accepted when working in warm weather, but again seen as somewhat lowerclass. The more formal the occasion, generally the more that must be worn. Certain types of fabric (e.g., silk) and color (crimson, yellow) are reserved for the wealthy or for the nobility.

Slaves generally wear a collar, usually of treated wood or fiberglass; this may be ceremonial or even ornamental, for certain valued house servants.

Ornaments: Only members of the highest castes—nobles and, within the city walls, wealthy merchants—may wear gold jewelry. The lower castes—shaaid and slaves—may not wear any jewelry, although slaves may wear livery.

Jewelry is very varied, and includes faceted gems. Iron, steel, bronze and brass are used as ornamental metals; carved wood, carved ivory, and tooled leather are also used.

Hair: Most Fehinnans of all classes wear their stiff, wiry hair cropped close to the head, sometimes with patterns shaved closer. Plaits (somewhat like dreadlocks) are fashionable among some of the upperclass youth of Illizbuah, often combined with beading, but this is regarded as daring and unorthodox. Those in mourning often let their hair grow out for a year or so.

Technology: Fehinna is among the most advanced countries in the world in the late Fifth Millennium. The following are some characteristic technologies:

1. *Agriculture.* Fehinna practices an extremely advanced form of intensive organic agriculture.

Land Tenure: The large estate is characteristic, with some parts rented out to tenant kinfasts and others directly cultivated with slave, hired or labor-tenant (labor service as part of the rent) workers. Typically, tenants in the lowlands pay more of their rent in labor and shares of their crop; in the piedmont uplands, cash rents and shares are more characteristic, but all areas have a mixture. A lowland tenant kinfast holding 60 acres would characteristically pay one-third of their grain and vegetables, every third piglet and lamb, and labor calculated to be one day in three for every adult. Special payments—e.g., entry fines, extra work in harvest time—are also common. Upcountry tenants gen-

erally pay less, and may send ox-teams and tools as
well as hand-labor. Farmers generally live in nucleated
villages of 200–700 people on their landlord's property; slaves and hirelings live in cottages attached to
the manor house.

Crops are rotated, with legumes (e.g., soyabeans,
alfalfa, peanuts) used to replenish nitrogen, and great
care taken to prevent erosion and maintain humus
content; rotation also reduces insect damage. Marl and
limestone are used to correct soil acidity; slopes are
terraced; all manure, human waste and crop residues
are carefully composted and applied to the soil. (So is
treated sewage around cities and towns.) Trash fish—
alewives—are also used as fertilizers in coastal areas.
Drainage and irrigation are applied where appropriate;
there is scarcely a wasted square inch in the Tecktahate, and maintaining maximum productivity is a religious duty. Field borders are usually live-hedges,
principally rosa multiflora.

The primary cereal is maize, followed closely by
winter wheat, the other small grains (barley, oats, triti-
cale), and rice in lowland areas. Root crops, sweet and
white potatoes, are an important source of starches
and are also distilled for alcohol. Fodder crops include
alfalfa, various clovers and grasses, kale, and beets;
they are preserved by both drying and ensilage. Bee-
hives are extensively kept. Livestock includes horses,
cattle, pigs, sheep, goats, rodents (rabbits and guinea
pigs) and poultry—including the four-footed turkey
(produce of pre-Fire genetic engineering), two-footed
turkeys, chickens, ducks, geese and pigeons. Breeding
is fully understood and carefully carried out; there
are many specialized breeds of livestock. Horses are
bred mainly for saddle and carriage work, or for
crossing with donkeys to produce mules. Draught
power is largely oxen, secondarily mules, with some
use of donkeys. Most cattle are kept for draught or
dairy purposes; bull-calves and overage animals are

the primary source of beef, but some fatstock is kept
for luxury beef production. Sheep and goats are used
for dairy produce as well as for meat, wool and
hides.

Most estates have an elaborate system of fishponds,
which produce fertile muck as well as carp, catfish and
trout.

Land not suitable for field crops is planted to vine-
yard and orchards (grape, peach, pear, apricot, pome-
granite, apple, etc.) with the type varying according to
location. Fruit is eaten fresh, as wines, brandies and
cordials, and in dried form and as jams. Except on the
western borders, real forests are rare, but less fertile
soils are often planted to managed woodland; roads
are generally tree-lined. These produce timber and
charcoal, and also serve as pannage ground for swine;
some of the larger provide hunting preserves for the
nobility. The nobility also have gardens, both truck
and ornamental, around their manor houses. Usually
these are fairly modest, except in the case of the very
wealthy. Ordinary country-dwellers cultivate truck gardens around their villages, and small herb- and flower-
gardens about their cottages.

Industrial crops include dyestuffs, cotton (south
of the Iaimz river), tobacco, flax (for linen and oil-
seeds), timber, etc. In general, cash crops are grown
for sale by the gentry on the land they farm directly.
Food crops and livestock products for sale in the
cities generally come from the same source, or from
share-rents paid by tenants and sold by their landlords. Some specialty crops (high-quality wines, dye
plants) are grown on a plantation basis, with landlords buying food for their workers, but this is still
rare, although increasing.

Methods are labor-intensive, since Fehinna is
densely populated. Tools include hoes, flails, sickles,
scythes—generally of wood, stone and ceramic, e.g.,
sickles of wood with tempered-glass blades fitted into

a slot, since metal is too expensive. Harrows, ploughs, seed-drills and multi-row cultivators are also used; woodsmen use steel axes and billhooks. Meticulous, intensive hand labor is characteristic, with a gardener's attitude even to field crops.

Processing and preservation: Vegetables and meats are preserved in sealed glass/ceramic jars, by pickling, salting, smoking, and in the upcountry in ice-cellars. Grain is ground in water- or wind-powered mills, which are also extensively used for fulling cloth, etc.

2. *Roads and bridges:* The main highways and bridges in Fehinna are owned, built and maintained by a division of the central government which is part of the military.

First-class highways—of which Fehinna has more than 10,000 miles—are built of rock and concrete. The first step in laying out such a road is surveying, with a straight path maintained even when extensive cutting and grading is needed. Ditches are dug 40' apart, and the earth fill used to build the base grade of the road, firmly tamped down. Over this is laid a layer of crushed rock, the individual stones being about the size of a small fist, 3'6" deep in the center, falling to 3' at each edge of the 25' broad roadway, which is edged with cast-concrete blocks. These stones are carefully fitted, then rolled and pounded. Good-quality concrete is then poured and worked into the crushed-rock surface until gaps are filled, and allowed to dry. A wearing layer of concrete is then laid, again 3'6" in the center and 3' at the edges; a layer of hard granite gravel is then rolled into the surface. Expansion joints several inches wide are left between sections of roadway every 35', and covered with fitted stone slabs laid flush with the surface in grooves cut from the concrete surface. These slabs are of standard size, 1' x 2'.

Concrete-pipe culverts are laid as necessary. Bridges are usually concrete reinforced with glass-fiber, using a long-chord arch form with piers of similar material as necessary. Piers are driven to bedrock or firm footing using caissons and pumps, and are faced with cut stone where possible.

Second-class roads are similar in size to the first, but are laid on a graded-dirt bed and are covered with a 3' to 2' layer of inch-sized crushed rock. This paving is graded, watered and rolled, and replaced as needed.

Third-class roads are graded dirt, laid out by the central government and inspected frequently, but maintained by local authorities using tax-labor from the peasantry.

Town and city streets are the responsibility of the municipal authorities.

Railroads—horse and miniature-elephant drawn—run on durcret rails.

3. *Building and Architecture:* Fehinnans use most materials from mud wattle-and-daub to brick and cut stone, but the largest structures are made with marl-based concrete, either alone or with glass-fiber reinforcement. The basic design for country homes is a hollow square or a C open at one end around a courtyard or series of courtyards; peasants have similar designs, greatly simplified, in rammed earth, mud or (on the western frontier) logs.

4. *Weapons and War:* Basic infantry weapons are a short double-edged sword and dagger, spears (for close combat troops), pikes up to 18' long, halberds (spear-axes) and bolt guns—a form of magazine-fed repeating crossbow powered by coiled springs. Pike troopers and boltgunners carry a small round shield that can be used one-handed or slung on a leather strap. Marines and other close-combat infantry use a tall, convex, oval shield with a forearm strap and handgrip. Cavalry use long single-edged swords with basket hilts and smooth 10' lances.

Armor consists of steel helmets, usually bowl-shaped, and with added lobstertail style neckguards for officers and cavalry. Body armor is overlapping articulated plates of leather (usually 3-ply bullhide, whale or sharkskin) boiled in wax and treated with preservative, on a backing of fiberglass. High officers may have steel supplements.

Large-scale warfare is similar to the pike-and-shot methods of 16th-century Europe, with the bolt gun taking the place of the arquebus. Gunpowder is known but little used, since primitive gunpowder weapons are no more effective than the other weapons available and much more expensive.

Fortifications are constructed of glass-reinforced concrete, often faced with granite blocks, and are both common and very formidable (e.g., walls 30 meters thick and 100 meters high). Towers, etc., are lavishly used.

Siege weapons are complex; durcret-made machinery, including huge coil springs and flywheels, is common. Models mounted on forts generally outrange mobile types, and include the functional equivalent of machine-guns. Flywheel-powered machines can throw tonne-weight blocks up to a mile.

Modern fortifications—the types used in Fehinna and adjacent kingdoms—are rarely taken by assault. Starvation and treachery are the most efficient agents for taking walled cities and castles.

Incendiary compounds—based on organic resins and alcohol—are widely used; mobile flamethrowers, glass balls of "clingfire" and heavy ship- or wall-mounted flamethrowers are all known.

The Fehinnan art of war is sophisticated, with disciplined full-time armies and a long military tradition. All-out war between the advanced states is rare because it is unlikely to be decisive; long sieges, economic warfare (devastating the enemy's countryside) and complex manouvering are the rule.

5. *Metallurgy:* Equivalent to early 19th-century

usage, but metals are relatively much more expensive. Steel alloys are made by crucible (wootz) process.

6. *Materials:* Materials include organic synthetics. High-quality glass fiber (produced by spinneret method) is used for reinforcement in organic resins—"fiberglass" and in concrete. Concrete-type compounds are also made with infusions of fiber and silica gel (durcret) to produce materials of quasi-metallic qualities. Ceramic bound with fiber (carbon fiber derived from rice husks) is also used, and "unbreakable" glass is common. Wood laminates used extensively. (Plywood, laminate beams, etc.)

7. *Mechanics:* Very advanced gear-train machinery, mostly made of durcret or treated wood. Fairly complete understanding of force ratios, sophisticated leverage, etc. Includes clocks, chronometers, adding machines (although the abacus is most common), power-looms, etc. Power sources are wind, water and animal power; some recent experiments with hot-air piston engines.

8. *Optics:* Fehinnans understand the wave theory of light, and are capable of grinding lenses and optical mirrors for complex telescopes.

9. *Chemistry:* Strong acids known; rule-of-thumb use of hydrocarbon chemistry from organic feedstocks.

10. *Ships and shipping:* Fehinnan ships are built of wood, wood laminates, and occasionally fiberglass for special uses. Sails are of linen canvas (with some glassfiber reinforcement) and cordage is of hemp or sisal. Larger ships are built in slipways or—for the very largest—drydocks, to blueprints. Merchant ships may range up to 2,500 tonnes, although most are much smaller.

11. *Mathematics:* Positional arithmetic, algebra, and the calculus. Sliderule in common use.

Food and Cuisine: The laboring majority of Fehin-nans live primarily on bread, usually corn-bread, with additions of soya meal; the other staples of their diet are fresh and preserved vegetables, e.g., tomatoes, greens, and fruit. Protein is provided by lentils, peas, beans, eggs, occasional poultry, dairy products—butter, cheese, yogurt—and more rarely meat, mostly pork or mutton. Coastal and river dwellers eat more fish.

Soups or stews are the staple of the working classes; soup or stew of potatoes or roots with other vegetables and some meat or meat stock, with bread on the side, and salads and fruit in season, is the typical main meal. Breakfast is generally wild-herb tea, with bread and perhaps porridge; the midday meal is peas or bean porridge, possibly with a piece of fat pork added.

Festival-day foods include grilled or fried meats, and various sweets and pastries.

Upperclass cuisine is far more elaborate and includes much more meat, fish and dairy produce. Fish is occasionally eaten grilled, but large lumps of meat—roasts, steaks, etc.—are regarded as uncouth and barbaric.

Currency and Banking: The currency is on a gold standard, the 50-grain gold "bit" being the basic unit. Silver is fixed at 1/25th the value of gold. Coins are rectangular, made by stamping an image (the Sun for gold, others for silver) on flat wire, which is then issued in fixed-unit coils. Individual coins are broken off at the perforations as needed. Small change is in copper and bronze.

The main banking center is the Sun Temple, which makes loans through its network of parish temples; usually these are secured against land or other real property. Commercial banks exist for financing trade; private lending (usually between relatives) is the general means for manufacturing finance.

Interest rates from the Sun Temple run between 5 percent and 12 percent per annum; commercial bank rates are much more variable.

(*Note:* Kinfasts can pledge members or children as security for loans, on written terms. If the loan goes into default, the persons involved become debt-bondsmen or slaves depending on the terms originally noted.)

Family Structure: Fehinnans of all the free classes practice the "kinfast" form of marriage common, with variations, to most of the peoples of Almerkun. Marriage is to multiple spouses, in Fehinna usually between four and eight, with up to twelve in some cases. Once established (usually first by a couple) a kinfast is "closed" when the desired number is reached; divorce and remarriage are possible but rare, and regarded as extreme misfortunes. The kinfast name of an established group is carried on by the children of the marriage. Generally, the daughters (or some of them; usually the firstborn pair) of an established kinfast form the next generation of the family, marrying males they either court themselves (generally in the lower classes) or which are found by their elders (more common for the propertied). Exchange of daughters between kinfasts exists, but is more rare than the converse. As the elder generation of the kinfast ages, they gradually hand over management of the family affairs—sometimes ceremonially—to the younger.

Among the propertied, sons are sent with a dowry to their new kinfast; when a daughter marries in to a kinfast a gift is made to the young woman's parents.

Blood descent is, of course, "matrilinal."

Authority within the Fehinnan kinfast is by a mixture of consensus and seniority, with seniority being more important among the upper classes. The "head" of the family is usually the eldest member of the kinfast, or the one so appointed by the parental kinfast.

Marriage is usually at about 22 for women and 26 for men; the lower classes marry earlier.

Children are regarded as children of the kinfast in common; there is a special bond between mothers and infants, but not nearly so exclusive as in monogamous cultures (e.g., small children will be suckled by any female spouse who has milk).

Virtually all land and most productive assets in Fehinna are owned by kinfasts, and descend through the generations to the next "phase" of the kinfast of name. Within the kinfast personal property is usually limited to clothes, ornaments, etc., although money and other goods *may* be owned individually.

The kinfast is the basic unit of Fehinnan society, and marriage links between kinfasts are the most important means of social interaction. Farms and businesses are customarily owned and managed as kinfast units; in urban areas, kinfast members may work at separate locations but will pool their resources. Related kinfasts form semi-clan groups, generally aiding each other, and relations of dependence and clientage will endure from generation to generation between noble and commoner kinfasts.

Adoption is quite common; a kinfast which produces a surplus of males or females will often "juggle" with related kinfasts of appropriate degree. Unkinfasted females who have children commonly give them over to their sisters' or parents' kinfast for adoption and rearing. The very poorest of the free population often have no opportunity to form kinfasts and their reproduction rate is much lower than the rest of the population.

Slaves may not marry, and have a rather low birthrate. In modern times male slaves are usually vasectomized; anciently they were infibulated or castrated;

this is still the case for those sentenced to the mines or other mass employment. Female slaves are bred at the discretion of their owners; house-born slaves are substantially more valuable than foreign-born or bought.

Sexual Mores:

Incest: Sexual contact between parents and children (or members of the kinfast of the parent's generation) is regarded with horror and is quite rare; the punishment for the adult is death by stoning.

Sex between siblings is not regarded as incest, but reproduction *is* so regarded. Sex-play generally begins in childhood between siblings and neighbor-children, and is regarded calmly as a natural thing; adults keep an eye out to make sure that no violence or harmful behavior occurs. Once puberty is reached the main concern is to prevent pregnancy; Fehinnans have advanced herbal contraceptives, and also employ barrier methods. (Nonreproductive practices are also encouraged among the young.) It is expected that as adolescents grow there will be a fair degree of experimentation, increasingly with non-siblings. Pre-marital pregnancies are usually terminated by abortion, and increasingly severe scoldings and other measures if they recur. When the time comes for marriage, the core of the next generation of the kinfast is generally two or more sisters, who marry and then court or are found an appropriate number of spouses from outside their sibling-group. Males always marry out, and care is taken not to bring in males of an inappropriate degree of blood-relation.

Under Fehinnan law and custom, "adultery" is defined as bearing a child to a male outside the kinfast without the consent of the other members; sex as such, unless it leads to pregnancy or to alienation of affection, is not adulterous—although it is considered

good manners not to have affairs of which the other
spouses disapprove. Kinfasts may, and fairly often do,
decide to have one of their members bear a child to
an outside male; for eugenic reasons, or as a means of
establishing a link with another kinfast. Within the kinfast, persistent sexual rejection is regarded as extremely
impolite.

As might be expected, Fehinnans consider bisexu-
ality as the norm, with heterosexuality and homosexu-
ality regarded with mild disapproval. In fact, in the
Fehinnan language the fundamental distinction is
between sex-for-pleasure (regardless of the gender of
participants) and reproductive sex. Sex-for-pleasure is
a matter of no great importance, but reproduction is
very important indeed. There are few taboos on any
form of sexual activity that does not cause physical
harm; sadism is regarded as a perversion, except
among some circles in the upper classes. In general,
rape between social equals is regarded as a serious
crime of violence, usually punished by enslavement or
mutilation.

Public sexual activity (that is, where strangers can
see) is regarded as vulgar, and is avoided except by the
lowest classes. Public display of affection—hugging,
kissing—is not disapproved of, except by some of the
starchier nobility.

In the home there are no particular restrictions
on sexual activity by couples or groups. In terms of
actual sexual acts, oral sex is more common than in
20th-century Western culture, and intercourse less
common. The usual positions for intercourse are
side-by-side or female atop and astride, except when
pregnancy is desired; in that case, "missionary" positions are preferred.

Exceptions: Class distinctions are very sharp in Fehinna. Slaves are at the disposal of their owners, and
have no right of refusal; sex with slaves is regarded as
a legitimate pastime of those lucky enough to possess

them. In law all the free classes have a right of refusal, but employers or landlords often have the *de facto* ability to compel their subordinates or tenants, particularly in the countryside, and coercion of that nature is quite common.

Prostitution exists, although largely in towns and cities; it caters mostly to specialized needs—e.g., sailors, travelers, those with extremely repulsive deformities—or to upper-class entertainment. It is regarded as a rather low-status occupation, but no more so than, for example, shoe-shining or other service jobs.

RACIAL TYPES OF THE FIFTH MILLENNIUM

Demographics: After the disaster of 2044, the human population of Earth was reduced from more than 8 billion to less than 1 million in about a decade—in effect, to pre-neolithic levels. Recurrence of the tailored viruses released at that time, together with ordinary disease, starvation, and the climatic upheavals accompanying the geological disturbances caused by gigatonne mines and crustal disruptions reduced the population further, to about 500,000 by the end of the 22nd century. Total population fluctuated at roughly that level for the next five centuries; humans died out over wide areas, and only luck and the profound toughness of Homo sapiens sapiens prevented extinction.

After roughly 2500 AD the return of ecological stability, the exhaustion of the viral plagues (many of which were designed to lie dormant for long periods) and the evolution of new social and technological forms permitted a recovery in numbers.

This was very gradual, with fresh setbacks from time
to time.

Population Table (approximate)

2100 AD	500,000
2600 AD	700,000
3000 AD	1,000,000
3500 AD	40,000,000
4000 AD	250,000,000
4500 AD	450,000,000
5000 AD	600,000,000

North and South America (Almerkun and Coylonta)
accounted for roughly 100 million each, Africa for 50
million, Europe and North Africa as far as the Brezhan
valley for some 120 million, and monsoon Asia and
east Asia roughly another 100 million each, with scattered populations elsewhere. Within each region population densities varied widely—the relatively dense
populations of the Mitvald Zee (Mediterranean) basin
contrasting with the sparse areas of northern Europe,
for example.

Patterns of Survival: Initially, survivors of the disaster were scattered in very small communities, ran-
domly assembled from individuals and small groups.
Many of these remained out of contact for centuries,
from the sheer difficulty of travel and also because
the plagues implanted a deep taboo on contact with
strangers. (For the same reason, there was a strong
incentive to preserve elementary sanitation and medi-
cal knowledge. Groups which did not tended not to
survive.) These early groups of survivors were often,
due to sheer chance and the greater survival-potential
of the rural and isolated, untypical of the predisaster
populations. Inbreeding within small populations
(made possible at all by the rigorous culling effect of
the harsh environment) often produced very uniform

gene distributions, and combinations of features
unknown before the disasters.

The prolonged period of slow growth or nonexistent
growth in population preserved many of these eccentric features, although the gradual return of trade and
other contact tended to produce regional rather than
strictly local breeding isolates. Once population growth
resumed—often quite rapidly in a given area—small
and eccentric local populations could spread quickly
and become characteristic over quite large areas.

Note: The following listing is of examples and is
by no means exhaustive; descriptions apply to typical
individuals. Recent centuries have seen a good deal of
mixture and travel.

Groups:

KOMMANZA

Location: North-central inland Almerkun, originally
in the Komman of Granfor (central Red River Valley
of Minnesota). Now common in northern tall-grass
prairie zone running in a crescent from northwestern
Iowa to the Rocky Mountains in north-central Alberta.
Rarely seen elsewhere.

Origin: Mainly europoid, amerindian (Lakota
Sioux), some negroid and oriental. Original group in
the 200–300 range.

Description: Tall, averaging 5'8" for females and
5'11" for males; extremely pale skin, often freckled,
but usually capable of tanning. Hair color most commonly light, in variable shades of ashblond, blond,
brown, red and black. Eyes usually blue, grey or
mixed-light. Scalp hair is invariably straight, usually
fine-textured and dense. Body hair is scanty. Limbs
tend to be long in proportion to the torso; hands long
in proportion to width, and feet are long and high-
arched.

Dolichocephalic skulls (index 72) with moderately robust bone structure. Narrow faces, high cheekbones, eyes slanted with partial folds, chins usually pointed, noses long and often curved.

Comments: Given to berserkergang, but it is uncertain if this is cultural or genetic in origin. Often startlingly athletic, but this (and the high average height) may be due to cultural patterns and the characteristic high-protein diet.

FEHINNAN

Location: Eastern coastal N. America, Virginia and adjacent areas.

Origin: Europoid-negroid mixture.

Description: Average stature 5'3" for females, 5'6" for males; olive- to brown-skin color, eyes brown to black, hair black and wirey to straight, features oval and somewhat blunt. Local variations, with more caucasoid admixture in western highlands.

Most Fehinnans are somewhat stocky.

ZAK

Location: Upper Brezhan river, pockets elsewhere. (central Russian Republic).

Origin: East-Baltic europoid, some mongoloid.

Description: Extremely small average stature, 4'2" for females, 4'5" for males. Pale skin, often incapable of tanning, predominantly dark hair of black or brown shades, generally straight; dark eyes. Light hair and eyes usually indicates outside admixture; body hair follows standard europoid pattern. Gracile bone structure, low sexual dimorphism.

Some evidence of dark-adaptation (e.g., very good night vision, extremely depigmented skin). Low natural metabolic rate, and at very low temperatures blood-flow to the extremities is spontaneously reduced, a cold-adaptation similar to the pre-disaster Yakuts and Samoyedic peoples.

Mesocephalic skulls (index 80), broad brow and cheeks but triangular faces, small regular noses, pointed chins.

Comments: Unusual degree of uniformity; the small size of the average Zak and the small pelvic arch (low even for the size-range) make inter-breeding with ethnic groups of much larger average size problematic. Average size seems to be spontane-ously increasing in recent periods, but slowly. Rumors of psychic powers.

The Making of Fifth Millennium

The world of the Fifth Millennium began as three separate settings in the imaginations of three authors, still teenagers, long before they met.

Karen Wehrstein's conception of Yeola-e dates back to age 12; the character Fourth Chevenga first appeared two years later (Friday, March 14, 1975, to be exact) when Wehrstein wondered what sort of life a person would lead who was granted both heroic abilities and foreknowledge that his life would be cut short.

The character Megan Whitlock was first conceived while Shirley Meier was in university in London, Ontario. For a literature class she was given the choice of writing either a short story or an essay; she chose the story, the first image a small woman standing on a rain-washed staircase, looking down into a city: F'talezon.

Shkai'ra Mek Kermak's-kin and her world started with an afternoon in winter woods near Ottawa, Ontario. The deep cold, the snow weighing down the branches of the trees, and a raven launching itself through the woods . . . and S.M. Stirling suddenly had the opening scene of his first novel, *Snowbrother*. That work took shape while Stirling was going through law school, which he believes may account for the savage and bloodthirsty tone.

Wehrstein and Stirling met at a party in Toronto in 1981 and were naturally drawn together; neither had ever before met anyone so interested in writing. At this time, though, violently opposing political and philosophical views precluded any collaboration. Stirling and Meier made friends at a convention in 1983; it was at a folk festival, watching Morris dancers, however, that they first wondered what would happen if Megan and Shkai'ra were to meet. Scrawling in a notebook passed back and forth, they began the first Fifth Millennium collaboration. The book grew slowly at first, mostly through correspondence.

The year 1985 marked the founding of the Toronto writers' group the Bunch of Seven, at whose first meeting Stirling introduced Meier and Wehrstein to each other. This was after he had extolled to both the others' virtues fulsomely for several months, leading each to expect the other to be much taller, more elegant and more sophisticated than she actually is. Reassured by their mutual mere humanity, the two women hit it off and began collaborating almost immediately on as yet unpublished works.

It was around this time that, despite no strong single common influences more specific than Tolkien and classical mythology, the three noticed that their respective fantasy settings and approaches had certain elements in common. All three used a time period several thousand years after a world holocaust, with technology at a pre-industrial but not entirely primitive level; diverse cultures created with extreme care to plausibility and detail; psychological realism and concern with growth and relationships; unexpected flashes of a dry but occasionally wicked situational humor; and a continual pondering of morality, particularly the morality of conflict and power.

It occurred to them that combining their worlds would give the resulting universe qualities of dissonance and discontinuity reflective of real life. A world built by one maker generally has a uniform flavor derived from the author's worldview. A world built by three has a sharp variousness whose synergy surprises even the authors!

The process employed in Fifth Millennium collaborations is very close-knit, almost a dialogue, in which the writers try to surprise, inspire and move each other. They agree beforehand who has creative control over which character, and sometimes the three, particularly Meier and Wehrstein, use improv theater techniques to realize scenes. Other divisions of labor play on their respective writing strengths. As a rough guide for readers wanting to know which geographical region of the Fifth Millennium world was created by which author: solo novels take place in that author's territory.

The Fifth Millennium Series